VELES

P. J. MARIE

Anxious Bean Publishing

VELES

First Edition

This book is a work of fiction. Names, characters, places, businesses, events, locales, and incidents are the product of the author's imagination. Any resemblance to actual persons, living or dead, events, businesses, or establishments is solely coincidental. The opinions expressed within these pages belong to the characters and should not be mistaken as the opinions or views of P. J. Marie, Anxious Bean Publishing, or any related affiliates.

Book Cover Design by ebooklaunch.com

Map design via https://inkarnate.com

ISBN: 978-1-7780028-0-9 (*paperback*)
ISBN: 978-1-7780028-2-3 (*hardcover*)
ISBN: 978-1-7780028-1-6 (*ebook*)

Anxious Bean Publishing
ON, Canada
https://www.anxiousbeanpublishing.com

For John, Dan, Julie, Devon, James, Ginny, Ryan, and my parents, without whom I wouldn't be here to write at all.

Thank you for listening to my ideas and supporting me. Thank you to those who read this in advance and gave me invaluable feedback. This would not be what it is without you.

VELES

P. J. MARIE

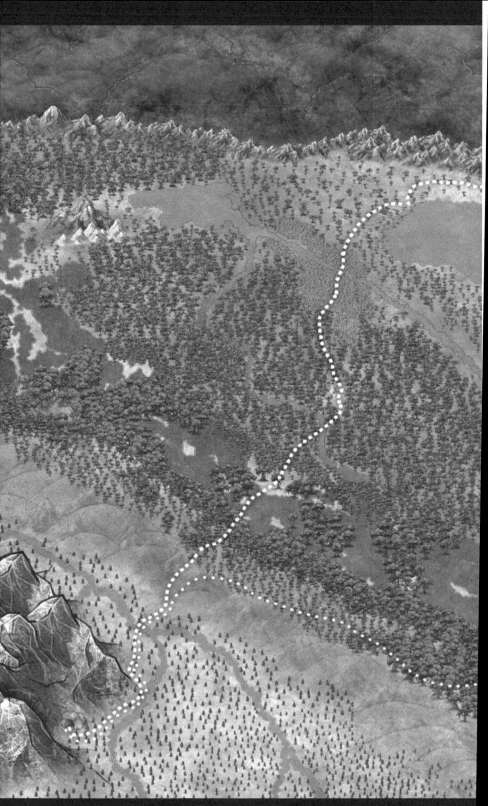

CONTENTS

Part One 1

  Mizuki 3

  The Altherrs 19

  The O'Kanes 40

  Aiden's Request 55

  The Map 72

  Leaving 90

  The Wolves 107

  The Wild 127

  Earnan 144

  The Return 164

  The Mountain Path 189

  Veles 207

Part Two 227

  Lilah 229

  The Accident 246

  Officer Wilson 266

  The Elk 288

  Incurable Changes 312

  The Great Destruction 334

Part Three 349

  The Truth 351

  Death 366

  Veles Reborn 378

PART ONE

Mizuki

Broken shards of rock slid down the edge of the mountain ridge as well-worn feet carefully made their way to the top, stepping around the larger broken pieces with practiced ease and balance. The movements were precise, steady, and purposeful – executed a hundred times before until they had become as easy as breathing. Dirtied hands gripped the top of the ledge tightly and pulled until bright blue eyes peered over the lip to look out onto the world beyond. It was barren and worn, laced with a painful history that made the girl's eyes crease as she surveyed the ruined land.

The tall ridge served as a wall. It separated the small village and wild green forest at the base of the mountains behind her from the dead and rocky world that lay beyond. It ran the entire length of the village and into the Wild to the south, providing their only protection from the horrors of the Dead Zone. She tensed as the wind picked up. It howled violently against the ridge and threatened to dislodge her from the precariously held position.

The storms were always worse beyond the ridge. The wind was wilder, the sun hotter, and the land more unforgiving. She gripped the rock more tightly and planted her feet wide as she squinted into the distance. Finally, the sun was up today after a long and cold winter. Spring had arrived, and with it, the view of the ruins had returned. During the winter months, everything farther than a stone's throw away from the top of the ridge was covered in mist, ice, and an endless storm of thick flurries. It was impossible to see anything then, and it would be a death sentence to attempt to climb this high.

She had tried it once when she was younger and far more foolish. It hadn't gone well. One sprained ankle and several bruised ribs later, she had tumbled to the bottom of the icy hill. She gritted her teeth at the memory. It had been painful, and worse yet, it had been stupid. One wrong roll on her way down the slick rocky surface, and she could have cracked her head open or broken a bone. It wasn't uncommon to die from such an injury, and even if you were lucky enough to live through it, your body was never the same. It would ache during the winter, and if the bones were not set *just right* you would limp for the remainder of your days. Worse than that was how it made you a burden on your family.

Looking back, she could hardly believe that she had been naive enough to try it – but then again, she had only been eleven. Now, at eighteen, she knew better. She had learned to wait for the snow to stop. She knew that just because the rocks might look dry, it didn't mean they always were and that sometimes ice still lingered near the spot she used as a lookout. So she knew that she had to wait until the sun's pattern changed – until it reached the point above the tallest trees in the village – for it to have warmed enough to melt the frost at the top of the ridge. After this, the second she was sure that it was safe, she would cautiously climb her way to the top to take the first look of the new year, and on bright clear days like today, she could see everything.

They were the same as they always were, the ruins, unchanged for the last ten years and a physical reminder of what had once been.

Her great-grandmother Miku had told her about them as a child, and her description had been remarkably accurate. The girl's eyes scanned over the vast empty expanse, searching for the odd broken shapes that protruded from the ground in the distance just to the left of the mountains. She nearly smiled when the clouds shifted to allow the sun to hit the cold dead surface, making the strange objects visible once more.

Sticks – as most of the people in the village called them, though not many had dared to climb the ridge to truly look. The majority of the village just believed the Elders' words, and the Elders called them *large sticks*, so that had become the accepted vernacular. And that was how the Elders preferred it. They didn't like it when people thought for themselves, asked too many questions, or listened to the words that her great-grandmother had spoken. They didn't like that she climbed the ridge either, and she knew that if she were ever caught doing it again, the punishment would be severe.

It had very little to do with her climbing the ridge and instead had everything to do with her being an *Altherr*. The Elders had not liked her great-grandmother Miku much at all for the same reasons they disliked her – she knew too much, thought too much, and questioned everything they told her.

She had only been eight years old the first time that she climbed the ridge. It was days after her great-grandmother had died – she was hiding in the thorn bushes near her home, quietly staring at the ground and wondering what was going to happen to her family. Her great-grandmother had always encouraged her to climb the ridge when she got older. She had even shown her the hidden path through the thorn bushes and the safest way to ascend the rocky ledge.

She hadn't meant to do it that day, to travel to the ridge in a wordless stupor, only to find her small hands grabbing at the rocks as her feet slipped against the jagged surface. Yet it had happened just the same, and she climbed the ridge alone, terrified, lost, and unable to stop until she reached the top and hauled herself up to look over the uneven edge.

The sight had taken her breath away.

Even now, ten years later, looking out into the expanse, she could still remember the feeling of that moment perfectly. She could still feel the warm sun and the way that the air had tugged at her short black hair as her eyes grew wide with wonder. The view was *exactly* as Miku had described. Not a single thing was out of place. The mountains were to the right, stretching to the north and east as far as the eye could see. A narrow path ran down the largest of them, Veles's Mountain, twisting and turning until it reached the base of the ridge. The trail was bordered by a sheer drop on either side and aligned with the double-gated entrance to the village, two towering walls of oak marked with Veles's symbol and covered in spikes. A great crevasse ran along the base of the mountains, separating them from the vast and empty landscape that stretched into the west. The overwhelming nothingness of the barren terrain was interrupted only by the eerie ruins that dotted the skyline before her.

She had hardly been able to see it that day as she was barely big enough or strong enough to pull herself up to look over the rocks. Yet as the sun shifted and the clouds moved, true to Miku's words, the ruins faded into view. They appeared as though they had risen from the dead ground just for her to see them, and at that moment ten years ago, she had known her instincts were right. Everything that her great-grandmother Miku had told her was true. She knew she would never question a word of it and *never* forget a single story.

After that day, she climbed the ridge any chance that she could during the spring, summer, and autumn, only stopping when the rocks became dangerous or when the weather turned for the worse. Every time she lifted her head over the edge and peered out at the land, she felt her heart calm, and her body would become quiet as she inhaled deeper than she could ever manage to do inside the village. She felt at peace here, breathing out the cool air, despite the wreckage that lay before her. She felt at home – and she felt closer to Miku.

She inhaled deeply, and her shoulders rolled back as her feet braced against the well-worn stone. Then her eyes fluttered shut as the calm settled through her bones just like it always did. It felt like ages since the last time she had been up here. She missed it. The winters always felt eternal without being able to climb the ridge to escape – yet, in some ways, it was worth the wait because the first climb of the spring always had the freshest air. Her bright blue eyes flashed open once more, and she began the familiar and steady routine of tracing every single bent and twisted remain she could find along the horizon, checking to make sure that they were all still there.

Rebar – that was what the large sticks truly were – old decrepit metal leftover from before the Great Destruction.

They were the remnants of massive structures that once used to fill the skyline like mountains. Miku had told her all about them, and she didn't care what the Elders said or what anyone else believed – she believed her great-grandmother, even if she was the only one who did. It wasn't something that she could explain. In the same way that an animal knows how to eat, run, sleep, and hide, she just knew. The feeling had hardened into her after the first climb when she gazed at the shattered remains of the past.

It was unshakable.

It was undeniable.

And it was the truth.

There had been a world here just over a hundred years ago. A world filled with people and creatures and things that she couldn't even imagine. Her eyes travelled across the irregular shapes, their outlines appearing like dead black trees across the endless rocky lands. They stuck out at odd angles, bent, warped, and damaged. She knew that up close they must be enormous, and she knew that the Great Destruction must have been devastating and powerful in order to bend and crack them like they were. They were impossibly strong, made from materials harvested from the earth and then beaten into shapes by humans. They had once stood hundreds of feet in the air, constructed to withstand the howling wind and the shaking of the earth.

Skyscrapers – that is what they had been called – giant concrete and metal structures that used to house hundreds, if not thousands, of people.

Yet even though her confidence in great-grandmother Miku was unshakable, the concept escaped her. She could hardly imagine hundreds of people together in one space, let alone thousands, and she certainly had no idea what concrete looked like. She knew it was similar to rock – except homemade – a mixture of water and powder and pieces of stone that people used to pour into shapes to build these great structures. She knew that large portions of the earth's surface had been covered in *pavement* or *asphalt* – which, according to her great-grandmother, had been very similar to concrete but thinner.

Why anyone would want to cover the grass with something hard, dead, and cold, she would never understand, but Miku had said it was how the earth was during the Before time. While she had never been able to picture this distant world in her mind, she knew it was real.

Miku had told her everything about it, everything that her own mother had taught her as a small child. Miku had explained it all in great detail, even telling her that people had managed to control water and bring it into homes. That people would travel all over in *vehicles* and *airplanes* – devices that allowed them to cover great distances in a matter of minutes. Miku had tried to describe it, even drawing a picture in the dirt with a stick to help illustrate. Yet trying to imagine it as a child had been like trying to see the air. It was there, and it was real – but she couldn't actually see it. So, begrudgingly, she had accepted that the world of the past was beyond the capability of her imagination.

Her hand carefully let go of the edge, reaching toward her chest and closing around the small pendant that rested against her sternum beneath her worn shirt. It was one of the few pieces of metal that the village still had. Most were used for various tools and weapons, though nearly all of it was rusted, dirtied, and old. They were relics from the past that the villagers had dug up over time. Each item found was brought to the Elders so they could decide how best to use it, and no matter how worn the item was, it was treasured and put to work.

This piece, though, was hers and hers alone. The Elders would never get their hands on it. Besides, she couldn't see why they would want it. It held no value for them, and it had no useful purpose, so aside from the satisfaction of taking it away from her, they didn't need it. But their dislike for her and Miku ran so deep in their blood that she didn't trust the Elders not to be petty or cruel and confiscate it regardless, so she kept the heirloom hidden beneath her clothes and securely fastened around her neck with a sturdy leather strip.

It was the only piece of her great-grandmother that she had left, and she would be damned if she was ever going to lose it.

Her fingers traced over the familiar shape, her thumb unconsciously running over the indents as she clung to the top of the ridge. It was old but not tarnished. It was silver and small – only roughly the size of the tip of her index finger – and it was the most valuable thing she owned in the world. It was a lotus blossom, which was appropriate because it had belonged to Miku's mother, who had been named after the flower. The back was engraved with her name, and even after all this time, the kanji symbols were still visible as faint, thin lines.

Gripping the ledge more tightly still, she let out a sigh and pulled herself further up the steep slant to rest her elbows over the edge. The toes of her leather shoes were barely touching the ground beneath her now, grazing the cold stone as she slumped her weight against the lip and watched the clouds begin to shift once more. Like always, they were moving quickly, spinning as they drifted across the light blue sky and sliced the sunlight into streams. No one else would agree with her, but she had always found this side of the ridge beautiful. Perpetually dead and wasted, sad and angry, yet oddly beautiful. Truth be told, as much as it terrified her, she was fascinated by it, and she loved it.

Everything, that was, except for those mountains to the north.

Steeling her nerves, she shifted her gaze to the Northern Mountains like she always did before leaving the ridge to head back home. She didn't know why she did it when every time she saw them, it just made her angry, sick, and buzzing with unresolved fear. Maybe she was hoping that one day she would be able to look and not feel that twist of panic in her gut. Or perhaps she was hoping that someday she might see *him*. Yet no matter how many times she turned her gaze, it always left her feeling the same.

Nauseated.

She could feel her legs growing weak and trembling beneath her as her heart rate started to increase.

The mountain.

The thing that plagued her village and ripped families apart. The place where the Elders said that Veles, the god of the earth, lived. Some in the village called him Terra, others Prithvi, but she had always called him Veles because that was what was taught to them in school and Miku had never called it anything else. Other names were discouraged. Yet all names were known despite this, and each of them was both feared and respected. They were whispered throughout the village, their lore a tale told by older children to their younger siblings to terrorize them – or by parents to make their children behave.

She knew that the kids usually meant it in good fun, but the fear was real, and for good reason. Veles's Mountain loomed over the village, *always*. It haunted them. It taunted them. It took from them; it destroyed families and kept the Elders in charge. It was the wretched thing that had shattered her home, her family, her life – killed her brother and all but consumed her mother.

She looked away from it, clearing her throat and forcing herself to swallow. Maybe one day she would be able to look at the mountain and not feel terror and sickness coursing through her veins, but today was not that day. So instead, her eyes traced the path that twisted around the mountain and led down to the edge of her village on the northern side. The double gates stood proudly, blocking the natural gap in the ridge and acting as the gateway into the Dead Zone. She could tell that the guards had been busy working there, adding even more wooden spikes, as if they thought that Veles himself might stroll down the hillside and knock on the gate looking for his next victim.

She swallowed again, feeling the panic in the pit of her stomach start to churn once more as she looked at the large gates, which were always closed. Today, it seemed she wasn't even strong enough to look at the pathway. Usually she could manage it, but this time it felt different, and she knew why. It was a Gifting year. Soon both gates would open. After ten long years they would open for the second time in her lifetime, and it would rip another family apart.

When she was eight, she hadn't realized the significance. She hadn't known what was coming, she hadn't understood the whispers around the village, and she hadn't appreciated just how deep the repercussions would cut.

But she understood now.

Slowly she lowered herself down from the ledge, dislodging her elbows from the rough surface until the flats of her feet touched the ground once more, and the mountain path disappeared behind the rough stone. Her view reduced to the rocky side of the mountain that vanished into the permanent mist that covered the peak. For that she was glad, because she never wanted to see the top of that mountain for as long as she lived.

She took another deep breath, forcing herself to focus and relax before she began her slow and steady descent back to the village. It didn't take her very long to navigate the ridge anymore, but it was still early spring, so she moved with extra caution. She paused by the large, jagged ledge halfway down, peeking around the corner to ensure that no one was by the fringe of the forest before moving on. It was the only place that someone would be able to see her up on the ridge. She had only been caught climbing it twice in her lifetime, and she had no intention of being caught again.

For the last three years, she had managed to keep her head down and maintain a clean record with the village Elders and the Praetorian Circle, and she wanted to keep it that way. Now that she was considered an adult, the repercussions would surely be worse, so she planned to reduce her visits this summer and be mindful of the times at which she climbed.

She moved quickly past the rock once she was sure the coast was clear, carefully completing a series of complex foot movements until she had navigated her way through the open section toward the bottom. Once there, the thorn bushes would give her cover, and she wouldn't need to worry about being seen. It only took her ten minutes to make it to the bottom at a brisk pace, and then she edged her way along the thick prickly bushes to the tiny opening that her great-grandmother had shown her on her fifth birthday.

It was narrow and low. She had to crawl along the ground on her hands and knees to fit, but it was the only way to make it through the thick brush that ran along the base of the entire ridge. She had briefly considered breaking down branches from the inside to make the tunnel larger, but she didn't want to risk it being discovered. So, just like she did every other time, she crawled along the cold ground, bracing herself on her forearms and knees, her chest all but scraping against the ground as she wiggled her way through until she reached the edge of the thicket and paused once more.

Peering through the small opening to her secret tunnel, she scanned the western edge of the village for any sign of people. There weren't any, which was to be expected. There were not many other family homes along this side of the village because it was too close to the ridge, which made people nervous. Most chose to live on the eastern side closer to the crops, the village Elders, and their small school. Yet this location suited her just fine. She preferred fewer people – it was quieter, calmer, and it made creeping around, listening in, and climbing the ridge much easier. She took another quick scan of the seemingly vacant space before she moved, pulling herself from the thorny brush and shuffling toward the edge of the trees to the south. There she momentarily hid behind an old oak and brushed herself off before continuing on and casually walking through the thin trees.

The village was small, though she didn't have anything to compare it to, so she didn't know for sure. As far as she was aware, there were no other villages besides hers. According to the Elders the Wild was uninhabitable, and even Miku had said that it was dangerous beyond the river to the south, though why that was, she wasn't sure. She knew that there were large animals out there because the hunting families had encountered them on their trips, but she didn't understand all the fear and mystery that seemed to surround it. Yet, she would never ask anyone about it. She had learned as a young teen that it was better to keep her questions to herself and figure out the answers on her own. As a child, she had gotten away with asking questions because some members of the village had found it endearing or cute – but now it was threatening, annoying, and troublesome, especially given her surname. So, she stopped talking to most people.

Come to think of it, she hardly talked to anyone but Aiden and her mother, and instead she had developed a keen ear and a talent for going unnoticed in the background. She rarely asked anything of her father either; over the last decade, they had fallen into a quiet and unspoken sort of agreement to just not talk about the village or why things were the way they were – or about anything else for that matter. And she avoided her aunt Mei and grandfather Kerin as much as possible because she neither liked nor trusted them.

She suspected the feeling was mutual. Their relationships with her father had always been tense, and it only seemed to worsen with time.

She stuffed her hands into the uneven pockets of her thin and worn hide pants, slowly weaving her way between the sparse trees toward her family's home. Most of the forest nearby, and that between the village and the river to the south, had been cut down to be used for timber. As a result, there were no longer any animals nearby, and everything from the southern end of the village to Glass Lake and the river was quiet, safe, and relatively sparse, with little cover. Aside from birds and small critters, there wasn't much life left. Because of this, the hunting families had had to push deeper into the Wild to the south of the river in order to find food. It was dangerous, and it wasn't uncommon for members of their hunting parties to come back injured after encountering unfavourable terrain or weather conditions. She had no idea how far they ventured because they never spoke of it, but at times they would be gone for days, tracking deer and snaring rabbits to bring back meat and furs to the village.

She was just glad that her family wasn't part of the hunting group. There were hardly any Altherrs left, and if anything were to ever happen to her father, she wasn't sure what would become of her or her mother. She tried not to think about it. It was bad enough that the one friend she did have belonged to a hunting family, and each time he went out she found herself plagued with nervousness for his return.

Her eyes darted to the path on her left, scanning to make sure that Mrs. Tran wasn't outside working on her sewing. The woman was nice enough, and Mizuki had never had any issues with her, but still, any time people did see her wandering around the village they tended to watch her suspiciously. She had grown used to it over time, but she avoided the main paths now as much as possible as a result. Today, it seemed, luck was in her favour, and

Mrs. Tran was nowhere in sight, which made the rest of her trip home easy since there were no other family homes along the way.

She rounded the corner, stepping out from the sparse trees at last and walking onto the worn village path. She could see her father, Kazuki, out in front of their home by the fire carving something, and she felt her heart warm.

He had always been incredibly gifted when it came to working with his hands. He was the best whittler in the village. He could take any type of wood in any shape and turn it into something beautiful with the small blunt blade that he carried around in his pocket. She had a collection of his small carvings in her room – a deer, a rabbit, a bird – just to name a few. They were her prized possessions, second only to the necklace that she wore around her neck. He had given her one every year on her birthday, and she adored them. They reminded her of life before losing Miku and her mother, though she could barely remember it now. Even after that day, after everything changed, he still gave her one every year.

They were, in an odd way, the only connection she had left to the man. It was like an unspoken expression of his regret over what had happened, his way of saying 'I still love you' without actually saying it. It was their form of emotional communication since they no longer seemed to have any emotions left. Both of them had buried their feelings in a hole deeper than Glass Lake the day that her brother died and her mother fell apart. So the carvings became their link. It was how she knew that underneath their cold exteriors, deep down, they both still cared.

Then again, maybe she was overthinking it.

They were just wooden figurines.

She walked quietly towards her family's home, knowing that her father had already sensed her presence as she saw his head tilt ever so slightly to glance up at her as he continued to work. She watched as Kazuki's dark hair blew in the wind. It was thick and long – she was going to need to cut it for him again soon. His sharp blue eyes were focused intently on the knife he was using to shape the small block of wood in his hands. Looking at it now, she could tell that it was going to be a bear, and she knew that it would be incredible when he finished it. Stress lines creased near his eyes as he worked, and his sun-tanned arms moved in gentle but sharp motions. He was careful and purposeful with each movement, transforming the block of wood stroke by stroke.

She pulled her right hand from her pocket, tucking the loose strands of her hair behind her ear as her pace slowed and the distance between them closed. Her hair was getting long, too – she would need to cut it soon as well. It was thick like his, jet black and mostly straight. She looked like him in nearly every way – except that her features were more delicate, and she was significantly shorter. The Altherr genes were strong, Miku had always said. Black hair, blue eyes, and solid bones. The surname had been protected through the last five generations because Miku's mother had never changed her name, and Miku had followed that same tradition, even after her partner, whoever he was, had died. It was one of the few topics that Miku never spoke about, hence why no one knew who had fathered her grandfather Kiren – which was probably just another thing that Kiren hated about Miku.

She let out a quiet sigh, pushing the endless stream of thoughts from her mind as she slowed to a stop a few feet away from her father, watching him turn the bear over and glance up towards her. His eyes skimmed over her petite form, lingering on her hair momentarily before he met her gaze once more.

"Where have you been?" he questioned, his hands stopping at last as he set the carving on his knee and slid the leather cover over his knife.

"I just went to Aiden's," she replied, keeping her voice level and her face impassive like usual. It was a practiced lie and one that she knew Aiden would cover for her – he was, after all, her best friend and the only person in the entire village that she trusted aside from her mother.

Her father stared at her for a long moment, his sharp eyes taking her in before he placed his knife and carving on the ground and let out a quiet sigh as he stood to his feet. He towered over her at his full height. Her eyes only reached his chest, and she had to crane her neck to meet his level and serious stare.

"If you're going to lie, Mizuki," he said, stepping forward and outstretching his hand. "Then make sure that you dispose of the evidence first."

He pulled two tiny thorns from the side of her hair. They were so small she had not noticed them, and she missed them while brushing herself off behind the oak. She doubted that many others would have seen them in her dark locks, but her father's eyes were keen, and he never seemed to miss anything. She could feel her body grow tight with tension as she swallowed hard and forced herself to hold his stern gaze.

"Sorry," she murmured, watching as his eyes creased and he flicked the thorns to the ground. He hadn't caught her in a lie in years, and she could feel the unease spreading through her body like a wave, but to her surprise, he simply let out another small sigh.

"Don't do it again," Kazuki said, his voice low.

He didn't clarify if he meant don't lie again or don't climb the ridge again, so she didn't ask, thinking it best to leave herself room for claiming a misunderstanding later. She simply nodded as he stepped back from her and returned to his seat by the fire.

She watched as he picked up his carving once more and turned it over in his well-worn hands. They were calloused and scarred like most others. Life was hard in the village, and the wear it caused her father seemed to grow exponentially as each year went by. At forty-two years old, he still looked good compared to some of the other village men, particularly those from the families that specialized in hunting and gathering foods in the Wild. But even confined to the village as the carver, carpenter, and all-around builder, he had begun to age more quickly in the last two years.

Most people in the village did not live much past sixty and certainly not past seventy. The village Elders and her grandfather were the exceptions to that. They were all over sixty-five and pushing seventy years of age. Yet their time was coming, and she suspected that they knew. The Elders seemed determined to try to hold out as long as possible, keeping their hand-picked successors at bay but diligently trained.

Allegedly, before the Great Destruction, people used to live over a hundred years with ease. No one alive today believed it, even if Miku had insisted that it was true. But Miku had also claimed that her mother was alive *before* the Great Destruction, which went against everything the village Elders taught. Naturally, this wild claim attracted even more doubt and skepticism from the other villagers and contributed to the animosity surrounding the Altherr name.

Though one thing the village did agree on was that their life expectancy was decreasing. She had heard the village Elders speaking about it once in hushed voices by the crops. It wasn't clear why, but people were dying younger, and the Elders were concerned. Miku had been another exception to that, not passing away until the ripe old age of eighty-five and surely disappointing those who had openly wished that she would die a lot sooner. Miku had explained that it was because her mother had done everything possible to give her a healthy start as a child, which was probably true. However, Mizuki didn't doubt that her great-grandmother's long life was primarily due to the woman's iron will and flat-out refusal to die.

"Aiden actually came by looking for you this afternoon shortly after you left, Mizuki," Kazuki said, pulling her from her wandering thoughts.

"He did?" she asked, watching as he nodded and flipped the carving once more to continue working on the head. She pushed her hair behind her ear again, turning on her heel as if to move away. "I should go see him."

"He's gone to help his da with the harvest in preparation for next week," Kazuki said, looking up at her once more. His blue eyes were hard, and there was a hint of something deeper behind them that made her stomach knot. She nodded knowingly, understanding precisely what Aiden and his da were doing. "He won't be back until late – so you can go see him tomorrow."

Kazuki paused. She saw his throat bob as he swallowed, and the muscle in his jaw twitched as he clenched his teeth. It was the most emotion the man had shown in years.

"He's going to need your support these next few weeks," Kazuki said, his voice almost soft. A beat of tense silence passed between them, neither one of them moving or breathing as everything unspoken from the last ten years seemed to hang between them thicker than the ice that coated the Dead Zone in winter. Then, as if the man had flicked a switch, his face became impassive as his voice turned neutral once more. "In the meantime, you can start dinner and check on your mother."

She watched him drop his gaze, his eyes returning to the carving in his hand as his knife resumed the systematic motions of slicing away tiny slivers of wood. Each shaving fell soundlessly by his feet, a physical manifestation of the unspoken words that had once again fallen painfully between them.

It hurt, in a lot of ways – knowing that this was the extent of *this* conversation – that they would never be able to pass this point or talk about it.

And it would always be like this.

She swallowed and nodded, even though she knew he wasn't looking, then turned towards their home. Sometimes burying everything felt easier; it kept her safe, secure, and free from the anguish of the past. But other times, like today, it didn't – and she had to force herself to bottle it all up as she retreated to their small family home.

The Altherrs

The Altherr family was small. In fact, it was the smallest household within the village, so naturally, their family home was also small. It was constructed from a mixture of animal skins and wood like the others. Only the school and Elders' Chambers were made entirely of wood – strong, sturdy, large, and unchanged since the time they were first constructed. Family homes were less permanent and tended to transform as households grew or shrunk through marriage and death. Mizuki's father had spent his entire life working alongside two other families to maintain the homes within the village. They built new ones when necessary and repaired the old ones to keep them standing. When she was younger, he had added a small expansion to their home along the eastern side so she and her brother could have their own space.

Living in the small side room now, she doubted that the two of them could have fit in it together for very long; her father probably would have needed to add a second expansion. As it was, her toes touched the animal hide wall when she stretched out in her bedroll at night, and her elbow brushed against the edge.

Her eyes trailed over the worn hide walls as she made her way toward the entrance. Miku had taught her as a young girl that the structures were modelled after the homes that several Indigenous peoples had used before the Great Destruction occurred, ages before the concrete buildings dotted across the skyline. But she didn't know much about the Indigenous peoples, or any other peoples for that matter. As it was, she barely knew anything about her own heritage. She couldn't read Kanji like her great-grandmother had been able to, and the language was long ago lost, save for a few choice words she wasn't allowed to say.

But Miku had told her that there were many peoples who had originally inhabited this land before those from different places around the world had come across the great seas. The *settlers*, as they called themselves, had been looking to expand their territory and find new trade. Miku had explained that at one point, before the Great Destruction, humans had lived all over the world – even on pieces of land that no longer existed and in every climate imaginable. She explained that it was the reason why people looked different, why they spoke differently, and why there were different languages. Even now, years later, Mizuki could see the remnants of it within the village – though, like hers, most families had lost significant aspects of their culture, and over the decades, everyone had become one people. They belonged solely to the village, unified by their desire to survive in a harsh world.

Family surnames, sparse words from lost languages, stories, and the occasional heirloom were the only vestiges that hinted at heritage. Appearance gave some indication as well, if one knew their history and what to look for, but the truth was, most didn't. It wasn't taught in their school, and frankly, it hardly seemed worth the time to learn it when they dedicated so much of their lives to preparing for winter, ensuring that the crops grew, and just surviving day by day. Miku had explained to her that before the Great Destruction, where people came from and their appearance had mattered a great deal. It had often caused issues and even resulted in battles between different lands and within the incomprehensibly large cities.

It was a difficult concept to grasp and one that Mizuki had always struggled to understand regardless of how old she seemed to get. She couldn't wrap her head around why people would care what someone else looked like. No one paid that any mind here. The village contained people of all different colours, heights, and appearances – and it had no bearing on marriages. The village only had two concerns. The first was to ensure that every member contributed to the village to ensure its safety and survival. The second was ensuring diversity since there were only just over thirty different family names – everything else was deemed unimportant.

In the last few years, the population of the village had stabilized enough that villagers were now allowed to marry whomever they wanted, provided that the families agreed and that the union was approved by the village Elders, who would check to ensure that the families were not too closely related. But before this, when Mizuki's great-grandmother was younger, the marriages had been assigned to provide the most variance possible. She knew that the Elders maintained an extensive family tree that documented each line in the village and carefully monitored the unions to ensure people who wanted a marriage weren't too closely related. The process was complicated but organized, and it had been maintained since the very beginnings of the village. She was told it was essential to their survival and the key to their success in the future – and it was about the only thing the Elders said that she believed.

This was undoubtedly yet another reason why the Elders despised Miku – the woman had flat out refused to tell them who had fathered Kiren.

Mizuki let out a sigh as she closed the distance to their home. She usually tried not to think too much about the village Elders or the pressures that they put on young adults to marry and have kids. It seemed like every year people were getting married younger and younger, and she was probably the only one in the village who hadn't been encouraged to do so. That made sense, given that she was fairly certain the Elders were hoping that her family line would die off and end with her, which was fine by her. She had no intentions of marrying or carrying a child – she had no interest in subjecting them to this life or the anguish and misfortune that was the Altherr name.

Now that she was thinking about it, she wondered if Aiden had been pressured to find a wife lately. He was old enough by the Elders' standards, and his family was in good standing within the village. It was difficult for her to picture him getting married, especially since he tended to ignore the other girls around their age, despite some of their efforts to try to catch his attention. She supposed that maybe he avoided the nagging more easily because he was part of the hunting crew, so he – like his da – was gone for lengthy durations throughout the year. Then, when he was home, he spent all of his time with his family or with her.

She fought against the urge to frown as she thought about it. She knew that when the day came, and Aiden finally did get married, she would see a lot less of him. More likely, she wouldn't see him at all, and that thought made her stomach twist. She didn't know how she felt about that, and she wasn't sure that she wanted to think about it.

Mizuki ducked inside the front entrance, her vision adjusting to the low light as she looked around at the three small rooms that made up their home, easily visible from the main door. It was a simple home compared to some of the others – cramped, tight, and sparse – and yet she loved it because it was theirs.

There was a small extension to the right that was just large enough for two bedrolls, and it was where her parents slept. To the left, there was the tiny eastern extension that had become her own private room. In the winter, they all hauled their bedrolls into the main area to sleep around the fire for warmth; she and Kazuki would take turns adding wood to the flames through the night while her mother slept. Their winters were thankfully bearable with the shelter provided by the ridge, but it was not uncommon for things to freeze, and snow was a regular occurrence, even if it didn't get overly deep. Now with spring finally here and the weather growing milder, they had returned to their individual rooms, leaving the space before her less crowded.

She blinked her eyes, removing her worn leather shoes and trying to force her eyes into focus as she stepped into the open main room. It acted as their kitchen and sitting area, and even though the main room was small, it was sizable enough to fit their table, three stools, a short cabinet and the small wooden chest that stored their cooking ware and dried foods. It all circled the stone hearth that was currently hosting a smouldering fire flickering somewhat pathetically. It looked like it had been abandoned sometime that afternoon, which was to be expected, but what she hadn't anticipated was the frail woman sitting on the stool nearest to the cabinet before her.

Mizuki let out a silent sigh, allowing a small smile to grace her lips as her legs carried her towards the table. She had been expecting her mother to be in bed, either sleeping or just lying there. To be honest, there was little difference anymore. The woman, Keelin, had become a shell. Once the best needleworker in the village, she was now hollow, empty, and void of any emotion or thought. Her fair blonde hair was thin like her frame – dull and lifeless. Her pale blue eyes, which had once been her best feature, now looked dim and gloomy, like the skies after a storm. They paired unnervingly well with her distant stare and unnaturally still body, and the combination gave her the appearance of a corpse that died a day or two prior.

In truth, her mother had died ten years ago. This empty creature before her was just a ghost that haunted their home and wandered about aimlessly.

Mizuki stepped closer toward her mother, keeping her face polite and her eyes warm as she studied the woman. They looked nothing alike, and it seemed that the only thing that Mizuki had inherited from her mother was her short stature. Yet even then, they held themselves so differently. Mizuki's body was small, yes, but strong. Thin muscles laced her limbs like cord from years of climbing the ridge and chasing after Aiden. She was lean but sturdy, and she was sound on her feet. Keelin, on the other hand, was fragile. She looked as though she would break and fall apart if someone sneezed too hard while standing next to her. Everything about her was weak and diminutive.

Looking at her was painful.

Once, when Mizuki was younger and Miku was still alive, she had complained to her great-grandmother that she did not like her mother. It was shortly after her brother had disappeared. She had told Miku that her mother had become annoying. She had told Miku that she hated Keelin because the woman had done nothing but scream and cry for days before falling completely silent and not making a sound. Her mother wouldn't look at her. She wouldn't even acknowledge that she existed, and her father had struggled to keep the home together.

It had been an awful time, and her memories surrounding it were vague at best. Back then, at only eight years of age, she hadn't really understood what had happened. All she knew was that her older brother was missing, her father was distant, and her mother was gone, even though she was still physically there. She had been scared and alone, desperate to understand. So naturally, she had gone to the only person who would listen to her – she had gone to Miku, and she had cried.

She could remember screaming as she got angry and said that she wished Keelin wasn't her mother anymore. Her great-grandmother had held her tight as she let it all out, allowing her a brief moment of safety to expel all the raging emotions that were too big for her body to contain. And then, once Mizuki had finally calmed down, Miku had scolded her.

Even now, nearly a decade later, Mizuki could still remember her great-grandmother's words. It was one of the few aspects of that time aside from Miku's stories that she could recite perfectly from memory. She could still see the look of agony on the old woman's face as she tried to help her understand and tried to explain to her what had happened. Mizuki had been far too young to carry the burden of the knowledge that her great-grandmother bestowed upon her that day, but she had stood there still and quiet, listening to every word.

Reflecting on it now and knowing everything that Miku had told her about the Gifting, about the cycle, and how the village worked – it all made perfect sense. That year had been a Gifting year, and it was the Altherr family's turn. It happened every decade. The cycle had been going on since her grandfather was a child, and each family was required to pay their dues. No one escaped it, and that year her brother had been selected to be sent up the path to Veles. It hadn't mattered that he was only ten years old. It hadn't mattered that he was a good kid. It hadn't mattered that he was smart and kind and helpful; the Elders insisted that the selections were random and that he had just been unlucky. Everyone else in the village readily accepted this, especially because he had been born in the previous Gifting year, and everyone knew that was a bad omen.

But she knew it was a lie.

She knew that her brother had been hand-picked because the Elders wanted to punish Miku for standing up to them. They picked him because they knew it would hurt her great-grandmother most; her parents' pain was just an added bonus. Kiren had allowed it. After all, the choices were limited. He was the head of their family, a Praetor within the Circle; he certainly wasn't going to offer up himself. The Elders couldn't select her aunt Mei because she was married into the Khatri family. They could have picked her mother, but it wouldn't have had the same impact, and since they couldn't actually lose Kazuki because they needed his skills to maintain the village, her brother had been the only remaining choice. He was deemed expendable. The only reason she herself hadn't been picked was that she was under ten years old, and even the villagers would have protested a Gift below the cut-off age.

She swallowed hard as she thought back to the bleary memories of that day, the day that Kiren had come for her brother, and the village had seemed to explode into chaos. It had been a blur, but she could still see the pieces and hear her mother's screaming. She could see the woman's pale hands clawing desperately at her husband as she tried to get to her son. She looked like a wild animal – vicious, desperate, violent. In an odd way, it was both the strongest and the weakest Mizuki had ever seen her mother, and it had taken her father a great deal of effort to keep his hold on her as Kiren dragged her brother away, yelling at Kazuki to get his wife under control.

The other villagers had been watching, nervously clutching at their children and spouses, undoubtedly thankful that it wasn't them. Some of them had looked at her mother with shame – as if they had honestly expected Keelin to just sit down and allow her son to go to his death. He was the youngest Gift ever to be selected, and Mizuki would bet her silver necklace that no other mother in the village would have ever allowed this to happen to their child. She also knew that it wouldn't happen, because no other family in the village was as hated as hers.

At the time, the scene had frightened her.

The sounds that her mother made were inhuman, and they had terrified her to her core. But now, the broken memory just made her sad. It hurt, and it made her angry because she finally understood. The noise that her mother was making had been the sound of a heart breaking. It was the sound of her world falling apart beneath her feet. It was a display of the Elders' true power and the control that Veles had over their village. When Miku had yelled at Kiren in a language that Mizuki didn't understand as he dragged her brother away, she had known then, deep in her gut, that she would never see her brother again, even if she didn't know why.

Her mother had sobbed for days, and time melted together. The yelling had seemed endless, expelled with a violent and vicious hatred until suddenly, one day, it stopped. Her mother stopped. The woman grew silent, and that had been so much worse. That had been what driven her to Miku weeks later in anger and heartbreak – the pain of being blatantly ignored. Her mother had sat and stared at the wall of their home without speaking or even acknowledging her existence. Her father had tried. He pleaded with Keelin for weeks, trying to get her to speak. React. To do anything other than sit there – but nothing had worked. Keelin's total disengagement from the world and her father's failure to bring her back broke Mizuki's heart.

But Miku had explained it.

She had explained *everything*.

Miku had pulled her away from her body and gripped her arms tight, forcing her to stand on her own two feet and making her listen to the sorrowful words she spoke. Miku told Mizuki that she was too young to understand her mother's grief and the frustration and anger that Keelin would hold against the village from that day forth. That her mother, in many ways, would never be able to live in this village again. She had told Mizuki to be compassionate. She asked her to be forgiving. She told her to love and care for her mother because the woman needed her now more than ever.

Miku told her to always live her life with kindness and to always seek the truth. She had begged Mizuki to never give up, ever, and to step up and always do what was right, even if it was hard. She had asked her to take care of her mother. She told her to be patient and kind – and to always know that even if Keelin never spoke again or never recovered, deep down, her mother still loved her. She would always love her. Keelin was just lost right now, but it wouldn't be forever. She told Mizuki that someday, maybe not until they had both passed away from old age, Mizuki would see her mother again, and she would know that all the kindness that she had shown over the years was seen and was treasured. Miku had been insistent that, despite her current condition, her mother could still see her, could still hear her, and that she appreciated everything that Mizuki did for her, even if she could not speak.

Mizuki believed Miku – she *chose* to believe her.

Her great-grandmother died a week later, leaving her alone with a distant father and a numb shell of a mother. It had been, and would forever be, the worst year in Mizuki's entire existence. Even now, nearly a full decade later, thinking about it made her heart ache. It stole her breath away and made the prospect of continuing on for yet another year in this bitter and cruel world seem like an impossible task.

But her great-grandmother had been right.

Regardless of how much it hurt, her mother needed her. Her father needed her. How Kazuki managed to continue working and putting food on the table for them after losing his only son and all but losing his wife was beyond her. She knew that living a life of hatred and anger would have been easier. Given everything that had happened, it would have been so simple to resent her mother and to hate the woman for leaving them. And as a kid, as much as she hated to admit it, it had been a challenge to resist giving in to her anger. It had been hard to learn to control her feelings and accept her mother for what she was.

But living a life of compassion had been the only thing that Miku had ever asked of her. It was the old woman's dying wish, and so, unquestionably, it became the only thing that Mizuki could do going forward. She knew it was the only way she would survive, and it was the only way she could feel close to her great-grandmother.

So, she spoke to her mother with love and kindness every day. She forced herself to interact with the mute woman, and she forced herself to love her. She told Keelin about her day. She told

Keelin what she had learned at school and where her favourite places to play were. It didn't matter that her mother never responded, and it didn't matter that the woman just stared blankly as she prattled on. She did it anyway – because she knew it was the right thing to do and because she trusted Miku. She trusted that deep down, somewhere in that hollow emptiness, a small piece of her mother still existed, that a tiny piece of Keelin was still alive and listening.

Over time, it became easier.

And she started to realize that she honestly did care for her mother and that, strangely, Keelin had become her confidant. Her mother became her secret keeper. She told the woman everything while hiding her emotions from the rest of the world – no matter how painful it was. The first time she saw her mother nod in response was on her tenth birthday, and Mizuki had felt her skin prickle. That single, solitary nod had been the only confirmation she needed; it gave her the strength to continue loving her mother unconditionally from that day onward.

"Good evening, mother," Mizuki said as she stepped towards the silent woman.

She couldn't help the smile that tugged across her lips as she leaned forward to place a small kiss on the top of the woman's head. She was the only human being that Mizuki ever graced with affection, and surely if anyone else in the village saw it, they would never believe their eyes. Out there, in the view of others, she remained stoic and closed off. Aiden was the only other person she ever allowed to see her smile, but she was largely reserved even with him, and she certainly never touched him or showed any physical affection.

Her mother made a tiny '*mm*' noise in response. It wasn't much, but to Mizuki, it was everything, and it was a massive difference from the complete silence she used to get several years ago.

"Dad asked me to start dinner. I thought we could have some of that dried deer meat and maybe some of the dried fruits left from winter storage. What do you think?" Mizuki asked, knowing that her mother wouldn't respond. She started to gather the items from their cabinet and continued on without missing a beat. "I need to give dad a haircut soon too. Maybe I can do that tomorrow morning before going to see Aiden. It's starting to hang low, and it's getting in his eyes – I'm sure it's a nuisance. Maybe I can give you a quick haircut, too. The weather is quite mild and getting warmer by the day. You won't need a jacket, and we can sit by the fire. Don't worry, I won't take too much off – but a small trim might be refreshing."

She turned to flash a slight grin at her mother as she placed the food on their worn wooden plates then set them out onto the small table. She took special care in portioning her mother's food and chopping it into bite-sized pieces before placing the dish in front of her. The woman would still eat on her own without assistance, but after she had nearly choked a few years ago, Mizuki didn't take any chances. She had just finished heating the water to make an herbal tea when her father entered the home, removed his leather boots, and made his way over to the table. He bent to kiss Keelin on the head like Mizuki had, murmuring a small greeting and not seeming to notice the way that his daughter's face fell back into its indifferent and blank expression in his presence.

They ate dinner in quiet conversation as per their usual routine, talking about the things that needed to be done and the chores that needed to be completed. They both included Keelin despite her non-responsive behaviour, and Mizuki made a mental list of everything that her father said so she could make sure that nothing was missed. Once they had finished eating, Mizuki cleaned up the table while her father went to help her mother wash up. When they returned, Mizuki was just placing new logs on the fire for the night since the temperature still dropped during the evenings in early spring. She stopped to say goodnight to her mother before her father led Keelin to bed.

Afterwards, she sat quietly around the hearth with Kazuki. It was what they did most nights, and yet despite this, she had never felt overly close to him. She eyed him from the corner of her gaze, debating what to say, if anything at all. He was working on a new carving, having finished the bear outside before dinner. They didn't usually speak, but today felt different. Given what was coming, her head was nearly spinning with questions, but she continued to debate in silence for a long while until it was dark outside and she was sure that her mother was sleeping.

"Did Aiden seem okay today when he stopped by?" she asked him, catching his eye as he glanced up at the sound of her low voice. She kept her face neutral as if this was a simple question – as if she were asking about the weather and not the future anguish that Aiden and his family were bound to experience.

Her father had stopped his carving; his eyes fixed on her as he raised his brow. She may never show her emotions to him, and his might be buried so deep they no longer existed, but he knew what she was really asking.

"He seemed like he was holding it together," Kazuki said. He watched her for another moment, and neither one of them moved. Mizuki assumed that the conversation was once again over, cut short by their inability to communicate with each other, haunted by all the unspoken things that had collected over the years. But to her surprise, her father seemed to study her for a moment then continued in a low voice. "That boy is worried, Mizuki – I think he is trying to appear unaffected for the sake of his ma, but it shows in his eyes."

Mizuki nodded as she dropped her gaze from her father. Aiden's ma was a perpetual worrywart, and emotional things always seemed to hit her harder than the others. She was a strict and serious woman, hardened by the challenging life of the village like everyone else – but she was, for as long as Mizuki had known her, rather emotional. And the next few weeks would be the most emotional and difficult ones that the village had seen in a decade. She twisted her fingers around the small piece of yarn that she had been playing with since joining her father at the fire. She could feel his eyes on her, and she knew without looking that he was tracking her movements and watching her fingers fidget.

"You care for him a lot, don't you?" Kazuki asked, and her hands suddenly stopped twisting.

"No," Mizuki said, the response quick as her throat tightened unexpectedly. The physical reaction to her father's words caught her by surprise, and she cleared her throat before continuing once more. "Well, not no. Of course I care for him – just – not like that. Not how you meant it. Aiden is my best friend. He is my *only* friend, and I'm worried about him. I'm worried that it might be him – and even if it's not – I'm worried that–"

She stopped, her voice catching as she looked up at her father. He was watching her intently, his keen blue eyes looking for any sort of break or falter in her usual indifferent expression. She could feel a tightness stretching across her chest, and she fought to keep her composure.

"I'm worried about what will happen to his family after." She forced herself to continue, her voice coming out strained despite her best efforts. She would never admit it to her father, but this upcoming Gifting and the knowledge that Aiden's family would be affected had been on her mind for some time. "It doesn't matter who is selected – it might break them regardless. I'm worried about the damage it will cause. I'm worried that they may not recover and–"

She hesitated again, wondering just how far she could push this. They had never made it this far into the conversation before, and now that the words were coming from her mouth, she was afraid to stop because she may never have the chance again. So, she inhaled deeply and made herself speak the words that she truly wanted to say.

"I'm worried that Aiden and his family might be punished for being so kind to me over the years," she whispered. "I'm worried that they're going to pick him or his da – and things will never be the same. And the whole thing just makes me feel sick because it shouldn't be happening at all."

Kazuki stared at her. The implication of her words hung heavy in the air between them, and she fought the urge to frown as she met his gaze. Sending someone up the path every ten years to appease a god so that they could continue to live life peacefully – it was the insane story that the village Elders preached. They taught it to every child once they were ten years old, and the village was content to follow it without question. She had never outright spoken about the practice with her father before, never directly called the practice insane or told him what she genuinely thought – but she knew she didn't have to. She knew that he knew, but she wasn't sure how he would react to her blunt words now. She watched as he shifted on his stool, the crease in his brow deepening as he took a quiet breath.

"I know that your great-grandmother told you things about the world," he said, his deep voice barely above a whisper. She struggled to breathe, the yarn between her fingers long forgotten as she stared intently and resisted the urge to shift to the edge of her seat as her father finally broached the topic that had been haunting her for years. "I know that Miku told you about what it was like Before and that her mother was around to see it."

He paused. A muscle in his jaw flexed as he swallowed, and Mizuki remained silent, unmoving as she waited for him to continue. He seemed to struggle; his hesitation visible before he finally spoke once more.

"But there has never been any proof that those stories were true, Mizuki," he said finally, his voice sounding flat. He was repeating the Elders' words verbatim, and she could feel her heart sinking in her chest as he continued in a monotone drawl. "The Great Destruction happened hundreds of years ago – there is nothing left and nothing to prove that Miku's words were valid. The village was in chaos for generations and plagued with illness until the Farr, Reyes, and Patel families rose up to become the first true village Elders. They unified our people, and they willingly risked their lives to walk the path and meet with Veles. They made a deal, and now we live in peace because Veles allows it. We are safe here because Veles deems it so, and we are expected to show our gratitude for that gift by giving one of our own every ten years. It is a small price to pay for the freedom to live in peace, protected from the Dead Zone and free of Veles's wrath."

Mizuki had gone stiff. Every muscle in her body tensed as she stared at her father and felt her carefully controlled anger starting to break free from its chains. Her thumb twitched against the yarn, and her eyes narrowed into a strained expression as she stared at the man before her in disbelief.

"You don't seriously believe that, do you?" she whispered, her voice sounding hoarse as it all but wheezed from her lungs. "That story about the first Elders climbing the mountain is deerspit."

He stared at her. His blue eyes had creased at her curse, but he let it pass as he shook his head.

"It is what the subsequent Elders have taught for years, Mizuki," he said without faltering. "The story isn't *deerspit* – the first Elders came back with proof, and the village prospered after their return."

"They came back with a scroll, feathers, and their word," Mizuki protested, her chest growing tight as her brain struggled to rationalize the words her father was saying. She had always assumed he knew better. She had always assumed that he didn't believe the Elders either but had resigned himself to follow their lies simply because he was trying to protect what little family he had left. Now, listening to him speak, she felt like she didn't know this man at all. "Miku said that the Elders were wrong, that Veles never demanded sacrifices. She said that the Elders probably never even made it to the top of the mountain, and she said that the Great Destruction wasn't ages ago like they claim. The village had only been around for a few years before the first Elders climbed that path."

"Yes, and great-grandmother Miku was also in her late eighties when she told you these things, Mizuki," Kazuki said, his eyes narrowing like hers as his voice grew stern. "She said a lot of things. None of which she was ever able to prove. Many people, including your grandfather, thought that she had lost her marbles quite a few years earlier because of the stories that her mother used to tell her. Stories that have caused problems and strained the village for decades.

"Her mother's claim that she knew what really happened to the world added a lot of tension and directly impacted the success of the village and this family," Kazuki said, his back stiffening as he spoke. She had touched a nerve, and for the first time in years, she could see that he wasn't entirely in control of his emotions, and his anger was evident. "She said a lot of things that didn't line up with what the village Elders taught, and she said a lot of things that didn't line up with what the rest of the village agreed was the truth. The *first* village Elders were the *only* ones to ever actually climb the mountain trail and meet Veles. Out of the three of them, only two came back alive – one was kept as penance for them intruding on his mountain that day, and the others were granted safe passage only because they agreed to his terms. The terms were simple and clear: we are not to take more than our share, we are to understand that we are part of this world and not above nature, and we are to show we understand it by providing a Gift every ten years – picked fairly and without bias. Gifting has been ongoing for many decades, Mizuki. No family is above showing their gratitude, and all families must participate in order to live in this world and prevent another Great Destruction. The Gifting is difficult, but we are better off for it."

"You mean a *sacrifice*," Mizuki said with a bitter coldness to her voice. That was what Miku had called them, and therefore that was what she called them as well. The term *Gift* was disgusting, and it made her sick to her stomach.

"Mizuki," Kazuki warned, his expression hardening as his voice grew low.

She looked down at her hands, her mouth pressing into a tight line as something uncomfortable shifted in her stomach. This was not how she thought this conversation would go. It was not what she thought her father would believe, and she refused to accept it.

"And you believe them?" Mizuki whispered, glancing up at her father once more and clenching her hands around the yarn as she tried to get control of her emotions. "The village Elders – you believe them?"

"I believe that our life was pretty good while we followed the rules set by Veles and enforced by the Elders," he replied. "I believe that since the Gifting started, the village has been better off. No illnesses have fallen upon us, crops and food have been plentiful enough to feed every mouth here, and the storms and panic that once used to rage within the village boundaries have diminished, if not completely disappeared.

"So you believe Kiren then," she stated, looking up to meet his eyes fully and fixing him with a tight stare that barely restrained her disgust at his words. "You believe what he said about the village getting better."

"I do," Kazuki said firmly, though there was a hint of pain in his eyes.

"But grandfather would have only been a boy," Mizuki argued. "He was a child before the Gifting started. How could he possibly remember what it was like before the first Elders climbed the path? I don't fully remember what the village was like the last time the gates opened, and that was only ten years ago. How can you believe that grandfather knows that things were truly worse before this ridiculous tradition started? How could he even remember that far back?"

Kazuki stared at her, his eyes raking over her tense form and clearly picking up on the resentment that laced her voice. She knew that her face had faltered. She knew that for the first time since she was a small child, she was openly revealing her emotions to her father and letting him see the hurt, the anger, and the disgust that laced her soul. And she knew that he understood what this was really about.

It was about her brother.

It was about the damage that losing him had inflicted on their family.

"Because what your grandfather says is in line with what the Elders have taught," Kazuki answered. Mizuki opened her mouth to respond, but he cut her off and continued. "It aligns with what many of the other families in this village believe and what their grandparents remember. It also aligns with what I myself have personally seen – which is that somehow, despite the ruins we live in and the challenges we face in our lives, we are still here. We are safe. We are fed. We can *see* the destruction that sits just outside our walls, Mizuki, yet those storms *never* reach us. We are protected, and our family was happy at one point – before Miku started to cause trouble."

His final words echoed between them, cold and heavy like a stone. He had been happy once, is what he meant. He had been content and safe until Miku caused a ruckus and brought destruction upon their family. A part of her had always wondered if he blamed her. A piece of her had always worried that Miku felt responsible for her brother's death and for tearing the family apart. And she wondered if her father had ever said those words to her great-grandmother before she died.

She felt her stomach twist as she forced herself to swallow and look away. She wanted to believe that her father didn't mean it. She wanted to believe that he was just saying these things because he had given up or because it was how he dealt with what had happened. Yet, she honestly didn't know if that was the case.

"It just seems unfair," Mizuki whispered, a sense of loss and desperation creeping through her body as she tried to wrap her head around this revelation. "It's not right. To ask a family to bear such a burden."

She glanced back up to him; her hands now wound so tight around the yarn she had been playing with that she could barely feel her fingers. He was looking at her with a solemn expression.

"I know it's hard, Mizuki," Kazuki said. "That's why the Elders developed a system to rotate by family every decade – we have thirty different families within this village, so each family name only provides one Gift every three hundred years. It's a small price to pay, and most people will never even see a Gift from their family. For our family – it hit harder because we are small. There were only the six of us under the Altherr name at that time, and there are only four of us left."

Her brow furrowed as she bit her bottom lip. Mizuki hated that her father insisted on calling the sacrifices Gifts as the Elders did. She hated that they would lose a family member once every three hundred years or so, and she hated that she was supposed to be happy about it. They should be calling it what it was – a human sacrifice based on a deerspit story that the Elders had never proven. It wasn't like they dressed the person up or slapped a bow on their head before sending them out the gate. Miku had said that calling the person a Gift didn't change what they were doing, and she was right. It didn't change the fact that they were sentencing someone to die, kicking them out of the village to face the hardships of the Dead Zone as they climbed the mountain alone and afraid.

They were sacrifices no matter how you tried to spin it, and Mizuki, like her great-grandmother, would never see it any other way.

"And you think the age," Mizuki said, her eyes growing hard as she looked at her father. "That ten years old is an acceptable age to become a Gift?"

Her voice had grown so low it was barely audible. Kazuki's gaze was unblinking as the fire cast eerie shapes on the inner walls of their home. His mouth tightened. She saw him stiffen on his stool once more, and she knew that she had pushed him with that question. She was no longer talking about the tradition in a general sense; she was now directly talking about her brother. Ten years ago. About how he had allowed Kiren to take his son away to die for the village.

The blame was unspoken, but implied – and she knew it had hurt him because she could see it in his eyes.

"We were unlucky," he said, each word firm, slow, and painful. There was agony in his gaze as he met Mizuki's narrowed stare. "I would not wish what we went through on *any* other family – but that doesn't mean that I don't support the system that the village has established. The Gifts were to be *unbiased* and *fair*. Death doesn't discriminate based on age, Mizuki."

She stiffened but said nothing.

It hurt her to hear that her father supported the tradition that had sentenced her brother to die alone at only ten years old. It was devastating to hear him defend the system that had destroyed her mother and had left her neglected throughout the majority of her childhood. After Miku had died, her father spared her the time that he could, but it often wasn't much. He had to continue working and contributing to the village. When he had spent time with her, he was always closed off and distant – and it had driven the wedge between them deeper.

It was why she had grown close to the O'Kane family, and why she had spent so much time with Aiden as a child.

She swallowed hard again, letting out a quiet exhale and forcing her fingers to untangle from the yarn. Some days, doing as Miku had requested was hard, and today was one of those days. She was struggling to find the kindness in her heart. Struggling to love her father unconditionally with understanding and forgiveness when the truth was, she didn't understand it at all. She didn't accept that those were his words, his beliefs, or that he actually accepted the death of his son as part of a ludicrous sacrificial practice.

Logically, she knew that it had been her family's year, and she understood why it had happened. She knew that her brother had been the *only* option for the family, but she also knew in her heart that they had picked him on purpose. They had wanted the Altherrs to suffer, and they had succeeded. Her broken relationship with her father was proof enough of that. Yet understanding it didn't mean she was okay with it. She would never be okay with it, and now after years of repressing it, she could not believe that her father, of all people, had apparently accepted it.

Kazuki stood, their conversation obviously over. He paused when he walked by her, seeming to hesitate a moment before he awkwardly placed a hand on her head and ruffled her thick black hair. It was a gesture that he had not used since she was a small child, one she had thought he had forgotten.

"Go see Aiden tomorrow morning, Mizuki," he said as his hand slipped from her hair, and he turned towards his room, where Keelin was already sleeping. "He needs you right now, more than you can understand – and I need you to support him."

With that, Mizuki was left alone at the hearth, staring at the log that crackled in the darkness. The heat radiated on her face and sunk into the bare toes that she had placed on the edge of the warm stone in front of her. Her fingers flexed as she held her shins, the yarn now abandoned on the table for another day as she leaned forward and rested her chin on her knees. The embers below the lingering log glowed dimly, and she could hear the breeze pick up outside, blowing gently across the hide walls of their home.

She loved her father; she knew she did.

She respected her father – he was an honest man who worked hard.

But she no longer related to him.

She no longer understood him or felt like she knew who he was. How could he support a village that had taken away his only son and turned his wife into a semi-functional vegetable? How could he defend them and agree with them? Was he that blind, or was he simply trying to cope?

Mizuki's face scrunched into a frown as her thoughts wandered, and she stood from her perch on the stool. She paused to place a final log on the fire before making her way to her room. Maybe she didn't truly understand what Kazuki had gone through. Maybe there were other aspects of the situation that she didn't know of that had formed his opinion or made him accept what the village Elders had done. Because no matter what he had said tonight – she didn't believe it.

She couldn't.

Maybe someday, she would find out what he truly thought. Maybe someday, they would be able to speak of this again without so much tension, without the chopped emotions or the discomfort that came from opening up and talking to each other. Maybe someday they could have an honest conversation – a real conversation. One that didn't leave her feeling like there were endless things left unsaid, things he was keeping locked away.

Perhaps, someday.

A part of her doubted it.

She honestly didn't know if it was possible anymore.

What she did know was that tomorrow morning, after she cut her parents' hair, she would immediately walk the familiar path to the O'Kane's home on the southern side of the village. She would greet Aiden's da with a wave if he were there, she would stand awkwardly and allow Aiden's ma to hug her even though it made her uncomfortable, and she would bring his little sister a new carving from her personal collection. Then, she would see Aiden.

And she would be there for him, in whatever way he needed her to be, because that is what Miku would have wanted.

The O'Kanes

The path to the O'Kane family home was familiar. Mizuki knew every rut, every twist, and every bump along the way. She could have run the entire length through the village blindfolded and not stumbled once. She had travelled it almost every day for the last ten years after all, and in many ways, Aiden's family had become an extension of her own. They were a taste of normalcy. They were her barometers for human emotion, and what rudimentary social skills she did have, she owed primarily to them.

They were also the only family in the village that didn't avoid her like a disease. They were the only ones who had allowed her to play with their child, and they were the only ones who treated her with any sort of decency. For that, she would always be thankful.

She would never be able to repay them for the kindness that they had extended to her over the years, and maybe that was why she felt so determined to make sure that they were okay. Perhaps that was why she had tossed and turned in her bedroll the night before, struggling to find sleep as she thought about Aiden, his sister, his parents, and what they were about to go through. She knew how hard this was, and she would never wish this pain upon any member of the village – not even the Elders.

It would be the first time that the O'Kane household lost a family member. They were one of the larger families within the village, so Mizuki knew it was possible that the sacrifice might be selected from the home of an uncle, an aunt, or a cousin, and it wouldn't necessarily be someone from Aiden's immediate home. Yet knowing that fact had done little to settle her mind or quell the sickness in her stomach. It had been building over the last month and had worsened after speaking to her father the night before. The loss that the O'Kane family was about to experience would damage them forever, regardless of who was selected.

She let out a quiet sigh as she walked. It had not taken her long to make her way through the village using the less travelled paths, cutting through a few sections of brush where possible to avoid curious gazes until she reached the south-eastern side of the village. Over the last month leading up to the sacrifice, people had seemed to grow interested in her and her family once more, and the appearance of Veles's symbol etched into trees and homes had increased. The Altherrs had always been the subject of gossip and rumours, but most people had forgotten and tended to avoid them. Yet as soon as the Gifting year had started, it was as if the entire village suddenly remembered what happened a decade ago and they became fixated on Mizuki's family. Now, people watched her and her father more than ever, and it left her feeling grateful to her past self for investing so much time in finding shortcuts and ways to sneak around unnoticed. It had spared her from the majority of the unwanted glances since the new year began.

It wasn't until she ran out of brush and she was forced to return to the open that she made herself step back out onto the main path. She nodded stiffly to Mrs. Lear, the old, nearly grey-haired woman who sat outside of her home with a battered set of knitting needles and seemed to pride herself on knowing the comings and goings of everyone on this side of the village. The woman had never spoken to Mizuki. Not a single word in eighteen years, but every time she saw the woman, her face would turn into a scowl, and she clutched the knitting project she was working on closer to her chest.

At first, this behaviour had bothered Mizuki, but now she didn't feel a thing. She simply completed her customary nod, then turned her gaze back to the main path, keeping her head down and her body curled inwards as if to make herself smaller while completing the rest of the short journey as quickly as possible. After all, Mrs. Lear was better than Mrs. Wilson – that woman could be outright hostile at times.

She didn't stop or remove her gaze from the well-worn dirt until the O'Kane home came into view and she had passed the other homes. Typically, Mrs. O'Kane was outside working on something – either repairing Aiden's hunting boots or trying to patch a pair of her husband's perpetually ripped pants, which was always troublesome because materials were hard to come by within the village. Families passed clothes down from generation to generation. Some clearly came from the Before because they had textures that she had never seen naturally. Anything new was made from hides, leather, and furs for the winter. Shirts, threads, and linens were made from flax, hemp, or soft tree barks – often haphazardly woven together in uneven pieces that never fit quite right. Maebh, Aiden's younger sister, was typically either helping, playing, or practicing her sewing. Regardless of the combination, there was always something going on out front. The O'Kane family home was full of life and energy, and the atmosphere was always warm, comforting and inviting. Yet today, it was anything but.

The tension was palpable.

Mizuki could feel it sinking into her skin like a weight as it inched down her spine. The air was tight. The abnormally warm breeze that had been ruffling her hair only seconds ago seemed to disappear entirely, and the sky grew dimmer as the clouds shifted over the early morning sun. Her eyes scanned over the home, silently taking in all the subtle hints of chaos and despair that were visible to those who knew the O'Kanes well. The woodpile outside was disorganized; pieces had been tossed there carelessly as if the collector had not truly been paying attention. There was a rip in the door flap that no one had bothered to fix – it had been there for over two weeks, and yet still no one had tended to it. Several of Maebh's toys were lying outside to the right, something that Mrs. O'Kane had never allowed in all the time that Mizuki had known her. The fire pit just outside hadn't been cleaned out; far too much ash had collected at the bottom, and on top of it sat the smouldering remains of a neglected fire.

These sorts of things were normal to some families within the village; many would walk by the O'Kanes' home and not think twice about what they saw, but not Mizuki. Her eyes were nearly as keen as her father's. She had spent years silently watching everyone in the village, learning their habits and collecting information – and with that skill had come an acute sense of perception. She knew that for the O'Kane family, these seemingly insignificant changes were massive. It was the equivalent of their home having been hit by a storm and turned inside out.

It made her stomach twist.

She didn't like it.

She couldn't even begin to imagine what state of mind Mrs. O'Kane must be in to allow her home to remain in such disarray, but before she could dwell on it, the woman had stepped out from the front flap of her home carrying a worn looking leather jacket with a tear down the left side. Her dark black and intensely curly hair, which was usually braided or tied into a neat bun, was hanging loose in a messy knot on the top of her head. Her skin was missing its usual healthy glow, and deep worry lines framed her light brown eyes. She hadn't been sleeping, that much was obvious, but it was her tight expression and nearly rigid body that stung harder than anything else. The woman had always been stern and serious, as were most adults within the village, but her eyes had always been kind, and her posture warm and welcoming. She was a loving woman to her core, but at the moment, she looked like an entirely different person.

Mizuki's feet stopped, and she stilled as she watched Mrs. O'Kane let out a silent breath and close her eyes. For a brief moment, she contemplated leaving or hiding in the bushes. Anything would be better than just standing there and staring at what appeared to be a private moment of weakness for the woman. Yet before she could decide what to do, Mrs. O'Kane moved, and as her head turned, her gaze landed on Mizuki.

"Mizuki," Mrs. O'Kane said, a distant warmth rushing into her eyes as she moved once more and made her way across the small distance between them.

All of the strain seemed to vanish from her body, her smile returned, and her welcoming nature took over. She was doing a commendable job of pretending to be alright, but Mizuki could still see the strain in the woman's shoulders as she walked. She wasn't okay, and Mizuki knew it. Her family would know it too, and yet there was nothing that anyone could do about it, so Mizuki just forced her face to remain calm as she raised her hand in greeting.

"Good morning, Mrs. O'Kane," Mizuki said as the woman covered the last two steps between them and pulled her into a tight hug.

It was the same routine every time she came to Aiden's, and yet no matter how many times it happened, she still tensed uncomfortably under the woman's grip. It wasn't that she didn't like the hug; she did, sort of. She had just never managed to grow used to it, no matter how much time passed. She let Mrs. O'Kane hug her because she adored the woman and because a small part of her craved the physical contact even if it did make her uneasy. And on very rare occasions, like today, she would even awkwardly pat the woman's back in return.

"So, how are you?" Mrs. O'Kane asked as she finally let go and stepped back to look at her. "How are your parents? I know that Aiden will be happy to see you. He's just inside putting away the rations."

"We're all fine, Mrs. O'Kane. Thank you for asking," Mizuki said as she absent-mindedly tucked her loose hair behind her ears. "How are you doing?"

"Oh, I'm doing just fine, dear," Mrs. O'Kane said warmly, smiling once more even though it looked tight and uncomfortable as it stretched across her lips. "I was just about to see if I could fix Finley's jacket – he got it caught yesterday while he was out with Aiden."

Mizuki's lips twitched at that, and her eyes creased in amusement. Finley, Aiden's da, had a reputation for damaging his clothes worse than anyone else in the village. Mizuki wasn't sure if it was due to bad luck or simply because the man didn't pay enough attention while he was out hunting. Regardless, the man was constantly ripping his clothes and bringing them back in tatters. He was both the best hunter that the village had seen in years and the most patchwork-clothed man ever to exist. Though the damage had seemed to lessen some after Mrs. O'Kane had threatened to stop fixing his clothes, telling him that if he weren't more careful, he would be forced to walk around in ripped pants and jackets until there was nothing left for him to wear.

"That must be a new record," Mizuki mused as she nodded to the jacket still clutched in Mrs. O'Kane's hands. "What has it been, a full two weeks since he last ripped it?"

"Fifteen days," Mrs. O'Kane said, her eyes crinkling at the corners. "The longest stretch yet, though I'll be honest, Mizuki, I'm not holding my breath that it will continue. A part of me wonders if his talent for hunting isn't tied to his ability to rip his clothes. Apparently, they struggled to find much on the last trip."

"I heard about that," Mizuki said as she walked with the woman back to their home, stopping just a few feet short of the door. "Do you think the deer moved south?"

"It's possible." Mrs. O'Kane nodded, her smile becoming even more strained. "But we're hopeful that's not the case. So, what brings you by this morning?"

"My dad said that Aiden was looking for me yesterday," Mizuki replied, her eyes darting to the hides that covered the entrance to their home. "Would it be okay if I go speak to him?"

"Of course, dear," Mrs. O'Kane said as she shook her head slightly, a strange look crossing her gaze. "You know you don't need to ask – but tell him while he visits, he can work. We need more kindling, and the two of you can collect it in the forest while you talk."

"Of course." Mizuki nodded, unsure of what emotion seemed to be lingering behind the woman's eyes as she stared down at her. "I'll make sure that we get lots."

Mrs. O'Kane gestured with her head to the entrance, then made her way over to one of the stumps by the fire. It was where she typically sat to mend her husband's tattered clothing, and based on the size of the rip in Mr. O'Kane's jacket, she would likely be at it for a while. Mizuki watched the woman sit down, then ducked inside the O'Kane household.

It was much larger than hers, though the general layout was essentially the same. Immediately inside the entrance, there was a small space for shoes. Then the room opened up into a large common area that housed a sizable wooden table, several stools, chests, and one large wooden cabinet. Their hearth was larger as well and slightly off-centred to the left so as to leave more open space. There were three rooms off the main one, and since Aiden wasn't anywhere in sight, she instinctively moved towards his.

"Aiden?" Mizuki called, making her way across the large common area.

"Mizuki?"

"Your ma said you were putting away rations," Mizuki said as she reached the small door to his room and peered inside. "Though right now, you appear to be slacking."

His eyes narrowed as he looked up at her, his sandy brown hair a ruffled mess as he lay stretched out on his bedroll.

"Hardly," Aiden scoffed, his face shifting into a grin. "I finished that already."

"You're so efficient," Mizuki teased, a half-smile tugging at her lips.

It was one of the rare moments where she could look down at him. Aiden was tall like his da, and he towered over her like a great oak bearing down on a tiny shrubbery. But even though it was an amusing change of pace, she felt her nerves shift somewhat uncomfortably. As children, they had spent the majority of their time together outside playing in the forest. Aiden had taught her how to fish in Glass Lake, track small animals, and read the weather patterns. As they had gotten older, their time together had changed. Their activities shifted from playing games and chasing after one another to talking and walking or completing simple chores, but it had always largely remained outside, except for the dinners that she had shared with him and his family. So regardless of how well she knew him, there was something about being in a small, enclosed space with him that made her nervous, and right now, standing in the door to his room staring down at him as he laid comfortably on his bedroll, she could feel herself growing flustered.

It was personal.

Too personal.

"My dad said that you were looking for me yesterday," Mizuki said quickly, folding her arms across her chest as she cleared her throat and leaned somewhat awkwardly in the doorframe. "I'm sorry I wasn't around – it was the first clear day, and I–"

"I know," Aiden said softly, cutting her off as he nodded in understanding. He was the only one who knew that she regularly climbed the ridge, and while he had never had any interest in going with her, he had always supported her in doing it. "I would have stuck around to wait for you, but I had to go out with my da for the Gifting harvest."

"My dad mentioned that," Mizuki said, watching his face and looking for signs of stress. She could see dark rings under his eyes. Ever since the Gifting family was announced a month ago, Aiden had been swamped, and they had barely seen each other. He had only just returned from a two-week hunting trip, and she had yet to see him since he got back, but it was clear that he had not been sleeping well while he was gone. "Is – is there anything I can do?"

He smiled at her again, but this time it looked nervous, almost tense.

"I wanted to talk to you," Aiden said, slowly pulling himself up into a sitting position. He ran his hand through his hair, his brow creasing as all the relaxation drained from his body, and suddenly he looked so much older. No longer the boy that used to help her catch frogs. "Maybe we can go for a walk to the lake?"

Mizuki nodded, her jaw clenching in anticipation as she moved away from the door while Aiden stood up. She knew what that meant. It was their code for something serious, and given the situation his family was in, it made sense. Whenever they spent time together, they would spend it in the forest near the southern edge of the village, and they typically didn't venture too far. But whenever they wanted to talk openly without the worry of who might be listening in, they always went to the boulder by Glass Lake. It was near enough to the village that it was within the boundaries for non-hunting families to wander so that if anyone ever did see them there, they wouldn't get in trouble. Yet it was far enough away that no one ever went there unless they had reason to.

"Your ma asked us to gather some kindling," Mizuki said as she led the way back to the entrance of the O'Kane home. "We can collect some on the way."

He nodded in agreement but didn't respond, his expression still laced with tension.

"Oh," Mizuki said as she paused just before the entrance, turning back to look up at him. "Is Maebh home? I brought her something."

At this, Aiden seemed to come out of his daze – his eyes creased and his boyish appearance returned, but he shook his head as he looked at her.

"You spoil her, you know? All the other kids are jealous of her collection. It's just like when you were little all over again, except for the part where the other kids aren't afraid of her," Aiden said, giving her shoulder a nudge as he smiled. Then his face seemed to fall again, and he swallowed hard. "But no, she's not home. She had to go to school today for the Gifting lesson. She won't be back until after lunch."

"Right," Mizuki said, her gaze dropping to the floor as her heart instinctively dropped at his words.

Every year the Elders would go to the school in the spring to present a special lesson on the history of the Gifting. With it being a Gifting year, she knew that the presentation would likely run long. She had never witnessed a full-fledged Gifting year lesson personally, having been too young to see it when her brother died and too old now to be in school, but she figured that the Elders were probably taking it as an opportunity to tell even more lies and sow fear into the minds of the children in the village.

She cleared her throat and pushed the thoughts away as she looked back at Aiden. "Well, could you give this to her later then?"

She pulled a small wooden figure from her pocket – a rabbit, which her father had carved for practice when she was eleven.

"Of course," Aiden said, taking the carving from her and moving back to his room to place it on his small storage chest. "It will be a nice distraction."

They left his home in silence, stopping to say goodbye to Mrs. O'Kane, who politely and sternly reminded them about the kindling. As they walked into the forest behind the O'Kane family home, Mizuki's thoughts wandered. She knew that Aiden wouldn't talk to her about whatever was on his mind until they reached their boulder, so she kept her eyes locked to the ground as they shifted through the trees and collected small sticks and branches.

The wooden carving had indeed been meant as a distraction for Maebh – and if there was anything else that Mizuki could have done or given to help the girl, she would have. Maebh was twelve years old, which meant that she was old enough to understand the Gifting and grasp the concept of what was about to happen to her family. She had learned about it in school since she was ten, and she knew it was coming, though she hadn't known that it was her family's year to contribute until a month ago. None of them had, not until the Elders announced it, and the change in the girl's behaviour had been instantaneous. She went from being excitable and full of life to quiet, reserved, and nervous.

The last time that Mizuki had seen the girl was when dropping off some spare material to Mrs. O'Kane the previous week, and Maebh's nails were bitten down to the stubs. While Maebh tried to play it off and pretend that she was okay, she clearly wasn't. Mizuki knew she never would be, and in many ways, she pitied Maebh more than she pitied her younger self. At least when it had happened to her family, she hadn't known what was coming. She hadn't had to experience the dread of anticipation that Aiden's family were going through now.

As they continued to make their way through the sparse trees, grabbing anything dry and small enough to carry, she couldn't help but feel like Aiden lingered closer. He never strayed much farther than a few feet from her side as they each held an armful of sticks and worked their way closer to Glass Lake. She watched him from the corner of her eye, taking in the strained flex of his muscles and the way he ground his teeth. In all the years that she had known him, she had never seen him this tense, and it made her nervous. Not because she was afraid, but because she didn't know what to do and she didn't know how to help him. She wasn't good with emotions to start with, but just because she didn't often express them, it didn't mean that she couldn't feel them.

She felt them.

And they hurt.

She bit her lip as she picked up a thick dead stick and tucked it under her arm. She had come over here to help him and to be there for him in whatever way he or his family needed, and she fully intended to keep that promise, but now she was sincerely doubting her ability to be able to do anything useful. She couldn't give him any sort of comfort or reassurance aside from telling him that it wasn't the end of the world. It might be the end of the current world as he knew it, but after some time had passed, he could make another.

He wouldn't be alone. She wouldn't abandon him, and regardless of how bad it hurt, he would survive. It would be hard, brutal even, but he would *live* even if it felt like he was dying, and she would help him and his family pick up the pieces when this was all over. It wouldn't be enough, because nothing would ever be enough to repair the damage done, but it was all she could do. So she was determined to do her best even if she couldn't express that to him.

She glanced at him again, watching as his hardened gaze flicked to their left and then their right, checking to make sure that they were alone before they changed course and headed west toward their usual meeting place. He looked so focused and yet so detached, and she fought against the urge to fidget with anticipation as the lake came into view and they made their way towards the large boulder that sat along the bank.

"What did you want to talk to me about?" Mizuki asked, double-checking over her shoulder that they were alone before she set her stack of kindling down on the ground. Aiden had done the same, and while his hands were now casually stuffed into his pockets, he was anything but relaxed.

"You know how they announce the sacrifice to the family Praetor a week before the Gifting?" Aiden asked, his amber eyes darting along the edge of the forest before he met her gaze once more.

"Yes." Mizuki nodded, biting back the anger that knotted in her chest at his words.

It was just another item on the list of things as to why she hated her grandfather Kiren and wanted nothing to do with the man. She hadn't known it ten years ago, but the head of each family, or the Praetor as they were called, was positioned on a council called the Praetorian Circle. They met with the Elders several times a year to discuss issues within the village, solve problems, and advocate for their families. Each Praetor was supposed to act as a representative for everyone who shared their surname. They were leaders; it was their job to protect the interests of their family, bring forward concerns from each household, and provide important information to the Elders.

The role came with a lot of responsibility; *Praetor* wasn't just a fancy title to be flaunted around. The Praetors were expected to be perfect role models – they were charged with enforcing the rules of the village within each household, and they were held accountable for the failings of the family when things went wrong. They were not the same as the Village Guard, who served the Elders and ensured the security of the village. Instead, they were heavily involved in the inner workings of the village and the decisions that were made regarding the village's future. It was not an easy position. That said, the role also came with several perks, including more food rations, larger homes, and a direct line to the Elders with the power to implement change and push for their household's interests.

Most Praetors shared the additional rations with their families and used their positions to aid those within their households that needed help. Her grandfather, Kiren, did not. He used the position as a way to distance himself from the Altherr name and gain the favour of the Elders. Yet that wasn't what made her hate him so. She didn't care that the man never shared the extra food rations with them and instead gave them to his daughter Mei, who shared them with the Khatri household. What bothered Mizuki and made her sick with disgust was knowing that her grandfather had *known* that her brother was going to die for a week – and that he had done absolutely nothing about it.

He didn't refute the Elders' decision.

He didn't tell her father so that he could prepare for the emotional blow.

He didn't say a thing, and, as Mizuki later found out from Miku before she died, he had refused to tell her father anything during the week leading up to the ritual. He hadn't been approved to, since the information was intended to be confidential, but still, her brother had only been ten years old. He was barely old enough to be selected, and Kiren had not only accepted it, but he had sat on the information and kept it to himself for seven days. Kiren had resented Kazuki for as long as she could remember. No one had ever told her why, not even Miku – but sitting on that information had been low, even by his standards. Mizuki frowned internally as she pushed the thoughts away and forced herself to focus on Aiden once more.

"Well, yesterday, when my da and I were out collecting the dogwood branches and kalmia for next week, he told me that my uncle is going to come by after the meeting," Aiden said, taking a small step forward as he lowered his voice. "He's going to stop by my aunts' and cousins' places too – to let us know who is selected."

"That's very kind of him," Mizuki noted, leaning against the rock by her side. "He could get in a lot of trouble for that if they find out."

"I know," Aiden agreed, his eyes creasing once more as he seemed to hesitate before her. "But that's not what I wanted to tell you."

"Alright," Mizuki said, watching as Aiden seemed to grow even more agitated and stressed. "What did you want to tell me then?"

"I–" He hesitated again, his eyes flicking over her carefully controlled face as if he was looking for something. He frowned, drawing his hands out of his pockets as he swallowed hard and then took another step closer. "I've been having dreams."

Mizuki's brow creased as she stared at him. It was an odd comment to make, and she wasn't sure where he was headed with it.

"Okay," Mizuki puzzled, careful to keep her tone calm as she spoke. "About what?"

"About this," Aiden said, his hands balling into fists at his sides. "About what's going to happen."

"It's perfectly normal to have dreams about the sacrifice," Mizuki said, her eyes tracing over the dark rings below his eyes once more. "Aiden – what's about to happen is–"

"It's not just about the Gifting." He cut her off, shaking his head as suddenly his eyes clouded with a storm of emotions. "It's about all of this – *everything* – all of the things that your great-grandmother told us."

Mizuki stiffened at his words.

They had been acquaintances before her brother had died, and Aiden had heard Miku tell many stories over the years. The rest he had either heard from her or heard from the rumours, gossip, and mockery throughout the village. As a boy, Aiden had always enjoyed the stories because that was exactly what he viewed them as – stories. She knew that one of the main reasons they had met was because he used to like to come by and hear Miku talk when they were children. She couldn't remember when or how it had started; her memories from those days were clouded at best. Everything before the last Gifting had nearly vanished from her mind after years of suppressing the memories of her brother. So it was almost as if Aiden magically appeared at her home with no context at all, but he never believed Miku's words; for him, it was free entertainment and nothing more.

From what she could remember, she and Aiden had only really become close friends after Miku died, and he had found her wandering alone in the forest that winter collecting kindling for her father. He had offered to help, she had said yes, and then his appearance in her memories grew much more frequent. As they got older and grew closer, she had told him more of Miku's stories, but she had always known that he didn't believe them. Yet she shared them with him anyway because he was the only one who would listen, he was the only one who didn't laugh, and he genuinely seemed to enjoy them.

Now though, looking at the incredibly serious and strained expression on his face, she felt even more nervous. They had not spoken about Miku or her stories for nearly two years, so for him to bring it up, something must have changed.

"Aiden, what happened?" Mizuki questioned, her voice so low it was barely audible. He knew that she took everything that Miku said seriously, and he had learned very early on in their friendship that she would not tolerate him joking.

"I saw it," Aiden said hoarsely, his expression becoming somewhat desperate as he spoke. "Mizuki – I don't know how to explain this, and I know that what I'm saying sounds impossible, but it was as if I saw the whole thing. As if all of her stories suddenly fell into place, and I could see all the dots connecting. I never really paid it much attention before. I know that, and I know it was incredibly selfish of me. My family has been very fortunate over the years, so I never had any need to worry or even think about it, but after I found out that it was our turn for the Gifting, I started to notice things. I started to listen to the way that the other Praetors in the hunting parties talked. Over the last month, I watched all their interactions, listened to their side conversations and eavesdropped on my uncle and da when they spoke. Since then, I haven't been able to sleep because every time I close my eyes, I see it, and I know it's going to be true."

Aiden let out a breath and ran a hand through his hair. His eyes creased in pain as he met Mizuki's gaze and took one final step closer. She could practically feel the heat from his body as he stared down at her.

"It's Maebh, Mizuki," Aiden said as he swallowed hard. His voice nearly broke as he spoke, and she could see something shining in his eyes as his fists clenched tighter at his sides. "They're going to pick Maebh. She's going to be the next sacrifice."

With those words, it suddenly felt like he had pulled all the air from her body.

Aiden's Request

"Aiden," Mizuki said, straightening from her leaned position against the rock as her voice faltered and she tried to find her words. "How do you know it's going to be *Maebh* – did your uncle say something?"

"No, he didn't say anything," Aiden replied, impatient exhaustion creeping into his voice.

"Then what did you dream?" Mizuki asked, her heart beating quicker in her chest as she looked at him curiously. "What did you see?"

"I saw the Gifting day," Aiden revealed before he swallowed hard. "I saw the mountain; I saw the path and a cave and a shadow with red glowing eyes. Then I saw the Village Guard. They came to our home, and they tore Maebh from my ma's arms. She screamed, and we yelled, but it didn't do any good, and they dragged her away as my uncle held my da back. He kept screaming for them to take him instead over and over again as my ma sobbed. It's the same thing every night, Mizuki – *exactly* the same and I can't get the images from my head. I can't get the sound of their screams out of my mind."

"Aiden, that could just be a nightmare and–"

"It's not a nightmare!" Aiden nearly shouted, his head shaking as his face pinched with pain. He stepped back from her and ran his hands through his hair in frustration before he dropped his voice lower once more. "They're not *just* dreams, Mizuki – I *know* they're not. I can feel it. There's something wrong with them, and it sits under my skin like an itch that I can't scratch. I don't know what's wrong with me, but I feel *off*. In the dreams, it's like I'm right there seeing it before my very eyes! Besides, it's not just the dreams, Mizuki – even my ma and da are nervous. They haven't said anything to me directly, but I keep catching them talking quietly when they think I'm not around. My uncle is on edge, and everyone keeps whispering while we're out hunting."

Mizuki eyed her friend carefully, taking in his extreme agitation with concern. She could tell that he was struggling to keep it together as he let out his pent-up fears, and she knew she needed to try to calm him down.

"That doesn't mean that it's Maebh, Aiden," Mizuki reassured him, watching as his eyes closed and he let out a deep sigh. "It could be one of your cousins."

"No, it can't," Aiden nearly whispered, his eyes opening once more as he took a step toward her and grabbed her upper arms firmly. She flinched in surprise at the physical contact but didn't step away as she tilted her head back to meet his eyes. She was close enough to see the tiny flecks of gold around the center of his irises and the agony that seemed to be radiating from their core. "After they announced that it was going to be my family for the Gifting, I started having trouble sleeping. I had that dream for the first time a week after the announcement. The second night that I had the dream, I left the house to go for a walk. I figured it was better than just lying there all night and stressing over it. Back then I thought it was just a coincidence to have the same dream twice, and I figured I was being paranoid. So, I went out – I thought maybe the fresh air would help. I was cutting around by the fields on the east – you know the path through the brush that we usually take when going to collect our rations? I took it out of habit; I wasn't trying to hide – I didn't think that anyone else would be up. It was late and dark, and aside from the Village Guard by the main gate, everyone should have been sleeping. The fields should have been abandoned, but they weren't."

Aiden swallowed hard, his voice dropping to a quick low whisper as he unconsciously gripped her tighter.

"I heard voices when I rounded the old oak tree, so I slowed down. I thought it might just be one of the guards wandering around or maybe a kid out causing trouble or something, but it wasn't," Aiden continued, and Mizuki felt her pulse start to quicken as he spoke. "It was the Elders, Mizuki. The *Elders* were out there in the middle of the night with my uncle and your grandfather – and they were talking in low whispered voices. They didn't have any torches; it was as if they didn't want to be seen. I didn't want to get in trouble for sneaking around, so I stopped and ducked into the thicket just next to the field, and I heard everything that they said."

"What did they say?" Mizuki whispered, staring at him intently.

"They're worried that there's going to be a sizable food shortage this year. Do you remember last summer? How they started to cut the food rations toward the end of the season?"

"Yes." Mizuki nodded. "They said that was because foxes and rabbits got into the food stores."

"Exactly," Aiden confirmed. "But that's not what happened – that story was deerspit. The land isn't yielding as much as it should be. The food wasn't spoiled and eaten by the wildlife last year; they never had it in the first place, Mizuki, but they didn't want people to panic, so they kept it a secret. Only a few of the Praetors knew, and most of the gatherers were kept in the dark about how much was actually harvested because they kept swapping shifts and moving people around.

"I heard one of the other Praetors whispering about it while we were on the last hunt, and he's married to the head gatherer," Aiden added. "It confirms what the Elders were saying by the fields that night – that the issue is with the crops, Mizuki. The soil isn't good anymore, and stuff isn't growing the way that it used to. Some of the reserve seeds have spoiled, and they're having a hard time getting things to germinate. They were talking about potentially expanding and trying to make another field further east past the river, but your grandfather was worried about the effort it would take to clear the land. My uncle was tasked with increasing the hunts and pushing further south to try to find food because they are worried that there won't be enough to get us through the next winter."

Aiden paused, leaning down closer and dropping his voice even lower.

"My uncle left the conversation after the Elders gave him orders to increase the hunt durations. That's why I was gone so long – that's why we went for two full weeks. But your grandfather stayed behind, and they continued talking once my uncle was gone. Mizuki, the Elders said that they might need to try to locate the Agronomist. At first I didn't know what they were talking about, I thought it might be a tool or something in the village, but then I realized that they were talking about a *person*," Aiden whispered, his body growing still as his words poured out more quickly. "The Agronomist is a man – he used to be part of the village. He was in charge of the crops, and he was the one who helped to set up the initial fields. Apparently, he knows things about the harvest and the land and the seeds that the gatherers just don't. I don't know what happened to him, they didn't say, but your grandfather really didn't like the suggestion. He seemed adamant that it was a bad idea to try to locate him, and he said that he was probably dead by now. The Elders agreed, but they seemed to think they'd have no choice but to at least try. Otherwise, we would start to face heavy losses in the next year."

"But that doesn't make any sense." Mizuki shook her head as her brow furrowed, and Aiden finally released his hold on her arms. "The Elders said that people couldn't survive out there much past the boundaries of the hunting zone, Aiden – even my great-grandmother never questioned that."

"I know," Aiden agreed, his voice becoming more strained. "That's what I thought too, but then your grandfather said something that changed everything."

"What?" Mizuki asked, her heart beating in her throat as she leaned in toward Aiden without even realizing it. "What did he say, Aiden?"

"He said that maybe it was time we tried to find the deserters and ask them for help," Aiden whispered. A warm breeze ruffled his hair as Mizuki's heart all but stuttered to a halt in her chest. "I nearly didn't believe what I heard, but then the Elders said that it was possible – that it might be a better chance than finding the Agronomist, given his old age. The others were younger when they left, so they might still be alive. The Elders want to put together a small group after the Gifting, send them out into the Wild down to the south to try and find the deserters."

"They said there were deserters," Mizuki whispered in disbelief. "Miku said they were real. She told me that a group left the village at one point because they disagreed with the sacrifices but–"

"I know, I remember," Aiden said quickly, waving his hand dismissively. "But the Elders denied it when I asked about it in class."

"You asked about it *in class?*" Mizuki's eyes shot wide in surprise as she stared at her friend incredulously. "Aiden! You're lucky they didn't beat you senseless for that. There's a reason why Miku told us those stories when we were alone."

"It was ages ago, and it doesn't matter now. The point is they were real, Mizuki – what your great-grandmother said about them was true." Aiden's eyes had gone wide, and his voice had taken a serious tone. "The Elders mentioned checking the unbounded map to try to figure out where they might have gone, and that was when everything seemed to click together – all of it. Everything that Miku told us and everything that you have been saying for years. It's all true! It *has* to be! That's why the hunting scouts are always Praetors. They lead the way a good distance ahead of the group. I always thought it was because they're more experienced, but I think it's because they keep an eye out for any signs of other humans. It explains why they've kept the hunting grounds restricted all these years – it's because they're afraid of running into the deserters. Because there are other humans out there living in the very lands that they said were dead, dangerous, and impossible to survive!"

"Okay, maybe," Mizuki conceded as she tucked the loose strands of hair behind her ear and desperately tried to process the implications of what Aiden had just said. "But what does that have to do with it being Maebh? How do you know she is going to be selected? I know you had the dream, Aiden. I'm not saying that I don't believe you, just – why are you so sure?"

"Because they *can't* pick anyone else," Aiden answered, his tone dropping flat as his eyes creased in pain. "I figured that out while on the hunt. After overhearing the conversation by the fields, something about it bothered me – I mean, aside from the obvious that the Elders have lied to the entire village, that the crops are failing, and that other people are potentially out there. There was something else about it that ate away at my mind, and I couldn't stop thinking about it the whole week leading up to the hunt. It wasn't until I was out there in the Woods watching the way that my uncle, my da, and the other Praetors were behaving that I finally figured it out.

"There *isn't* anyone else for them to pick, Mizuki," Aiden whispered, his shoulders dropping as he met her gaze. "My uncle is a Praetor; they'll never pick him. My da is the best hunter that the village has, and with the crop issues and food shortages, they can't afford to lose him. They can't pick my ma because she's one of the main gatherers, and they will need her in the fields this summer. The rest of my aunts, uncles, and cousins under the O'Kane name are either too young, key members of the gatherer group, part of the hunting group, or they're involved in the crop planting crews. There's not a single one of them that's expendable.

"That leaves Maebh and me," Aiden said, his voice so quiet now that Mizuki shivered at the low sound. "We are the only two O'Kanes who could possibly be selected, and out of the two of us – I contribute more. Maebh is only a child. She's replaceable in their eyes, and she is the only O'Kane of age and expendable. And my da knows it. My uncle knows it. The other Praetors have been dancing around him uncomfortably like they all just *know*, but no one will say it.

"You were right." Aiden let out a sigh, and his eyes slowly traced over her face as he spoke. "You have always been right; the selections aren't random. The village can't afford to randomly sacrifice someone, even if they only do it once every decade. Could you imagine if they drew straws and they ended up picking my uncle or my da? Or if they had selected your father ten years ago? The village would fall apart – we're too small, and most people have significant roles. There's no way that they randomly make their selections, the village Elders are far too smart to leave it up to fate because they can't risk losing indispensable people. This whole thing is calculated, it always has been, and I think that the Praetors have always known."

"Aiden," Mizuki murmured, her head shaking once more as she found herself at a total loss for words. The sudden and unexpected urge to reach for him briefly flickered through her body, but the confidence to do it was lost.

"It's going to destroy my ma," Aiden whispered, his voice trembling as he looked at her. "I – I think she suspects it. She's always been clever, and I think that's what she has been talking to my da about when they're alone, but my da won't confirm anything. He keeps trying to avoid her. To be honest, I think he was actually happy to go on the two-week hunting trip because then he didn't have to be around her. He didn't have to lie to her and evade her questions or see Maebh when he suspects what's coming."

Mizuki opened her mouth and closed it, then repeated the process twice more before she finally snapped it shut and hesitantly reached out her hand to grab Aiden's arm and give it a reassuring squeeze. She wasn't good at this comfort thing – or at physical contact, but it seemed to be what he needed as he stared out into the trees behind her then swallowed hard.

"I wanted to tell you sooner," Aiden said, his eyes glazing over as he spoke. "I wanted to tell you about the conversation by the field the very next day, but the morning after my da dragged me off to check the snares. He made me help around the home until late in the night, and when I went by your place the next day, you were in the middle of helping your father. After that, it was like my da was purposely trying to keep me busy – or maybe he was just attempting to keep himself busy. I'm not sure, but I couldn't get away from the house to come see you. He caught me trying to sneak out twice in the middle of the night that week before the hunt. I think he knew I was trying to go see you because he lectured me on proper etiquette and told me if he caught me again, he'd tell my ma."

"And then you were dragged off on the hunting trip," Mizuki surmised, and Aiden nodded as his gaze slid back to hers.

"And I was barely able to stop by to let you know we were going," Aiden said quietly. "But I lost my chance then, too, because my da came with me to help carry that wood for your father."

She watched him let out a deep sigh, his eyes closing and his expression pinching as if he was carrying the weight of the world on his back.

"Mizuki, I need you to tell me that I'm not crazy," Aiden whispered, his voice pleading as he opened his eyes once more. "*Please.* I need you to tell me that this isn't all in my head – it's been driving me crazy for the last three weeks. I haven't been able to sleep, and I can barely concentrate. I nearly broke my ankle when we were trekking home because I wasn't paying attention; all I could think about was seeing you and telling you what happened. I tried yesterday but–"

"I wasn't there," Mizuki whispered, feeling her heart drop in her chest as she spoke the words. Aiden had needed her yesterday, just like her father had said, and she hadn't been there for him. She had been off climbing the ridge and not even thinking about him until she had gotten home and her father had told her he'd come by. Her arms curled around her middle as she fought to keep her emotions from showing on her face.

"It's not like that," Aiden said, his eyes searching over her face as if he could see the shame and disappointment that she was hiding. Out of everyone, he knew her best, and he always seemed to know what she was thinking no matter how blank her face was. "You know that's not what I meant. I only had a minute before I had to go out with my da for the harvest yesterday. I wouldn't have been able to tell you all this anyway. I had just wanted to see you."

"You're not crazy," Mizuki said abruptly, shaking her head firmly as she wrapped her arms tighter around her body. She could feel the same sickness that had curled in her stomach the night before twisting in her gut now as she looked up at him determinedly. "You're not. I believe you, Aiden – of course I believe you."

He smiled, but it wasn't happy. His lips barely twisted, and it almost looked painful.

"I'm sorry," he murmured, and Mizuki could not stop her brow from furrowing in confusion at his sudden and completely unnecessary apology.

"What?"

"I'm sorry I didn't believe you before," Aiden clarified. "I'm sorry that I treated Miku's stories like entertainment, and I'm sorry that I didn't take it as seriously as you did."

"Aiden," Mizuki murmured, shifting uncomfortably at his words. "You don't have to be sorry; I was never upset with you over that."

"I know," he breathed, stepping closer once more. "But that doesn't change the fact that I regret being a blind idiot for the last ten years."

"You were a kid, Aiden," Mizuki said, her arms constricting around herself further.

"So were you," Aiden murmured. "But you believed it. You didn't once doubt it."

"You had no reason to doubt the Elders," she countered, fixing him with a firm gaze. She didn't want him to feel guilty about doubting the stories that Miku had told them as kids. No one else believed them, and Aiden was no different; he'd had no reason to believe them. "You listened to her, you listened to me – and that's what counts."

"Maybe." His eyes creased, and she could see his smile soften as he looked down at her and his eyes searched her face. Then his gaze shifted back to the right, and she could see him hesitating before he spoke once more. "Do you know what my da said to me when we were out gathering the dogwood branches and kalmia for the offering?"

She didn't answer. She simply shook her head and waited for him to tell her as a strange look crossed over his face.

"He'd just cut down a dogwood branch and was about to tuck it into the basket, but instead, he stopped and looked at it. He stared at it for such a long time that I started to wonder if something was wrong, but then he turned back to me, and he said, *'put silk on a goat, and it's still a goat, Aiden. Keep people safe, fed, and protected, and they will see what you tell them to see because fear is more powerful than reason,'*" Aiden recited, his voice growing low once more. "And then I could see it, Mizuki – the doubt in his eyes like he was questioning everything, and he had finally seen the village for what it truly was."

"Did you talk to him about it?" Mizuki asked, untangling her arms from around her middle. She watched as Aiden shook his head and swallowed hard, his gaze still locked to the forest behind her.

"No," Aiden whispered, his voice becoming hoarse. "What could I have said? What would it do? They all know, Mizuki, everyone in the Praetorian Circle seems to know and talking about it would only make it worse. My da can't do anything about it, and neither can my uncle. Most of them believe that Veles is real. I've heard them talking about it for years, they all believe the teachings of the Elders, and they all believe that the Gifting is required. Just on the last trip I heard two Praetors talking about it while on night guard before we came home, and they both agreed it's necessary. If anything, I think they support the process even more because it's *not* random. They think the process protects the village and that the loss of one expendable person every decade is a minor inconvenience. Had the process truly been random, it probably would have caused more of an uproar, but because they pick families and people who don't overtly impact the function of the village, no one questions it. No one cares if it doesn't affect them directly, and everyone else in the village doesn't know and just accepts it."

"So, what about you?" Mizuki asked, studying Aiden's face closely. "What do you think?"

"What do I think about what?" Aiden asked, his gaze shifting back to her once more.

"About Veles," Mizuki clarified. "Do you believe in Veles?"

"I don't know," Aiden whispered. "I don't know what I believe anymore, but I know I can't sit here for two days and wait for my uncle to come and tell me that my baby sister has been picked for the Gifting – that's why I wanted to talk to you. Mizuki, I need your help."

His eyes were shining as he reached for her once more, leaning down closer and gripping her upper arms firmly. She knew that whatever he was about to ask was going to be big. She had known him nearly her whole life, and she could tell from the way that he was holding on to her as if she were his last and only lifeline in the world, that whatever he was about to say would forever change their lives – or possibly end them. And yet, the words slid from her mouth so easily. She didn't even hesitate as she spoke them, and the nervousness fluttering in her stomach seemed to fall away as an odd stillness shifted through her body.

"What do you need me to do, Aiden?" Mizuki whispered, her back straightening as she spoke. She saw his face crack with relief before he pulled her against his chest and hugged her hard.

"Thank you," he whispered, his breath ghosting against her hair. She stiffened, her arms awkwardly pinned to her sides until he stepped back once more to look at her. "I need you to help me steal the unbounded map from the Elders' chambers."

"You want to *steal* from the Elders?" Mizuki nearly blanched, her eyes growing wide with surprise. "Aiden, if they catch us, you know we'll be dead, right?"

"I know." Aiden nodded, his face shifting into a grimace. "Which is why I understand if you say no, but that's not even the half of it."

"What's the other half, Aiden?" Mizuki asked, meeting his gaze and letting out a breath.

"We steal the map," Aiden said slowly, watching her face for reaction as he spoke. "Then we go find the deserters or try to find the Agronomist – just like the Elders talked about by the field. From what I heard, it sounds like they might have already mapped out possible locations to search, and they know the direction that the people headed off in. If we can find them, we can ask them to come back to the village with us. Miku said they left because they disagreed with the Gifting, but the Elders acknowledged that they were probably still out there. That means that they must be existing *without* providing gifts to Veles. So maybe Veles isn't real, or maybe your great-grandmother was right and he never wanted them. But either way, if we can find the deserters and get them to come back to the village with us, it will prove that we don't need a Gift. The second the other families see that there are other people out there, alive in the world that the Elders said was uninhabitable, they will start to question everything – it will force the Elders to acknowledge the lie. We can save Maebh, Mizuki – all we need is one of them."

"There's only just over a week until the Gifting, Aiden," Mizuki said, panic fluttering in her stomach once more. "They could be weeks away. From the stories we heard, they left ages ago – we have no idea how far they have travelled since then. There's no guarantee that we'll be able to find them and get back in time."

"I know, and that's why we need the map," Aiden affirmed quickly. "Look, I know it sounds crazy, but I've thought it all out. They announce the Gift the day after tomorrow. My uncle already told us that he would breach protocol to come and tell us who was selected. So, we steal the map tomorrow night and look it over. I know the lands to the south – I've hunted in them for years. I can get us to where we need to go. I think I already know which direction we have to head anyway. The Praetors leading the hunting parties always avoid the southwest, so I bet you anything that the unbounded map shows that as the direction that the deserters travelled."

"Okay, so we steal the map, look it over and then what?" Mizuki asked, a million questions floating through her mind as she ran the scenario in her head. "We just head out into the Wild?"

"No." Aiden shook his head and met her gaze intently. "We wait until the Elders make the announcement. The meeting with the Elders to reveal the Gifting choice isn't until after sunset. So, that day we pack, and we prepare. Use your mother's old bag, pack enough food and supplies for a week of travel. Make sure to pack extra clothes. Hide the bag in the thicket by your home or in your storage chest and be ready. When my uncle comes by to tell us – that's when we decide. If it's Maebh, I'll meet you here by the lake that very night after the moon is at its highest. If it's not Maebh, we return the map and pretend as if nothing happened."

"So if it's one of your cousins, you're fine with letting them die?" Mizuki asked, her brow arching at him in disbelief.

"No," Aiden scoffed as he crossed his arms over his chest and fixed her with a look. "I only said that because I know that's not going to happen. It's going to be Maebh, and once that's confirmed, we meet here, and we go find the deserters."

"And what if we can't find them? What if they all died or they're too far away, and we can't reach them? The sacrifice happens at noon on the seventh day after the announcement is made – if we leave that night, we will have less than seven days to find them *and* get back. That's not a lot of time, Aiden," Mizuki breathed as she clutched at the necklace that hung beneath her plain and fraying shirt.

She could feel her heart beating hard in her chest as her mind raced, and she tried to consider every possible option. They didn't have a lot of time, no matter how she looked at it. They had only eight days to figure this out, but she knew that they would never garner support from anyone in the village without some sort of proof. No one would believe Aiden if he said that he heard the Elders speaking about the deserters. The Elders would deny it, her grandfather would deny it, and the cold hard truth was that no one in the village would care. It wasn't their family that was being affected by the sacrifice, and they wouldn't need to worry about anything themselves for at least another ten years. Based on what Aiden had heard the Praetors saying, some of them even supported the process, and they supported how the selections were made because it was done with the village's wellbeing in mind.

Besides, her great-grandmother had spent decades trying to convince people that the sacrifices were unneeded and look where that got her. She was considered a nut bag, and people avoided being associated with her. There was no way on earth that they could do in eight days what Miku had tried and failed to do in decades. She let out a tight exhale, meeting his gaze once more.

"Have you thought about just taking Maebh and leaving the village?" Mizuki asked though she felt like she already knew the answer as she spoke it. "I would come with you – your ma and da might even come with us too."

"I know you would." He smiled at her, but his eyes just looked sad. "And I did think of that, but it won't work. If I take Maebh and leave, they'll come after us because she is the selected Gift – they will hunt us down like animals and drag us all back to the village for the Gifting. They'll probably kill the rest of us to make a statement once the gates close. We would never be able to get far enough away with her. She's too small, and she won't be able to keep up. And even if the three of us somehow did manage to get away, which I seriously doubt we would be able to do, they'll just punish my parents, my uncle, and my cousins in Maebh's place."

"But you don't think that they would come after just the two of us or punish your uncle or family if we go missing?"

"They might," Aiden admitted, letting out a low sigh as he tilted his head to the side and looked at her thoughtfully. "But the truth is they hate you, and they don't like me any better. If Maebh is selected as the Gift, and I go missing – they won't be happy, but they might not bother too hard with trying to find me because I'm not worth *that* much to the village. I'm a decent hunter, sure, but they could manage without me, and it would be one less mouth to feed this upcoming winter. They'll still have Maebh as their Gift, so I would just be treated as a runaway. No offence, but they will probably just blame you for my disappearance. They'll assume we ran off together, and frankly, we both know that they'd be all too happy if you up and disappeared one day. It's possible they might let me go without consequences to my family just to get rid of you."

"True." Mizuki snorted, rubbing her temples with her fingers as she breathed out another low exhale. "Aiden, this is insane. You know that, right? You know that we could die out there? That your ma and da could lose you and Maebh in the same week – you know that it would kill them, right? They will be devastated when they find out that you left."

"I know." Aiden nodded.

"And you know that we might not find the deserters or the Agronomist," Mizuki continued as she started to pace in a small circle before him. "And what if we don't? What's your plan then? Do we come back to the village empty-handed and beg for forgiveness? They'll cut off my head before they let me speak, and they'll probably hang you by association. Or do we just live out in the Wild forever and keep searching for the deserters until we inevitably die? What's your plan for if we fail?"

"If we don't find them, then it changes nothing," Aiden said, the solemn tone of his voice freezing her mid-pace. She met his amber gaze once more and saw the sadness radiating behind it. "If Maebh is selected as the Gift, there is nothing else we can do – there is no one we can appeal to. Even if I could somehow convince my ma, da, and uncle to stand up against the other Praetors, it still wouldn't work because the people of this village are terrified. I love my aunts and uncles and cousins, but do you seriously think they will argue if Maebh is selected? It spares them from losing a sibling, a daughter, or a son, Mizuki, and when push comes to shove, they will let it happen because they're thankful it's not them. The truth is they live in fear of the mountain, they live in fear of the Elders, and they know that the entire village stands behind the Gifting. They don't want to find out what might happen if we don't send someone up that path – just like Miku said, they will blindly follow because it is easier, safer, and they are afraid of being wrong.

"Even my da knows that," Aiden said. "It's why he's done nothing – because he's afraid. If he stands against the Elders and the Praetors without any solid proof, the consequences will be grave. It will impact the entire family, and a part of him is terrified to question Veles. I know you don't truly believe in Veles, Mizuki, but even Miku didn't deny his existence. She never once said that Veles wasn't real.

"And that's why I want to find the deserters – that's why we *need* to find them. They're proof that Veles didn't demand sacrifices, as Miku said. If we want to have any hope of changing the village and putting an end to this, we need them," Aiden insisted. He let out another low sigh and stepped towards her once more. "If we don't find the deserters or the Agronomist, we either stay in the Wild, or we come back the day before the Gifting and see if we can convince my ma and da to leave with us and bring Maebh – and we just make a run for it. If they catch us and kill us, then we die – but at least we tried. It's better than just sitting here and letting this happen, and it's the only solution I can come up with that has any hope of working. Two years from now, people will have forgotten that Maebh was Gifted. They'll go on with their lives happy and normal as if nothing has changed, and my family and I will still be there picking up the pieces. I saw what it did to your mother – I saw what it did to your father, what it did to you, and I'm not going to let that happen to my family. Not when there is something that I can do. Not when there is still hope and not when I know that there are people out there who can help us put a stop to this.

"Mizuki." Aiden stepped even closer, his voice dropping low again as he reached out once more and placed both hands gently on her shoulders. "I know you have responsibilities at home taking care of your mother and father. I know that what I'm asking of you isn't fair – I know it's insane. I know I'm asking the world of you – but I can't do this without you. I need your help getting that map. I want you to come with me to find the deserters, but I know that it's not fair for me to ask that of you, and I understand if you say no. If I have to, I'll go alone, but I do need your help tomorrow night as a lookout if I'm going to have any chance of finding those people."

"It's insane," Mizuki said, closing her eyes and letting out a sigh before she looked up at her best friend once more. "You're insane."

"I know." Aiden winced, his face faltering as he tried to gauge her blank expression. He hesitated, his eyes creasing once more. "I'm sorry, I shouldn't have asked this of you and–"

"No, it's insane that you thought for one second that I *wouldn't* go with you," Mizuki interrupted, her brow creasing as she gave him an open look of disbelief. "I asked you what you needed me to do because I'm going to help you, and that means helping you until the very end, regardless of how crazy your plan might be. I believe you, Aiden. I trust you – and you're not wrong. We would never make it past the river if we tried to run with Maebh, and if we don't do something, nothing will ever change. So, I'll help you get that map, and I'll be ready two nights from now because of course I'm going with you."

"Mizuki," Aiden whispered, his face splitting into a strained smile as he pulled her tight to his chest and hugged her once more. "Thank you."

"You're welcome," Mizuki muttered into his jacket, ignoring the way her stomach knotted as he held her.

It was the third hug she could remember receiving from him, the second having happened only moments ago and the first being years prior, when they were just kids. But as her arms curled around his lean frame and her nervous, shaking hands gripped the back of his jacket – it was the first time that she had ever hugged him in return.

The Map

Gathering the supplies for her pack had been surprisingly easy. She hadn't exactly expected it to be a challenge, but in the back of her mind, she had been anticipating that something would go wrong. Yet it hadn't. The following morning Kazuki went to work like he usually did, leaving her home alone with Keelin, and the day became exceptionally ordinary.

Mizuki had prepared her mother's breakfast, combed out her hair, and spent a few minutes braiding it into a fancy plait as she prattled on to the woman about the weather and how the spring flowers were just starting to poke up out of the ground. She behaved as she usually would have. She collected kindling from the forest nearby and mended a few torn items of clothing before cleaning out the ash from the hearth. Everything about her appearance that day was calm, controlled, and perfectly normal in every way.

Yet on the inside, she was spinning, and she felt like she might vomit at any second as she silently gathered the majority of her limited clothes and carefully packed them into her mother's old bag. She had used the pack for adventuring as a small child, but she hadn't had any need for it in recent years. When she had pulled it from the bottom of her small storage chest, she sat there on her bedroll for a long moment just staring at the worn leather material, remembering the way that she and her brother used to fight over who got to use it. Then, swallowing hard and fighting against the rampant nerves in her stomach, she got to work. First, she packed dried meat, berries, and tree nuts. She added her hide water flask, favourite knitted hat, extra socks, and medical supplies. Then she added some thin thread, a needle, flint, and the knife that Kazuki had given her on her sixteenth birthday.

She kept the pack hidden in her storage chest all day as she slowly and secretly added more and more items, staying mindful of the weight. Then, once it was finally full and she had everything that she could possibly think to include that her father wouldn't notice was missing, she carefully covered the pack and left it hidden in her storage chest as Aiden had directed. She even managed to take her mother on a short walk around their home before preparing dinner and starting the fire for the night. By the time Kazuki returned, exhausted and worn from his hard day of labour, Mizuki had managed to calm down and finally get control of her spiralling anxiety. Even with knowing that she was going to be sneaking into the Elders' Chambers in just a few short hours, she kept her expression emotionless.

They ate in quiet conversation like they always did, and Keelin went to bed after dinner just like every other night. Everything about the day aside from packing supplies and preparing to leave had been entirely normal and uneventful. Yet as Mizuki sat around the fire with her father and absently twisted yarn between her fingers, watching the flickering glow of the flames fill the small space between them, she couldn't help but feel like she and the world around her had somehow permanently changed.

"How was Aiden today?" Kazuki asked, his voice low as he gazed at her over the small carving he was working on before the fire.

"I didn't see him today," Mizuki answered in honesty, catching her father's gaze as she unwound the yarn from her fingers and prepared to start the cat's cradle over. "He had to help his da reset the snares, and they needed to make some more arrows for the next hunting trip after the ritual. I think they are doing alright, though – or at least they are managing."

Kazuki nodded, his eyes shifting back to the small carving once more. Silence passed between them for a long moment as

Mizuki kept her attention focused on her yarn, careful to keep her face blank and her hands still despite the lingering nervousness festering in her chest.

"I'm glad that he has you," Kazuki said. His words startled her gaze back up to his, and he met her stare with a level look. "You've been a good friend to him, Mizuki."

Her brow creased as she looked at Kazuki in confusion, and her shoulders shifted into an awkward shrug.

"I haven't done anything more than what any other person would do," Mizuki mumbled, hooking the yarn from her left hand under her right index finger.

"Except that that isn't true, Mizuki," Kazuki disagreed. "I ran into Mrs. O'Kane on my way home today. Not only did you help with the firewood yesterday, but she said that you helped her patch some clothes. But more importantly, she said that Aiden seemed better after seeing you. She's been worried about him, and most people have been avoiding them ever since the announcement was made."

Kazuki stared at her for a long quiet moment, and Mizuki's hands stilled before her as she watched the fire shift across her father's face.

"You're a good kid," he said, his voice taking an odd tone that she had not heard before. "Better than most in this village want to admit and better than most here deserve. I can't take credit for how you turned out; I know that. But I am proud of who you've become, Mizuki. And I know that Miku would be proud as well."

She stared at him, speechless – unable to come up with anything to say as the wood cracked beneath the heat of the flames and sparks shot up into the air. She could feel the tension in her chest shifting up into her throat as all the emotions that she kept locked away churned in her stomach. He had never told her that he was proud of her before. He had never said anything of the sort, and as he said it, she couldn't help but feel a sickening guilt slide down her spine as she thought about what she was going to do.

"Don't forget to add another log to the fire before you go to sleep," Kazuki said as he stood from his stool and shifted around her to make his way to bed.

She felt his hand drop onto her head as he passed, his fingers gently ruffling her hair in that familiar way that made her heart ache for the past – longing for the time before the Gifting, before her family had been torn apart. The contact vanished nearly as quickly as it had happened, and just like that, Kazuki had ducked into his room, closing the hide hanging behind him, and she was left alone by the fire feeling burning down her throat.

She was going to break his heart.

What little remained of it would be devastated if he found out what she had agreed to do. If she got caught, if Maebh was selected and they left the village – her disappearance would kill him. She felt her eyes prickle with tears as she swallowed hard and forced her body not to allow the emotions any foothold. She was willing to risk her own life on the journey to try to make a difference if Maebh was selected tomorrow night, that much she knew for sure. Her only wish was to make it home so she could see her father one last time and explain to him why she did it, so she could apologize for causing him pain without reason.

She sat there for a long moment, clutching the necklace beneath her shirt and willing herself to calm down before she finally got up and placed the final log on the fire. She couldn't afford to lose focus, and she could not allow herself to be distracted by thoughts that would not help her tonight. So she went to her room, closed the hide hanging behind her and laid down on top of her bedroll, not bothering to change or get inside it as she stared at the ceiling. Then, just as she and Aiden had planned, she waited. Waited until her father fell asleep and until the village was still and silent. Until the night was so dark, it was hard to see, and the only sounds that could be heard were the wind and the owls as they hunted for mice and small critters. Then, silently, she crept from her bedroll, pulled on her jacket, pocketed her small paring knife, and snuck from the Altherr home into the darkness to go meet Aiden.

It took several long minutes for her to navigate her way around the outermost edge of the village, toward the crops on the east. There were two buildings that made up the Elders' Chambers: the Hall, a large wooden structure that contained the Meeting Chambers and the Documents Room, and the

Residence, where the village Elders lived. Both buildings were located just next to the small section of trees and brush that ran along the eastern fields, and thus she and Aiden had decided that the best way to approach was from the south, using the same brush that he had hidden in when he had overheard the conversation regarding the state of the crops.

It wasn't far away, but she took her time as she moved, letting her eyes adjust to the dark as she stopped every few feet to listen and ensure the coast was clear before continuing on. When she finally reached the thicket of trees and bushes where they had agreed to meet, her heart was racing in her chest, and her jaw was clenched so tight it was starting to ache. She didn't say a word as she stepped to his side, only nodding as he gently touched her shoulder and then gestured for her to follow along behind him through the thin trees and brush.

Initially, Aiden had insisted that he be the one to break into the Hall and get the map, but after several intense minutes of discussion by the lake the day previous, he had finally relented and agreed to allow Mizuki to sneak inside instead. While the Elders' Chambers were not heavily guarded, there was always a single guard located near the entrance to the Hall, which made it nearly impossible for Aiden to sneak inside, given his size. Whereas Mizuki was small enough that she could climb in through the vent on the top of the long wooden structure.

It had been years since she had been inside the Hall, having only ever been brought into it once after getting caught climbing the ridge as a kid. Yet she remembered the layout, and she knew from her one visit and years of watching her father work and discussing the structure's designs that the large building was made up of two distinct rooms. At the front of the Hall was the Meeting Chamber. It was large, open, and contained very little aside from a massive hearth, tables, and chairs. It was typically where the Praetorian Circle met and where the Elders would meet with village families to discuss important topics. But aside from being their point of entry, there was likely nothing useful in that section of the Hall. She and Aiden both agreed that the map would be in the back room – the room that only the Elders and a very select number of Praetors were granted access to. It was called the

Documents Room, and she suspected that not only did it contain the unbounded map but that it was also the place where the village Elders stored the records of their history.

Getting inside would be a challenge because there was no rear door on the wooden structure. The vent on the Document Room was much too small for anything other than a squirrel to fit through. So, their only chance was for her to climb in through the vent of the Meeting Chamber and access the Document Room from inside. It was a simple enough plan, and they figured that they could manage it fine. The problem was getting out. The Hall was quite tall, tall enough that Mizuki sincerely doubted she would be able to climb back up and out of the vent once inside. They discussed it at length the previous day while collecting up the last bits of kindling, and they were not able to come up with a good plan. What they had was weak, and she could feel her stomach knotting as they silently closed the distance toward the large wooden structure. Once she had the map, Aiden would distract the guard by the entrance of the Hall, and she would slip out the front door.

It wasn't ideal, but it was their only choice.

They hadn't had the time to come up with anything better, and they couldn't afford to try to wait for a better time to steal the map because they would need it the very next day if Maebh was selected and Aiden's fears were proven true.

Mizuki could feel her body starting to tremble with fear as they slowly and silently crept their way to the edge of the brush, avoiding the belladonna that grew near the edge as they darted across the darkened path and pressed themselves up against the rear wall of the building. She shuffled along against the cool wood as Aiden moved, following his every step carefully and moving tightly behind him until they reached the northern corner of the Hall, and he put out his arm and gestured for her to stop. It was the best place to climb given the slope of the roof, and it gave them the most cover because of the trees to the north. With only a sliver of moonlight in the night's sky, Mizuki sincerely doubted that anyone would see them. As it was, she could barely make out Aiden in the darkness, and he was standing less than two inches away on her left.

She waited in silence as Aiden peered around the edge of the building, and when he finally turned back to her and nodded, she felt her muscles tighten in anticipation. This was it. The coast was clear, and they were making their move. She could just barely see the gleam of his eyes in the night, and yet she could nearly feel the stress and concern radiating from him as they shifted positions to execute their plan.

She exhaled hard as she moved to stand in front of him, and he kneeled to the ground. Reaching out above him, she grabbed the wooden wall behind him as best as she could while she placed her right foot on his shoulder. She felt his hand grip her ankle, tightening around it firmly as she looked down to meet his gaze, and he nodded once more. She swallowed, then pulled her left leg from the ground, placing it on his other shoulder so she was standing on him while tightly gripping onto the side of the building. He waited until she had her balance, then, slowly, he stood, and she shifted her hands up the wall as he lifted her into the air. Once he was on his feet, the roof was nearly at eye level, so she grabbed onto the edge and started to pull herself up. It was far easier than she thought it would be with Aiden lifting her into the air by her calves, and in less than a minute, she managed to crawl on top of the Elders' Chambers and lay flat along the roof.

She could feel nervous sweat forming across her brow as she looked around from her high vantage point and gazed down at the village. The Elders' Residence was dark, the paths were empty, and there wasn't a sign of human life anywhere. Biting back her fear, she cautiously crawled along the roof on her stomach, keeping her weight spread out across the beams. She made her way towards the opposite side, where she could just barely see the outline of the vent and the steady stream of smoke that poured from the hole. The hide that was stretched taut above it to keep out the rain vibrated in the gentle breeze that blew through the village, and her heart raced.

She reached the vent only a moment later and pulled out the paring knife from her pocket. Working quickly, she cut the tie that kept the hide stretched over the opening and rolled the material back so she could peer into the Meeting Chamber of the Hall. She squinted, looking around the dark room for any sign of movement, but there was none, only the faint glow of the fire shifted in the large open space. All she could hear was the wind and the night. Not even the guard at the front was making a sound. She re-pocketed her knife and inched her way onto her knees in front of the small vent. It would be a tight fit, and looking at it now, she knew that there was no way that Aiden would have been able to fit inside.

She twisted her body around, dropping her legs into the hole as she sat on the edge, and she took a deep breath. The drop was at least twelve feet. If she didn't land carefully, not only could she hurt herself, but she could also land in the hearth or draw the attention of the guard. She swallowed hard, sliding into the hole as she gripped the edges of the roof and lowered herself into the large wooden structure as if she were a squirrel hanging from a branch. She could feel the heat of the fire against her feet when she was all the way in, dangling from the tips of her fingers. She fought the instinct to close her eyes as she hung there, then swung her body to the side and let go. Her stomach lurched into her throat as she fell, the warm air of the massive room rushing up past her face until suddenly the ground met her feet, and she landed just to the left of the sizable hearth. Her legs buckled as she landed, her knee hitting the ground hard as she rolled to the side with a soft thump before pressing her spine against the stone hearth as she rapidly looked around.

She stiffened as she heard a noise by the front entrance, her wide eyes locked to the dark space as she waited, heart racing, to see if the guard had heard her fall. But after a tense moment, Mizuki heard the sound of a light snore over the crackle of the low fire, and she let out the breath she didn't even realize she had been holding as she closed her eyes in relief.

The guard must have fallen asleep.

It wouldn't be the first time – it wasn't uncommon to see the Village Guard snoozing while on watch. As much as they took their roles seriously, they had no true concerns regarding the safety of the village. The last time the village had experienced any discord was a decade ago when Miku was still alive, and that had only been verbal. In Mizuki's entire life, she had never once seen a guard draw their bow or pull out their knife. They had no reason to expect her, or anyone else for that matter, to stage a break-in, especially not in the Elders' Chambers. If someone were going to steal something, they would likely take food, supplies, or goods from the supply buildings.

Not documents.

That said, she had no intention of sticking around any longer than necessary, at the risk of testing the guard's vigilance. So, she silently stood to her feet and grabbed one of the small torches lying on the table next to the hearth. She took a moment to light it, then quietly made her way around the hearth, through the tables and chairs, and past the massive linen hanging of Veles's symbol toward the back of the room. Thankfully, they had both known that the main fire would be burning, and she would be able to use it for light. It took too much effort to restart it, and the Elders never let it die until well into summer. Smoke could be seen pouring from the roof of the large wooden structure nearly all year long – but she had sincerely doubted that the fire in the documents room would be lit.

Her suspicion was proven correct when she reached the door at the back of the massive Meeting Chamber and pushed aside the thick hides hanging over the entrance. It was dark, cool, and eerily silent. Her eyes quickly scanned over the room, taking it all in and trying to decide where would be the best place to start looking. She didn't have all night; eventually, the guard would come in to place more wood on the fire, and she couldn't risk Aiden standing behind the Hall all night waiting for her signal.

Letting the thick furs and hides fall closed behind her, Mizuki stepped into the room fully and willed her racing heart to slow as she began to look around. There were wooden shelves along the three walls – no doubt constructed by her father or grandfather sometime over the last few decades. They were covered in books, scrolls, and random artifacts that she didn't understand. She stared quietly at a small and strange-looking black box that had a stick coming out the top before her eyes shifted back to the books.

Some looked ancient, others looked newer, but she knew that anything bound or containing colour must have been from before the Great Destruction since books like that simply didn't exist anymore. They had paper, yes, and they had the means to write whether it be with graphite, paints, or even on occasion chalk – but they had no means of binding books. Every book in this room that was straight cut and wrapped with a sturdy cover came from the Before time, and they had all been found during hunts or located around the village. Her eyes skimmed over the words that were visible along the spines of the books on the left side of the room, and she stopped to pull one out and look at the cover.

'*An Introduction to Electrodynamics*'

She couldn't make out the name of the author, it had long since faded away and the book was covered in dust. She slid it back onto the shelf and frowned. As a kid in school, she had witnessed the Elders coming by to read to them, and she knew that they occasionally allowed their teacher to use some of the books from this collection for instruction. But seeing the extent of the collection now, it was clear that the vast majority of the texts were not shared.

Most people in the village were taught how to read and write, but their education was largely focused on survival and skills needed to get by. As a result, her writing was sloppy, and her ability to read was limited. She had no idea what the title of this book meant, even though Miku had taught her more words than most people in the village knew, and she was certain that if she opened the book up, she would not be able to read the majority of it.

Her gaze quickly flicked over the rest of the shelf, and her frown deepened. There was a lot of information here that the Elders were not sharing. In just a few short seconds, her eyes had seen the words leadership, survival, and crafting – and none of those books had ever been shown at school. Sure, they may allow some of the Praetors access, and she could see a few books related to food, crops, and weather – but knowing that this was all here and that the majority of the village was denied permission only made her hatred of them grow. She turned away from the endless volumes of hidden knowledge to start looking for the map.

She spent a few quick minutes scanning over the shelves along the left side but saw only books, then continued her search across the shelves along the back. The second shelf was promising. It was covered in scrolls, yet no matter how many she pulled out to unravel, there was nothing that even resembled a map. She found notes on each family in the village documenting their heritage, family lines, and health risks. She found ledgers recording the crop yields and even found what appeared to be plans for expanding the village toward the south, but she didn't see anything that looked like a map. She had just finished going over the documents on the large table in the center of the room when she heard a voice, and her body froze with panic. She couldn't hear the words that had been spoken, but she could have recognized the tone anywhere.

It was Kiren, her grandfather – and he was talking to the Elders.

"Oh no."

The words came out as a hoarse whisper as she looked around desperately for someplace to hide, but there wasn't much in the room, just the shelves, a few small cabinets, chairs, the hearth, the large table in the center of the room that she had already searched, and another smaller one along the back wall that was draped with a dark knitted fabric. A faint tapping sound rapped against the back wall of the small room, and her eyes darted to it as her chest clenched tight.

"Aiden," she breathed, rushing across the room as carefully as she could and tapping back to let him know that she was there.

She could hear voices at the front entrance, and suddenly it felt like the already small room was closing in on her as her panic grew and her pulse quickened to a painful beat. Without stopping to think, she quickly shook out the torch and darted over to the small hearth in the left corner of the room. She jammed the torch into the pile of ash to smother it out, cursing under her breath as she did so, and the voices grew louder.

There was no time for anything else and no way she would be able to leave without being seen. So, she did the only thing she could do and rapidly buried the entire torch in the ash before diving for the table along the back wall while the sound of voices grew closer, and her grandfather approached the very room where she was trapped.

"That's the second time that John has fallen asleep on duty," Elder Clark said as Mizuki pulled her feet under the table and curled into a tight ball against the wall, clamping a hand over her mouth to quiet her breathing. "I expect you to take care of that, Kiren."

"Of course," Kiren replied as light filled the room and the two Elders and her grandfather entered the small space. "I'll speak with Omar tomorrow and ensure that it doesn't happen again."

"Good," Elder Farr said as he moved toward the center table and roughly pulled out a chair. She could see the giant black feather that hung from his neck – just one of the few that had allegedly come from Veles; the rest were securely stored within the Elders' Residence. "Have you spoken with Keller yet and finished the list? I want to send out the parties immediately after the Gifting. We don't have any time to waste if we're going to have any hope of rectifying this before it becomes a problem."

"I did," Kiren confirmed as she heard the sound of two more chairs being pulled out.

She held her breath as she stared through the small holes of the dark fabric, her hand trembling against her lips as she willed her body to remain motionless and silent. With the flicker of low light from the torch, it was unlikely that they would find her unless they looked under the table – but that didn't stop her heart from beating so hard and fast that she started to worry they might hear it explode in her chest. She hoped that Aiden didn't do anything to try to help; he couldn't afford to get caught lurking around the Hall with the upcoming sacrifice.

"We have compiled a list of the best candidates," her grandfather revealed, pulling something from his pocket and setting it out on the wooden table. "Largely Praetorian based from the existing scouting group, with the addition of a few sons and future successors – all men that we can trust."

"Good." Elder Clark's voice sounded firm as she heard the sound of something scuffing across the table. "I've spoken with Keller directly, and he assures me that no one knows of the crop shortage outside of the key group. He will lead the exploration under the guise of it being a search for new hunting grounds. It will be easy to pass off given that the deer have moved further south."

"*Have* they moved further south?" Kiren questioned. "Or do you think that the deserters have expanded their territory to the north?"

"It's possible," Elder Farr admitted, his voice dropping lower. "When they left, we suspected that they would venture down to the Southern Mountains. The initial scouting of the area around the village indicated that there is another large lake a few days beyond the mountains – Dante and Anya would have known that when they left. With the Dead Zone to the north and west, there are only so many places that they could have gone. They would need fresh water, and as far as our documents show, there is nothing of value to the east unless you pass the chasm – and I highly doubt that they were able to accomplish that. So, it stands to reason that they travelled south."

"Yes, but they could have moved significantly south over the years," Elder Clark challenged, and Mizuki heard the man get up from his chair. His feet shuffled across the dirt floor until he reached the right side of the room, the side she had yet to search, and she heard him shuffling things about before he pulled out a large book. "Don't forget that the initial scout who climbed the Southern Mountain said that there was another possible habitable site beyond the lake. They would have known that too."

"Possibly," Elder Farr conceded, though his tone sounded displeased. "But they left with no resources and hardly any people. So it is far more likely that they headed to their death, or they made do by the smaller lake near the back of the mountains in order to survive."

"How long do you want to have the teams search?" Kiren asked as Elder Clark made his way back to the table.

"For as long as it takes," Elder Farr said.

"We have no other option," Elder Clark sighed as he sat back in his seat, and Mizuki heard him unfold a large piece of parchment. "We believe that they travelled south along the ridge to the mountains here."

Mizuki heard him tap the table as he pointed at whatever document he had just unfolded.

"There are some old tunnels and crevasses on the northern face they could use for shelter. But after that, assuming that they made it that far, they likely would have moved and set up a base camp along the small lake before they attempted anything else," Elder Clark continued. "My guess is that's where the Agronomist went, too. Ideally, Keller and his men will find him and bring him back within the village boundaries where we can use him. However, if the man is dead as you suspect, Kiren, then Keller will press on and look for signs of the deserters by the lake."

"In the likely event that they find nothing," Elder Farr added. "Then Keller will assess the area around the lake to see if it might be suitable to grow additional crops and act as new hunting grounds. We can look to establish a small outpost there and plan to have the harvest brought up to the main village. As you said, Kiren, the effort it would take to clear the land to the east of the existing fields is worrisome, especially given the state of the soil. It may not be worth the effort."

"And if Keller finds them?" Kiren asked, his head shifting to look between the two Elders. "What's the directive? Do you wish to have Keller bring them back – are we extending an offer of peace? Are we making an alliance?"

"No," Elder Farr said, his voice so dark and empty that Mizuki felt a shiver run down her spine. "Keller is under the impression that we are largely looking for new land. Should the deserters exist, and Keller finds them, it is his current understanding that we are going to make a request for help. But the village cannot afford to do so. It would destroy our way of life and only add additional resource strains to this village. If Dante and Anya's people are still alive – there is no guarantee that they are thriving. They may be in worse shape than us, and we cannot support any growth in population at this time. Under no circumstances are any of them to be brought back to the village or is any offer of unity to be extended. The teams will be sworn to secrecy just as the scouts are. We will talk with Keller next week to discuss the details, but he will be given clear directions – he and his teams are to take what we need then eliminate the threat that the deserters pose to this village."

"Understood," Kiren said, and Mizuki saw his shadow nod as the Elders leaned forward across the table. "And the first betrayers?"

"They shouldn't be an issue," Elder Farr said coldly. "They're long gone."

"It goes without saying that this assignment is critical for the success of the village," Elder Clark whispered, and she heard him shuffling more papers around. "Should anyone breathe a word of this around the village, the consequences will be severe."

"Of course." Kiren nodded again. "I'll make sure that Keller understands the implications of his actions."

"Good," Elder Farr said. "We don't expect that there will be any issues given the Gifting ceremony next week, but it wouldn't hurt for him to hear it from you or for you to use Kazuki as an example."

Mizuki's hand tensed over her mouth, and her eyes grew wide as she heard her grandfather agree. She couldn't believe what they were saying. She couldn't believe that the Elders were going to task Aiden's uncle with killing the deserters should he find them in the Wild – he was a hunter, not a guard. She could feel nausea spinning in her stomach as she watched them sit around the table, entirely unbothered by the idea of killing innocent people who had apparently left the village in peace with little but the clothes on their backs.

The trio spoke for several more long minutes, discussing the status of the crops and reviewing the list of names that Kiren had prepared for the scouting assignment. It took everything that she had not to move. Her legs had gone numb, and her back was screaming in pain by the time they finally stopped speaking and stood from the table. She had no idea how long she had been there, but when they finally left and the light and voices faded, she couldn't seem to make her limbs move. She remained motionless in the dark for a long while until she heard a faint double knock on the wall behind her head. She jumped at the sound, biting back a groan of agony as she stiffly crawled out from under the table and knocked back to let Aiden know that she was okay. She grimaced as she stretched her legs and limped back to the door to peer out into the Meeting Chamber.

It was empty.

Silent.

The large warm fire burned with a low crackle of flames, but there was no sign of life in the entire room. Swallowing hard, she crept back out to the main hearth and lit a second torch. When Mizuki returned to the small room, she didn't hesitate – she moved to the shelf on the right side of the room where she had seen Elder Clark move and began searching for the map. She found it only a moment later, folded and stuck inside a massive tome that was so old the text on the cover had worn off years ago. She pulled the piece of worn-looking parchment from the pages of the massive book and shifted to the main table where her grandfather and the Elders had sat only moments ago. Then she carefully unfolded the paper.

It was a map of the village. The very same one that she had seen as a child, except that this one expanded significantly to the south and east and hinted that the village had, at some point, ventured incredibly far out into the Wild to survey the land. Her eyes traced along the familiar ridge that she climbed every year, down past Glass Lake and below the river to the south to where it looked like mountains had been sketched in with dark ink.

That was where they needed to go.

That was their destination.

Yet when her eyes traced back up toward the village, she felt her heart drop into her stomach. The space between was marked with thick brush. There was something else splotched across the paper that smeared through the land between their destination and the village, and it filled her with dread. There was no way they would be able to cover this distance and return within a week. It was impossible. Yet they had to do it. The Elders were going to locate and slaughter the deserters right after the sacrifice, so they couldn't wait even if they wanted to. If they did, those people would be dead along with their hopes of trying to save Maebh and change the village.

She folded the map back up and quickly tucked it into her pocket before putting out the torch and shifting to the back wall once more. She knocked three times, waited, then knocked twice more. Silence rang in her ears for what felt like an endless moment before she heard Aiden knock back. She let out a breath and turned to make her way from the small room back to the entrance of the Hall, where she would wait for Aiden to distract the guard.

It didn't take long.

Even she heard the *thunk* in the bushes to the right, and she knew Aiden had thrown a rock against a tree. Pressing herself flat against the inside wall and peering through the gap by the hide door, she watched John, the now awake and alert Village Guard, stand from his seat and step toward the noise. There was a second loud *thunk*, and Mizuki slipped from the door as the guard shuffled toward the thicket where the sound had originated.

She could hear him calling out into the night behind her as he looked for troublemaking kids. She darted in the opposite direction, her soft leather shoes soundless across the dirt path as she disappeared into the night, running until she reached the brush and ducked inside. Her legs shook beneath her as she crawled deeper and deeper into the thicket, away from the Elders' Chambers and toward the bottom of the village. She didn't stop until she reached the large elm tree at the edge of the brush, collapsing against it and clutching at her chest.

At the snap of a twig on her right, she nearly jumped out of her skin, only to clutch at her chest once more in relief as Aiden's shadow stepped into view.

"You got it?" Aiden whispered, his voice so low she had to lean in only inches from his face to hear him.

"Yes." Mizuki nodded, breathing hard as she pulled the paper from her pocket with trembling hands and held it out to him.

"Oh, thank Veles," Aiden murmured, letting out a sigh of relief. She could see the concern stretched across his features as he leaned in close and whispered once more. "I thought they were going to catch you in there. What the hell were they doing?"

"They were discussing the search and the crops," Mizuki whispered, letting Aiden take the map from her and tuck it into his pocket. "They wanted to review the list of names that Kiren had come up with."

"The teams my uncle will be leading." Aiden nodded in understanding.

"Exactly," Mizuki breathed, finally feeling like she had caught her breath, though her limbs had still yet to stop shaking. "But Aiden – it's not what you thought. They're not looking for the deserters to request help."

"What?" Aiden's face contorted, and she could feel his breath on her cheek as he leaned closer once more. "What do you mean?"

"Aiden," Mizuki whispered, her heart pounding in her chest as she met his gaze in the darkness. "They're going to kill them. They're going to have your uncle Keller kill the deserters if he finds them."

Leaving

Mizuki piled the additional wood she had collected along the side of her home and wiped the sweat from her brow. It was midday, the sun was warm, and the sky was clear. She could hear the voices of other villagers out and about completing tasks; they were enjoying the abnormally warm day, but an odd and uncomfortable sort of tension hung over them. It was selection day, and every single person in the village would be itching to know which member of the O'Kane family would be heading up the mountain in just seven days' time. Their fascination with the sacrifice made her feel sick, but she did her best to ignore it and instead focused on her tasks and worked in silence as she avoided the glances sent her way.

She had already gathered wood earlier that week, but given her plans to leave the village tonight with Aiden, she wanted to get as much done to help her father as possible. Without her around, he would need to take care of her mother, look after the home, and find a way to work his usual job since she sincerely doubted that the Elders would give him a day off or allow him to go look for her. As such, she had spent the majority of the day in the thin forest to the south scavenging whatever food she could find and trying to complete as many tasks around their home as possible while pretending not to be exhausted from her daring escapades the night before.

Thankfully, that morning when her father had seen her, he had not commented on her weary state. He had looked at her for a long moment during breakfast, but he hadn't spoken a word. So she figured that he assumed the dark rings around her eyes were a result of her worrying about Aiden and his family – which wasn't entirely wrong.

After leaving the map with Aiden the night before and agreeing to meet at the boulder by the lake tonight, she had snuck back home and laid down on her bedroll, only to find that her racing heart and wandering mind would not allow her any rest. It wasn't until what felt like hours later that sleep finally found her, and when it did, it had not been restful. She was almost glad to be woken up by the sound of her father moving around in the main room because it was better than the terrifying dream she had been having about a dark shadowy figure with red glowing eyes.

Now, many hours later, she could feel the exhaustion sitting heavy in her bones, and she wondered how in the world she and Aiden were going to manage trekking to the Southern Mountains and returning before the sacrifice. She had never been trained how to read maps like Aiden was. She had no idea if the map was drawn to scale or if there was a way to figure out how long it would take to get there. From what she had glimpsed while inside the Document Room, it seemed an impossible task – she would just have to trust that Aiden could get them there, that he knew what he was doing, and that he would keep them safe on the journey.

She let out a sigh of relief as she stacked the final pieces of wood and straightened to stretch her back before heading back into her family's home. It would be another hour or so before Kazuki got home, and she planned to use that time to take her mother to the bathhouse, fix dinner, and mentally review her list to see if there was anything else that she needed to pack for tonight. She gathered the small basket of their bath supplies from the smaller storage chest, draping the rough, worn towels over her arm before fetching her mother from her stool and leading the woman outside to the bathhouse. It was late enough in the day that it should be largely empty by now, which made it her favourite time to go. She had long ago given up going in the morning unless it was before the sun rose, or going in the evening, because she couldn't stand the way that the other women stared at Keelin.

On occasion, her father would take her mother, and he would use the small room he had added to the bathhouse for those who wanted more privacy. It was an unspoken rule that the room was reserved for Praetors only, and it was almost always in use, but Mizuki didn't care. On the occasions where she found it empty, she used it without hesitation. So, as she led her mother down the dirt road toward the bathhouse and found the small room vacant, she snagged it without question, quickly grabbing two buckets of water from the heated reserve behind the building before closing the door to the room.

Like always, she dedicated her time and care to Keelin, carefully washing her mother's hair and taking the time to comb out the small knots before rinsing away all the soap and drying the woman off with a towel. It wasn't until after her mother was dressed in a fresh set of clothes and seated on the small bench in the corner that Mizuki finally stripped off her own clothes and began rapidly scrubbing her hair and body clean.

By the time she finished lathering her hair with soap, the rinsing water was cold, and she shivered as she dumped the bucket over her head and blinked the water from her eyes. It wasn't until she reached for her towel that she realized her mother was staring at her, her dull eyes looking faintly curious as they fixated on her legs. Running the towel over her head to stop the water in her hair from dripping down her face, she glanced down at her leg and froze. There was a purple bruise forming across her right knee – the same knee that had hit the ground the night before when dropped into the Elders' Chambers and rolled across the ground.

She swallowed, forcing her face to remain indifferent as she quickly dried off the rest of her body and pulled on her new clothes.

"I must have bumped my knee the other day while helping to collect kindling," Mizuki said dismissively, moving back to her mother and helping the woman up from her seat before gathering their belongings. The woman said nothing, but her eyes were now locked to Mizuki's face, and it almost looked as if she was thinking. Mizuki forced her lips into a smile as she rubbed the last bits of water from her hair and heard a knock against the wooden door of the small room. "Alright, let's go – we still need to make dinner."

She ignored the rude look she got from Mrs. Lear as she passed the old woman and led her mother from the bathhouse. It was the same look that she had gotten the day before on the way to Aiden's, and so Mizuki simply nodded before ducking her head and shuffling her mother down the path.

When they returned to their home, Mizuki tended to the fire, leaving her mother on her usual stool with a bit of thread to play with as she pulled out food and supplies and started to cook. It wasn't until she was halfway through preparing the meal over the fire that she realized Aiden might not have any medicinal herbs to pack and that she better bring enough for the both of them. The hunters usually got them from the supply houses before going out, and those were meticulously monitored by the head Praetorian gatherer, whereas Mizuki collected her own herbs in the forest during the summer months and then dried them to store for the winter. They didn't have many left over from last summer's collection, but she did have a few that would be useful to prevent infection if they got injured along the way, and having additional sprigs wouldn't be a bad idea.

Eyeing Keelin to make sure that the woman was still staring blankly at the red thread that was being mindlessly twisted around her fingers, Mizuki shuffled behind her back to the storage chest and fished out several sprigs of dried goldenseal and comfrey. Then, she grabbed some ginseng and more woundwort just to be safe.

It was always better to have fresh, but aside from a few small clusters of comfrey, she knew it was much too early to find anything growing in the Wild, so dried sprigs would be better than nothing. Silently closing the chest once more, she moved to her bedroom and knelt before her storage chest, opening the wooden lid and moving the clothes that concealed her mother's pack before gently stuffing the linen-wrapped dried herbs into one of the side pouches. It wasn't until she had re-covered the pack and was about to put the lid back on the small wooden chest that she felt eyes on the back of her head, and she stiffened.

Panic flooded her body.

She hadn't heard Kazuki come home, and if she didn't lie and sell this right, not only would she not be able to leave tonight, but Aiden would get caught too. Her mind raced as she swallowed hard, her brain desperately spinning to come up with an explanation that would be believable and would leave Aiden out of it so he could go on his own. She clenched her jaw tight, forcing her face into a blank expression before casually placing the lid back on the chest and turning to face her father. Only it wasn't her father standing in the doorway.

It was Keelin.

The woman's dull grey eyes were locked to Mizuki's face, and there was a tiny crease between her brows. Mizuki could feel the relief flooding her body as she let out a sigh and slowly stood back to her feet.

"Dinner is almost ready," Mizuki said, smiling at her mother and pushing her hair behind her ears. "Let's go set the table."

She stepped toward the door, expecting her mother to shift back into the main room, but Keelin didn't move. She stood there unblinkingly, staring at Mizuki with more clarity than she had ever seen. It was eerie and unnerving, and Mizuki could feel the unease sliding down her spine as her smile started to falter.

"I just thought those herbs might be useful," Mizuki stuttered as Keelin remained unmoving in her door.

Silence stretched between them as Mizuki stared at her mother, and Keelin continued to watch her in silence. The woman's gaze dropped down to her knee, to the bruise that she had been staring at earlier in the bathhouse, and Mizuki stiffened once more.

"It's nothing," Mizuki insisted, her fingers twitching nervously at her side. She could feel her heart starting to beat more quickly as her smile completely fell away.

Why was this so hard? She lied to Kazuki all the time. She could spew deerspit like no other, and evading questions was as easy as breathing for her, yet suddenly, as her frail and mute mother stared at her bruised knee, she could feel her palms growing sweaty as guilt coursed through her chest. Keelin hadn't spoken a word in nearly ten years. She hadn't interacted with anyone or done anything, but as the woman's dull gaze met Mizuki's once more, she felt her emotions surge. There was a question behind the woman's eyes. It was silent – foggy – but Mizuki was certain that it was there as the woman stared into her eyes and remained entirely still.

"They don't deserve to go through what we did," Mizuki found herself whispering as she stared at her mother and her throat grew tight. "The O'Kanes – they're good people, and Maebh is just a child."

Keelin's gaze shifted over her daughter's face as Mizuki's eyes began to sting with tears.

"I know if I leave, it will hurt you and dad," Mizuki said, swallowing hard. "But I can't stand by and watch another innocent person be Gifted to a god that we don't even know exists. Not when I know the *Gifts* aren't random and that they're using them as a way to control the village. The Elders made a mistake, mom. Aiden heard them talking, and we have the chance to change things."

Mizuki stepped toward her mother, her brow creasing in pain as all the emotions that she had been burying for years began to leak from the box that she had stuffed them in. She could feel them spreading through her body and showing across her face. She couldn't stop them, and she couldn't breathe as her eyes welled with unshed tears.

"I know you tried to save him." Mizuki's voice broke as she whispered the words and reached out to touch her mother's hand. Keelin didn't move at the contact, but she blinked and stared at her daughter intensely as Mizuki squeezed her hand tight. "I'm sorry that you couldn't – I'm sorry that I didn't understand, that I was so awful to you back then, and that it took me so long to see how hard you fought for him. I know that what I'm about to do will hurt you both, but I think you understand.

"I have to go," Mizuki breathed, a single tear falling from the corner of her eye and trailing down her face. "Aiden needs me, and we have to try. We could stop this. We could end the Gifting. So please, please know that I'm doing this for the right reasons.

That tomorrow if I'm gone, I didn't just leave you and dad or run away. I'm going to do everything that I can to come back – I promise. I promise that I won't leave you here alone, not unless that choice is taken from me and we don't make it, but I will fight with everything that I have to come back to you. I promise."

She felt another two tears slide down her face as she bit her lip hard and tried to stifle the wave that was surging through her. She didn't know why she was saying this. She didn't know why she couldn't stop the words or why her heart felt like it was breaking. Maybe it was the guilt of abandoning her mother, or maybe this was something much deeper, but as her mother's gaze met hers once more and the woman's lips parted, she felt her heart falter in her chest.

"Go."

The word was whispered, broken and hoarse like the creak of an old branch in the wind. It was rough from years of never having been used. Yet despite being small and weak, it cut through Mizuki's heart and flooded her soul with warmth.

Ten years.

Keelin had not spoken a word in ten years, and Mizuki had to clamp a hand over her mouth to stop the sob that wracked her lungs. She could see her mother. She could see Keelin – a hint of who the woman used to be lingering behind the dull eyes that were looking at her clearly for the first time in ages.

It had been a lifetime. The woman had missed so much, and yet she had been listening all along, just as Miku had said. Mizuki grabbed the woman, pulling her into her arms and hugging her tight as a deep pain radiated from her chest. She felt the woman's arms wrap around her, and it was everything she could do to remember how to breathe as her mother hugged her for the first time in a decade.

It had taken every bit of her strength to pull away from the woman and lead her back to the main room. Her hands shook as she wiped the tears from her eyes and forced herself to set the table while trying to calm down. She couldn't stop looking at the woman. She couldn't seem to get control of herself, and it took making a cup of tea and sitting with her forehead pressed to the table while breathing deeply for several long minutes to finally slow her heart.

When Kazuki came home, Keelin said nothing.

The frail woman sat at the table like she always did, silent, her eyes downcast while they ate. Kazuki watched Mizuki closely, but he didn't comment on anything as they went through the motions of their normal routine, and he left her sitting by the fire at the end of the night. She remained there longer than she usually would have, staring at the fire and watching the flames flicker until she heard the familiar gentle snore of her father from the room on her right. She had known that leaving would be hard – she had expected it – but when she forced her limbs to move and stood stiffly from her seat by the hearth to add the final log, she found it hard to swallow.

She could feel her eyes burning again, and something long forgotten in her heart was breaking as she made her way to her room and pried open the small storage chest. Mizuki dressed in the dark, adding an extra layer as Aiden had directed before pausing at her door and grabbing one of the small wooden figurines that lined the edge of her room. She placed the carved deer on the table in the main room, facing it to the north and staring at it for a moment before she finally shouldered her pack and snuck out into the darkness. The deer had been her brother's, and she hoped by leaving it there for her father to see, he might understand that her leaving was tied to something greater, something bigger – and that she wasn't just abandoning them.

She moved along the thorn bushes by the ridge, her chest heavy with guilt and fear as she made her way to the lake. A part of her was hoping that Aiden wouldn't be there, that Maebh hadn't been selected, and they could forget this whole plan. But a larger part of her knew that there was no turning back. Aiden had been right, and Miku's stories were proving to be not only the true history of the village but also a forewarning for what was to come if things did not change. She stepped carefully through the widely spaced trees, avoiding fallen sticks and keeping her eyes focused on the surrounding darkness as she closed the distance to their boulder. Her fingers toyed with the hem of her leather and fur jacket as she stepped out into the clearing and slowly made her way to the large rock.

Her pulse quickened as her eyes searched through the shadows. For a fleeting moment, she thought the lake was deserted, and her heart fluttered in her chest only for it to immediately falter as a tall figure by the boulder shifted out from the shadow and came into view. It was Aiden, and he was standing there with a pack on his back and a bow held tight in his hand. She felt her face fall as a quiet exhale left her lungs, and her heart dropped into her stomach like a rock.

It had been Maebh.

Her steps didn't falter as she closed the distance to their boulder and then turned to the right to fall into step beside him as he started to lead the way around the lake to the west. She didn't say anything as they moved – because there was nothing to say – she just followed his lead and kept up with his quick but silent pace as he slung the bow over his shoulder, and they marched off into the night. He moved even more silently than she did, and she realized as they walked that she had never seen him hunt. She had never seen him move like this before, and she had never been this far from the village. Her head turned to glance over her shoulder, her eyes just able to make out the edge of Glass Lake near the southern side of their village before Aiden led them into the forest, and it disappeared from sight.

The second they were under the cover of trees, he doubled his pace to nearly a run, and Mizuki's fingers dug into the straps of her pack as she forced her legs to keep up. She could already feel her muscles groaning in protest after too many late nights and from sneaking into the Elders' Chambers, but she ignored the pain and pressed on. They moved in silence for a long time, Aiden easily navigating through the trees and leading them farther and farther away from the village without a word. She chanced a glance at him as she ducked under a low hanging branch and then darted across a well-worn footpath.

He didn't look good.

She could barely make out his features, but she could see the tension in his body. He looked stiff and uncomfortable. There was anger in the way he carried himself – and something else she wasn't sure how to describe as they stepped across a thick, broken branch and then weaved through another set of trees. She wanted to say something to him. She wanted to offer him some sort of comfort or reassurance, but she didn't have any. They both knew that this idea was insane and that the odds of them coming back were so low it was almost laughable. Besides, she knew that there was nothing she could say to make him feel better about Maebh being selected, so she just bit her tongue and diligently followed along behind him.

Her legs burned. It wasn't until the trees started to get thicker, and after they had passed several large trees with coloured markers barely visible in the moonlight, that he finally spoke and slowed their pace to a brisk walk.

"I left a trail along the eastern side of the lake," Aiden said, his voice barely audible as he held up a branch for her, and she stepped beneath it. Mizuki turned to glance at him, struggling to see his face in the darkness. "They won't notice it right away, but when they do, it will make it look like we headed east."

"That was a good idea," Mizuki noted as they moved past another large tree with markers, and Aiden steered them to the right. "Were you able to look over the map?"

"Yes." Aiden nodded, his low voice tight. "We're going to need to move quickly and cut through directly. If we had more time, I'd take us there by following along the ridge down to the south. It would be an easier path – less risk of animals or getting lost. It's the path that my uncle will most likely take next week, but the ridge juts too far west, and we would never make it back in time. Our only chance is to cut through directly – through the forest, through the Woods, past the edge of the normal hunting grounds, and straight through the Wild. We'll need to cut through the swamp that they marked on the map too."

"That smear was a swamp?" Mizuki questioned, her eyebrow arching in surprise.

"Yes," Aiden said, and she could hear the grimace in his voice. "And I've never seen it before, so I don't know what we're in for – but it's the only way."

"Then we'll take it," Mizuki said, nodding in acceptance even though her heart was beating nervously in her chest again. "I trust you – you'll get us there, Aiden."

They moved in silence for another few minutes, the movements becoming automatic as Mizuki's muscles finally gave up complaining and simply did what she asked of them. They had just reached another large tree when Mizuki caught sight of the lake on her left and realized that Aiden was circling them east once more. She didn't realize Glass Lake extended so far south, but she followed him out into a small clearing where he stopped to fill three water pouches. She kneeled beside him, pulling the empty one from her pack and filling it up as his voice filled the air once more.

"When the meeting ended with the Elders, my uncle came straight to our house," Aiden murmured, his voice drawing her gaze. "He didn't even have to say anything. It was written all over his face."

Mizuki watched as Aiden closed the final water pouch but remained crouched by the lake, the faint starlight reflecting across the dark surface.

"My ma collapsed, and I – I've never heard her make those sounds before," he said. She heard him shift as she gripped her water pouch tightly. "She sounded like a dying animal, Mizuki – I hunt them, I know what they sound like. But I didn't know it was possible for a person to make that noise."

Aiden turned to look at her, and she could just barely see the glassy look of his eyes in the darkness as his head slowly began to shake.

"We're going to make this right, Mizuki," he whispered, his voice growing firm as his gaze seemed to harden. "We have to."

She stood as he rose from the lake, not trusting herself to speak as he repacked the freshly filled water pouches and then gently grabbed her shoulder and steered her back into the trees.

"Come on, let's go," Aiden said, leading them back into the cover of the forest and onto a smaller, less worn path. "I want to make it through the forest and over the river by daybreak, and most of the way into the Woods before nightfall. We're going to need the majority of our time to cross the swamp, and I have no idea what's waiting for us on the other side. So we're going to jog until sun-up. If you can't keep up, tell me, and I'll carry you."

"Alright." She nodded in agreement, forcing her legs back into the rapid pace that Aiden set them on.

They moved through the darkness in silence. Mizuki could hear only the sound of her own breath, rapid and hard, each exhale crystallizing in the cool night air before her. She had lost track of where they were the second that Aiden pulled them away from the lake and back under the cover of the forest. Each tree looked the same at night, and in the darkness, she could barely spot the hunting trail that they were supposedly following. She had no idea how Aiden could navigate in the dark, but then again, she doubted she could do it even if the sun was shining bright and she had the map open before her. He moved with such confidence. His feet and breath were silent. Had he been trailing along behind her, she wouldn't have known, and it only made her feel even more out of her depth as the muscles in her legs began to complain once more, and her bruised knee started to ache.

Morning broke with the sound of birds. Their low chatter and early morning whistles echoed in the tall trees above them as the first glimpse of sunlight began to peek through the clouds, and with it, a deep crimson red filled the sky. Aiden grimaced at the sight, his face scrunching as the trees finally started to thin and the sound of rushing water filled the air.

"It seems like the world isn't going to make this easy on us," he muttered, leading her down a now visible path and over some small stones.

"Red sky in the morning, sailors take warning," Mizuki murmured, looking up at the rising red sun as they broke through the treeline and reached a small river.

She remembered the saying from when they were kids – it was something that Aiden had taught her and something that his da had taught him. Apparently, it originated from well before the Great Destruction and was used by men who built large wooden objects to cross great oceans. The Elders had never put much stock into sayings that predated the village, but Mizuki found herself frowning as they darted across the shallow river. In all her life, she had never seen the phrase proven wrong. With the rising red sun came the rain, thunder, and often violent winds – and with it still being early spring, she knew the threat of dropping temperatures was still very real.

"We're making good time," Aiden said as he held out his hand and offered to help her climb the rocks that lined the opposite side of the river. She took it gladly. She was far too tired to be too proud to accept his help. They had run all night, and Aiden planned to run them all day. Her legs were already shaking, and the idea of climbing these boulders on her own was too much. If not for all her years of climbing the ridge and running around after him in the forest, she doubted that she would have made it this far.

"That's good," Mizuki grunted, gripping his hand tight and hauling herself up the rock that Aiden had easily scaled before her. "Is this the path that you normally take?"

"Sometimes." Aiden nodded, helping her up another ledge before the boulders seemed to even out. "Though usually it takes us longer to get here because we're setting and checking snares. Here – we should stop to eat. It gets rougher up ahead before it drops down into the Woods, so this is a good spot."

Mizuki nodded in agreement, too tired to think of anything to say as she pulled her mother's pack from her back and wiped the sweat from her forehead. Her shoulders were aching in pain, and she bit back a groan as she rolled the stiff muscles in her shoulders and collapsed onto the hard ground. She eyed Aiden as she pulled out her dried foods, her hands shaking a little from exhaustion as she did so. He looked out across the boulders, his eyes scanning the horizon in the dim light before he removed the hunting bow from his shoulder, dropped his pack to the ground and sat down to join her. He hadn't even broken a sweat yet, and he didn't appear to be tired as he bit into a piece of dried deer meat and met her gaze.

"How are you holding up?" he asked, his eyes tracing over her weary-looking frame as she nibbled on a few berries before pulling out the first water pouch that she had filled at home.

"I'm alright," she said, rolling her eyes at him when he arched a brow at her doubtfully. "I'll live, Aiden, don't worry about me. So when do you think they will notice that we're gone?"

"If we're lucky, not for a while," Aiden said, taking a sip of his own water before pulling out a few tree nuts from the side pouch of his pack. "Given what happened last night, my parents will be distracted this morning, and when they do notice that I'm gone, they'll probably just assume that we went for a walk by the lake or in the forest somewhere near the village. My da will probably get upset – he'll think I'm being selfish and avoiding the whole thing while my ma might not even notice. She fell asleep holding Maebh last night, and she isn't going to leave my sister's side. I doubt anyone will realize that we're truly gone until much later, and hopefully they won't start seriously looking for us until closer to dinner time when we don't return."

"True," Mizuki murmured, biting off a piece of dried meat and chewing it thoughtfully. "It wouldn't be the first time that we disappeared for the day. That will give us a solid day's head start. Do you think that's enough?"

"It's going to have to be," Aiden said, his amber eyes looking strained as he met Mizuki's gaze. "The hunting crew can move fast, Mizuki – it's why I've been pushing us so hard and why I laid that trail along the lake to the east. If they don't take the bait and they head this way first, they could catch up."

"Then we should get moving," Mizuki said, tearing off a final piece of meat and repacking the rest of her food.

Aiden nodded in agreement, doing the same before shouldering his bow and pack. She fought back a groan as she pulled on her pack once more, her shoulders straining under the weight. The brief break had done nothing to help, and if anything, it had left her feeling even worse than before. She could feel a dull tremor in the muscles of her legs as she walked next to Aiden's side, and she knew that the rest of this day was going to be nothing but pain.

She hadn't had any grandiose expectations or any misconception of luxury for the journey. She had known from the start that this was going to be brutal and exhausting and filled with dangers. But as they set off across the rocky boulders and began making their way towards the area that Aiden had deemed the 'Woods,' Mizuki found herself beginning to wonder if she was realistically going to make it. She was incredibly fit by most standards, and her endurance had always been good, but even she had limits. She had told Aiden not to worry, but as her bruised knee continued to ache with each step, she found she couldn't help but worry.

"Aiden?" Mizuki asked quietly as they jumped across a small crevasse and continued to pick up speed.

"Mhmm?" He turned to glance at her, his brow arching as they shuffled across the next set of broken and uneven stone.

"Why did you ask me to come with you?" Mizuki asked, her breath already coming in pants as she paused and waited for Aiden to hop down a particularly steep drop. She sat down on the ground, swinging her legs over the edge and grabbing Aiden's shoulders as he reached up to help her down the tall ledge. He set her down carefully, and as she looked up at him, she realized that he was still holding her waist.

"Because I trust you," he answered, staring at her for a moment before he finally let go and began moving once more.

"I know that," Mizuki said, watching the graceful way that he easily hopped across the rocks. He had two hunting knives strapped to his leg, a quiver of arrows strapped to his back, and a pack likely twice as heavy as hers, and yet he didn't seem bothered by any of it. She was entirely out of her league here – surely, he knew that. She could feel the guilt and worry starting to build in the pit of her stomach as she wondered how long she could truly last. She didn't want to be the reason that they failed. "But you can clearly move faster than me – I'm slowing you down. Why bring me along? I'm a risk."

"You're not a risk." Aiden shook his head, glancing over at her and giving her a look she couldn't fully process. "You're my partner in this."

"Aiden," Mizuki said, glancing ahead at the seemingly endless land that stretched before them. "I'm being serious, I–"

"And so am I." Aiden cut her off, stopping in his tracks to turn and face her directly. He fixed her with a strange expression, one that she had seen previously but had yet to decipher, before his eyes creased. "Are you changing your mind?"

"What?! No!" Mizuki said, surprised that he would think such a thing. She looked up at him, frowning in frustration. "Never –

I said I would go, Aiden. And I trust you to get us there. I just don't want to be the reason that we fail."

She let out a sigh, fighting against the panic that was building in her chest as she forced her face back into its usual impassive form.

"I don't want to slow you down," Mizuki clarified, her eyes tracing over his face as she tried to understand the emotion that was radiating behind his gaze. "I'm with you on this – I just don't want to fail you."

"You're not going to fail me," Aiden said firmly as he took a small step towards her. He towered over her, and she had to tilt her head even more to meet his gaze. "You're my *best* friend, Mizuki – you mean more to me than anyone else in the village, and you're the only person I can trust."

"That's a really nice sentiment, Aiden," Mizuki said, her voice wavering as she swallowed at the heat of his closeness. "But I might not be able to keep up with you. I'm already starting to struggle, so I need to know that you'll leave me behind if you must. You can't jeopardize this for me – this is bigger than us. This is our chance to change the village. So if I can't keep up with you, then you need to leave me behind."

"I'm not going to leave you behind," Aiden stated, his head shaking as something sad and earnest crossed his face. "I can't do this alone, Mizuki, and more than that, I don't *want* to do it alone. I asked you to come because I need your help. I need someone to watch my back when we get into the Wild, and I trust you to do it. You're fast, Mizuki, faster and stronger than you think, and far more nimble than most. You see things that others don't, and you know more about medicinal herbs than anyone on the scouting squad. You're smart – you're a problem solver. If we get into trouble, you can get us out, and if I get hurt, you can keep us alive.

"I didn't ask you to come because you're my only friend or because there was no one else to ask," Aiden said, his tone gentle as his hand reached out to tuck a stray lock of hair that had fallen loose behind her ear once more. "Given the choice between you and anyone on the hunting squads – I would pick you every time, no questions asked."

Mizuki swallowed hard. She could feel her heart starting to race once more, but it didn't seem to have anything to do with the physical exertion of their journey as Aiden stared down at her. She forced herself to nod as she watched a myriad of thoughts flicker behind his eyes.

"So give yourself some credit," Aiden said, lowering his hand and finally stepping back. "You're more important than you think, and you're better at this than you realize. I wasn't joking when I said that we made good time getting this far. You can do this, okay?"

"Okay," Mizuki whispered, her hand instinctively coming up to tuck the hair that Aiden had already moved behind her ear.

"Then let's go," Aiden said, a small smile tugging at his lips as he tilted his head toward the looming cluster of trees at the base of the rocky ledge. "We still have a long way to go."

The Wolves

Navigating the Woods was so much worse than climbing the boulders by the river. As the sun rose high into the sky, Mizuki found herself longing for the cold, rough rocks and the open terrain. She would have climbed those boulders without complaint all day if it meant getting out of the thick trees and having the ability to see where they were going. In the Woods, it was warm, dizzyingly repetitive, and claustrophobic. She hadn't truly appreciated how thin the forest near the village was, and now, dodging endless branches while trying to avoid getting tangled in the underbrush of the trees, she was glad that she had not been born into one of the hunting families.

Aiden looked perfectly at home. He continued to lead them at a remarkably fast pace using only the coloured markers on the trees, the sun, and a few key features of the landscape as a map. She tried to memorize their route; from what she could tell, it seemed like they were following the yellow marker path now, heading directly south below Glass Lake and straight for the Southern Mountains, but keeping track of their trail was difficult.

They moved mostly in silence, only speaking on occasion, such as when Aiden pointed things out or when Mizuki motioned for him to stop so she could collect early spring berries from a thick bush. It wasn't until well into the afternoon when the sun was at its peak, and the diffused streams of light were beating down on the tops of their heads through the new spring leaves that Aiden finally slowed. He motioned for them to stop, shifting over towards a small fallen log before dropping his pack and kneeling to the ground.

"See these here," Aiden murmured, pointing to the soft dirt floor.

"Yes." Mizuki nodded, doing her best not to wheeze as she pulled the pack from her shoulders and set it down with a heavy thud. She collapsed on the ground beside him, huffing for air and gritting her teeth tightly as the muscles in her legs burned. "Tracks."

"Wolf tracks," Aiden specified as Mizuki leaned in for a closer look. She noted that the print was wide and large – larger than her fist, with four toes facing forward and a smaller fifth one on the inside step. "There is a pack in this area. My uncle never found the den, but they cut through here to hunt to the east."

"Shouldn't we keep going then?" Mizuki asked, turning to look at Aiden as she clutched the stitch in her side. She wasn't sure how much longer she could continue at their rapid pace, but she didn't think it was a good idea to linger near wolves either. She had never seen one – but she had heard enough stories from Aiden during her childhood to know that she never wanted to encounter one of those four-eyed creatures.

"They don't hunt during the middle of the day, so we're okay right now, but we'll need to try to gain some more distance before nightfall," Aiden replied, twisting his head to give her a reassuring look. He turned and pointed to his right, gesturing to the west as he spoke. "My uncle thinks that their den is a fair ways to the west, over there. We've monitored their movements for the last few years, and from what we can tell, they hunt during the early mornings and late evenings. Their territory seems to span from the ridge on the west over to the chasm on the east, but they don't seem to venture much past the edge of the hunting grounds or into the Wild because the trees get too thick."

"Thicker than this?" Mizuki asked in disbelief.

"Yes," Aiden confirmed, his eyes looking amused as he pulled out some food from his pack. "Much thicker. That's why I've been pushing so hard. The Wild is a jungle Mizuki, it's tough to navigate, and our pace is going to slow quite a bit when we hit it. But we won't get there until late morning tomorrow."

"And once we do, we won't need to worry about the wolves," Mizuki concluded, watching as Aiden nodded and handed her a piece of dried meat. She took it without question, leaning back against the fallen log by his side. "Another reason to push to get there as quickly as possible, but what about tonight? What are the chances we'll run into them?"

"I'm not sure," Aiden admitted, his brow scrunching with thought as he popped a few of the fresh berries Mizuki had collected into his mouth. She watched him chew in silence for a moment before he continued. "I've never been out here at night in anything but a large hunting party. We usually travel in two or three groups of five, we split up to hunt, but at night we camp together in a big group. The wolves have never bothered us, but we sleep around a fire, and we always keep night watch. I honestly don't know what to expect tonight, especially since we've not had much luck with the deer as of late. That's why I want to get us to the hunting group's usual campsite before nightfall. It's near a small rock formation, so it will give us cover in case the rain comes, and we'll at least have something against our backs while we sleep, but we'll still need to be careful."

"Alright," Mizuki agreed, taking another bite of the dried meat that Aiden had given her before washing it down with a swig of water from her pouch. She brushed the sweaty hair from her forehead and straightened her legs to stretch them out. She had already taken off her jacket and tied it around her waist, but she still felt much too warm. "Then lead at whatever pace we need to maintain to make it there, and I'll keep up."

"Mizuki," Aiden said, eyeing her as he pulled out his own water pouch and then paused before taking a drink. "If you're tired, I can carry you for a while."

"No." Mizuki shook her head, repacking her water and grabbing a few of the fresh berries for herself. "Thank you, Aiden, I appreciate it – but not yet. I'll probably need your help later, so I'd rather go for as long as I can on my own first."

"Alright," Aiden said, his eyes tracing over her stretched-out legs before he met her gaze once more. "But if it gets too hard, let me know."

"I will," she agreed, nodding as she popped a few more berries into her mouth and tried to steady her still racing heart.

They ate the rest of their lunch in silence, then packed up and continued on. She followed Aiden's quick pace for the next two hours until her legs were shaking so badly that she thought they might give out. They finally stopped to relieve themselves, after which Aiden took her pack. With him carrying both bags, it was easier to keep up, but their pace began to slow as the sun started to drop into the west. The birds grew quiet, and Mizuki could see a tightness forming in Aiden's shoulders as they both glanced up at the sky in concern. It was only a few moments later that a low growl of thunder split through the air, and Aiden began to usher them forward at a faster pace once more. She ran along beside him, her heart racing in her chest as she ducked and dodged tree branches. Then a thunderous crack rocked the earth.

"Aiden, how much further?" Mizuki called out over the roll of thunder, ducking under the next branch. "If it pours before we get there, we won't be able to start a fire."

"I know!" Aiden called back, another low groan rumbling through the sky as the first flickers of lighting flashed to the west. "We're not going to make it – we need to get wood now."

He quickly slowed to a stop, pulling off both packs and untying the jacket from his waist. She watched as he dropped it on the ground, spreading it out like a blanket before glancing up to her once more.

"Grab sticks, kindling, and whatever else you can that's dry from the ground," Aiden instructed, moving into a thicket behind him to start collecting pieces. "We need enough to last us through the night – make sure you get some firestarter too. That rain is going to hit before we get there."

Mizuki nodded and shifted off to the right, quickly grabbing anything dry that they could burn while being careful not to wander too far or lose sight of Aiden. They worked in frantic silence for several tense minutes, dumping branches, leaves, dried grass, and sticks onto Aiden's jacket before she removed the one from her own waist to drop on top and bundle it up.

"Give me my pack," Mizuki said, knotting the sleeves of her jacket around the bundle of firewood as Aiden re-shouldered his bag. "I won't be able to carry the stick bundle as well as you."

"Alright." Aiden nodded, handing her her pack as she stood before grabbing the bundle of firewood from the ground. A loud crack cut through the air, and Aiden looked up with a grimace. "Well, at least this will help cover our tracks and prevent them from gaining any ground. I don't think the Elders will send out a search party in a storm, so if they haven't left yet, they're not going to tonight."

"Leave it to you to see the bright side of things," Mizuki breathed, forcing her aching legs to move as they set off at a rapid pace through the trees.

Her breath came heavy and hard as the sky grew dark and the lightning grew closer. She could practically feel the charge in the air as the hair at the base of her skull stood up, and her skin prickled as the cold air rushed in. Aiden's breath began to fog in the air as he easily hurdled the next log to cut through a thick patch of trees. It was getting dark. Too dark for her to see much farther than a few feet ahead of them. Lightning flashed above, and a massive groan of thunder shook the earth beneath their feet. They managed to cover a few more feet before the sky opened up, and the rain came flooding down as the wind ripped through the forest like a blade.

She stumbled against the nearest tree, groaning in pain as the sharp, cold water stung against her face and blurred her vision. She hadn't realized just how much the ridge protected the village from these storms, and she and Aiden struggled to push forward while he clutched the bundle of wood to his chest.

"Almost there!" Aiden yelled, his voice barely audible over the wind and rain as he urged her forward through the next patch of trees.

Her teeth chattered from the cold, her body shaking as the warmth of the afternoon travel was entirely washed away and replaced with a freezing cold. They pushed on into the darkness, only slowing when the wind blew so hard it threatened to knock them over. The giant trees creaked and swayed around them, and she knew that if they did not manage to start a fire tonight, they might not wake to see the morning. The air might not be freezing, but with the wind and the rain, it was still cold enough to put their lives in danger.

Just when she was sure her legs couldn't take another step, they broke into a small clearing, and Aiden gestured for them to shift west. She nodded in understanding, sprinting across the water-logged ground behind him until a dark, uneven shape came into view. It was the rock formation, and she let out a painful sigh of relief as they darted towards it and ducked under the low-hanging lip.

"There's a small hole big enough for our packs there!" Aiden called, gesturing to the dark rocks as he moved toward the tallest part of the overhang to set down the bundle of firewood and pull off his pack. "Get them stored! I'm going to get the fire started!"

"Okay!" Mizuki yelled, shrugging the pack from her shoulders as a massive flash of lightning lit up the small shelter.

She raced over to the small hollow that Aiden had pointed out, blinking the water from her eyes and ducking as the lip of the rock grew lower. She shoved her pack into the hole, making sure it was safely tucked away before returning back to Aiden to grab his and do the same. Her breath crystallized in the air before her, her limbs shaking as she shoved the heavy bag into the hole. She pushed the sopping wet locks of hair from her face before turning to move back to Aiden. He was just as drenched as she was, his messy hair sticking to his forehead and dripping water into his eyes as he worked to start the fire. It took him several tries, deep concentration showing on his face with each flash of lightning as he muttered curses under his breath until the spark finally took.

"Finally," Aiden breathed, dropping the flint contraption he had been using and grabbing more dried grass and leaves from the bundle. He carefully tucked the firestarter into the flames, urging the fire to take hold and grow as Mizuki selected some small sticks to add to the pile. They worked at it for what felt like forever, and when the fire finally took hold, Mizuki's hands were shaking hard.

"Do you think we'll have enough to last the night?" Mizuki asked, eyeing their collection of wood suspiciously before gazing back at Aiden.

"I'm not sure," Aiden replied, but the doubt in his voice was obvious. "Maybe, if we keep it small and if the wind doesn't change."

"Have you ever been out here in a storm before?" Mizuki asked, watching as water poured down from the rock overhang and the dark sky continued to flash.

"Only once," Aiden sighed, his voice barely audible against the sound of the storm. He glanced over at her, his expression flashing with concern at her shaking frame. "We need to warm you up – and get these jackets dried out. Here, come here."

She let him guide her deeper under the ledge and sat down close to the fire as Aiden got to work. He returned to his pack to pull out a small bit of rope then hooked it along the overhang to create a clothesline. Mizuki rubbed her hands together over the fire as Aiden removed the wood from their wet jackets and piled it on the ground to her left before hanging the coats above the flames to dry. It was clear that he had done this before and that the small overhang had been picked as a shelter for good reason.

It blocked the wind from the west and north and sloped just enough to keep the majority of water from draining inside the overhang. The hunters had chipped away at the rock over the years and taken advantage of its natural nooks and crannies to make it more functional. The recess for their packs had likely been natural, but it had since been made larger, and it would protect anything stored within from getting wet in case the rock formation did flood. In a matter of a few short minutes, Aiden was back at her side with food, water, two old tin cups, and a small, mostly dry towel.

"We should change," Aiden said, adding another small stick to the fire as he sat down next to her. "You'll never get warm in those wet clothes, and we can't afford to get sick. You go first; I'll watch the fire."

"Thanks," Mizuki murmured, forcing her stiffening limbs to move as she stood from the hard ground and made her way to the back of the underhang where their packs were stored.

She tried not to think about the fact that Aiden was less than ten feet away as she pulled out dry, thicker hide clothes and forced her shaking hands to peel the soaked plant-fibre shirt from her body. She used the small towel Aiden had given her to dry off before she donned the new clothes, tugged her favourite knitted hat over her head, and then pulled out the linen-wrapped dried herbs from her pack, along with her small wooden bowl. She used some of the water from her clothes to make a woundwort paste, asking Aiden if he wanted any before smearing it over her bruised knee and aching calves. When she was done, she wiped her hands clean, rolled her pant legs back into place, and then grabbed two slices of ginseng before heading back to the fire.

"Your turn," Mizuki said, hanging her drenched clothes on the line before taking her previous seat and handing Aiden one of the ginseng pieces. "Eat this – it won't taste good, but it will help to keep you from getting sick."

"Thanks." Aiden smiled, taking the ginseng and holding out a tin of heated water. "Drink this – it will help to warm you up."

She gratefully accepted the tin of warmed water that Aiden gave her, popping the ginseng slice into her mouth before clasping the warm cup tightly between her hands. She could feel the heat radiating through her body as she took a sip and tried to ignore the bitter, earthy taste of the herb. She kept her eyes firmly fixed on the flames, her body still trembling from the cold as the storm continued to rage. A moment later Aiden reappeared, hanging his wet clothes before dropping to the cold, hard ground by her side and handing her some of the food they had packed.

She forced herself to eat it even though she wasn't hungry. She knew she needed the nourishment, and frankly, she was surprised that she wasn't feeling ravenous after being on the move for the last day. Instead, the only things she felt were fear, nervousness, and deep, heavy exhaustion that clung to her bones. She could feel her eyes drooping and her shoulders starting to sag as her exhausted limbs gave up. The woundwort paste on her knee and calves was helping, and with the warmth of the fire finally easing the cold in her body all, she wanted to do was sleep.

"How are your legs?" Mizuki asked, forcing her eyes to stay open as the wind violently changed direction and the rain began to tilt to the south. The adrenaline that had kept her going to this point was officially spent, and she had to force her head to twist so she could look at Aiden in the low glow from the fire.

"They're okay," Aiden said, his eyes shifting over her with a look of concern. "I'll be honest, Mizuki, I'm amazed that we made it this far and that you're still standing."

"Well, to be fair, I'm sitting," Mizuki murmured, a small smile tugging at her lips as Aiden rolled his eyes. She accepted some of the tree nuts that he handed her and popped one into her mouth, chewing slowly as she thought. "I don't think I could stand right now if I had to. Are you sure you don't need any woundwort paste? I can make some more up."

"I don't," Aiden assured her, his eyes creasing as he smiled at her. Another crack rumbled through the air, and they both jerked at the noise, their heads snapping up to look out beyond the low overhang. "We should get some sleep – I'll keep watch for a bit to make sure that the fire doesn't go out, but nothing will be hunting in this. We should be okay until morning."

"Alright," Mizuki said, trembling as she pulled her knees up to her chest and wrapped her arms around them. "But if the storm stops, wake me up for night watch. You need your rest too, Aiden."

"I will," Aiden agreed with a nod. He watched her for a moment, his eyes creasing as she continued to shake, and her eyes started to close. "You're still cold."

"Only a little," Mizuki acknowledged, forcing her eyes back open to glance at his worried face once more. "I'm not going to get hypothermia – I can throw on another shirt."

She shifted to get up once more, but Aiden shook his head.

"That won't do you any good if your body isn't producing any heat. Here–," Aiden stood from her side, moving the woodpile closer so it was in reach before motioning for her to scooch forward.

"What are you doing?" Mizuki asked, shuffling closer to the fire and watching as Aiden stepped behind her, only for him to sit down, lean against the rock wall and straddle her with his legs.

"Keeping you from freezing to death," Aiden replied, pulling her back against his chest and carefully wrapping his arms around her. She stiffened in his hold, her heart rate increasing as she swallowed hard. "Relax – I'm not going to do anything."

"I didn't think that you were," Mizuki retorted, her tired eyes narrowing as she turned her head to glare up at him. Her mouth went dry as she realized how close his face was, and she quickly looked away and cleared her throat. "So, is this how the hunting group sleeps, too?"

She felt his laugh; it vibrated through his chest and into her body like the heat that was already seeping through her thick hide shirt.

"If the occasion calls for it – yes," Aiden said. The deep rumble of his voice was almost soothing, and she could hear the amusement in his tone. "Though usually, our fires are much larger, we're a lot more careful of the weather when we're out, and the guys don't get cold as quickly as you do. They have a lot more meat on them."

"That makes sense," Mizuki murmured, her body relaxing in his hold as her eyes started to drift closed. "You're sure it's safe for us both to sleep?"

"No," Aiden admitted, a small sigh leaving his lungs. "But I sure hope so."

Mizuki nodded, her body flinching as another deafening crack of thunder rocked through the ground, and the rain grew louder. Had she been at home in the safety of her bedroll, she would have lain awake listening to the storm and likely stayed up all night. But now, resting against Aiden's chest and feeling more drained than ever before, she found that she couldn't have stayed awake even if she wanted to. Even with the racket just an arm's length away, her eyes fell shut, her pulse began to slow, and she drifted into a deep but uneasy sleep.

The smell of wet earth and smoke filled her lungs as she inhaled. She felt warm and safe – but there was a dull ache coming from her legs and shoulders that made her frown in confusion as her eyes slowly fluttered open. She blinked, her half-asleep mind trying to make sense of the grey rocks and small, smouldering fire near her feet. She blinked again, realizing that there were two sets of legs before her – her own and someone else's – and her brow creased further as she jerked to sit up only to be held firmly in place around the middle as a low whisper echoed near her ear.

"Don't move."

She froze at the sound of Aiden's voice, her brain instantly making sense of everything surrounding them as all the pieces and memories from the last two days fell into place. She had fallen asleep in Aiden's arms, but he had not woken her up for night watch, and now he was sitting rigidly behind her and gripping her tight. She blinked again, her eyes rapidly searching the small space under the overhang and peering out into the darkness that lay beyond their small shelter. Only the faintest hint of light was visible; the sky was dark, with a grey drizzle still lingering from the storm the night before. She instinctively knew that something was wrong from the tense way he was holding her, but no matter how hard she squinted, she couldn't see anything.

"What is it?" Mizuki whispered, her voice so low it was scarcely audible as she forced herself to remain still against Aiden's frame.

"I heard something," Aiden whispered, his hand leaving her side and slowly shifting to point off to the left just outside the shelter. "There."

She looked to where he pointed but again saw nothing. She could barely make out the nearest trees and the thin trail of smoke coming from the remains of their fire. So she craned her head forward and listened. She could hear the wind as it shifted through the trees, faint and weak compared to the force of the gales the night before. She could hear the slow drips of water that fell to the ground off the shelter and the soft patter of light rain that continued to fall, but what struck her more than anything was the lack of other sounds.

"No birds," she whispered faintly, feeling Aiden nod behind her. They both remained seated and still, their breaths puffing like little clouds in the cool morning air. She had woken up enough times after a storm to know that the birds always sang, even if it continued to rain. She could feel her heart starting to race, her panic starting to grow as she swallowed hard and willed her eyes to see into the dark. "What do we do?"

"We need to pack up," Aiden whispered, his hands moving once again as he unwrapped his arm from around her waist and gently leaned forward to reach his calf. "Quietly – but as quickly as you can. Take this."

She could see from the bottom of her gaze that he was undoing one of his knife holsters and transferring it to her leg, but she kept her eyes firmly locked to the place where Aiden had heard the noise. She remained entirely still as he worked until she felt the leather pull tight, and Aiden patted her calf twice to let her know he was done. Then they both shifted, Aiden sliding back and silently crawling to the small hole where they had stored their packs while Mizuki tentatively stood and began taking down their damp but no longer drenched clothes. Her tired legs ached beneath her as she carefully rolled each item and handed it to Aiden, who had moved back to her side. He stuffed everything into his pack, not caring what was what and keeping his eyes fixed on the darkness as the wind shuffled through the trees.

Her skin started to prickle with the distinct feeling of being watched as she slipped on her pack and glanced over to Aiden. He already had his pack on, and he was holding his bow ready with an arrow nocked. He glanced at her, his eyes gesturing down to the knife on her leg before he looked back out into the dark, grey drizzle. She reached down and took out the knife without question and tried not to think about how much it shook in her hand. She had to remind herself to breathe as Aiden shifted and motioned for her to follow. She held the blade near her hip, moving toward him and standing so close next to his side that there was barely an inch of space between them.

She followed him out from their cover, inching soundlessly to the edge of the overhang as her eyes rapidly scanned the darkness for movement. They had just stepped out into the misty rain when suddenly Aiden was shouting, and her heart was constricting in terror.

"GET BEHIND ME!" Aiden yelled, unleashing his arrow at the dark and silent form that lunged from the treeline on the left.

His shot missed, and the arrow struck the ground as the large animal darted to the right and dove back into the bushes. Before he could pull another from his quiver and before she could even process what was happening, the creature rushed them once more. A vicious snarl cut through the air as Aiden shoved her out of the way seconds before being knocked to the ground.

"AIDEN!" Mizuki screamed, sliding in the mud as she struggled to find her footing. She staggered to her feet, knife in hand, and saw Aiden on his back with his bow lodged in the creature's mouth.

The monster on top of him was as black as night and larger than any animal she had ever seen with her own eyes. Foam frothed from its mouth as it snarled, and her eyes rapidly traced over its form. It looked wrong – too thin and scruffy to be healthy, too terrifying and violent to be real. Both sets of eyes were locked on Aiden, one green, one yellow, its pupils dilated in rage as the bow between its teeth cracked.

Without stopping to think, she charged towards it with her knife, legs pumping as she rapidly closed the distance until she was close enough to strike. The blow landed on the creature's side, a painful yowl tearing from its lungs as its green set of eyes locked to her face. It dropped the bow and lunged toward her, the knife still protruding from its side as it knocked her to the ground. A sharp, piercing pain shot through her left leg, and her brain briefly registered the sensation of being bitten before the scream left her lungs and the wolf dragged her through the mud. It shook her hard, struggling to get a good grip on her leg as her body slid and jerked against the ground. Her nails clawed at the dirt, and her pack grew heavy with mud. She could hear Aiden yelling – there was a sharp yowl, and the pressure on her leg disappeared. She gasped in pain, struggling to breathe as she coughed mud from her mouth and rolled onto her side.

"MIZUKI, MOVE!"

She twisted away instinctively, covering her head with her hands and narrowly missing the two sharp claws that grazed by her face as a giant ball of fury and fur slid through the mud at her side. She forced herself to her knees as a low growl split the air, desperately looking around to try to locate the creature once more.

She spotted it, and she screamed out for Aiden as the wolf lunged for his neck. It missed, grabbing his shoulder instead and tugging him to the ground. Its right paw swiped, the large dewclaw catching across Aiden's face and splattering the ground with blood. Mizuki scrambled to her feet as Aiden's scream of pain rang out through the trees. Fighting to stand and sliding in the mud as she limped her way toward him, she desperately looked for something to use as a weapon.

But despite the blood that covered his face, Aiden's hands didn't stop moving, and she watched him stab the creature twice more in the chest with his knife before it squealed in pain and darted into the bushes. She could hear it running loudly and clumsily through the trees as it howled, abandoning stealth and silence as it fled the rock formation, and she rushed to Aiden's side.

"Aiden!" she yelled, no longer feeling the pain in her leg as she careened to a stop and dropped into the mud at his side. He was holding the left side of his head, his muddy hand covering his eye and temple as his face contorted in pain. "Are you okay?"

"Fine," Aiden groaned, his head turning in her direction. "Are you okay? Your leg – did you break anything?"

"I'm fine," Mizuki breathed, trying to pull his hand away from his face. "Don't worry about me – Aiden, your eye!"

"I know," he said through gritted teeth, clamping his hand back over his damaged eye and grimacing in pain.

"Let me see it," Mizuki pressed, reaching for his hand once more only for Aiden to swat it away.

"We have to go, Mizuki – we can't stay here."

"And we can't go anywhere until I do something about your eye, Aiden," Mizuki countered, her voice laced with frustration. "If that gets infected, you'll die."

"I know," Aiden said tightly, this time grabbing her outstretched hand and holding on to it. "There's a small stream just south of here – the water is clean. You can look at it there."

"Fine," Mizuki said, gripping his hand tight and helping him from the ground. She gathered the damaged bow from the mud, slinging it over her own shoulder before looking across the muddy battlegrounds for anything else that might have gone astray. Then she ran her hand across her sternum, checking to make sure that her necklace was still safe before she let Aiden lead her into the trees.

They travelled in tight silence for several minutes, their breathless pants filling the air as they moved through the trees. Each step left her calf aching in pain, but she gritted her teeth and ignored it as they pushed forward at a run and made for the sound of rushing water. She didn't even realize that she was still holding Aiden's hand until they reached the stream and slowed to a stop.

"Sit down," Mizuki ordered, gesturing to a small rock along the bank as she pulled off her pack and the bow, then dropped to her knees to rinse her hands in the water. She shook her hand dry before reaching for her mud-covered pack and pulling out a small block of soap and a fresh, soft bark-linen wrap. She glanced over to Aiden, who had removed his pack and was watching her through his single eye. She grimaced. "This is going to hurt."

Cold sweat poured down her spine as Aiden screamed out in pain. She had never heard him make that noise before, but then again, she had never seen someone nearly lose their eye in a wolf attack either. She cleaned the cuts as best as she could, knowing that Aiden would never see from his left eye again as she did it. It was still there in the socket, but it was damaged beyond repair and damn near impossible to open as Aiden instinctively clenched shut.

Despite this, she managed to rinse it clean. Then she pulled out her herbs and made a thick paste that would protect against infection and numb the pain. She coated his eye, layering it several times before covering the surrounding wounds with the same mixture. She stitched two deeper cuts closed with the thin thread that she had brought, then she cleaned the bite on his shoulder and smeared those with paste too.

The entire time she worked, Aiden gripped the side of her muddy shirt tight, sweat forming across his brow as he fought against the pain and tried not to pass out. She had always known that he was strong, but she didn't realize how strong until this moment. She pulled fresh strips of linen from her pack, wrapping them around Aiden's head and over the wounded eye before tying the makeshift bandage in place. When she was finally done, she remained kneeling before him, unable to look away as he let out a shuddered breath.

"We need to do you next," he whispered hoarsely, his right eye red from pain and the tears he hadn't been able to hold back. "Let me see it."

Mizuki nodded, shifting to sit down on the ground and pulling up her left pant leg to look at the damage. It wasn't nearly as bad. Her leather shoe had prevented a significant amount of damage – as had her pants. But there were still four distinct puncture wounds, a few other shallow marks, and a deep bruise forming around her calf just above the ankle.

"It's not that bad." Mizuki shrugged, glancing back up at him, and he frowned as he looked at the wound on her leg. "I can patch this up quickly – no stitches necessary. It will just be a bit swollen."

"Make sure you add some of that woundwort paste," Aiden said, his one-eyed gaze shifting to meet her own. "Otherwise, that will get infected."

"I will," Mizuki agreed, setting about cleaning and wrapping her leg.

"I've never seen anything like that," Aiden murmured, holding the small wooden bowl of paste for her as the tight grimace on his face finally started to lessen. She knew it was the numbing agents in the paste, and she let out a silent breath of relief knowing that her medicine was working and that the pain would continue to subside.

"I thought you've seen wolves before," Mizuki commented, smearing the new batch of paste over the freshly cleaned puncture wounds and grabbing a small damp piece of linen.

"Yes," Aiden confirmed, his brow now creasing with worry as he looked at her. "But not one like that. This one was smaller."

"*Smaller?*" Mizuki started, her eyes widening in surprise as she looked up at him. "You mean they're normally bigger?"

"Usually." Aiden nodded. "But they've always been afraid of us, and they've always hunted in packs. That one looked starved. It was alone, and I think its leg may have been injured before it attacked. I don't get it – I've never heard the other hunters tell stories about wolves attacking people before, and they love trying to scare the juniors. It's just never happened."

"Your ma said the deer moved south," Mizuki offered, wrapping her leg and tying the linen in place. "Maybe they don't have any food. Maybe they're desperate."

"Maybe," Aiden agreed, handing her the now empty wooden bowl as she began to pack up. "How's the leg?"

"It's alright, I promise," Mizuki said sincerely, standing and testing her weight on the limb. It hurt, and she knew that it would get worse before it got better – but it wasn't broken, and she could still use it – she had gotten lucky. She gave Aiden a small, reassuring smile before reaching out her hand to help him up off the rock. "How are you? Does it still hurt?"

"A bit," Aiden admitted, grimacing as he stood and reached for his pack. "But the herbs have helped a lot. Thank you, Mizuki."

"Of course," Mizuki said, watching as Aiden began to put on his pack once more. "I know we don't have a lot of time – but maybe we should rest for a little bit?"

"We should," Aiden agreed, turning back to look at her after grabbing his damaged bow from the ground. "But we can't – we need to put as much space between us and that shelter as possible. As it is, we've already stayed too long. They'll be able to smell the blood, and if the rest of the wolves are starving like that one, they'll come after us. It's possible that one was only left behind because it was injured. I don't want to stick around to find out what happens when the pack gets back."

"Alright," Mizuki agreed, concern growing in the pit of her stomach as she swallowed hard and reached for her pack. She didn't like the idea of pushing forward so quickly with Aiden's injury, but she knew he wasn't wrong. "Then we push on – but Aiden, if you start to feel sick or lightheaded, you need to let me know. I can't carry you if you pass out."

"I will," Aiden said, giving her a tight smile as he held out his arm and gestured across the river.

She followed his direction, shoving away her nervousness as they cut across the stream and continued to move south. But her trepidation followed them as the dark, grey sky began to lighten and the rain continued to drizzle. The Woods remained eerily quiet, and her eyes darted through the trees as Aiden's pace began to quicken. She could see the tension in his shoulders again, but she knew it wasn't from the pain. His head shifted constantly, eyeing the dull darkness of the surrounding foliage and looking for any signs of life as the Woods continued to get thicker and thicker.

She tried to ignore the ache in her calf, reminding herself that it could have been worse and that the injury was nothing in comparison to Aiden's. She tried to pretend like she wasn't terrified every time the wind moved a branch or something cracked in the trees around them. She tried to convince herself that they were still going to make it – that they weren't just marching to their deaths – as they passed a large, marked tree, and Aiden noted that they were getting very near to the edge of the hunting grounds. She tried, desperately, to believe that everything was going to be fine and that nothing was following them through the trees.

She was doing rather well at convincing herself; that was, at least, until a howl broke through the air, and Aiden yelled at her to run.

They took off at a sprint, Mizuki panting hard and her feet colliding loudly against the muddy ground as another howl sounded to the east. Fear shot down her spine. She could feel sweat collecting across her skin as her wet, muddy clothes stuck awkwardly to her body and her injured leg ached in pain. They raced through a section of brush, Aiden urging her to go faster as a third howl sounded to the west. She may not be a hunter, but she didn't need to be to understand that they were now prey, and they were being surrounded.

The muscles along her side cramped; her face was scratched as she ducked under the next branch and urged her legs to go faster. Aiden grabbed her hand, tugging her forward as they darted around the next marked tree and jumped over a fallen log. She could hear her heart beating in her ears, and the sound became deafening as her pulse raced dangerously fast. Then, suddenly, the noise of their feet wasn't the only one rushing through the trees, and she heard the terrifying sound of paws against earth gaining ground behind them.

"Don't stop!" Aiden panted, gripping her hand tighter and somehow doubling their speed. They crashed through a section of trees, not even blinking as the thorns tore at their skin and ripped at their clothes. "Down!"

Mizuki dropped to the ground, tumbling into a roll as Aiden dragged her down and something massive lunged over their heads. She barely had time to look over her shoulder and see the immense black wolf, frothing at the mouth and snarling in rage, before Aiden hauled her from the ground once more, and they darted into the next batch of thick trees. It was bigger than the other wolf – taller but bone thin as well. This one had yellow and blue eyes, and both sets looked desperate as it skidded to a stop and twisted around to chase after them.

"On the right!" Mizuki shouted, hearing another one approaching as they ducked around a thorn bush and rolled under a low branch to evade the wolf that bounded at them from the west. The trees were getting closer. The brush was getting thicker. Vines were dangling from the trees, making it impossible to navigate. Mizuki's heart felt like it was going to burst in her chest as they struggled through the thicket, and she heard the wolves approaching once more.

"Aiden?!"

He grabbed her hand again, gripping it tight.

"Jump!"

He screamed the word just as she saw it, a steep hill sloping down to a green-looking lake that was spotted with small patches of land. Using the last bit of strength she had left, she pushed off the ground, jumping into the air and off the ledge as she clung to Aiden's hand. Warm air rushed past her face as they dropped more than ten feet and landed in the water. Her leg screamed in pain as it collided with the bottom, but she didn't have even a second to think about it as Aiden tugged her forward, half-swimming, half-walking away from the ledge toward the nearest patch of land as the wolves snarled behind them. She struggled against the muddy bottom, her lungs gasping for air as Aiden all but dragged her to a tiny patch of land and hauled her out of the water.

Grunting in pain, they both collapsed against the damp surface. Mizuki's face pressed against the thick moss as she inhaled sharply and groaned. She forced herself to glance back despite the fear that was possessing her body and saw four wolves pacing along the top of the ledge. Two were foaming at the mouth. All four were thin and ragged, but none of them followed them into the water, and as much as she was happy about that, it made her stomach twist with unease.

"Aiden," Mizuki wheezed, turning to look at him as he lay panting by her side. "Where are we?"

"I have no idea," Aiden groaned, rolling onto his elbow and looking out around them. "We passed the last marker just before jumping – this is the swamp, Mizuki. We're in the Wild now."

The Wild

"So, what do you think the odds are that someone could drink this water without dying?" Mizuki asked, carefully holding her hands above the stale, waist-deep water as she walked through another patch of the green slime that seemed to cover the majority of the swamp's surface. She turned to glance at Aiden, who was walking along her left, hands raised in a similar fashion.

"Well, given the colour, the smell, the shallow depth, and the fact that I'm nearly entirely sure that this swamp is not fed from Glass Lake – I'd say it's pretty low," Aiden responded thoughtfully, his gaze shifting to meet hers as he raised an eyebrow in question. "Why, thinking of taking some back for the Elders?"

"It's tempting," Mizuki said, unable to stop the small smirk that touched her lips as she shook her head in amusement.

After confirming that the wolves weren't going to follow them into the swamp, Mizuki and Aiden had laid on the small patch of grass for several long minutes, waiting to catch their breath as their heart rates slowed. It wasn't until after they had checked each other over for injuries and ensured they still had all their belongings that they finally stood to face the swamp and examine their surroundings.

It was like nothing either of them had ever seen before.

The air was warm, humid, and unmoving. Tall trees grew out of the water, their trunks thick with visible, spindly roots disappearing into the stagnant green liquid while smaller dead and broken pieces stuck out all around. Nearly everything was a shade of green. Moss crept up the tree trunks, and vines dropped down from the canopy above. Strange birdcalls filled the air, the noise echoing as if the sound was bouncing off the trees and growing louder each time, broken up by periods where the intense chirping seemed to fall instantly silent, only to start up once more as a loud croaking buzzed from the trees.

She had no idea what creatures were making the sounds, but they saw things that she had never imagined possible. A pure white bird on impossibly long legs waded through the water to their left while a short, stout bird with blue feathers watched them walk by from the safety of the tree on their right. They had stopped once already on a small patch of damp, mossy land to eat while Aiden looked at the map. Now, as they slowly moved through the water and into the unknown, they responded to the strange new world with the comfort of small talk.

It had never been Mizuki's favourite thing, and she had never been particularly good at making conversation. She and Aiden typically didn't talk for the sake of talking, and their conversations largely centred around the happenings in the village or the task they were completing. But the discomfort of talking for the sake of talking was easily outweighed by the unsettling feeling of the mysterious world around them, and with every step she took and every word she spoke, she found it easier and easier to open up to Aiden – almost as if she were at home rambling on to her mother.

And she was surprised to find that in some ways, she actually enjoyed it. Then again, she supposed it wasn't that surprising since she had always enjoyed Aiden's company.

"I was just wondering about it since the wolves didn't follow us in here," Mizuki said, glancing at Aiden once more and clarifying her earlier statement. "Do you think the water is unsafe?"

"Maybe," Aiden said, turning to look at her once more with his one good eye. "I thought of that, but maybe they just can't swim. It would be too deep for them to walk across, and the small patches of land are too spaced out for them to be able to jump their way across."

"I suppose that's true." Mizuki nodded, her gaze shifting along the surface of the green water once more. She didn't like that she couldn't see the bottom, and she tried not to let her fear get the best of her as she wondered what was lurking beneath the surface. "But then the deer wouldn't be able to cross either."

"Probably not," Aiden agreed.

"Then how did they move south?" Mizuki asked. "The map shows that this swamp extends nearly all the way from the ridge to the chasm. They would have had to go around it, which I guess they might have done, but it just seems unlikely."

"You think the deer are gone," Aiden concluded, meeting her gaze once more as his voice dropped low with concern. "I've been wondering that too. If the deer had moved around the swamp to the south, the wolves would have followed. I'm starting to wonder if there just might not be any deer left."

"You think we hunted them all?" Mizuki asked, a heavy feeling sinking in her chest as she spoke the words.

"I'm starting to," Aiden muttered. "I never put much thought into it before now, but I'm not sure how much effort was put into preserving their numbers."

"All the more reason to try to find the Agronomist," Mizuki murmured. "Because even if the deserters are still alive, I can't see that they would cross this mess to hunt when they'd have to drag the body back home. It just makes me wonder what else the Elders have lied about."

"What do you mean?" Aiden asked, and she could feel his gaze on her temple as they moved through another section of green slime.

"I mean all of this, Aiden," Mizuki said, gesturing around them. "They told everyone that the Wild was dangerous, which it is – but they also said that people couldn't live out here. They told everyone that there was nothing past the hunting grounds. No life, but this looks like a lot of life to me. How many birds have we seen since coming here? And what about all that croaking and clicking? Aiden, there is a whole world out here with life everywhere. What if there are more people too?"

"You think there might be others – more than just the deserters?"

"Maybe," Mizuki murmured, biting her lip as her eyes flicked around them once more. She couldn't explain why, and she wasn't about to tell Aiden, but something about all of this was making a piece of her heart ache in pain. "Why not? Why would we be the only ones to survive the Great Destruction? What makes us so special? And what about the first betrayers that my grandfather mentioned? Miku always said that the world was massive – maybe there are others out there, but they're just too far away for us to ever find them?"

"So *this* is the sort of stuff that you think about when you go all quiet," Aiden said as he stopped and turned to look at her.

She could hear the amused smile in his voice, and she let out a breath of frustration. This was exactly why she never truly talked to anyone but her mother. If people knew half the thoughts that she had, they would surely think she was crazy.

"Aiden, I'm being serious," Mizuki sighed, pushing past him and ignoring his stare. Her step was cut short as Aiden grabbed her shoulder, and as she turned around to look up at him, she was surprised to see that he didn't look amused in a mocking way at all. He looked serious – in an almost impassioned sort of way.

"So was I, Mizuki," Aiden said, dropping his hold on her shoulder and stepping toward her. "I didn't mean that in a bad way. The way you think, and the things that you come up with, it always surprises me."

"Most would say that's not a good thing," Mizuki muttered, crossing her arms over her muddy shirt and looking up at him with doubt.

"Well, most people in our village don't think at all, do they?" Aiden countered, a small smile tugging at his lips as he looked down at her. "They're happy not asking questions. They're content so long as things are going well – but not you. You're always thinking, and that's one of my favourite things about you. I always want to hear what you're thinking, and I wish you would share it more often."

Mizuki eyed him carefully, searching for any sign of teasing but finding none, as he continued to look down at her with sincerity.

"You're serious?" Mizuki said in disbelief. She wasn't sure she understood why he was telling her this or why her stomach was starting to knot as she looked up at him.

"I told you I was," Aiden said. His words were gentle as his eye traced over her face, then he shook his head and let out a sigh, gesturing for them to keep moving. "The way your brain works has always fascinated me, Mizuki – even if you are a little obtuse on the more obvious things."

"The more obvious things?" Mizuki questioned, turning to follow after him and struggling against the muddy bottom of the swamp. It wasn't so bad when they moved at a steady pace, but any time they stopped in the water, it was as if their feet had sunk into the earth. "What do you mean?"

"Maybe I'll tell you someday," Aiden teased, turning back to offer her his hand as he winked. The effect was muted given that his left eye was covered by linen, but she narrowed her eyes at him anyway before she gave up trying to dislodge her foot and begrudgingly grabbed his hand for help.

"Fine, don't tell me," Mizuki muttered, ignoring his laugh and gripping his hand tight for balance as they continued to push through the swamp. "I didn't want to know anyway."

They moved in silence for the next while as the sun grew hotter and the day grew later. The drizzle had stopped shortly after they reached the swamp, and now the bright blue sky was clear, with not a single cloud in sight. She tried not to think about how she was still holding Aiden's hand even though she had already gained her footing or what he had meant by his words. The nervous, spinning sensation in the pit of her stomach hinted at something she wasn't sure she wanted to know. So, she pushed it all down and kept her eyes focused on the water, the green, and the trees as she looked for any signs of danger.

There were none.

At least not any that she could see. Twice while walking, she felt something brush up against her leg, and she gripped Aiden hard as they quickened the pace. After one such incident, they crawled onto the nearest mound of land and spent several long minutes staring into the water, looking for any sign of movement. But the surface was too dark, the water too muddy, and the path that they had walked remained silent, without a single ripple of movement across the surface. So, they begrudgingly got back in and continued on their way.

Wiping the sweat from her brow with her free hand, she fought back a groan as her exhausted legs began to cramp. Before setting out across the green liquid, they had packed away their jackets and hats, but it was still far too warm. Just when she was wondering how much farther she could walk, she spotted land ahead, and she let out a deep sigh of relief. The sun was starting to sink, the birds were growing quiet, and bugs were buzzing over the water and biting at their skin.

"We're almost there," Aiden huffed, exhaustion showing across his face as he began to pick up the pace. "So close."

"I never want to cross this thing again," Mizuki panted, forcing her legs to take another step as she heard something shift in the water. "Aiden?"

"I heard it," he confirmed, his head turning as he looked around. "I don't see anything – I can't see anything in this. Just keep moving. We're almost there."

They moved even faster, and Mizuki's body grew tense with each step as she glanced around nervously. It was getting harder and harder to see; the light was fading too fast. Something brushed against her right leg, then the water behind her rippled, and she nearly jumped with terror.

"Aiden, it touched me," Mizuki whispered, her voice shaking as she gripped his hand tighter and tried to fight back the panic that was growing in her chest. "It's behind us."

"Maybe it's just a fish," Aiden whispered, but he tugged her closer and began moving even more quickly. "We're less than twenty feet – when I say go, run."

"Okay," she whispered, feeling the brush against her leg once more and biting her lip to stifle a whimper. The water rippled behind them again, and this time Mizuki could have sworn she saw something long and silver moving on their right.

"GO!" Aiden yelled, gripping her hand so tightly it hurt as he began rushing through the shallowing water, paddling with his free hand to move faster.

Mizuki tore along beside him, pushing herself forward with everything that she had as the land grew closer and closer. Her heart was beating in her throat; she didn't even realize that she wasn't breathing as she raced toward the shore and began clambering up the muddy bank with Aiden. Her fingernails dug into the short, damp grass as she pulled herself out of the green sludge that collected around the edge and tugged her legs out of the water. Turning to look behind her, she saw the water ripple, a flash of silver vanishing from sight as whatever had been lurking along beside them dove back under the surface.

"What – do you think – that was?" Mizuki panted as Aiden helped her stagger away from the swamp.

"No idea," Aiden wheezed, clutching at his side in pain. "But I don't want to find out. Come on – I'd rather not know if it can walk on land. The trees should clear up ahead and transition into rocks like by the river. We might be able to reach it before dark. There might be something there we can use for shelter."

"Anything would be better than sleeping in here," Mizuki breathed, her legs shaking as she stumbled against Aiden's side.

He slipped his arm around her waist to hold her up as she fought to catch her breath. She didn't complain as he continued to support her while they navigated through the thick jungle-like terrain. At this point, she honestly wasn't sure how she was still standing. Her pack was heavy and wet, her muddy clothes and wet shoes added extra weight she simply had no strength to bear, yet her shaking legs continued to move her forward. She was fairly certain that she was operating on sheer willpower alone – but she knew even that had its limits.

When the thick trees finally started to thin and the ground grew less damp, Aiden started to gather small sticks and branches. She did her best to help him, but her arms struggled to hold much as she stumbled through the trees beside him, and the sky grew dark. By the time her feet hit rock, and the jungle faded into sparse trees, she couldn't feel her legs. Her eyes were half-closed, and her shoulders sagged and ached under the weight of her pack. If not for Aiden muttering a constant stream of reassurances, she might very well have fallen asleep on her feet.

"There," Aiden breathed, gesturing with his head to a large rock before them. "We'll stop there."

She nodded in agreement, too tired to say anything as they closed the distance to the large rock at a sluggish pace, and she collapsed on the ground by its base. The sticks she had been holding clattered as they hit the ground. She could smell the stink of the swamp clinging to their clothes as she looked around at the barren, rocky land and forced herself to take off her pack and pull out their supplies.

Only the faintest hint of light remained in the sky, and soon it would be too dark to see anything. As it was, she couldn't see more than a dozen feet before them, and she still needed to unwrap and reclean her leg wound before she fell asleep. She didn't trust the water in the swamp, and she didn't want to risk the bite getting infected.

"I'll start the fire," Aiden said, dropping to his knees and nodding in agreement to what she was doing. "Get that cleaned – mine are fine. They didn't get wet."

"Okay," Mizuki sighed, forcing her shaking hands to roll up her wet pant leg.

She grimaced as she unlaced and pulled off her ruined leather shoes. They were caked in mud and worn through in several places along the bottom. She could feel the blisters that had formed on her feet as she tugged off her socks and frowned at the state of them.

"I'll need to check your feet, though, Aiden," Mizuki said, glancing up to see him positioning the wood so they could sleep with the rock behind their backs. It wasn't nearly as good as the hunting spot, but it was definitely better than sleeping in the swamp or out in the open with nothing. "You might have cuts, too."

"I know I do." Aiden grimaced, finally taking off his pack to get his flint and stone. "I'm not sure these shoes are going to make it back."

It took fewer tries than the night before for him to start the fire, and by the time he got it going, Mizuki had managed to clean her leg using half a pouch of water and re-wrap the wound. It was worse than earlier, the bruise was deep purple, and it was swollen nearly twice as large, but she bit down the pain as best as she could.

They used the other half pouch of water and empty herb linens to wipe away the mud from their feet. With Aiden having insisted that she use what remained of the woundwort on her leg, they were officially out of herbs and down to their last pieces of ginseng. They both ate the bitter root in silence, ignoring the itch of the bug bites that covered their bodies because to itch them would be a mistake – one that could possibly be fatal without additional herbs. So instead, they sat there uncomfortably, eyes heavy with exhaustion as they forced down some berries and the last of their water.

"According to the map, there is a stream a little way beyond this, and then the base of the Southern Mountain should be right there." Aiden pointed, his voice laboured as Mizuki leaned back against the rock and stared into the darkness. "I hope."

"I hope so, too," she murmured, too tired to ponder the closeness between them and why it didn't bother her as he sat back against the rock by her side. She traced her thumb over the familiar etching of her necklace, trying to find some comfort in their otherwise bleak conditions. "Otherwise, we're in big trouble."

"Do you regret coming yet?" Aiden asked, his voice low as his head rolled to the side so he could look down at her. "You could have been asleep in your bedroll, safe, clean – no danger of being eaten."

"And miss this?" Mizuki murmured, her eyes glancing up at the familiar night sky before she turned to look up at him.

He was so close she could see all the tiny marks that covered his skin and the faint shadow of scruff along his jaw. It felt strange, and yet she couldn't help the tired smile that crossed her face as she let out a deep breath and closed her eyes. She relaxed against his side, her limbs going limp as the exhaustion set in.

"No," she whispered, not minding when she felt him wrap his arm around her shoulders and pull her to his side to keep her warm. "I'm glad I'm here, Aiden – there's nowhere else I'd rather be."

When she woke the next morning, she was fairly certain that her body had become a solid, immovable object. Her legs felt heavy, breathing hurt, and her arms weighed more than the pack that she had been carrying for the last two days. She could feel Aiden pressed against her side, or maybe she was pressed against him; she wasn't sure. But he was definitely sleeping because his breath was slow and long, and she could feel each puff ghosting across the top of her head as he exhaled.

She tried to move, but every muscle in her body screamed out in pain, and so she gave up and deemed the task impossible. She settled on cracking her eyes open instead while silently hoping that no other terrifying creatures were lurking around them. As the dull grey light of morning flooded her vision and she blinked her eyes clear, she felt the air in her lungs vanish as she was left breathless at the sight.

"Aiden," she whispered, her eyes opening wide. He murmured something near her ear, and his arm gripped her tighter, but he didn't move. "Aiden!"

"What?!" He jerked, his eye popping open and his body tensing as Mizuki sat up and forced her body to move.

"The mountain! Aiden, look! The Southern Mountains – they're right there!" Mizuki untangled herself from his side and staggered to her feet. The pulled tendons in her legs and swollen calf caused her to stumble back against the rock as she pointed her arm to their right to point to the incredible sight.

"Veles be damned," Aiden breathed, hauling himself up from the ground to stand beside her.

The smouldering remains of their fire continued to smoke on the ground just three feet before them, but beyond that, the view was breathtaking. Her wide eyes scanned over the terrain hungrily, her heart racing with excitement and wonder as she tried to take it all in. The flat-top rocks they had slept on stretched out before them then dipped into a valley. She could see the river that Aiden had spoken of weaving through the valley's center, around the rocks and grass and odd dark green trees. Colourful flowers dotted the land along the bank and swayed in the gentle breeze that whispered over her mud-caked skin. It was beautiful – peaceful – but the most incredible thing about it was the tall, rocky mountain that jutted from the earth and seemed to pierce the sky.

Before she even realized it was happening, she was hugging Aiden tight as her eyes burned with tears. She didn't know who had grabbed who, but she didn't care as all her emotions came rushing up in one giant wave. She gripped him tight, swallowing hard as she fought for control and tried not to cry.

"I can't believe it," she whispered into his chest, scrunching her eyes tight and biting her lip as she sniffled. She let go and ran her hand across her eyes, forcing herself to inhale as she looked back out at the valley and struggled to find words for what she wanted to say. But there were none. There was nothing, and she couldn't describe the enormous feeling in her chest as she turned back to look at Aiden and grinned wider than she ever had in her life.

"We made it," Aiden whispered, his visible eye watering with unshed tears as he continued to hold her tight. He looked terrible in the morning light. Dark rings lingered under his eyes. The bandage around his head was dirty and stained. His face was smeared with mud and blood, just like hers. Yet, at that moment, he somehow looked better than the day that they had left – because now, they had hope. "Let's go – I'll bet you anything that water is safe to drink."

They grabbed their packs from the ground, throwing them on with renewed energy as they set off across the rocky plateau. It took longer than she thought it would to cross the rocks and make it to the valley with both of them limping, but when they did, she felt her body calm and heart quiet.

The tall, dark trees smelled fresh. Their leaves were not truly leaves at all; instead, the branches were lined with thin needles that stuck out in all directions. The grass was soft. The low, rolling flow of the river filled the air like music as they made their way barefoot toward it. Neither one of them had bothered to put their shoes back on, and instead, they carried them in hand until they finally reached the river and they collapsed on its bank.

If places like this existed, surely there were others.

Surely people were living out there. Not just surviving, but thriving in the land that the Elders had said could not support life. As she dipped her hands into the cool water and washed the caked mud from her skin, she saw three rabbits darting across the opposite bank and felt her pulse flutter. Everything here was so beautiful, and it made her wonder if this was what the village had looked like years ago.

Was it their fault that the deer were gone, the trees were thin, and the soil no longer grew crops large enough to feed the village? Had they done something wrong?

The thoughts swarmed her mind as she washed the mud from her arms and then tore off her pack. They agreed to face opposite ways because neither one of them wanted to leave the other after everything they had been through. So Mizuki trusted Aiden not to peek as she pulled off her blood and mud-covered clothes and left them on the bank before stepping into the river.

She shivered as she washed away the stench of the swamp, even ducking her whole head under the cold water and combing her hair out with her hands before adding a little bit of soap. The low temperature helped to soothe the ache in her muscles, and she knew it would reduce some of the swelling in her calf. She did her best to dry off with the small towel she had packed, but it was still damp from the rain in the Woods – though thankfully, none of her goods seemed to be coated with swamp slime aside from what she had been wearing. She took time to rinse out her muddy clothes, hat, and battered shoes before wiping the dried mud off her pack and putting on the last unsoiled clothes she had left. Then she rubbed her hair dry with her towel, feeling more alive and human than she had felt in days.

Once they were both decent, and Mizuki had re-wrapped her leg, they moved upstream to refill their water pouches. Then shifted barefoot through the grass to a small rock before sitting down to eat.

"We should be able to reach the mountain base by midafternoon," Aiden said as he pulled out some food and handed her one of the newly refilled water pouches. "That's the easy part. The hard part will be trying to find him. You said Elder Clark mentioned that there are tunnels in the mountains?"

"Yes, along the northern front, but I couldn't see where he was pointing," Mizuki said. "Was there anything marked on the map?"

"Nothing useful." Aiden shook his head. "The scale is too small for them to have been able to provide detailed markings like that, and they didn't add any notes. But at least we're on the northern side, so there's that. When we get closer, we can pick a point, mark it, and start searching along the base."

"Alright." Mizuki nodded in agreement, handing Aiden a few berries and taking a bite of dried meat. She chewed thoughtfully for a while, her eyes scanning over the terrain and looking for anything that might give away the location of a shelter. As far as she could see, there was nothing, and her brow furrowed as she glanced back at Aiden in question. "Would there be anything to give it away? Smoke? Trees? Is there something that the hunting group looks for when you're trying to find shelter?"

"Water," Aiden said simply, his eye narrowing in thought as he stood back up from the ground and climbed onto the small rock. She watched as he looked around, popping a few berries in his mouth as he looked up the river then turned back around to watch the water flow away. "This river curves to the south – you said there was a larger lake beyond this mountain?"

"Yes," Mizuki confirmed. It didn't show on the map, so she had no idea how far away it was. "The Elders seemed to think it was where the deserters would head."

"Well, the river is coming from the west." Aiden pointed, his brow furrowing as he eyed the base of the mountain and squinted into the sun. "We're downstream of the source, and I bet you it curves around these mountains and feeds into the small lake. There might be a few rivers that do, but my point is the river gets closer to the base down there."

She looked to the left where he was pointing, to the northeastern edge of the mountain.

"If I were picking a place for a shelter, that's where I would go," Aiden said, his head nodding in agreement with his words.

"The storms always come from the northwest; it wouldn't make any sense to build a shelter on the northern front of the mountain unless you're on the eastern edge. It's why the village is so protected – because of the way the ridge curves. I think we should head to the east."

"That makes sense," Mizuki agreed, forcing her legs to move as she stood and looked where Aiden was pointing. She could only just see the curve of the river, and judging by the way the odd trees grew thicker in that direction, she had to agree it would make for better shelter. "Let's go east."

They finished eating quickly, packing up their wet, but now mostly clean, clothes and shoes before setting off along the river. They moved in determined silence, refreshed in the cooler air now that the stink of the swamp was gone from their bodies. Yet, despite the nervous excitement churning in her stomach from their success, Mizuki refused to let herself lose focus. She kept her eyes and ears open as they moved, cautiously watching every tree and rock for signs of a threat.

She ignored the ache in her spine, the groan of her shoulders, and the agony that was her calf as the numbing agents from the herbs finally wore off and the wolf bite began to throb. She glanced at Aiden in concern as they moved, sticking close by his side and monitoring the way that his face was growing tighter with pain. She knew that his eye must be killing him, but he didn't utter a word about it as they cut across the grass and began to approach the base of the mountain. It felt strange to admit it to herself, but it was so much larger than she had realized from afar. Standing at the base, it looked like the ridge, just a giant wall of rock and stone and the odd tree that grew out at a strange angle – but looking up and craning her neck, it seemed to extend into the sky forever.

"How's your leg?" Aiden asked as they passed the third tiny crevasse and deemed it unsuitable for a shelter. The hole was so small even Mizuki couldn't fit through it, and she seriously doubted that the Agronomist could – not that she knew what he looked like.

"It's fine," Mizuki lied. She knew that Aiden wouldn't believe her, especially because she was limping, but there was no point telling him it hurt. They had no herbs, they had no time, and they had to keep going. She ignored the churn in her stomach as she thought about going back to the village, cutting through the swamp, and navigating the Woods again. She didn't know if she could make it, and even if she could, she wasn't sure that the world would allow them passage a second time, given how harsh it had been the first. "How's your eye?"

"It's fine," Aiden replied, clearly lying, as they passed yet another small hole along the mountainside. He frowned in frustration. "This would barely fit a rabbit."

"We're going to find it," Mizuki reassured him, not truly believing her own words as she pushed on alongside him and the afternoon grew late.

She was beginning to wonder whether it was possible for a person's legs to simply fall off – or for them to just stop working altogether. She was debating the merits of the thought as the sun began to set when Aiden suddenly stopped and grabbed her arm.

"There," Aiden whispered, gripping her tight as he pointed to a small crack that ran along the side of the mountain. "If I were to pick a shelter – *that* is what I would pick."

Mizuki's gaze shifted to the small hole, her eyes tracing over it as the warm red glow of the sun cast shadows across the grass. The split was narrow but tall – tall enough for a grown man to fit through if he turned sideways, and it was protected by the way the rock had become uneven after the split. It created a lip that jutted out farther to the north that would block wind and rain from getting inside. It was small enough that a wolf wouldn't be able to fit, maybe rabbits or something smaller could, but anything that posed a real threat would struggle to get through the opening.

"What do we do now?" Mizuki whispered, her voice dropping low as she stared transfixed at the small crack. They were running out of time – the sun was starting to lower, and they couldn't be out here searching all night. She figured Aiden was thinking the same thing as he nodded and took a step forward, stowing his damaged bow in favour of drawing his remaining hunting knife.

"We see if anyone is home," Aiden answered, his gaze scanning along the ground before the opening. He squinted and dropped to his knees, brushing his hand over soft grass blades that looked crumpled. "If not, we stay here for the night and keep searching in the morning. But based on this – I think there might be someone here."

Mizuki followed him as he gestured forward, regretting that the knife he had given her was currently lodged in a wolf somewhere out in the Woods. They squeezed through the opening, Aiden going first, his blade out in front of him as they moved as quietly as possible. She bit back a groan as her calf began to pulse with pain from the strained angle of navigating the small opening until suddenly the faint glow of light flickered along the stone walls, and the crevasse opened into a small cave. She stumbled from the opening, colliding with Aiden and letting out a groan as loose rocks clattered to the ground. Her mind barely processed the fact that Aiden was standing rigidly still until a voice echoed out, and she stiffened at the sound.

"I wondered when you'd come."

The voice was feeble, and as Mizuki gripped Aiden's sleeve for balance and leaned around his body to look into the small cave, she nearly gasped in disbelief. A frail old man was sitting by the fire. His shoulders were slumped and rounded. His hair was white, and his gnarled hands were weaving long thin leaves together into some sort of mat.

"But now I find myself wondering how bad things must have gotten for you to become desperate enough to risk making this journey, Farr. Or did you manage to convince Clark to take it for you? Truth be told, I was hoping not to run into either of you ever again."

"I'm not Elder Farr," Aiden said, and the man sitting by the fire stilled. The gentle sound of the moving leaves stopped as his tanned and knobbly fingers placed the half-made mat on the ground. "Or Elder Clark. My name is Aiden – Aiden O'Kane, and I came here with Mizuki Altherr."

"O'Kane," the man said slowly, his head still downturned and his gaze fixed at the ground. "And Altherr... I've not heard those names in many years."

Aiden shifted, holstering his knife as he inched towards the old man.

"Are you the Agronomist?" Aiden asked as he slid another step forward, and Mizuki inched along behind him, unable to let go of his arm. "Because that is who we have been looking for."

"Do you even know what an agronomist is, Aiden O'Kane?" the man asked, a hint of amusement lacing his weak voice as he lifted his head. Mizuki's grip on Aiden tightened as the man's face came into view, and she felt Aiden stiffen once more. There was a large scar that ran down his face and cut over his eye, while another cut across his cheek. His eyes were clouded and white, and they searched the space before him as though they could not see to whom he spoke. "It's a farmer, an agriculturalist – it's a *job*, boy, and nothing more. It's not a name, nor is it my title any longer. My name is Earnan."

Earnan

"Why don't you sit down," Earnan said, his hand gesturing out to the ground before the fire as he coughed and continued to stare somewhat imprecisely in their direction.

Mizuki stood frozen at Aiden's side, her fingers knotted into the rough fabric of his long-sleeve shirt so tightly that she could no longer feel them as her eyes danced around the small cave. There was a worn bedroll against the back wall. Tattered clothes were hanging from a rope that was strung across the rocks. A pile of sticks and wood lined the left side. Next to it was a collection of dried herbs, an old pack, what looked to be a stack of ancient books, parchment, and oddly shaped containers stacked along a crudely built wooden shelf. There were odd symbols on the walls, etched into the stone and painted onto the surface. The only one she recognized was that of Veles.

The space was cramped.

It was worn and well lived-in, but it was dry and warm. She could see the smoke from the small fire trailing up into a crack that ran along the rock above their head. It acted as a natural vent, and she realized that not only was this the perfect shelter as Aiden had described but that this man had been using it for a very long time. The Elders had never said when it was that the agronomist had left the village, and seeing his old frail form, she felt lost for words – she still couldn't believe that they had actually found him, and he was still alive. She wasn't sure what she had been expecting to find when they squeezed into this cave, but an old, frail man with shoulder-length white hair who could barely see had certainly not been it.

Aiden shifted at her side, slowly taking another step forward and reaching to remove his pack and bow. She swallowed hard, pushing aside her nervousness and forcing her body to follow his lead. She tried to think of something to say. She tried to think of something to ask the man as she set her heavy pack on the ground and sank to the cool stone to sit by Aiden's side. Yet, despite all the endless questions that had circled in her mind along the journey, and those that had formed when she first heard about the agronomist, she couldn't seem to decide what to say as she stared at him. He seemed to sense that they were both nervous and struggling to find their words because he spoke once more in a low and gentle voice.

"Are you injured?" Earnan asked, his cloudy eyes shifting over them as he squinted in the low light. She wasn't sure how much he could see, whether he was fully blind or still had partial vision, but despite the eeriness of his gaze, there was kindness behind his eyes that made her racing heart slow.

"A little," Aiden said, his eye locked to the strange old man as he looked at him curiously. "But we're alright."

"I have herbs if you need them – there." Earnan pointed to the pile that Mizuki had already spotted, then returned his thin arm to rest across his lap as he tried to muffle another cough.

With her eyes now adjusted to the dim glow of the fire, Mizuki could see that his skin was weather-worn and rough. He could have blended in with the stone behind him in the dark; he seemed very nearly nature itself by the way he moved and the soft way he spoke. He stared at them for a moment longer, then his head tilted to the side, and his face shifted into a curious expression.

"They didn't send you, did they?" he said.

"No," Aiden breathed as his fingers gripped the fabric of his pants and he glanced around the small cave. His brow furrowed as he looked back at the man, asking the same question that had just floated to Mizuki's mind. "How did you know that?"

"Elder Farr and Elder Clark would never allow an Altherr to leave the village to come find me," the man said, a slow, gentle smile twisting across his face. "Did Miku send you?"

Mizuki stiffened at the mention of her great-grandmother, her eyes growing wide with questions as she leaned forward toward the man across the small fire.

"You knew my great-grandmother?" she breathed, her voice a hoarse whisper as she watched the man nod in confirmation.

"I did," Earnan revealed, his smile growing wistful as his misty gaze shifted in her direction. "She was my most dear friend. How is she?"

"She's dead," Mizuki whispered, watching as the man's smile faded and his eyes grew heavy with grief. "She died ten years ago, just after the last Gifting."

"Well," Earnan said, his soft voice wavering as his lips shifted into a tight smile. He wheezed painfully once more. "She always did say that she would die before me. I disagreed, but it seems that she won in the end."

Silence stretched between them as the man let out a low sigh and closed his eyes. She glanced at Aiden, but he looked just as lost as she was as he stared at the old man.

"How did you find me, then?" Earnan finally asked, his eyes opening once more as he reached to his right to pull out a small container.

"We heard the Elders talking," Aiden answered, his eye closely watching as Earnan unwrapped some linen and pulled out dried tree nuts and berries. "The crops aren't producing the way that they used to. There was a food shortage last summer, they had to ration the crops, and they're worried that it will happen again because the soil is no good. They were discussing coming to find you – to try and bring you back to the village to help."

"And you came all this way to tell me?" Earnan asked, his misty gaze shifting back to Aiden.

"No." Aiden swallowed. "We came to ask for your help."

"And what could an old man like me possibly do to help you?" Earnan asked. "My sight isn't what it used to be. I would not be able to fix the crops even if the Elders themselves dragged me back to the village. Not after what they have done to the land."

"We're not here about the crops," Aiden said, his body tensing at Mizuki's side. "They are a problem, and they do need to be fixed, but we're here for you. We need you to come back to the village with us – tonight."

The old man snorted, resulting in a small coughing fit as he shook his head.

"I would never survive the journey," Earnan said, and his eyes creased with sadness as he looked at them. "I'm amazed that the two of you made it in one piece. The Wild is not a place to go wandering alone. Though you always were rather tenacious as children."

"You knew us?" Mizuki asked, shuffling forward another inch. "When did you leave the village?"

"Shortly after your second birthday, if I remember correctly," Earnan hummed, his brow creasing with thought. "But my memory is not what it used to be, and that was a long time ago."

"So you've been out here for sixteen years? How did you survive for so long?" Mizuki asked, the questions finally beginning to pour from her lips as her initial nervousness fell away. "How did you make it this far? Why did you leave? Why didn't you stay?"

"I wasn't given a choice," Earnan answered, his gnarled finger rising to point at the scar along his face. "It was either Miku or me – they didn't care which, but one of us had to go, and I wouldn't let it be her."

"But they needed you," Aiden said, confusion drawing across his face. "They needed you for the crops – why would they send you away?"

"The Elders had stopped listening to me long before that day," Earnan wheezed, his head shaking as he spoke. "They had the same information I did, Aiden O'Kane, but they chose to ignore the majority of it and carry on overburdening the soil because at the time the crops were plentiful, the process was well established, and it was easier. They didn't agree that it would become a problem, and they weren't interested in my warnings. They were more concerned about Miku and the ground she was starting to gain gathering support in the village."

"If she was gaining ground, why didn't you do something?" Mizuki whispered, watching as the old man's expression grew sad.

"The both of you here today is the answer to that question, Mizuki," Earnan said, and his voice grew weaker. "This fight extends well past the bounds of your lifetime. We *did* do something, and we lost. The Praetorian Circle was happy with their arrangements, and they weren't interested in change. They didn't want to think critically, not when they were guaranteed safety, food, and shelter. They had no reason to believe us. No reason to question it when one look over the ridge or a single week in the Woods did nothing but reinforce the Elders' teachings. This world is a harsh and bitter place. It is not easy to survive, and many of those who now aid the Elders have spent their fair share of time being reminded of that truth day in and day out. They didn't like that we were stirring the fire and upsetting the balance that they had worked so hard to establish.

"The comforts that you enjoy in the village today were hard-earned, Mizuki," Earnan murmured, his gaze growing distant. "Life used to be much more difficult before the Elders gave the village structure and order. Thus, the Praetors resented us nearly as much as the Elders did. Just before your birth, there was a supposed hunting accident and a crop shortage. Things grew tense, and the blame was placed on Miku and those that opposed the sacrifices. We suffered harsh consequences, the village started to grow unstable, and it threatened our very existence as humans. So, Dante and Anya left the village with the small group of supporters that Miku had managed to gather. They had long since realized that the village was a lost cause, and taking their chances in the Wild became preferable to staying when they realized the lengths that the Elders were willing to go to maintain their control.

"Sometimes, when I think back, I can't believe that the Elders let them leave," Earnan said, his head shaking as he spoke. "Maybe Farr and Clark truly believed that people could not survive in the Wild, or maybe they thought that Dante and Anya would return sometime later begging for forgiveness. Either way, I suppose it was a win for them. It removed the faction of the village that had always given them trouble, and it lessened the strain on their resources. If Dante was never seen again, the rest of the village would assume that he and his followers died; if they returned, it only proved the Elders right. It wouldn't surprise me if Farr had some of the more loyal Praetors spread rumours about finding bodies in the Woods just to safeguard the support he already had.

"I think their only regret was that Miku did not leave alongside them. They had assumed she would, but your great-grandmother refused to leave without you and your brother, and Kiren wouldn't allow Kazuki or your mother to go. So, she stayed behind, and so did I. But things only got worse after that," Earnan recounted, pausing to cough as his eyes dropped to the small flames. The food he had pulled out remained untouched on the linen wrap before him as his eyes grew sad. "The next year was hard. With Miku's supporters gone, the Elders grew motivated. They were determined to remove the stain of her existence from the history of the village to prevent another divide from taking place. They didn't like that we had both stayed behind; we were too dangerous, and they couldn't allow us to gain any new support. So with the crops growing well and the deer plentiful, they no longer needed me, and the *choice* was extended – either I left, or Miku was dragged into the Wild. I knew she wouldn't make it out there alone, and I knew she couldn't leave you and your brother behind – it would destroy her. So I left the following season. I had hoped that things might get better and that the Elders might relax when they no longer felt threatened."

"Well, they didn't," Mizuki whispered, her voice wavering and her throat growing tight as she stared at the hunched man. "Miku continued to tell her stories. Most in the village simply called her crazy and ignored it – but the Elders didn't feel the same way about it because they Gifted my brother ten years ago."

Earnan's head shot up, his clouded gaze creasing with pain as he looked at Mizuki, and she felt the corner of her eyes start to sting.

"They came by that morning, and they dragged him away without even letting us say goodbye," Mizuki whispered. "Miku died a few weeks later."

"And now they're Gifting my younger sister," Aiden said, his fingers knotting the hide fabric of his pants even tighter. "She's only twelve years old, Earnan. She's just a kid."

"Please," Mizuki breathed, her chest clenching tight. "You have to come back with us – we need you to tell them that the Gifting serves no purpose."

"They won't believe me," Earnan murmured, his weak voice growing hoarse.

"But they have to," Aiden insisted, his desperation audible. "You're living proof that humans can survive in the Wild and that it isn't all some Dead Zone like they've been telling everyone in the village. There's life out here! Places where people can live without needing sacrifices!"

"Miku and I already tried that; people died, and it nearly destroyed the village," Earnan whispered as his gaze shifted back to Aiden.

"But it's different this time!" Aiden argued, shaking his head in denial. "It has to be! Some of the gatherers know about the crop shortages – it's proof that you were right! Some of them will remember you. You've been living in the Wild for sixteen years without Gifting anything up the mountain, and you're still alive!"

"You don't understand," Earnan said sadly as a look of pity crossed his face. "You don't know the Elders as I do. You don't know what they have done, what they are willing to do. They will spin this in their favour."

"How?" Mizuki challenged, watching as the old man's gaze shifted to her.

"They will say anything that they need to say in order to keep control – that's all this has ever been about. They will blame the crop shortage on my return or my living in the Wild without Veles's blessing. They will claim that I am a spy for Dante and Anya and a threat to the village. The people will believe them because they don't want to see the truth," Earnan said, his voice so weak now he sounded like he was struggling to speak. "Put silk on a goat, and it's still a goat. But keep people safe, fed, and protected, and they will see what you tell them to see because fear is more powerful than reason. The ones who might believe us already know, but they choose not to care. They choose not to see because they are comfortable. The others are too afraid to even begin to believe."

Aiden stared at the man in silence, his body rigid as he sat before the small fire.

"My da said those words to me when we gathered the dogwood branches and kalmia," Aiden whispered.

"And I spoke those words to him well before you were born," Earnan replied hoarsely. "You have courage – the both of you – to have made it this far. I pity you and your family, Aiden O'Kane. I truly do. Your da was always a good man – though I fear that might have been his downfall. But this battle has been going on since before you were both born. It started from the very moment the world ended. You came here expecting to find answers, and while they are not the ones that you sought, they are the truth. The village will not change. The Elders will not relinquish control, the Praetorian Circle will continue to serve them without question while the others simply follow, and there is nothing that I can do to help save your sister. The fear of Veles is very real for good reason."

"But we have to go back," Mizuki murmured, her head shaking in denial as everything Earnan said circled in her head. He wasn't wrong – this had not been what they were expecting to hear, and now as she sat on the cold, rocky floor of the cave and the final threads of sunlight disappeared from the small opening, she wondered what on earth they had been hoping to find.

Had they seriously thought it would be so simple?

Locate the agronomist and bring him back, have him tell the village that sacrifices weren't needed and that the crop shortages were the result of the Elders' poor planning? How could she have thought it would work?

Looking back on it now, she felt almost foolish. Of course the Praetorian Circle knew. Of course the Elders would deny every shred of proof that they dragged back to the village while blaming the recent food shortages on Earnan, them, and anyone else they found alive in the Wild. She could feel her doubt and panic starting to rise as her brain rapidly tried to process the new information.

Had it been a mistake to come here? Had they just lost any chance that they had at trying to save Maebh by choosing to go after Earnan instead of just running away with the girl?

She shook her head, tucking her still damp hair behind her ears as she forced her weary mind to think clearly. Had they tried to run with Maebh, they never would have made it. Knowing what she knew now about the Wild, Aiden's sister wouldn't have been able to survive, and the Village Guard would have chased them down in full force because Maebh was the chosen sacrifice. It had been much easier for just the two of them to slip away unnoticed, and the truth was that she believed Aiden's initial suspicion to be true – she doubted that anyone had bothered to come after them at all. Besides, had they taken only Maebh, their families would have paid the price. So as much as Earnan's words were not what she wanted to hear, and as much as the situation surrounding the village and the sacrifices was more complicated than she had realized, it didn't change the fact that they had had no choice but to continue.

No matter what happened going forward, coming to find him had still been a better option than sitting around in the village doing nothing.

"We have to go back, Aiden," Mizuki repeated, turning to look at him and swallowing hard. "We have to try."

"We're going back." Aiden nodded in agreement, and she suspected that he had reached the same conclusion. "We can't stop now."

"If you return to the village, they will kill you on sight," Earnan said, his white eyes fixing them with an intense stare.

"And the alternative is what?" Aiden countered, his determined gaze shifting back to the old man as he got to his feet and gestured around at the small cave. "Living in this cave until I die of old age or until the village inevitably expands their hunting grounds, and they find us? We're just supposed to wait to die?"

"You head south to find Dante and Anya," Earnan answered, his head tilting back to look up at Aiden as his voice strained. "They will take you in."

"And just leave Maebh to die?" Aiden questioned, his face twisting in disbelief. "Let them send my baby sister up the mountain – not to mention how many countless others, just so that they can stay in charge while they blame all their failings on a god that doesn't exist? I don't think so! That's deerspit, and you know it! I didn't come all this way just to give up and abandon my family. We didn't run for two days straight, wade through a swamp, and nearly get eaten by wolves to run away now. You're coming back to the village with us whether you want to or not. If I have to – I'll carry you myself!"

Earnan stared at Aiden for a long while until a deep sigh left his lungs, and he coughed once more before gesturing back to the ground with his crooked hand.

"Sit down," Earnan said, picking up the dried food that had been abandoned by his side once more. "If you wish to return to the village, I won't stop you, but travelling at night in these areas, especially through the swamp, is a death wish. You will leave in the morning."

"And what about you?" Aiden said, his hands clenching into fists as he remained standing by Mizuki's side. "Are you coming with us?"

"I'm dying anyway," Earnan wheezed, his white gaze flicking back up to Aiden as he held out a small cluster of berries to Mizuki. "Don't worry – I'm not sick with anything you can catch. But whether I die here or in the Wild, it makes no difference to me. I'll go with you, but you must be prepared to return to the village on your own as I don't expect that I will survive the journey. And I hope, for both of your sakes, that you have a better plan than just showing up. If the Village Guard catches you before you manage to find and rally support, you will not make it for more than a few hours. When is Gifting day?"

"Three and a half days from now," Aiden answered. "They usually do it around midday."

"That's not a lot of time," Earnan said, another deep sigh leaving his lungs as he looked at them both with pity. "You both need to get rest tonight. Use the herbs that I have to mend your injuries – we will leave first thing in the morning."

"Okay," Mizuki agreed, accepting the berries that Earnan held out as she tugged on Aiden's pant leg to get him to sit down.

"Thank you, sir – we appreciate it. We ran out of our own supplies."

"It's no trouble," Earnan said, waving his hand dismissively as Aiden finally sat down and took some of the berries that Mizuki handed him. She knew he wasn't happy about spending the night, but if Earnan said these lands were dangerous at night, it was hard to argue.

They ate in awkward silence. The sounds of the night echoed softly into the small cave as Earnan placed more wood on the fire and coughed hard into his arm. Mizuki watched him move, noting the way that his body seemed to sag more than before and how his hand didn't fully close as he gripped things. She watched him for a while as they continued to eat, then got to work making woundwort paste so they could clean and dress their injuries.

"Excuse me, Earnan?" Mizuki finally asked as she smeared the fresh paste across her leg and held the bowl out to Aiden so he could take some. Earnan's head tipped in their direction, and she noted that the scar looked deeper and far worse in the low flicker of light. "How old are you?"

"I'm not sure," Earnan said after a small pause, his gaze becoming thoughtful as he groaned and shuffled back onto his worn bedroll. She waited patiently as he spiralled into another coughing fit and panted hard before he could continue. "I never knew my birthday, and I don't remember much now from my early years. Miku was convinced that I was born before the Great Destruction – as was her mother, but of course, the Elders would say otherwise. If I had to guess, I would think that I am nearing a hundred."

"That's incredible," Mizuki murmured as she finished with her leg and began to tend to her cut and blistered feet. She could feel a heavy exhaustion settling in through her muscles as her body begged her to sleep, but she found her mind unable to slow. "How did you get these supplies? Do you collect them yourself?"

"Mostly." Earnan nodded, his eyes drifting closed as he laid down on the small bedroll. "But Dante still comes by to check up on me, and he leaves me supplies and wood. I told him not to bother anymore, that I was well past my expiration date. Though he seems not to want to listen to an old man."

"You've seen Dante?" Aiden asked, his attention shifting away from his blistered feet to look at the old man once more. "The others that left? You know where they are?"

"Of course." Earnan nodded again, his voice growing weaker as his body grew limp. "They live a mostly nomadic life through the mountains and down into the valley in the south. They migrate with the seasons, and they follow the herds. They seem quite happy."

Mizuki turned to look at Aiden, arching a brow at him as Earnan's breathing levelled out and he became lost to sleep.

"Before we leave, we should leave a note for Dante and Anya – warning them that the village will be looking for them and that we brought Earnan back with us," Mizuki murmured, smearing the rest of the paste across her toes and over a particularly large blister on her heel. She used some of the clean linen strips they had packed to wrap her feet since she knew that her shoes and socks would provide little protection the following day. "They will be concerned if he is missing, and Dante could come by again before your uncle starts his search. I think it's a good idea – you know, just in case this goes wrong."

Aiden nodded in agreement, and they added another log to the fire before she cleaned his eye, packed it with fresh herbs and re-bandaged the wound. They took the time to set up Aiden's clothesline and hang their damp clothes, knowing that they would never properly dry if they remained packed away in their bags. When they were finally done and had cleaned up their supplies, they settled in for the night against the cool stone wall.

Yet despite the fatigue that riddled her body and the warm safety of the small cave, she struggled to find sleep as she stared up at the strange ceiling and mulled over what Earnan had said. She had no idea how they were going to convince the people of the village to believe them, and that was assuming that they made it back at all. Her family was a lost cause. No one would listen to Kazuki, and Kiren would stand by the Elders until the end. Their best bet was going after Keller and hoping that his uncle had some compassion. If they could swing him to their side, as a Praetor, his opinion held weight, and they might be able to use it to convince others to question the Elders. It wouldn't be easy, and she could already feel the doubt clouding her soul.

It wasn't until much later that sleep finally took her, and she dozed off next to Aiden, gripping the sleeve of his jacket tight as images of red eyes danced through her dreams.

The next morning, she woke to the sounds of movement and Earnan's harsh cough and rolled over to find that Aiden was already up and packing their bags. Earnan was seated on his bedroll, looking thinner than the day before and somehow even older. He was holding a small stack of books and parchment tightly on his lap, and he couldn't seem to stop wheezing. Aiden had taken everything out of their packs and was going through their supplies, sorting them into two piles.

"I can't carry Earnan and my pack," Aiden explained when he noticed that she was sitting up and watching him in silence. "Once he is too tired to walk, you'll need to carry our supplies, so we can only take what you can carry."

"That makes sense," Mizuki agreed, rubbing the sleep from her eyes and stretching her legs. They were still incredibly sore, and she could feel that she had pulled and bruised muscles across her body that she didn't even know she had. She tried not to think about how on earth the three of them were supposed to get back in three and a half days when it had taken them two days and running through the night to get here in the first place. Especially when they needed to try to get back as quickly as possible so they could gather support, arriving just before the Elders started the Gifting ceremony wouldn't do them any good, but with both of them injured and Earnan unable to stop coughing, it felt like an impossible task. "I'll put on a few extra layers, but otherwise, we can leave the clothes behind. It's more important to bring our supplies."

Aiden nodded in agreement, moving over so she could come to kneel by his side to help. It took them until the sunlight stretched across the small opening of the cave to finish packing their supplies and preparing for the journey home. Then, she and

Aiden took turns washing their faces in the river, refilling their water pouches, and relieving themselves before regrouping at the cave entrance and preparing to head out. She chewed on a small sprig of mint as she layered her clothes, handing one to Aiden and longing for the soft-bristled brush Kazuki had made for her to clean her teeth. She hadn't bothered to bring it, though now she was starting to regret that decision. They left a note for Dante on Earnan's bedroll, using charcoal and a spare piece of his parchment, then they helped the old man exit the cave and make his way into the meadow.

They set off at a slow pace, Earnan walking on his own and Aiden carrying Mizuki's pack as they made their way across the soft grass. She could feel it through the holes in her shoes, and she was sad to leave the place behind – especially since she knew what was coming next. She wasn't looking forward to the hard rocks or damp heat of the swamp.

She carried Aiden's damaged bow across her chest, the knife from her father now securely tucked into her jacket pocket. The weather looked favourable, a light cool breeze brushing through the odd needle trees, stirring up their fresh scent as the flowers swayed in the wind. If they had any luck, there would be no rain, but she didn't trust their fortune. These last few days had taught her not to expect anything. She knew the winds could change, and nature could turn against them in the blink of an eye.

It took them far too long to cross the river and reach the flat top rocks where they had camped the previous night. The sun was already starting to set in the sky, and Mizuki could see the frustration on Aiden's face as he tried to balance rushing Earnan along beside them with being mindful of the man's health and the fact that he wouldn't be able to carry Earnan the whole way back. They had to let the man walk on his own for part of the journey, so it made sense to let him walk the easy grounds of the meadow, especially since he was familiar with it. They needed to conserve their energy for the swamp, the thick trees of the Wild, and the dangers of the Woods. However, Earnan wasn't the only one moving slowly.

Mizuki was struggling to get her legs to function. Despite the paste that she had covered them in the night before, they screamed in pain with every step that she took, and she could see that Aiden was having just as hard a time. Their bodies were beaten; they had nothing left to give, and each step was agony.

Yet they didn't stop.

They couldn't stop.

They had no other choice. Maebh was counting on them, and the hardest part was still yet to come. They had barely made it onto the rocks when Earnan stumbled, and Aiden dropped to his side to see if the old man was okay.

"Do you need some water?" Mizuki offered, reaching into the pack that Aiden was carrying to pull out one of the pouches, but Earnan shook his head, waving in refusal as he coughed violently and held his chest.

"No – thank you," he wheezed, struggling to catch his breath. "I just – need to rest."

Aiden grimaced as he stood back up and looked around. The daylight was already starting to grow dim. The Southern Mountains were still visible behind them, and they had barely covered any distance across the flat-top rocks. She could tell that he was upset with their progress, but there wasn't anything that she could do about it.

"We'll rest here for a few minutes," Mizuki said, turning to stand closer to him as she spoke. "Then I'll take the pack, and we can walk until nightfall. We might be able to get halfway across the rocks. I know it's slow, Aiden, but we'll just have to make up for it tomorrow."

"I know," Aiden said, letting out a deep sigh and running his hands through his messy hair. "You might as well sit down. We'll move again when he stops coughing."

Earnan didn't stop coughing.

The man's wheeze only grew worse, and eventually, Aiden tore the pack off his back and replaced it with Earnan, regardless of the old man's worsening condition. Mizuki's legs struggled under the weight of their combined belongings as she hauled her pack onto her shoulders, and they began to move across the flat-top rocks at a quicker pace. She could tell from the determined glint in Aiden's eye that he was pushing himself hard, and concern filled her mind. There was still a lot more to go, and he needed to make sure he didn't burn himself out, but as the darkness grew and the mountain faded from sight, she realized that despite his determination, they were not going to clear the rocks.

"Earnan?" Mizuki asked, trotting along at Aiden's side and ignoring the pains in her leg. She made a mental note to wrap the bite tighter tomorrow. "Are there any animals out here that we need to watch out for?"

"Bears," Earnan wheezed, fighting back another coughing fit as he turned his head against the back of Aiden's shoulder to look at her. "But they probably won't bother us."

"Bears?" Mizuki repeated, her eyes growing wide. She jumped over the next gap between the flat-top rocks and saw Aiden's face pinch from the effort. "You've been living around bears for sixteen years?"

"There's plenty of other food," Earnan coughed, struggling to inhale. "They have never been a problem."

"That might change," Aiden panted, glancing over to look at Mizuki as he carefully navigated the thin cracks. "The wolves weren't a problem either, but they attacked us in the Woods on our way here. They're starving."

"Then they're desperate," Earnan whispered. "I warned Farr not to over hunt the deer."

The man's eyes drifted closed, his breathing becoming ragged as Mizuki shot Aiden a worried look. The limited number of days to return home might not be their biggest issue. Earnan seemed to be struggling to hold on, and she found herself wondering what was wrong with the man for him to be this sick. She kept her questions to herself, not wanting to waste his energy as they pressed on into the night. Aiden didn't stop or slow down until it grew so dark that running across the flat-top rocks was dangerous, and he was forced to set Earnan on the ground. Mizuki tended to the old man, making sure that he was okay as Aiden pulled out some of the dried wood that they had stored in their pack and arranged it to make a fire.

"What's in the books that you brought?" Mizuki asked, trying to distract the old man from the pain that was clear on his face as she took out some food. Aiden had packed the books into the bag as well, but she hadn't yet looked them over.

"They're the – history of the village," Earnan panted, his misty eyes shifting in her direction as she gently cupped his hands to place food in them. "The real history – and details about the crops, so if I – I don't make it. Maybe you can try to – fix the soil. And a map – a map of the swamp. You can use it to cross more safely tomorrow. There is a land path through it to the east. Take the books with you – make sure you bring them home."

"You're going to make it, too," Mizuki said firmly, her eyes flicking over to Aiden, who had finally managed to light a small fire. He was listening to their conversation, and his eye looked worried as he glanced at the old man. "We're *all* going to make it."

"We all have to die sometime," Earnan said, coughing once more as a small smile touched his lips. "People weren't meant to live so long."

"What do you mean?" Mizuki asked, pulling out some dried deer meat for Aiden before looking back at the old man.

"It became unnatural," Earnan whispered distantly. "Before the destruction – it brought out the worst in us, and we brought this upon ourselves."

"You mean the Great Destruction?" Mizuki paused, looking at the old man in confusion. "You're saying that *people* did that?"

"No – no," Earnan breathed, his voice growing weaker and his eyelids drooping. "Veles did."

"Veles?" Mizuki asked, her brow arching in surprise. It was the story that she had heard growing up, but she had not expected this man to believe it.

"Veles is very real," Earnan whispered, his gaze shifting to her once more. "But we were the ones who started it."

She turned to look at Aiden, who was sitting motionless across the fire. He was watching the old man with a cautious expression.

"You think Veles is real?" Aiden asked in disbelief, drawing Earnan's white gaze in his direction.

"I *know* Veles is real," Earnan answered, his hand moving to return the berries that Mizuki had given him. She took them without question, watching in silence as the man laid down against the cold rocks without eating a thing.

"How do you know?" Aiden questioned as the crackle of the fire filled the night.

"Miku's mother saw him," Earnan whispered, his eyes fluttering shut as he let out a heavy sigh. "Along with several others from the village before the Great Destruction. It was a different time then; people were different, the earth was different – and yet nothing has changed. People are still the same, and it will happen again and again and again just like the times before until there are no more of us left."

Earnan let out a low breath, his body growing limp as a chill ran down Mizuki's spine.

"But we all have to die sometime," Earnan whispered again, his voice trailing off as he drifted into sleep. "It's the most natural thing in the world."

Mizuki sat in silence by the flames, watching the slow rise and fall of Earnan's chest. Miku had never told her that. In all the years and all the stories, Miku had never once told her that her own mother had seen Veles before the Great Destruction. Her gaze shifted to the fire, and she stared at the flames for a long time until Aiden finally shifted to come and sit by her side.

He told her to eat. She wasn't hungry, but she ate the berries that Earnan had returned to her anyway and chewed on a small piece of meat as her mind spun in circles. She couldn't explain the sensations that seemed to be washing over her body as she looked out at the vast empty space around them and felt her heart sink in her chest.

She felt so small. So small, so naive, and so totally insignificant out in the huge world of unknowns.

She swallowed hard, dreading what would happen in the next few days. Even if they did somehow make it back, and even if they did, against all odds, find a way to convince the village that Maebh didn't need to be sacrificed – she wasn't sure where to go after that.

How did she go back to the village when she knew that Dante and Anya were out there with others living in the Wild? How could she live in the village when there was a world brimming with life of all shapes and sizes surrounding them? And what was she supposed to do with Earnan's final words – and his claim that Veles was real?

She closed her eyes and let out a sigh. Forcing her mind to quiet, she laid back against the hard rock and pulled the lotus pendant out from her fraying shirt. She gripped it tight as she stared up at the stars and wondered what else she didn't know. The history with Miku and the village was so much more complicated than she had realized, and the Elders and the Praetors were so much more dangerous than she had thought. She felt Aiden lay down beside her, his arm brushing against hers in the dark, but neither of them spoke.

There were so many questions that she needed answered, and so many things that she wanted to know. But as the warmth of the fire spread through her body and the sound of Aiden's gentle breathing filled her ears, she sunk into a deep and heavy sleep.

Morning broke with dull grey light. She could hear the faint sound of birds as they flew overhead, and the smell of smoke filled her lungs. Aiden was awake, and he was pulling out food from their pack and placing it out on the rocks.

"Hey, you're awake," Aiden said, glancing up at her movement and closing the pack once more. "I'm going to go take a quick look ahead and see if there is a better way to get off these rocks. I don't think jumping over cracks with Earnan is going to go well. Last night I nearly broke my leg. Can you wake him up?"

"Of course." Mizuki nodded, rubbing her hands over her face and willing her aching body to move.

"And make sure you eat," Aiden added before he stood and bit off a piece of dried meat. "I'm going to try to get us through the swamp today."

She nodded again in agreement, then forced herself to stand and stretched her hands over her head as Aiden darted to the north around the rocks, searching for a better path. Letting out a low groan, she moved to grab some food and called out to Earnan. She popped a couple of berries in her mouth, chewing slowly before turning to look back at the old man who hadn't moved.

"Earnan?" Mizuki repeated, groaning in pain as she shifted away from the small fire and made her way over to the man. "We're going to be leaving."

But the man didn't move at her call, and he continued to lay motionless next to the small fire. Mizuki felt her pulse quicken as she kneeled down beside the old man and gently touched his shoulder.

"Earnan," she whispered, already knowing that he couldn't hear her.

She swallowed hard, forcing her other hand to grip his shoulder so she could roll the man onto his back to see his face. As his stiff body flipped, she felt her stomach sink. Earnan's skin was cold, his misty white eyes open to the sky, dull and lifeless. As she looked down at the peaceful expression left on his face, her eyes pinched in pain.

Earnan, the agronomist, was dead.

The Return

"We can't leave him here," Mizuki said as she stared at the old man's body.

She had experienced death before, many times over the course of her eighteen years within the village, yet somehow this felt different. It felt heavier and bitter. Perhaps because she felt responsible as she looked over the frail man and wondered if he would have lived longer had they just left him behind in peace or tried to carry him the whole way. She let out a sigh and closed her eyes as her heart ached with pain.

"Not after we dragged him from his home and made him come this far," she whispered. "We can't leave him out in the open like this, Aiden – an animal will find him and pick his bones clean."

"We don't have time to bring him back," Aiden murmured as he shifted next to her side.

When he had returned from scouting a route across the flat-top rocks, he found her kneeling beside the old man in silence. One look at the man's wide-open eyes, and Aiden dropped to his knees by her side and wrapped an arm around her shoulders. Now, standing over Earnan's motionless corpse, they seemed to struggle to decide what to do as the implications of his death hit them hard. They would be going home alone, and their chances of saving Maebh had just drastically decreased.

"As it is, we might not make it back in time, Mizuki."

"Then we bring him with us until we find somewhere to leave him," Mizuki said, turning to look up at Aiden before she glanced around the empty expanse of rocks. "There must be a crevasse or a nook around here somewhere that's large enough. Did you see anything when you were looking for a better path?"

"There was a crack just to the east," Aiden said. He looked exhausted in the dull morning light, but he let out a deep sigh as he nodded in agreement. "It might be large enough to fit him. We can try it, but if that doesn't work, we have to leave him. You get the pack; I'll carry Earnan."

Mizuki nodded in agreement, accepting the compromise while silently hoping that the gap Aiden had located would be large enough. She couldn't stomach the thought of leaving the old man out on the rocks, exposed to the weather and creatures that wandered this region, but she knew that Aiden was right, and they didn't have time to wander around looking for a grave. As it was, it took them far longer than Mizuki had anticipated to carry Earnan east to the large gap. While Aiden gently placed the old man in the tight space, Mizuki wandered the nearby formation searching for loose stones to mark the impromptu burial grounds.

If they somehow survived, made it back to the village, and convinced the others of the truth, she wanted to come back. She wanted to be able to find this man again so they could burn him properly in the meadow by his home. That was, of course, assuming that no creatures managed to pry him from the rocks. Once Earnan was carefully stowed, and Mizuki had marked the location, Aiden pulled out the map that the old man had brought along and looked for the land path through the swamp.

"He must have spent quite a lot of time around the swamp before his vision faded," Aiden said as he smoothed the worn bit of parchment out on the rock before them. His gaze narrowed as he scanned the hand-drawn terrain and then looked up at their surroundings to try to pinpoint their location. "Or maybe Dante gave this to him. Either way, see this—"

Aiden pointed to the map, and Mizuki nodded at the small trail that was sketched across the swamp. There were little notes scrawled around the border of the parchment as well.

"This is the land passage through the swamp. From the way he has drawn it, it looks like a bunch of little islands – like those patches of land that we stopped on when we first cut through. But according to his notes, these are close enough together that we could hop our way across," Aiden said as he scanned the map once more. "We might be able to cut through the swamp without getting in the water."

"That's good," Mizuki said, looking up and seeing Aiden's furrowed brow. "Isn't it?"

"It is," Aiden agreed. "But it's much further east. We're going to lose time taking that route, and when we get to the other side, we won't be near any of the hunting trails or markers. Though I suppose that could be better. We'll be farther away from the wolf den and nowhere near the hunting shelter. If anyone had come looking for us in the last few days, they wouldn't be looking in this area. We'll have to cut our way through some thick forest, and it will be pretty rough until we reach the river to the south of Glass Lake, but it will be safer."

"I think we should take it," Mizuki insisted, watching as Aiden turned to look at her once more. "Aiden, we won't survive another wolf attack. I took what was left of Earnan's herbs and linen wraps, but there isn't that much. We can't afford to get injured again. We got lucky cutting through the swamp the first time, and I'm not sure we should chance it again when we still have three days to get back."

"I know," Aiden said, letting out another sigh of frustration. She watched as he ran his hand through his messy hair and looked around the flat-top rocks in deep thought. "Alright, we'll take it. But we'll have to push hard. This route is longer, and I have no idea what to expect when we get to the other side, so we can't let up."

"We'll push hard," Mizuki said. "We can make it."

Her stomach knotted as she spoke the words, and she could see Aiden's expression soften into something she couldn't name as he looked at her. She wasn't sure she believed her own words, but she knew if she didn't try to be optimistic about their situation, they would be doomed before they even started.

"We have to," Aiden said, giving her a small smile as he folded up the map once more and stood to his feet. "Let's go."

They set off into the late morning light, Aiden carrying the pack and quiver while Mizuki donned the damaged bow across her chest as a cool breeze ruffled their hair. Their pace was quick by normal standards but a far cry from the speed at which they had travelled when they first left the village. Yet, there seemed to be nothing that she could do about it. No matter how hard she tried to push her legs to move more quickly, there was only so fast that they would go. Every muscle ached, and the rough surface of the rocks scratched at the bottom of her feet through the holes in her shoes despite her best efforts to protect them with linen wraps and socks the night before. It took them until the sun was at its highest to locate the spindly tree drawn on Earnan's map as a marker for the land path through the swamp. Then, it took them another long while to navigate through the thickening jungle as they made for the swamp.

Despite the fact that Earnan had said bears roamed the meadow, Mizuki longed to return to it as the temperature grew warmer, and the small flying bugs that had assaulted them the first time began to attack their faces and hands once more. Even after the encounter with the wolves in the Woods, the swamp was her least favourite part of the trek, and she couldn't wait to get back to the familiar-looking trees that surrounded the village.

After several long minutes of cutting through vines, the trees thinned, and they reached the edge of the swamp. It only took them a few minutes longer to locate the land path, and they both sighed in audible relief when it appeared just as the map had shown.

It was a string of islands. Each small patch of land varied in size and shape, and they dotted across the stagnant green waters in an uneven and twisting path. They were close enough together that one could, as suggested by Earnan's notes, with careful footing and balance, jump from patch to patch without needing to set foot in the swamp waters. It wouldn't be easy, and based on the unbounded map, they were crossing the widest section of the marshlands. Still, assuming that the trail of land stretched the full way across, Mizuki thought it was far favourable to shifting through the green slime and encountering that silver creature once more.

So, with no time to worry that the land bridge may be incomplete, they set off across it with Aiden taking the lead. He tested each small island before he signalled for Mizuki to jump over and join him. The process was slow and exhausting. Every time she landed, her knees threatened to buckle, and she grunted in pain at the effort. On several occasions, the land patches were water-logged and muddy, which made it difficult to cross and ruined their footwear once more. Four times she nearly slipped into the swamp when landing on the slick muddy surface, and twice she stumbled and fell to her knees, only for Aiden to grab her and haul her to her feet.

One of the islands was so muddy that Aiden almost got stuck as his foot sunk into the muck. It had taken nearly all her strength to help pull him out before they quickly scrambled to the next island. Then they forced themselves to jump again and again as they continued their way across.

It was awful, and the whole process was made worse by the heat. The lifeless air was thick. There wasn't even a hint of a breeze or anything to cool them down as the sun grew hot overhead. Mizuki ended up removing her two extra hide shirts and tying them around her waist with her jacket because she was sweating so badly, she thought she might pass out. Yet she forced her eyes to remain focused, glancing from side to side as they moved, searching the water in between jumps for any signs of danger. But there was nothing, not even a ripple on the surface as their breathless panting grew louder and the strange birdcalls filled the air.

When they reached a particularly large patch of land, and the sun began to set, it became clear that they were not going to make it out of the swamp before nightfall. Aiden grimaced as he acknowledged their problem, and Mizuki frowned as they both reluctantly agreed that they would need to spend the night. Sleeping in the swamp had been something that they were hoping to avoid since they didn't know what to expect during the night, and any wood they could collect was too damp to burn, but as the sun grew even lower, they were left with no option. It was too dangerous to continue in the dark based on how the journey had gone thus far. If they tried, they would end up slipping into the swamp waters or breaking a leg in another sticky pit of mud.

So, they began looking for a place to sleep.

It took them a while. They had to veer off course along another string of land patches, but eventually, they found one large enough that it had a small cluster of trees that they could use for shelter. Panting from exhaustion and shaking on their feet, they made their way into the center of the trees and cleared a space just large enough for the two of them to fit. They had only barely managed to collapse onto the damp ground and pull some vines around them for cover when the darkness rapidly crept in.

Night came more quickly in the swamp, Mizuki learned – with the tall, thick trees and crowding vines, the lowering sun simply faded from existence, and very quickly it was impossible to see anything. They pulled some food from the pack and ate in tense silence while strange noises began to echo through the thick air around them. They didn't bother removing their shoes or replacing the now muddy and disgusting linen wraps that covered their feet under their socks since new ones would only be ruined the next day. It was uncomfortable and far too warm, yet she hoped the temperature wouldn't plummet during the night because they would be sleeping without a fire.

At the sound of a splash to their right, Mizuki tensed, and Aiden grabbed her hand. Her wide eyes searched through the darkness, looking for what made the noise, but she saw nothing, not even the outline of the trees that surrounded them as she instinctively gripped Aiden's hand in return.

It took nearly every bit of courage she had to close her eyes that night, and if not for the exhaustion that riddled her small body, she never would have been able to sleep. She didn't say a word as Aiden looped his arm around her, and she didn't even question her instinctive response of curling toward him in the dark as they leaned back against a moss-covered tree. If they were lucky enough to wake in the morning and live through the next few days, she might allow herself to think about why it felt so natural to be by his side, but for now, she couldn't afford to. With everything going on, her heart was heavy with dread, and she didn't have room for anything more. So, she clenched her teeth and tried to ignore the eerie sounds of the swamp.

Warmth was the first thing to cross her mind as her eyes slowly fluttered open and cool air brushed over her face the next morning. Yet as she blinked and looked around at all the green, she realized that the heat she felt wasn't coming from the air, which had grown colder – it was coming from the body that lay beside her.

Aiden was holding her tight. His arms were wrapped protectively around her as he clutched her to his chest, and they both laid in a tangle of damp moss and vines. Her face was burrowed into his shoulder, and her arms were wrapped tightly around his waist. Swallowing hard, she tried to suppress the nervous knotting in her stomach and the heated blush that crept up her neck as she forced her stiff body to pull away from Aiden's warmth. Never in her life had she ever been so close to another human being, and it just made all the exhausted and unfamiliar emotions that had been collecting in her chest over the last few days all the more confusing.

At her movement, Aiden stirred, and his single eye opened as he groaned and sat up beside her to look around. They had somehow, against her expectations, lived through the night, and the swamp looked remarkably similar to how it had been the day before. She could already see a tall white bird shifting through the waters to their left, its yellow stick-like legs barely disturbing the surface as it hunted around for food. The sun was starting to filter through the thick trees, and for a moment, it almost looked peaceful as they both sat there in quiet reverie, unsure of what to say to each other. Then another splash sounded in the distance, and her spine stiffened with fear.

"Ready to go?" Aiden asked.

She nodded, noting how rough his voice sounded in the morning. She could feel his gaze burning along her temple, but she couldn't seem to meet his eyes directly.

"Yes," Mizuki murmured, struggling to her mud-caked feet and grabbing the damaged bow from the ground as she brushed herself off. "Let's get out of here. I've had more than enough swamp for my lifetime."

It took them half the day to make it through the remainder of the swamp, and with each passing minute, the temperature grew more unbearably warm. When they finally reached the northern bank and jumped onto the solid ground, Mizuki sighed in relief. They stopped to eat, drinking water from their pouches and resting in the cooler air of the Woods before they continued on once more.

Aiden hadn't been wrong. This section of the Woods was thicker than what they had trekked through when heading toward the swamp, and without the tree markers and the hunting trails, it took them longer to navigate through the underbrush as they made their way north. Twice they stopped and remained incredibly still after hearing the faint rustle of a nearby bush. Yet each time it proved to be nothing, only small animals scurrying through the dense brush after being startled by their presence.

As they walked, their pace slowed, and Mizuki could see Aiden's shoulders beginning to sag under the weight of their pack. She offered to carry it, but he refused, giving her a tight smile and saying that he was fine as they pressed on through the afternoon. By evening it had grown cold, the sky grew dark and then out of nowhere, it started to rain. It slowed their pace even further as they both struggled to keep going and fight against the winds that were cutting through the trees. Mizuki pulled on her two extra hide shirts, her leather jacket, and her hat to try to keep warm, but they did little to remove the chill that seemed to have settled into her bones. She held Aiden's hand for balance as he guided her through a section of dense brush, but she didn't let go as they continued past it into the darkness. Instead, she squeezed his hand back when she felt him grip her reassuringly when the rain grew worse, and it soaked them to the bone.

They gave up when she stumbled over a dead log and nearly collapsed to the ground in exhaustion. She had finally reached her limit, and as much as she didn't want to admit it, she simply couldn't walk anymore. Even with the slower pace of the previous two days, her legs were shaking so badly she could barely feel them, and they refused to carry her weight. Without the tree markers or the trails, and with the sky covered in thick clouds, it didn't matter that she couldn't continue because Aiden couldn't navigate in the dark without the stars. So, he lifted her from the ground and held her up as they agreed to stop and started looking for somewhere to sleep.

They found shelter in an old oak, the broad tree base half-rotted away and hidden behind a thicket of thorns. Mizuki bit back a groan of pain as they crawled beneath it, and the sharp little spikes tugged at her skin. The space was cramped, and in order to fit, she had to sit between Aiden's legs just like how they had slept that night at the hunting shelter, but as she leaned back against his warm chest, she found that she didn't care. The awkwardness she had felt that morning about being so close to him was gone, replaced entirely by survival instincts and a deep appreciation for him as they gripped each other tightly and shivered in the cold. Even if they had been able to gather wood before the rain hit, neither one of them had the energy to start a fire as they nestled into the old oak tree and fell asleep to the low growl of thunder that rumbled through the air.

The next morning the rain had reduced to a slow drizzle, and the process of hauling herself from the ground felt like an impossible task. Everything hurt, and her body entirely rejected the motion while her mind dreaded it. Yet somehow, despite the fact that she felt like she would never be able to stand again, her limbs moved, and her will to go on won out. They set off at a slow and feeble pace toward the village, agreeing not to push too hard since they still had a full day and night to get back, and they both knew that they would need their energy for when they got closer.

She held his hand the entire way after stumbling three times. Aiden had offered to carry her, but she knew that he didn't truly have the energy, so she took his hand instead and gripped it tight. Once she had it, she once again found that she didn't want to let it go.

He navigated them through the thinning trees as she glanced at him from the corner of her eye and watched their surroundings. She was getting better at keeping track of their movements, and with the sun in the sky she could confirm their direction of travel. Yet even still, she knew that she would have been lost without Aiden, and with each step she took, she started to realize that she would have been lost without him years ago. Mizuki had grown far more attached to him than she had realized, and even though she didn't always show it or even acknowledge it – she needed him, and she couldn't help but feel like maybe he needed her too.

They didn't reach the riverbank below Glass Lake until nightfall, and by that point, despite the slow pace that they had maintained all day, they were both struggling to walk. They stopped along the bank to refill their water pouches, washing their faces, feet, and shoes in the cool stream and allowing themselves a few minutes to breathe before they crossed into the forest and took the final steps out of the wolves' territory. They had gotten lucky in their second pass not to encounter the desperate and starved creatures, but they didn't want to spend any more time in the Woods than they had to.

"We'll need to walk through the night," Aiden whispered as they made their way into a small clearing and dropped down to the ground by a tall maple in exhaustion. He slid the pack and quiver from his shoulders and grunted in pain as he pulled off his wet, freshly washed boots. "We lost too much time in the rain yesterday and with taking the land path through the swamp. Gifting day is tomorrow, and we have to get back before sunrise, or we won't stand a chance of sneaking in and finding my uncle."

"I know." Mizuki nodded, grimacing in pain as she stretched out her legs and bit back a groan.

The objective remained the same – they needed to find Keller O'Kane and try to swing the man to their side. She just hoped that Aiden's uncle was as decent a man as they both believed him to be and that he would listen to them. Failing that, if he refused to stand up to the other Praetors and support them, they hoped that he would have enough kindness in his heart to at least allow them to make a run for it with Maebh before the rest of the village woke.

It wasn't much of a plan.

If Keller refused to help them, they would not get far, and that was assuming that he let them go. They were both too injured, too worn, and too tired to sprint through the forest and evade the Village Guard – but at this point, they didn't have any other options. The situation had changed, and the village was so much more complicated than they had realized. They had stepped into the middle of a deeply-rooted feud that the Elders had been fighting for decades. They had been naive and foolish to think that bringing Earnan home would change anything, and the old man had all but shattered their hopes of success while opening their eyes to the ruthlessness of the village Elders.

The truth was, Mizuki realized, that they had been doomed to fail from the start – and slowly, in the most heartbreaking way, she was starting to understand why her father had said what he did that night by the fire. It was a losing battle. One that had already been fought and lost time and time again because the Elders had control, the Praetors were happy, the world around them was harsh and brutal, and the village was too afraid to try anything else.

No one cared that there was a sacrifice every ten years so long as it wasn't them or their family, and since the Elders used it to remove problems from the village, the practice was accepted.

She forced the circling thoughts from her head, knowing that dwelling on them and the situation would do her no good. They were where they were, and now they simply needed to deal with it and be prepared to fight tooth and nail when they got back to the village. Maybe they could convince Keller to go find Earnan's body with them and bring it back as proof. Maybe they could reveal the crop shortages or show the unbounded map to the rest of the villagers who didn't already know about it before the Elders realized they were back. Maybe Keller had allies they could appeal to, and maybe her own father would finally take a stand.

All she knew for sure was that she would try anything and do anything to make them listen – because after six days in the Wild with Aiden, and after everything that they had been through, she would not stop fighting until the village saw reason or until the Elders took her life.

She just hoped they were able to realize the first option before the second.

"Do you think they will have any patrols out in the forest?" Mizuki asked, glancing over at Aiden, who was collecting small sticks from the ground around them and gathering them into a tiny cluster. She removed her wet shoes and pulled out the last of

Earnan's herbs and linen wraps from their combined pack. Then she set about making a new woundwort paste in her small wooden bowl as Aiden started the tiny fire.

"I don't know." Aiden shook his head, finally answering and glancing up at her as the small fire sparked to life. The flames wouldn't last more than a few hours with the modest collection of wood he had assembled, but she didn't suspect that they were planning to stay here very long. He took some of the woundwort paste that she offered him, smearing it over a sizable blister that covered his heel as Mizuki tended to her own injured toes in the dim light. "They don't usually have patrols, but with the ceremony tomorrow, it's hard to say. There will likely be a guard stationed at my home, but I doubt they are out in the forest looking for us. By now they will have assumed that we deserted, but even if they are out, they wouldn't be this far east. So, at least we have that in our favour – if we cut northwest from here through the rest of the forest, we should come out near the bottom of the village below the crops. We'll be able to sneak around to my uncle's while staying away from the trails near the lake."

"Alright," Mizuki agreed, wrapping her foot with fresh linen strips and pulling on her last pair of socks as Aiden did the same. "How long do you think it will take?"

"If we run – a couple of hours. If we walk, maybe five or six?" Aiden said, stretching out his legs and looking off to the north. "I've never been in this area, so the truth is, I'm not sure."

"Then we shouldn't chance it," Mizuki said, packing away their supplies once more and pulling out the last of their food after rinsing her hands clean. She handed Aiden a strip of meat and pulled her knitted hat down over her ears for extra warmth as the flickering firelight danced across her skin. "We need as much time at the village as possible, so we shouldn't stay here much longer."

"I agree," Aiden said with a sigh, his gaze returning to her and tracing over her body. Even in the low light of the small fire, she could see his worry. "Can you make it?"

"Does that matter?" Mizuki asked, a sad smile shifting across her lips as she looked at him. He looked terrible. Absolutely beaten and worn, and she knew that she must look just as bad. "Whether I can or not – I have to. There is no other choice."

"I can carry you." Aiden offered again, gesturing to the pack that sat between them. "We're almost there. We can leave the pack behind and just take the books."

"No, you're just as exhausted as I am, Aiden." Mizuki shook her head. "But we should empty the pack anyway, only bring the books, the water, and anything else we truly need."

"Alright, if you're sure," Aiden said as he looked up to the sky.

She watched his expression grow tight as he stared into the night. She couldn't imagine what must be going through his head as he let out a low sigh and closed his eye. As much as this affected her, it was his sister they were trying to save and his uncle that they depended on. She knew the apprehension must be tearing him apart, and if Keller refused to help, Aiden would be devastated more deeply than most of the people in the village were capable of understanding.

"We'll rest for just a few hours," Aiden said finally, opening his eye once more and shifting across the ground to sit by her side. "Then we'll head out at a steady pace until we get within an hour of the village. Once we're there – we go as fast as we can for the final stretch, and we don't stop until we reach my uncle's."

"Alright." Mizuki nodded in agreement, leaning forward to pull out the books that Earnan had given them.

She handed one to Aiden at random, then took another for herself and leaned back against the tall maple behind them. The cool night air grew colder as the stars grew brighter in the sky, and her breath started to crystallize before her nose. She felt Aiden shift closer. Then, as he had done the past few nights, his arm wrapped around her shoulder, and she realized that she had been shivering. She murmured a quiet thanks, keeping her eyes on her book as she felt his warmth start to inch through her body. She had no idea how he was so warm all the time, but as much as her heart beat nervously at the contact, she was grateful for it, because the small fire was doing little to keep her from freezing.

She did her best to focus on the book, her eyes struggling to stay open as her mind grew weary in the low light. Yet with every page she turned, she only felt her heart sink in sadness, and her mind burned with more questions. A good number of the words contained between the pages she couldn't read. They were either smudged, too poorly written to be legible, or she simply didn't know what they meant. Even then, she could glean enough to understand the image that they painted of the village. This book was Earnan's journal. A personal account of what had happened within the village over the last few decades. It documented key events, and it specifically named people who were involved in the feud within the village and which sides they had taken. Miku's name came up a lot, and twice she found sections written in symbols that had clearly been entered by her great-grandmother directly.

There were too many pages for her to be able to read them all, so she skimmed as best as she could while Aiden absorbed the one beside her. Neither of them spoke as the pages flipped more quickly, and their bodies grew tense with dark realizations until Aiden slowly closed the book on his lap.

"They're having issues with the soil because they're not rotating the crops enough," Aiden murmured as he stared into the small smouldering fire. He subconsciously gripped her tighter, his thumb brushing along her arm as his brow furrowed in thought. "Earnan noted that the land was never very good to start with. I guess they had a really hard time getting anything to grow when they first started. Earnan said they would need to take years off, let the land grow wild for a season and then clear it again in order to restore the nutrients, but they refused in the last few decades. They didn't agree that it would be a problem, the fallow years were too hard on the village, and they didn't want to go looking for new grounds or food sources."

"Earnan suspected that the Elders fabricated the crop shortage shortly before Dante and Anya broke from the village," Mizuki replied. "And it wasn't the first time. There were several notes in here about unexplained food shortages or things being spoiled in the past over the last several decades. It always seemed to happen when tension in the village was at its highest – and it was always blamed on Miku or anyone else who defied the Elders. People struggled in the winters, and in one case, Earnan noted that someone died from eating something that had gone bad. And there wasn't just one hunting accident in the forest, Aiden – there were several, and those are just the ones that Earnan knew about. There were a few other families that were starting to listen to Miku toward the end, but then someone died while out hunting, and two others were injured.

"Then the Lears lost their son in the Gifting before my brother. Mrs. Lear's husband had started to side with Miku, Aiden – that's why it happened," Mizuki said quietly, her heart sinking in her chest as she thought about the way that the old woman glared at her every time she walked past. They sat in silence for a moment before Mizuki swallowed and forced herself to continue, revealing to Aiden the other piece of information that had shaken her to her core. "At the start of his journal, Earnan mentions the first betrayers – that was what Kiren had mentioned when I was stealing the map, remember?"

"Yes." Aiden nodded, his gaze flicking toward her.

"I didn't know what he was talking about, and I'm still not entirely sure of the details." Mizuki hesitated, her eyes dropping down to the book in her hands once more. "But based on what's in here, I think they were the very first people to split from the village. He mentions family surnames that don't exist in the village anymore – the Kozaks, the Kades, the Gills, the Tangs, the Browns, and a few others, including his own family name. His name was Earnan Sanchez, Aiden – and he didn't have any family within the village."

"You mean there were others that left before Dante and Anya?" Aiden asked as he twisted around to face her fully.

"Yes," Mizuki confirmed, looking up at him once more. "A lot of others from the sounds of it. Dante's last name was Boyko, and Anya's was King – they left with the Hill and Scott families. Aiden, this has been going on for generations, and our village keeps getting smaller. Earnan noted that the first betrayers left shortly after the village first formed. Apparently, Miku's mother believed that they crossed the chasm to the east to find a new home. They left after a fight broke out, and they were never seen again. My great-great-grandmother was the one who told Miku and Earnan about them."

Mizuki stared at Aiden as her brow knitted together, and then she dropped her gaze back to her lap as her voice grew low.

"I don't know why Miku never told me," Mizuki whispered. "She never once mentioned the first betrayers."

Silence passed between them until Aiden let out a low sigh, and she felt his body grow limp by her side.

"It's so much worse than I thought it was," Aiden whispered, and she felt him lean his head against hers as his voice grew rough. "How are we going to do this?"

It wasn't truly a question, and even if it had been, she didn't have an answer for him. So she sat there on the hard ground leaning gently against his side as they both stared out into the cold silence as the last of the flames died out. She waited until Aiden moved – until he couldn't sit any longer, and he finally shifted to get to his feet. They left everything that they didn't need on the ground by the tree. Then they re-layered their clothes, tied on their mostly dry shoes, and carefully packed the books. Mizuki made sure her small paring knife was still securely in her jacket pocket before she pulled her hat down over her ears once more and ditched the damaged bow on the ground as Aiden donned the mostly empty pack.

Then they set off into the night.

She didn't question it when he took her hand and gripped it tight. They moved in silence through the trees, steady but quick, ignoring the groan of their muscles as they made their way toward the village. Despite it taking hours, time seemed to race by as they grew closer and closer. Before she knew it, the village was upon them, and her heart was racing in her chest. She wasn't ready for this, and she could feel her stomach knotting in sickness as they started to run through the trees and dart through the bushes.

The crops were almost in sight. She recognized the land as the first light of morning broke through the sky. Aiden moved faster and faster, his feet still nearly soundless as they cut around a cluster of trees and darted under the low maple branches. Her heart was thudding now. Her legs were screaming in pain as she forced her limbs to keep up with his impossible pace. The muscles in her side spasmed. She could feel her knees threatening to buckle as the empty fields came into view, and they darted up toward Aiden's uncle's home.

They were almost there.

The dull light grew brighter, and the first morning birds began to sing as Aiden dropped her hand so they could both begin to sprint.

She could see it.

Her feet ached in pain. Her lungs were burning for air – but she could see it. Keller O'Kane's house was just in the distance.

They darted into the next section of trees and cut around a collection of oaks as they made for the brush that would lead them up behind Keller's home. Her legs were going to give out. Her lungs could barely breathe. Surely her heart would fail with the next painful thud. Just as her feet skidded across the ground and they banked around a large oak and darted to the north, she heard the snap of a twig before something collided across her chest.

All the air was crushed from her body, and she dropped to the ground with a heavy wheeze. Aiden screamed out in pain; the sound sliced through the air like a knife as something thudded to the ground by her side. Her vision blurred, and her mouth fell open in a silent scream of agony as her body refused to inhale. Blinking rapidly and gagging as a desperate wheeze finally left her lungs, she looked up to see a tall blurry figure standing above her. Then everything started to happen all at once, and it moved too quickly for her to track.

A deep voice sounded to her right as she was hauled from the ground. They did it so easily she felt like a small child, and it took her brain a moment to process what had happened. A Village Guard had struck her across the abdomen and knocked her to the ground as she and Aiden rounded the oak tree. They'd shot him with their bow. She could see the arrow jutting from his thigh as more voices sounded in the distance, and suddenly they were being dragged into the village as Aiden screamed her name.

"MIZUKI! *MIZUKI!* LET GO OF HER!!"

Her head rolled to the side as she finally caught her breath, and her legs instinctively began to kick at the man who was carrying her.

"AIDEN!" she screamed, trying and failing to get her bearings as she scratched at the man who was holding her.

There was so much commotion.

Too much movement.

She kicked and clawed as they dragged her across the ground, and her hat was lost to the chaos. Her eyes rapidly darted around as more voices broke out, and she tried to see what was going on as the sky grew lighter. Aiden was being dragged across the ground to her left, still trying to fight against the two guards who were holding him despite the arrow lodged into his leg.

"KELLER!" She heard him scream as familiar homes started to flash by along with the faces of shocked and curious people. "KELLER O'KANE!"

"KELLER!" Mizuki screamed with him, trying to turn around and look behind her only to be lifted fully from the ground and thrown over the guard's shoulder. She fought against him, but it was no use. Her legs had nothing left to give, and she couldn't combat his strength, so she just screamed even louder. "KELLER – PLEASE!!"

But all their screaming seemed to do was create more confusion and chaos as people from every home burst out into the cold morning air to see what was going on. Before she even realized where they were, she was dropped to the ground with a thud, and the familiar mud of the open village center swam into focus as she grunted out in pain. She tried to get to her feet, she tried to run – but she was slammed back down to the ground with a painful thud as the air was knocked from her lungs once more. She kicked out again, hoping to hit one of the guards, but froze when a familiar deep voice boomed through the air.

"WHAT IN VELES'S NAME IS GOING ON HERE?!"

The village became quiet, the uproar growing still as Elder Farr shifted out into the open space holding a walking stick tight, a long black feather swinging from his neck. He looked livid. Angrier than she had ever seen him. His face was pinched into an ugly expression as the small crowd parted before him, and Elder Clark came into view at his side. Her eyes traced along the edge of the impromptu gathering as she laid unmoving on her back, searching for any signs of a familiar or friendly face.

181

Wilsons, Smiths, some of the Khatris and Zhangs – not one person who had ever given her family support or kindness, let alone human decency.

"We found the deserters lurking in the forest, just as you expected Elder Farr," the guard who was standing above her said.

"We weren't *lurking* in the forest!" Aiden spat, forcing himself up to his knees with a grunt as he turned and glared his one eye at the guard. "We were coming back from the Wild!"

"Be quiet!" the guard that was holding him yelled as he grabbed Aiden by the collar of his jacket and jerked him back down. Aiden groaned out in pain as the leg with the arrow collided with the ground.

"Stop it!" Mizuki screamed, scrambling onto her knees and looking up at the crowd almost desperately as her gaze shifted to Elder Farr. "He's not lying! We went to the Southern Mountains – we know about Earnan and the others who left! They're still alive!"

She was jerked back violently as the guard behind her grabbed her arms and forced them behind her back, but the village had gone quiet at her words, and Elder Farr's expression grew tight. Her eyes searched the crowd again – Lears, Hamiltons, Reyes, Millers – then she spotted Keller.

"Keller!" she cried out, fighting against the guard who was holding her. "Mr. O'Kane, please! You have to believe us! We found Earnan! We know about the crops! Please listen to us!"

"You expect us to believe that the two of you survived in the Wild and made it to the Southern Mountains in a week," Elder Farr said, his voice so low it was nearly a whisper as he stepped forward. He fixed her with a cold stare. "If you found other people – then where are they? Why are you alone?"

Mizuki gritted her teeth; she knew if she said that Earnan was dead, it would only give the Elders more power, and she wasn't going to tell them where the old man had said Dante and Anya were living. If she did, Dante and his people were as good as dead.

"He was too weak to come back with us," Mizuki lied, her eyes flicking around the crowd again. "But he sent us back with books and records – records that show you knew about the crop problems years ago!"

"We've had persistent crop problems since the moment that Dante and Anya first defied Veles's command and left," Elder Clark said, stepping up next to Elder Farr as Mizuki saw some people in the crowd nod. The gathering was growing larger, and she could see people peering over shoulders as they tried to get a better look. "The gatherers all know this. We have been dealing with the aftermath of their indiscretions since before you were born! But we have always managed to pull through because of our devotion!"

"Keller," Aiden groaned, hauling himself back up to his knees once more as he looked at his uncle desperately. "*Please* – we can prove it! There is life out there – we saw it! People are living out there, and they are thriving!"

"Then prove it." A deep voice sounded, and Mizuki turned to see her grandfather step through the crowd. "You cannot make such wild claims and have nothing to support it. Where is your proof?"

"We have books," Aiden panted, struggling to remain on his knees.

"Books?" Elder Farr scoffed, his face pinching tight again as he looked down on them. "Books and papers that you undoubtedly wrote while hiding out in the forest."

He stepped toward the guard who was holding out Aiden's pack and took the bag from him. It only took him a second to fish out a few of the loose pieces of parchment that Earnan had given them since the pack was largely empty, and he made a show of reviewing them with disgust.

"These are the ramblings of an insane woman, none other than Miku Altherr – who *repeatedly* put our village in danger and threatened our way of life," Elder Clark said as he looked over the papers as well. "She left these in your possession before she died – ahh, and I see that you and Aiden have added to it, no doubt to try to spin things in your favour."

"Those are Earnan's," Mizuki spat, fighting against the guard's hold and glancing at Aiden, who was gritting his teeth in pain. "There are books in there too! Real books about crops and the unbounded map!"

"Lies," Elder Farr hissed, his eyes narrowing at them as he dropped the bag and the papers into the mud. "Earnan stole those books when he left!"

"Aiden?!"

Mizuki's head jerked to the right as a fresh round of commotion broke out in the crowd, and Mrs. O'Kane's voice cut through the air. Aiden's da was holding her back, and Keller was rushing toward them as several of the Village Guards made their way over.

"Ma!" Aiden called, jerking in her direction before groaning out in pain as the guard holding him in place struck him over the head. He slouched from the impact, his shoulders shaking as he forced himself to remain on his knees. "Uncle Keller! *Please* – Elder Farr, Elder Clark – *please* listen to us! There are people living out in the Wild – we've been there, we've seen them! We don't have to live in fear of the mountain. We don't have to do this! Maebh doesn't need to be sacrificed, Veles never asked for Gifts, and we have the proof!"

But as the words left Aiden's mouth, Mizuki saw Elder Farr's eyes glint as the faint flicker of a smile crossed his lips. Her brain made the connection too late, but as Kiren shook his head and Elder Clark looked at them in disgust, she realized their mistake. Aiden never should have said Maebh's name. He never should have brought up the sacrifices or claimed that Veles had not asked for Gifts. She could see the realization donning on his face as the energy of the crowd instantly shifted from one of curiosity and concern to one of anger and disgust. Everything was unravelling, and the small hope they had of getting people to listen was gone because now this was personal. She watched as Elder Farr stood to his full height, and when Elder Clark nodded in their direction, the guard gripped her tighter.

Then the rhetoric began to pour from the Elders' mouths like one of their rehearsed sermons.

"It is the Gifting that allows us to live," Elder Clark admonished, his sharp gaze frigid and his voice laced with disgust. "The promise of one life, regardless of age, gender or health, that keeps us equal! That keeps us safe! That shows we understand that none of us are above Veles! None of us are above the natural law!"

"And you come here – after deserting your village, leaving your families in pain and anguish for seven days to try to prevent the very thing that will allow us all to continue?!" Elder Farr carried on, his voice growing louder as those in the village nodded in agreement. "You believe you are better than your friends and family? That you are better than all the others who live in this village? Better than all those who have been Gifted before you? Better than all those who have died to give you life, than those that stand here today and have risked their lives and their health to keep this village strong?!"

"No!" Mizuki yelled, desperately tugging against the guard who was dragging her up from the mud and onto her feet once more. "Please! *Please* listen – we have proof!"

But her voice didn't even cut into the outcry that had broken out around the small muddy space as villagers shouted at them in rage, and the Elders continued to bellow over top of them. She could feel her feet dragging in the mud as the guards shoved her forward toward the Elders. Her eyes scanned around desperately as her body shook in pain.

This couldn't be happening.

How could this have all gone so wrong?

She could hear Aiden trying to scream at his da and Keller over the chaos as the Elders continued to preach. His ma was screaming so loudly that her voice had gone raw, and three men were holding her back as Aiden's da started to yell at Keller. She felt like she was drowning as it all echoed in her ears. Everything was starting to spin, and she fought to breathe as she looked up into the cold eyes of her grandfather, who was standing just a few feet away.

"Kiren," Mizuki panted, groaning in pain as the guard kicked her behind the knees, and she collapsed onto the ground at the Elder's feet next to Aiden. She forced her gaze back up, pleading for reason as she looked at the man above her. "Grandfather – please!"

"You have brought disaster upon this village," Kiren said, his voice heartless and his eyes like stone as he stared down at her.

"And more shame than even your great-grandmother ever managed."

"What you have done is inexcusable!" Elder Farr bellowed, his voice carrying through the crowd as the guards forced their arms out before the Elders. "Veles will never forgive us! Our crops, our village – our entire way of life is now doomed because of your fool-hardly, vile, and utterly shameless act of selfishness! Our only hope of survival is to pray that he will be forgiving. To pray that he knows that you two acted alone and that you do not reflect the stance of this village!"

"*Please*," Mizuki whined, her eyes stinging in pain as the guard forcefully turned her arm over and pried her fingers open. "Please, you have to listen to us! Just come with us into the Wild – *let us show you!*"

"You have no place to ask for anything!" Elder Clark roared, his voice like thunder as Kiren pulled something from his pocket and held it out to them. "You abandoned your people. You abandoned your families – you knowingly planned to risk the safety of everyone in this village for your own selfish wishes, and you have done it for the last time, Mizuki Altherr!"

"Your actions are punishable by death!" Elder Farr said as he took the item that Kiren had held out and turned back towards them. "But I will not deny Veles his vengeance – and we will offer you both as penance!"

Mrs. O'Kane's scream cut through the air as the crowd surged and chaos broke out once more. People were shouting and fighting. Guards were yelling and moving into the crowd as children cried, and she heard Maebh's voice shrieking somewhere off to the right. Elder Farr grabbed her hand, and before she could even try to pull away, he sliced her palm open with a small, sharp knife. She screamed out in pain as the wound burned and her eyes filled with tears. It was worse than the wolf bite, worse than the bugs, worse than the sun, the cold, and the ache in her bones. She heard Aiden scream to her left next, and she barely registered the low whisper that ghosted by her ear.

"Eighteen years I've waited for this moment." Elder Farr's cold voice was like death, and his words sent a shiver down her spine as the long black feather dangled before her nose. "But *finally*, the Altherr name can die as it should have long ago. Say hello to your great-grandmother."

She was hauled from the ground before she could respond and dragged to her feet. She fought against the guard, kicking and screaming and using every last bit of strength that she had until she heard her name through the chaos that surrounded them.

"Mizuki!?"

Her head jerked to the side as she fought to see into the crowd around the massive guard who was hauling her toward the gate.

"DAD!!" she screamed, her voice breaking as she searched through the faces and clawed against her holder. "DAD!!"

"MIZUKI!"

Her head snapped further left, and she found him through the insanity. Her eyes locked to Kazuki's gaze, and she felt her stomach twist – it was as if someone had shoved white-hot coals down her throat as every emotion she had ever buried surged up from the ground and burst from her lungs.

"DAAADDD!!"

She could feel her throat tearing as she screamed for her father, and the man's face contorted with a mess of emotions as he lunged into the crowd and began shoving people aside. She had never seen him move like that. She had never seen him look like that. His eyes were blazing as his yells bellowed over the crowd, and suddenly screams cut through the air behind them. Aiden's ma broke loose, shoving aside two guards and rushing towards them.

A terrible groan rocked the air, and her soul filled with terror as she realized the gates were opening. She could hear Aiden fighting at her side as he called for his family and tried to break free. She screamed and kicked, she dug her heels into the ground and scratched at the man holding her, but her eyes never left her father as the man was grabbed by guards, continuing to fight as they were dragged further and further apart. She barely managed to call his name one last time when the shadow of the gate crossed over her head; then she was lifted into the air and thrown to the ground.

She grunted as the impact rattled through her bones. Her vision blurred, the sounds around them amplifying and disorienting as she rolled onto her side and struggled up onto her elbow. It was all she could do to breathe; all she could do to open her eyes through the pain that was coursing through her body after being tossed to the cold stone ground. Through it all she could still hear the screaming, still hear the Elders as they called for peace, justice, and forgiveness as a second loud groan split through the air.

Horror filled her blood. For all her adamance that Veles wasn't real, that the Gifting wasn't necessary, and that this entire thing was a sham – her fear at that moment was real and paralyzing. This was where people were sent to die. This was where she and Aiden would die. Veles or not, they would never survive in the Dead Zone. They had no supplies – no food, no water, no shelter.

They would never make it.

Groaning in agony she forced herself to sit up, her eyes barely catching a glimpse of her father as he fought against the Village Guard before the massive gates slammed shut. Mrs. O'Kane's shriek cut through the air, Mizuki's chest constricted in pain, and she saw nothing but the great wooden spikes that lined the edges of the mountain path and rear of the gate as a cold and biting gust of wind ripped across her skin.

The Mountain Path

Mizuki forced herself to her knees, her breath coming in sharp shallow pants as the world seemed to spin around her and her body shook with terror. Before she could stop herself, she vomited violently on the ground, gagging as she struggled to stand, and tears prickled at the corner of her eyes.

This couldn't be happening.

This couldn't be the end. After everything they had done and everything that they had been through – how did they end up here?

She could still hear the chaos on the other side of the double gate, but as she staggered to her feet, an arrow struck the rocky ground on her right, and she froze. Her gaze shifted up the tall wooden beams of the outer gate, past the spikes, and up to the skyline above. Her eyes blurred in the cold wind as she craned her neck to look at the top of the massive wooden structure, and she stiffened when she saw Village Guard lining the ridge with their bows drawn.

"Aiden," Mizuki said, stumbling toward him. He was still on the ground and struggling to get up. He must have landed on his injured leg when they threw him out of the village because fresh blood was starting to trickle from the wound.

"Mizuki," Aiden grunted, rolling onto his side and clutching his right leg tight. His only visible eye was watering in pain, and his voice sounded broken. "I'm so sorry – this is all my fault."

A second arrow struck the ground, this time only a foot away as she grabbed him around the middle and started to haul him from the ground.

"Aiden, we have to go," Mizuki groaned, the effort of lifting him up making her back ache with pain. "They're shooting at us – we have to go, now!"

Her legs shook violently beneath her as she helped him up and all but dragged him along the cold stone path. He was breathing hard, and she could feel him trembling as they staggered up the narrowing stone away from the village gates. She heard two more arrows crack as they hit the ground behind her, and she forced Aiden to move quicker.

"I'm so sorry," Aiden said again as he hobbled faster despite the blood coming down his leg.

"It's okay," Mizuki said, looping his arm around her shoulder to help support his weight as they moved.

"Nothing about this is okay," Aiden grunted, his eye pinching tight as another set of arrows collided against the stone beside them. "Nothing about any of this is okay."

She gripped him tighter, ignoring the burn of her muscles and the sharp pain that was shooting down her spine and up her legs. Her cut palm felt like it was on fire, and her stomach was threatening to turn over once more. Yet her mind couldn't stop racing.

Was this how they got people to move up the path? Throw them out and then shoot arrows to force them to ascend the mountain? Was this what had happened to her brother? How many had chosen to stay at the base and die by the Village Guard's hand? How many had they shot simply because they could?

Endless questions circled her mind, but she didn't stop, and she forced her unsteady legs to keep moving. Every step was like agony, and by the time they finally staggered out of range and around the first bend of the narrow path, she could hardly breathe. Aiden collapsed to the ground behind a large, jagged boulder, and Mizuki dropped to her knees at his side, tearing off her jacket and removing one of her hide shirts. She didn't hesitate as she pulled out her paring knife and quickly sliced the spare garment into pieces.

"Don't!!" Aiden hissed, grabbing her hands as she made to reach for the arrow that was still sticking out of his leg. He gripped her hands tight, sweat forming across his brow as he tried to fight against the pain. "Don't take it out. It might be barbed – I'll bleed to death if you remove it. It'll just rip a giant hole in my leg."

"Okay," Mizuki breathed, squeezing his hands tight as she met his gaze. "I won't take it out – I promise, but I need to wrap it and cut it shorter."

He nodded, clenching his jaw as he let go of her hands, and his own began to tremble. She took the strips of her shirt and began wrapping them around the arrow in his leg, tying them tight to prevent bleeding but being careful not to cut off the blood flow. She added a second large strip, then a third, and knotted the bundle securely before grabbing her knife once more and carefully sawing the end of the arrow off. Aiden's eye shut tight as she worked. She tried not to jostle the injury, but no matter how careful she was, it seemed to hurt him, and when the end finally broke off, Aiden rolled to the side and vomited against the boulder.

"Give me your hand," Mizuki said, reaching for him once more as he wiped his mouth along the sleeve of his jacket.

He gave her his left hand, and she grimaced at the depth of the wound that was cut across his palm. Pushing down the sickness in her chest, she wrapped it before doing the same to her own and pulling on her jacket once more. Then she dropped to the ground by his side, tucked her knife into her pocket, and closed her eyes. They sat in silence for a long time until she felt Aiden shift at her side.

"I never should have asked you to come with me," Aiden whispered, his voice hoarse as the wind picked up, and they both shivered against the boulder.

"Don't." Mizuki shook her head, opening her eyes and turning her head to look at him. "Don't say that."

"I shouldn't have," Aiden repeated as he turned to look at her, and his eyes shone. "This is all my fault, Mizuki – you're going to die out here, and it's all my fault."

"I could have died out there," Mizuki countered, awkwardly squeezing his forearm in an effort to be reassuring as she pulled her legs closer to her body for warmth. Her eyes pinched as she looked at him, and she shook her head at the absurdity of his statement. "We almost did die out there, Aiden – how is this any different? We knew the risks, *I* knew the risks, and I went anyway. I agreed to go."

"I know, but I thought we would make it," Aiden said, a devastated expression crossing his face as his eye searched her face. "That's why it's different. Even after everything that Earnan said, I still thought we would make it. I still thought we stood a chance – I thought Keller would listen, and I thought we could do it."

"We did do it," Mizuki murmured as she looked over Aiden's strained expression. "We found him, and we made it back. We saved Maebh, Aiden, and we caused enough of an uproar that maybe Keller, your parents, my dad – maybe someone in that village will start to question what's going on. We did exactly what we set out to do."

"Sort of," Aiden scoffed. "But I was supposed to keep you safe."

"You did," Mizuki said, and she found that she meant the words as she spoke them. "I don't regret it, Aiden. I'm not missing out on anything being here like this. I never planned to live a full life in that village. I was never going to marry, have kids, or grow old. That was never my plan, and I doubt that it was anyone else's plan for me either. I didn't belong there – I never did. I always figured I would leave someday. I just thought that I would head in the opposite direction, but what we did was worth it. We saved your sister. We found Earnan, and we know that there are others out there in the Wild. We know the truth, and I wouldn't change that for anything."

Aiden shook his head, a small snort leaving his lungs. She could see something shifting behind his gaze as he looked at her and let out a low sigh. "You really don't have any idea, do you?"

"Any idea about what?" Mizuki asked, her brow arching in question. But Aiden didn't offer up any explanation; he just let out another sigh and turned his gaze toward the barren landscape that surrounded them as he reached for her hand and gripped it tight. She let him take it, and she didn't push for answers as she sat by his side until he finally spoke once more.

"So, what do we do now?" Aiden murmured.

"I don't know," Mizuki breathed, her eyes shifting to the path that carried up the mountain on their left. The sight of it sent a nervous shiver down her spine. She had meant what she had said to Aiden – she didn't regret what they had done. From the moment she left the village, she knew she might die. She just never thought it would be on the mountain path, and while a part of her found it cruelly befitting given the history of the Altherr family, it didn't mean she *wanted* to die, and it didn't mean that she wasn't afraid. "But we can't stay here. I don't trust that the Elders won't send someone up the path tonight to make sure that we left."

"Earnan said that Veles was real," Aiden said as he slowly shifted his gaze to look up the path.

"What are you thinking?" Mizuki asked, turning to look at him.

"Maybe Veles is just a man," Aiden said thoughtfully, turning to look at her. "Or what if there are people here too. Maybe someone survived the Gifting and made it up the mountain. As far as we know, no one besides the Elders have ever made it to the top and come back, and you can't see the rest of the path once it curves around the eastern side."

"You think someone is living up there?" Mizuki asked him, her voice laced with disbelief.

"I don't know." Aiden shook his head. "But I made you come with me this far, and I'm not going to let you die on the mountain path a hundred feet away from the village. There was water running through the Southern Mountains – maybe there's water running through these ones too. No one has ever seen the other side of this mountain, Mizuki – even the Elders don't know what's out here. Maybe all this land isn't barren. Maybe there's life out there."

"So we keep going," Mizuki concluded, nodding in agreement. She wasn't sure that she believed they would find anything out here, but she knew they couldn't stay where they were. They needed to get as far away from the village gates as possible, and they needed to try to find some shelter.

She got to her feet before helping Aiden from the ground, then looped his arm over her shoulder once more. The sun was rising to their right. She could see it getting higher in the sky as its rays stretched out across the desolate land that surrounded them, and a faint warmth started to shift through the air. She had a sneaking suspicion that they were in for rough weather as the wind picked up and a faint red glow followed the sunrise. She had climbed the ridge and stared in this direction enough times to know that the weather changed quickly and viciously. With nothing but a narrow dirt and stone path that led toward the base of the mountain and sharp drops on either side that plummeted into jagged rock crevasses, they were completely exposed. The sun would be hot during the day, the nights would be cold and unforgiving, and they would be battered by the rain and wind.

She gritted her teeth hard as they staggered forward, Aiden struggling to put weight on his leg as they set off at a slow and steady pace. She figured they would last a week without food, three days if they couldn't find water, but possibly less because of their injuries. Her mind raced through all their options as they moved toward the unknown, and the fear that shifted along her spine grew deeper.

What if there were bears on this side of the ridge? What if there was something worse? What if her father, Aiden's parents, and his little sister were now facing punishment for their indiscretions?

Yes, they had saved Maebh from being sacrificed, but that didn't mean that she was safe. She gripped Aiden tighter, her brow creasing with concern as she tried not to think about the look on her father's face as he had darted into the crowd and desperately tried to battle his way toward her. With the immediate threat of arrows now gone and her panic calming, she could feel her heart breaking once more as she thought about her mother and father.

Would they live through this? Would Kazuki ever be the same after losing both his children? Would she ever even know?

Chances are, they would never see the village again, and she would die on this path by Aiden's side. She couldn't decide what was worse, never knowing what became of her family, Aiden's family, and the village – or finding out that they had been injured, banished, or punished in some other way. It was a question that haunted her. She could still hear their screaming in her mind, and she knew in her heart that Kazuki yelling her name was the last words she would ever hear her father speak.

"They're going to be okay," Aiden said, his low voice echoing by her ear as he hobbled along by her side. She turned to glance at him, realizing that she had been gripping him increasingly tighter as they walked. She swallowed hard as she looked at him, another wave of sickness rocking through her chest as she nodded. "They're smart, Mizuki – and the Elders can't afford to lose them all. They're going to make it through this."

"I know," Mizuki murmured, turning her gaze back to the small path and staggering in the increasing wind. "They'll be okay."

She wasn't sure if she believed it, and she doubted Aiden was as confident about it as he had sounded, but she forced herself to shove it down as she held him close and pushed her legs up the hill. They walked until the sun grew high in the sky, and the intense heat burned the back of their necks as the cold air continued to claw at their skin. It was an unbearable combination, and it only grew worse the farther they got from the village.

They stopped near a large, jagged rock formation to rest, neither of them speaking as they looked out to the west and stared at the ruins that darted across the skyline. They looked the same as they always did, but the calm feeling that usually surged through her chest as she looked at the Dead Zone from the safety of the ridge was missing. Instead, all she felt was dread and a continued churning sickness. She had no idea how long they sat there, but after a while, as her eyes started to water from the wind, she stood to her feet once more and helped haul Aiden from the ground.

They pressed forward again, their pace slow and uneven as Aiden struggled to walk. He was doing a good job of pretending to be okay, but she could see the stress lines around his eye and the muscles in his jaw flexing as he clenched it tight, fighting against the pain in his leg. Her stomach growled with hunger as the sky grew dark, the air grew cold, and thunder echoed in the distance. They had nearly reached the base of the mountain when the rain started, and she shivered as the wind threatened to tear their bodies from the narrow ledge.

"We need to stop!" Mizuki yelled over the wind as her feet slipped on the slick rock, and Aiden nearly tumbled to the ground.

"We can't stop here!" Aiden yelled back, holding onto her for support as they both clambered up the path. It was too dark to properly see, and as lightning flickered through the sky, her foot came dangerously close to the edge of the narrowing trail.

"I don't think we have much choice!" Mizuki grunted, slipping once more and hearing the edge of the path crack beneath her weight. They made for the side of the mountain, stumbling and staggering as the rain and wind beat against their bodies. The next flash of lightning lit up the sky, and her eyes saw a tiny shadow along the base wall. "THERE!"

Aiden followed her as she steered them towards the shadow, running her hand along the rough rock surface as they moved until they ducked into the tiny alcove. It wasn't much – the small indent in the side of the mountain was barely deep enough for them to sit in – but it stopped the wind from tearing at their bodies, and it kept the rain off their heads. Grunting from exhaustion, they fell against the hard wall and slid to the ground. She could hear the storm getting worse. She could feel the thunder through the sharp rock behind her back as she curled against the wall and leaned into Aiden's side. He wrapped his arm around her once more as they tried to get as deep into the small alcove as possible. When they could scrunch in no more, she gripped her necklace tightly and found herself doubting more and more that they would find anything in this forsaken land.

Somehow, she must have managed to sleep, because her mind had been filled with images of dark creatures and burning red eyes as her own slowly drifted open and her body shuddered in the cold. Everything was stiff, and everything hurt. She could hear the light drizzle of water dripping off the ledge above them as the dull grey light of morning came into view.

Aiden was still sleeping. She turned to look at him and felt her heart sink with worry. The dark ring below his eye was even darker, which wasn't surprising – but there was a sickly colour shifting across his skin. Her gaze dropped to the wound on his leg, and she wondered if it might have gotten infected as she carefully pulled herself from his hold and staggered to her feet.

She didn't feel well, but she supposed that after everything that had happened, it made sense. Stepping out onto the narrow mountain path, she looked around. She could just barely see the village, the Dead Zone was covered in mist, and the sky to the west looked as if it was ready to break into another raging storm at any second. She shivered as she swallowed, gritting her teeth to stop the chatter. She could see the path curving to the left, wrapping around the eastern front just as Aiden had said before it disappeared from sight. She had no idea where it would lead them, and not a clue if it continued up or simply weaved between the multiple rocky mountains that scattered the north.

For all she knew, it simply dropped off into a pit and didn't go anywhere – but what she did know was that they had to keep climbing, and they needed to move soon. The wind was coming from the northwest, and it was bringing that massive storm with it.

Turning away from the view, she moved back to their small alcove to where the small stream of water was trickling over the edge, and she tilted her head to take a drink. It was freezing cold, and she was fairly certain it wasn't clean, but it was better than nothing. Letting out a quiet breath, she started to remove the makeshift bandage from her left hand – intending to wash the wound in the small stream of water, but she paused when she realized that she couldn't feel it. Her heart quickened in her chest, and she felt her body stiffen as her mind churned.

The injury had burned the entire day previous. She remembered it aching sharply as she helped haul Aiden up the path, and she remembered that it stung horribly as she collapsed into the stone alcove – and yet now there was nothing. She stared at her hand, willing her fingers to move and watching as they barely shifted at her command.

"No," she whispered, the realization slowly sinking in.

She grabbed the ruined bit of hide with her right hand and rapidly began to uncoil the bandage. It couldn't be, they wouldn't have – would they? She could barely breathe as she tore off the remains of her makeshift bandage, and as the laceration that spanned across her palm came into view, her heart plummeted into her stomach.

"*No*," Mizuki whispered, her eyes stinging with tears as her stomach rolled violently. She grabbed at the sleeve of her jacket, ripping it up her arm as her legs began to tremble and her head began to shake. "No, no, no–"

Thin black tendrils crept from the wound across the palm of her hand like a spider's web and laced up her arm. The cut itself was swollen – festering with purple and black pus. She could see the veins in her hand and arm. They were dilated and pulsing, and the entirety of it was numb. She could barely move her fingers, and she couldn't feel anything below her wrist as she touched it.

Poison.

There would be no Village Guard coming up here to make sure that they died because they had already guaranteed it. They didn't care how far people made it up the path, so long as they were out of sight from the village when they died, and she doubted that anyone ever made it to the top. There would be nothing there. It didn't matter how hard they pushed, how far they went, or what they did – they would die in this barren wasteland like all the rest.

The truth hit her hard, and she stumbled back into the alcove and dropped to the ground beside Aiden once more. She didn't know what to do. She didn't know what to think. The faster they moved, the quicker it would spread. But she didn't have any herbs to treat it with, and she wasn't even sure what the poison was made of. Even if she did have herbs – treating the infection would be risky, and she could end up making it worse.

She closed her eyes and forced herself to breathe. This was why they had gotten sick the day before. This was why she felt strange now. She had assumed that it was because of the exhaustion and everything going on, but it was their bodies reacting to the poison as it started to spread throughout their veins. She swallowed hard and forced her eyes back down to the injury once more. Her stomach turned as she looked at it, and then her eyes shifted over to Aiden's sickly sleeping form.

He looked even worse than she did, and as her gaze shifted along his body, her eyes trailed over the wound on his leg and she stilled in understanding. They had poisoned the arrow, too. That's why Aiden was worse than her. It was spreading through his body from his leg and his hand.

For all she knew, his eye might be infected from the wolf attack, too.

She could feel her heart beating dangerously fast as she forced her gaze back to the sickly-looking wound on her palm for the third time. The black tendrils had crept past her wrist and were an inch above the joint. It was obviously already in her bloodstream, and she suspected that it involved belladonna because of the numbness. If she had to wager a guess, they only had a few days before the poison caused irreversible damage. It would spread up their arms, leaving the limb numb and lifeless until it reached their chests and hit their hearts. She didn't have much exposure to poisons, and what she knew was limited to what Miku had taught her years ago, but she suspected that it wouldn't end well if they couldn't find treatment before it hit their chest.

When it did, their hearts would probably stop. That, or their lungs would cease to function. Both of which sounded like terrible ways to die, but that was assuming they even got that far. They might fall off the mountain or die of dehydration before then. Or maybe the poison would simply kill them in their sleep.

She didn't know, and she found herself clutching her necklace tight as she closed her eyes and tried to steady her heart. She needed to calm down. She needed to figure out what to do. They couldn't stay here – to stay was to die. Forcing herself to breathe out, she re-wrapped her hand. There was no point in washing it – nor was there any point in panicking because it wouldn't do her any good to lose control.

So, she took a deep breath and forced her eyes open.

They had to keep going. Their only chance at making it now was to continue up the trail and hope that they found some herbs. It was unlikely – but it wasn't impossible. Plenty of herbs grew along the ridge, so she knew that they could thrive even in the worst of conditions, even in between cracks in the stone. It was too early in the season to find woundwort – but they might be able to find some comfrey, and possibly even some arnica.

Letting out a low sigh, she turned back to Aiden and gently shook his shoulder. They needed to get going before the storm grew any closer, but she didn't know if she should tell him about the poison. She figured she probably should, but as his tired amber eye cracked open and his face grimaced in pain, she felt her mouth go dry, and the words died on the tip of her tongue.

She could tell just by looking at him that between the two of them, he would be the first to go if they didn't find any herbs, and she found she couldn't stomach the thought. He struggled to stand as she helped him from the ground, and she could feel her eyes stinging as she looped his arm over her shoulder once more, and they moved back out onto the path.

They paused so he could drink. Then they set off at a slow and steady pace up the narrow trail as Mizuki gripped him tight and ignored the stabbing pain in her heart. She would tell him later. She would tell him tonight, maybe, if she could find the words to say.

They travelled all day mostly in silence until the sound of breaking rocks falling into the crevasse startled them mid-afternoon. They both froze when they saw an odd-looking brown creature climbing up the side of the mountain. It scaled the jagged rocks with an ease and speed that she would have never thought possible, and they both stood and stared in awe. At first she worried that it might be dangerous, but when the creature spotted them, it quickly darted off, and she saw that both sets of eyes were outward-facing like the deer they hunted from the Woods. Her fear was then quickly replaced by a dull flicker of hope, and she saw Aiden smile from the corner of her gaze as they both watched the animal disappear into the mist that surrounded the mountain.

If it was living here, it meant that there was water and food, and Mizuki couldn't help but grin as they set off once more and made their way up the path. As the air grew colder and the sun disappeared behind the clouds, her hope started to falter. The path was growing more treacherous, and there wasn't a hint of green nor any other sign of life as her legs struggled to keep moving. By the time they stopped for the night and collapsed next to a small rock formation that jutted up from the side of the path, she could hardly move, and Aiden could barely stand. Any hope she had of finding herbs or water was gone, and she leaned close to Aiden's side in defeat as her windburned skin stung in pain.

The next morning, her low spirits dropped even further as her eyes fluttered open and she saw Aiden. He had wrapped his arm around her again while he slept, but he looked worse than the day before. He struggled to stand as they made to head out, and he was sweating heavily despite the cold. The awful sickly tinge to his skin had grown a deeper shade overnight, his breathing had become ragged, and as she looped his arm over her shoulder and looked up to meet his gaze, she realized that he already knew, because he was looking down at her in the most agonizing way. Pain radiated from his face as he clutched her tight and his lips shifted into a sad smile.

Aiden was dying, and he knew it.

Yet he forced his legs to move, and he didn't utter a single complaint as they walked on. By noon the storm was rolling in, and she had yet to find any cover. The path was barren, no more than a few feet wide, and it was a mess of mud and rock as the rain began to come down. They struggled to keep going. Her feet kept slipping across the wet surface, and twice they fell as Aiden lost his balance. She groaned out in pain and frustration as they hauled themselves up from the ground once more. She couldn't see where they were going; the sky had grown dark, and the fog around the mountains refused to dissipate even though it was raining.

"I'm not going to make it," Aiden panted by her side as his legs shook beneath him.

"We're going to make it," Mizuki grunted, gripping him more firmly and forcing her legs to take yet another unbearable step. "We just have to find another alcove – just until this storm passes."

"No, *I'm* not going to make it," Aiden clarified, groaning in pain as he forced them to stop. He pulled his arm from around her shoulder and leaned back against one of the small rocks that littered the path. He looked at her in the growing darkness, his face exhausted as he shook his head. "I'm slowing you down, Mizuki. You have to leave me behind."

"I'm not leaving you behind," Mizuki said, clutching at her cramping side and fighting to stay on her feet before him. Her legs wouldn't stop shaking, and even without the weight of Aiden on her shoulder, she felt like she was going to collapse.

"Mizuki–," Aiden argued, but she cut him off and shook her head firmly.

"No," she said, flat out refusing to hear it as she looked at him hard.

She shuddered as the cold wind tugged at her waterlogged jacket and made her stumble on her feet. The storm was getting worse, and she knew if they didn't get off the open path soon, they would be knocked off of it and sent falling to their deaths. She understood what Aiden was trying to do, but she refused to accept it. They had come this far, and they were in this together.

"I won't do it," Mizuki said, her gaze narrowing into a glare. "So just stop – okay? We'll figure this out."

She wrapped her arms around herself as she took a few steps forward and looked up the path. She could see it turning up ahead, and it looked like it doubled back on itself, which might give them some kind of shelter.

"I think there is something up ahead!" Mizuki yelled over the wind as the rain started to pour harder. "It's not that far – we can make it, Aiden."

"Fine."

She heard his faint voice echo behind her, and she let out a sigh of relief as her shoulders dropped. She hadn't wanted to argue with him. She turned back to face him, but just as her foot shifted across the stone, a horrendous crack cut through the air. She jerked as lightning flashed through the sky, and she realized too late that the crack wasn't from the thunder. Fear sliced down her spine like a knife as she twisted toward him.

"Aiden?!" Mizuki cried, her eyes growing wide with panic as the rock that Aiden had been leaning on fractured away from the edge of the path. Her hand shot out. Her body lunged forward. Everything seemed to slow down as she watched Aiden reach for her while the ground beneath his feet broke away.

"AIDEN!!" Mizuki screamed as she dove for him, her hand just narrowly missing his as he tumbled over the edge. She grunted hard as she hit the ground, struggling up onto her knees and scrambling toward the edge of the path. "AIDEN – AIDEN!!"

She gripped the edge tight, ignoring the violent shaking in her body as she lay down in the mud to peer over the edge into the darkness below as she screamed his name. The wind tugged at her body and threatened to push her off the opposite side. She had to lay as flat as possible to search the edge of the crevasse.

"Mizuki!"

Her eyes darted to the left, her ears barely catching the sound of his voice through the growing storm. She squinted into the rain, willing her eyes to see as the next flash of lightning struck through the air. It all looked the same, nothing but rock and darkness, rain and mud, until she saw a hint of movement and clawed her way along the path to get above it. Then she saw him, a flash of lightning illuminating the chasm just enough that she could make him out. Aiden was lying on a small ledge roughly twenty feet below her, and she could just barely hear him groaning in pain as he clutched at his leg.

"AIDEN!" Mizuki yelled, leaning further over the edge and hoping that the rocks didn't break beneath her weight. She squinted as the cold, hard droplets began to sting against her face like little cuts. "I see you! Are you okay?! Can you hear me?!"

"I hear you!" Aiden yelled back. He went quiet as a huge gust of wind rushed over the path, and Mizuki's nails bit into the stone to keep her from dislodging. "Mizuki – I – I can't move! I think I broke my leg!"

Cursing into the wind, Mizuki's eyes searched the edge of the path. There was no way to get down to him – it was nearly a sheer drop. The ledge was much too small for the two of them, but even if she could climb down, she would never be able to get him back up with his leg broken. She turned around, looking across the path through the rain. If they had supplies, had rope – clothes, something, *anything*, she could fasten it to one of the other jagged rocks that littered the path and try to pull him up. But they didn't have anything, and she could feel her panic growing as her throat started to tighten.

She couldn't do this.

She couldn't help him.

If the roles had been reversed, maybe he would have been able to climb down and pull her up, but she wasn't strong enough to lift him on her own.

"Aiden, I'm coming down!" Mizuki yelled as she peered back down at him through the rain.

"WHAT?!" His voice rang out through the wind, and she could just barely see him twisting to look up at her as the sky flickered with light. "Are you insane?! You'll die!"

"I'm not leaving you!" Mizuki screamed, her heart thudding in her chest as her eyes filled with tears. "We're both dying anyway!"

"NO!" Aiden yelled back up, and she could hear the anger in his voice. "Go up the mountain, Mizuki!"

"We don't even know if there is anything up there!" Mizuki screamed, barely managing to yell the words before she had to duck her head against the next gust of wind. "If I'm going to die – I'm going to die with you!"

"Mizuki, I swear to Veles if you come down here, I will never forgive you!" Aiden screamed at her. "If you even think about trying it, I'll throw myself off this ledge before you even get one foot over the edge! Go up the mountain!"

Mizuki eyes turned back to the path that extended to the north. She felt like she was going to be sick. She couldn't leave him here, but she knew she couldn't go down to him either. Going to him meant death for both of them. There would be no coming back from that drop – but so long as she was still able to move and was still on the path, she could try to find a way to help him.

"I'm going to come back!" she yelled over the edge, struggling to her knees in the storm and forcing down all the emotions that were raging through her chest. She could feel her eyes prickling with tears again. "I'm going to find something to help, and then I'm going to come back! Don't move, Aiden! Hold on to the ledge!"

"Mizuki!" Aiden called, and she could just see the outline of him as thunder rumbled through the mountains. "Mizuki, I need to tell you something!"

"No!" Mizuki yelled, shaking her head as she fought back the urge to be physically sick. "You're not saying goodbye – not yet! Just hang on! I'm coming back!"

She screamed the words as she got up from the ground and staggered her way up the path. She didn't know what she was looking for, and she didn't have a clue what she was hoping to find. She just knew that she couldn't stop. She knew she couldn't give up, and she couldn't leave him there. Not after everything they had been through, not after everything Aiden had done for her – not after all these years.

He was her best friend.

Her only friend.

He was everything to her.

He was – he was –

She couldn't finish the thought, and she felt her body shaking as tears started to pour down her face. She pushed herself up the path, her feet skidding across the mud and stone as she navigated by the light of the storm and struggled not to slip off the edge. She fell to the ground when the wind caught her body, and the rain washed her feet out from beneath her. Her worn leather shoes weren't helping, so she tore them from her feet and threw them aside as she hauled herself up once more.

With every step she seemed to slide five more backwards, and she could feel the skin of her hands tearing against the stone every time she slipped to the ground. It grew darker. Colder. Sweat poured from her skin as she grunted in pain and crawled her way up the path. It had doubled back at least four or five times now; she had long ago lost count, and it had grown steeper at each turn.

She was panting for breath and clawing at the mud as a massive gust of wind tugged her body down, and she skidded across the ground. It was all she could do to hang on; she felt some of her nails crack as they dug into the stone, her arms and legs hugging the surface as she fought not to get thrown off. Then, when the wind finally slowed, she forced herself up and kept crawling. It happened again and again, and each time she thought it was the end. Then each time the wind faded, she would clamber further up the path. She couldn't feel anything anymore. She didn't know how she continued to move, but scratched her way up the next incline.

Aiden was waiting for her.

Aiden *needed* her.

She was all he had left, so she couldn't stop.

She wouldn't stop.

Even if it cost her life, she would find a way to get back to him because he meant more to her than she had ever allowed herself to recognize. It was the right thing to do, and it was what Miku would tell her to do – and she would not leave him to die alone. She would find a way to help him, and if there was nothing at the top of this path that she could use, then she would fight her way back down to be with him when the poison took hold.

Heaving from exertion, she pulled herself up and over the next ledge, rolling into the mud and coughing and gagging as she struggled to breathe. She wheezed out in pain as she rolled onto her stomach and slowly raised her head to look up at the path – and she froze, for there was no path.

Her eyes widened in disbelief as her gaze shifted across the large flat plateau. It was more than thirty feet wide, stone, mud, and rocks extending out from the side of the mountain like a massive shelf. Yet that wasn't what stilled her and made her heart stutter in her chest. What stole her breath away was the dull flicker of firelight that she could see through the sheets of rain.

And it was coming from a large, open-mouthed cave.

Veles

The warm glow was unmistakable.

The low light flickered through the darkness like a beacon of hope, and it made her heart stutter within her chest. The storm had grown so bad she could barely see, and she laid there in the mud for a long time while staring at the light, unable to move. If there was a fire in that cave, it meant that someone lived here, and if someone lived here, it meant one of two things. She could find help, herbs, and a way to save Aiden – or she could be in even more danger. She didn't know what to expect, and she could feel her muscles tensing as cold terror started to shift down her spine.

What if this was Veles? What if he lived here? What if all the stories were true? What if Earnan was right and the Elders really had spoken to a god, and she was about to trespass through his home?

A loud crack of thunder rocked through the air, jerking Mizuki from her straying thoughts. She couldn't stay here. The wind was getting worse, and it was tugging at her body, threatening to yank her off the flat plateau. She would never know the truth unless she moved, and Aiden would die if she didn't at least try to find something within this cave to help him.

Drawing a ragged breath, Mizuki hauled herself from the wet and muddy ground, her legs vibrating beneath her as she struggled to stand in the harsh wind. She staggered toward the cave, teeth chattering in the cold. As she grew closer, she could just barely begin to make out the details of the cavern, and she collapsed under the weight of her soaked clothes as she stumbled through the curtain of water that was pouring over the lip of the opening. Shaking on the dry ground, she looked around and felt her heart still once more.

It wasn't a small, cramped cave like the one that Earnan had been living in along the Southern Mountains. This was something else entirely, and an acute nervousness began to spread through her body.

The inside was warm. It was as if there were an invisible barrier at the entrance that prevented the wind and rain from passing over the threshold. She could feel the heat of the large fire against her face as she trembled and fought to breathe. The sound of the storm was lessened, the once deafening thunder now only a gentle rumble as the lightning that continued to flicker in the sky behind her cast flashes of white light across the large rocky shelter.

The space was tall and wide – more like the Meeting Chambers in the Hall than a cave, though the entire thing was carved out of the mountain stone, and there were deep gashes that marked the ground in odd patterns. The fire was burning in a hearth, wood was stacked beside it, and an old metal pot was resting on the edge of the stone. Herbs hung along the ceiling and walls from strands of string, and stone jutted out from the side of the cave like shelves. They were covered with small containers, cups, bowls and pitchers. A wooden chair was sitting before the fire, and a leather pack was resting against the wall nearby. A collection of odd symbols were scratched into the stone, similar to the cave that Earnan had been living in, but just like with Earnan's cave, the only symbol she recognized was that of Veles.

Her brow furrowed as she stood from the ground and swayed on her feet. It looked as if a human was living here, based on all the belongings, and it looked as if they had been living here for a while. Her eyes flicked across the space once more, and she saw thick vines and flowers growing along the back wall of the cavern. By all logic, they shouldn't be there. She had never seen that much green growing from stone, and yet it draped down the walls thick and luscious as if it were thriving.

None of this made any sense, and she got the distinct and uncomfortable feeling that she wasn't supposed to be here.

She couldn't explain it, but it wasn't just nerves. There was something unnatural about this cave that made her skin crawl with uneasiness. She didn't know what it was, but that didn't matter – she wasn't going to be staying for very long. The vines could work as rope; all she needed to do was cut some down and carry them back down the path. Taking a breath, she shoved the uneasiness aside and forced her legs to move once more.

She could already feel the numbness in her arm creeping up to her shoulder, and she knew they were running out of time. Moving to the fire, Mizuki climbed on top of the old chair and pulled down the woundwort that was hanging from the ceiling. She didn't hesitate as she ripped the disgusting hide wrap from her left palm and grabbed a small bowl from one of the rock shelves. Rushing back to the entrance of the cave, she gathered water from the stream pouring over the entrance and moved back to the fire to make a paste. It only took her a few moments. Then she smothered the wound with it while silently hoping that it didn't make the injury worse.

Ripping off her mud-caked jacket, she dropped the garment to the ground with a soft thud, then tore off her second shirt. The hide was soaked, but it was cleaner than her jacket and better than nothing. She quickly cut it into strips, wrapping two around her left palm to secure the woundwort paste before shoving the others and the knife in her pants pocket. She paused as she looked at the remaining paste in the bowl. She needed to find a way to bring it to Aiden since she wasn't sure if she would be able to get him up the path. Unable to come up with a better solution, she took out a few of the hide shirt strips and coated them with the paste before repocketing them once more.

She didn't bother putting her ruined jacket back on. Cold as it was outside on the mountain path, the heavy weight of the soaking wet leather and muddy furs just slowed her down. She was already struggling to support her own weight as it was, and the wet material did nothing to provide warmth. So, she left it on the stone floor near the hearth, opting to only wear her frayed, long-sleeved plant-fibre shirt as she headed toward the vines.

She made it halfway there when she faltered, and her head jerked to the right. There was a tunnel leading out the back of the cave. She hadn't seen it when she had first staggered in and looked around, but now she could see a faint glow coming from the other end. She hesitated, her heart beating quickly in her chest as she stared down the dim tunnel and nervously tucked her wet hair behind her ears.

Was there someone back there? Was there more to this cave? Could there be other things here that could help? Or maybe it led out the other side of the mountain?

Her eyes shifted back to the vines, and her body tensed. The vines would probably work, but rope would be better, and from what she could see this place was littered with different objects. She knew she couldn't waste any more time, but there was something about the faint glow illuminating the tunnel that was drawing her attention. Before she could even fully think about why she was doing it, she slowly stepped into the tunnel and inched down the hall. It narrowed as she walked, but the walls were still easily several feet wide when it jolted to the right and opened up into a smaller cavern.

She paused at the mouth of the space, her eyes widening as she sucked in a quiet breath. The room was a bedroom – or at least that's what she assumed it was based on appearance. There was some sort of large bed in the corner made of dried plants and sticks. It was way too large for a person and circular in shape. She wondered what could possibly sleep in such a massive, nest-like bed – then she felt her stomach knot as her eyes spotted several long black feathers jutting out from the tangled mess.

They looked *exactly* like the one that Elder Farr wore around his neck.

She swallowed, forcing the surge of panic back as she tore her eyes away and made herself examine the rest of the room. Her eyes traced over to the small fire that burned in the opposite corner, and she frowned when she saw that there was nothing here that would help her with Aiden. Twisting on her heel to return to the main area of the cave, she froze as her eyes traced over a small rock shelf that jutted from the side of the small room. It was just like the ones in the main cavern, but this one wasn't littered with plates or pitchers or herbs. This one appeared to be covered in small trinkets, and what caught her eye was the three small paper items propped up against the wall.

They were pictures.

She recognized the small, paper-like cards from the very limited few that she had seen back in the village as a child. There were hardly any left. Most had been lost in the Great Destruction, but the Elders had some from the Before time that were kept in the Documents Room, and a few families within the village had old, worn pictures of their long-dead relatives. Her family didn't have any, but Aiden's did, and they had always disturbed her in some way. There were people in the village who drew, and they had made portraits of family members and friends – but these old relics of the past were lifelike captures that just felt too real.

Despite the exhaustion that clung to her body and the way her legs shook, she forced herself to move across the room toward the shelf. She couldn't help it – she had to know. If she somehow managed to pull Aiden up from the ledge, she wanted to know if this was going to be a safe place to bring him – and right now, her confidence in that was shaken, given the large black feathers that littered the makeshift bed behind her. Logically, she knew it could just be a coincidence. It was possible that large birds lived within these mountains, and the first Elders simply gathered stray feathers that they found along the path like whoever was living here. Yet even she doubted her mind's weak attempt to rationalize the similarities between the feathers.

Staggering the final few steps, she stopped before the stone shelf and reached a trembling hand out to the first and largest photo. It was covered in something hard and clear that had prevented the picture from getting worn over time.

The people within it were alive with life, smiling, laughing, and sitting around some kind of table. They wore strange colourful clothes, necklaces, and other things on their body that she didn't understand. They all looked similar, green eyes, brown hair, tanned skin, straight teeth, and crease lines by their eyes as they smiled – a tall man, a woman, and two girls who looked to be early teenagers.

The second photo was of the two girls from the first, and they were once again wearing strange clothes that seemed over-elaborate and impractical. They were both smiling brightly and standing outside on a pleasant day. The tallest of the two was wearing a strange pointy gold-coloured hat on her head, and she had her arm wrapped around the shoulder of the shorter girl. Mizuki had no idea what the gold hat was or why the taller girl was wearing it, but it looked like they were having fun.

Placing the photo back on the shelf, Mizuki reached for the third one, and she paused.

This one was nothing like the others, the edges were worn and battered, and the photo looked damaged, like it had been folded or touched many times. There were two girls in the photo. One with loose brown curls and green eyes that she recognized from the others even despite the wear. But this time, the girl's face was gaunt, and her skin looked ashen. She appeared older than in the other photos, and there was a scar that ran down the middle of her forehead that hadn't been there before. Her smile looked tight, and her body looked too thin. She was sitting on a chair with some kind of untouched food before her, but her eyes were focused on the girl to her left.

It wasn't the same young woman from the other photos – this girl looked completely different, though the material was so faded it was hard to make out all her features. Straight black hair, lighter skin, and possibly blue eyes? It was hard to tell, but something about the expression on her face looked exhausted and sad. It tugged at Mizuki's heart, and she couldn't stop staring at the image as she tried to see behind the crease lines that had long ago ruined the photo.

Both girls were wearing much simpler clothes than in the previous two images. Bright, colourful, and impractical had been replaced with dull, grey, and simple. Only the new girl on the left seemed to be wearing a necklace, but it was cut off by a crease line, so she couldn't tell what it was. They were clearly close, based on the small amount of space between them, and yet as she stared at it, Mizuki couldn't help but feel like there was tension hidden behind their smiles, and it made the discomfort along her spine grow.

Why were these photos here?

Was it possible that Aiden was right, and someone had survived the sacrifice and made it up the path? Maybe they lived here, and these were family heirlooms? Maybe the feathers really didn't mean anything?

As she set the photo back down and stepped away to gaze at the room once more, she felt her stomach knot. The photos didn't align with the bed or the feathers. Neither did the fire or the wood – or anything else that was here. Unless there was a trail off the plateau that she hadn't been able to see in the dark that continued around the mountain, and unless there was a forest on the other side, how would someone have gathered this wood? Why would they leave the fire burning if getting wood was such a challenge?

She staggered back from the odd room. The sinking feeling that had been lurking in her gut since she entered the cave was compounding with each step.

She shouldn't be here.

She didn't like this.

There was something about this place that was wrong, and she couldn't explain it. Swallowing hard, she turned away, pulled the knife from her pants pocket and darted back to the vines in the main cavern. Her arms shook as she reached up to cut down the thickest of the green strands, and she struggled to rip them from the walls as her left hand failed to do what she asked.

As she worked, her heart continued to race, and she could feel cold sweat collecting across her brow as a shiver ran down her spine. She wanted to leave. She couldn't tell if it was the poison, the hunger, or simply just the cave, but as she ripped down more and more vines, her panic started to grow as an eerie feeling of being watched settled over her body and a dull clicking noise filled the air.

People weren't supposed to be here. She couldn't explain the thought as it entered her mind, but she knew instinctively that it was true.

She took down six strands, ignoring the dull noise and repocketed her knife before she pulled the vines away from the wall so she could tie them together. She had to use her feet to help tighten the knots since her left arm was barely working now, and a quick glance down the collar of her still wet shirt confirmed that the black tendrils had reached her shoulder. Either the woundwort wasn't working, or she was simply too far gone to be saved.

Forcing the concerning thoughts from her mind, Mizuki coiled the vines on the floor, looping them over themselves before she grunted and lifted the heavy bundle from the ground. She staggered as she hauled them over her shoulder, panting from the effort and swaying on her feet as she moved toward the mouth of the cave once more. She could see lightning flashing through the sky, the low growl of thunder still dull until she crossed over the threshold and was immediately bombarded by the elements.

Cold rain washed over her body in sheets. The wind bit at her burned skin and tried to tug her off the large plateau as the mountain shook beneath her feet. She would be lucky if she made it back to Aiden at all in this. Every step she took as she crossed the plateau threatened to be her last as the terror of the storm surged against her once more. She had just managed to get nearly halfway across the plateau when a massive gust of wind sliced over the surface and caught her across the chest.

It was as if the air had been sucked from her lungs in the pressure change, and she was knocked backward, colliding with the ground and skidding through the mud. The noise was unbearable, and she screamed out as she rolled across the ground through the wall of water and into the cave once more. She coughed out mud and gasped for air as she rolled to her side and opened her eyes. At this rate, she would never make it back to Aiden, and she could feel her eyes starting to burn with tears as she forced herself to inhale. Pulling herself up on her elbow, she looked back at the entrance as the ground shook beneath her, and she froze.

She felt her body grow numb as her eyes widened with fear. Her lungs forgot how to breathe, and her heart stuttered in her chest as every muscle in her body stiffened.

An enormous creature had landed heavily on the plateau, its spiked wings beating to a stop and sending three more massive gusts of wind across the surface. They spanned nearly as wide as the entire ledge, and they were covered in long, black feathers. She felt her heart drop in her chest as the creature folded them behind its back and stood to its full height. Mizuki stared as her mind failed to process the image it saw through the curtain of water.

This wasn't possible.

She could see two large red eyes glowing through the darkness – and they were staring at her. Cold fear washed through her body. She couldn't move. She still hadn't inhaled. She was almost certain that she had died in the gust of wind, and this was just some dream she was having as her heart took its final few beats, but then the creature moved as a second flash of lightning cut across the sky and lit up the plateau.

The ground shook with each step it took, and as it moved through the curtain of water and into the light of the cave, she realized it was shifting. It moved on all fours, but with every step it took, the grotesque shape transformed into something worse. Almost humanoid – but entirely wrong. Taller, uglier – a bungled mess of things that didn't belong, and her mouth fell open in a silent scream.

Its wool-covered hind legs bent the wrong way. Antlers sprouted from its head while razor-sharp talons extended from three toes and cut deep lines into the stone as it moved. Quills jutted out from the spine between its feathered wings, and they stopped just above a scaled tail that dragged across the ground behind the thing as it closed the distance between them with burning eyes. A deep and horrible noise left its distorted face as it stalked across the ground, and suddenly her limbs began to move as a fresh wave of terror rushed through her veins.

If this abomination was what the first Elders found when they climbed the mountain, they had lied to the entire village.

This was no god.

This was a demon, and she was going to die here.

She could feel it in her bones as she scrambled back against the ground. Her left arm gave out beneath her as she fought against the vines that had tangled around her body when she was thrown back into the cave. She didn't even make it three feet before the creature was upon her, and her blood ran cold as it reached out to grab her from the ground. She couldn't look away. She desperately wanted to close her eyes, and yet its red burning gaze demanded her attention as its black, slitted pupils narrowed in rage. Her hands came up instinctively, and the words left her mouth before she could even think.

"Please, don't!" Mizuki exclaimed, her voice breaking as she thrust out her hands, and her whole body trembled against the stone ground.

She blinked in shock as the creature stopped, and she stared at it wide-eyed until she realized that its gaze was locked to the wrapped gash on her left palm. The feathers around its neck flared, and the quills running down its back fluttered like leaves in a breeze as it raised its hackles. Its eyes slid over her body in one slow movement, taking in her small form before it looked to the vines along the back wall, and its eyes narrowed once more.

Then it looked back to her once more, and she flinched. She could see it thinking, its burning gaze filled with rage as a look of comprehension slid across the massive creature's face. It eyed the wound on her hand once more as she struggled to decide what to do, but before she could think, the combined abomination let out a snort, and she watched in stunned silence as the creature turned away, shaking its head as it stalked toward the large hearth.

Without moving a muscle throughout the rest of her body, Mizuki followed its movement with her eyes. She watched as the huge monstrosity continued to contort and change shape until it was standing very much like a human before the flames. Its hind legs still bent the wrong way, its feet were still clawed with talons that cut into the stone, but it stood on two legs now as it towered over the fire and its antlers nearly brushed the ceiling.

Its hands were somewhat human, though large nails extended from each finger, and the skin was scaled like that of a serpent. The wings remained folded, smaller, so they fit in the space of the cave while its long tail trailed on the ground behind it. It eyed her dirty jacket in disgust, then reached for something along its side. Mizuki watched transfixed as it detached a small leather pouch from its body and dropped it along the edge of the hearth before reaching for a sprig of some herb she didn't recognize.

It was working, moving, going about its day and behaving as if she wasn't even there. Mizuki's brow furrowed in confusion as her hands dropped limply back to her sides, and she watched dumbfounded while the creature pulled a bowl down from the shelf and began to crush the dried herb within it.

It didn't make any sense, and though her lungs had finally remembered how to breathe, the rest of her body remained paralyzed as she stared at the creature in disbelief.

What was this thing?

Was it Veles?

Or was this someone from the village?

How long had it been here, and where did it come from?

The questions raced endlessly in her mind, but she couldn't seem to focus on any of them as they spun uncontrolled. She couldn't seem to form a single coherent thought as all the unease and terror that had filled her soul moments ago continued to course through her veins and kept her rooted to the ground. She could hear the echo of her quick breath as she panted, her heart beating against the bones in her chest, and even though she could feel her legs, they refused to move as she watched the creature in silence.

Yet it continued to ignore her.

She swallowed hard, her mouth dry with fear as she finally forced her eyes to glance back to the storm that raged outside the cave. She had to get back to Aiden. None of her questions mattered if he died. She *had* to move. She had been sitting here for far too long already. She needed to leave and make her way back down the path.

She glanced back at the creature, wondering if she could move without the thing noticing – or if it would even care? It didn't seem to. Its back was mostly turned to her, and it appeared uninterested in her presence.

Her eyes dropped down to the vines that were coiled around her body and scattered across the ground. She couldn't leave without them. If she did, Aiden would die, and coming up here would have been for nothing. Trembling uncontrollably, she held her breath and shifted across the ground. The creature didn't acknowledge it, continuing to ignore her as she silently crawled further into the cave to reach for the vines that had blown away.

She kept her eyes glued to its back, shuffling one knee at a time and gathering the green strands into a pile once more as she struggled to use her left arm. She had managed to gather nearly half of them when her next pull scuffed a loose rock, and the creature by the fire stiffened. She froze, her heart racing in her chest as she watched the beast's feathers and quills bristled at the noise.

Then a low growl filled the air, and fear rocked through her body, sharp and paralyzing as its head started to turn. Its face had changed since the last time she saw it, its elongated snout was shorter, and its bone structure was even more human in shape, just like the rest of its body. Then its mouth opened, and the most wretched and twisted sounds poured from its lips.

"If you are here to die – do it outside."

The noise made her wince, and her eyes watered in pain as she dropped her hold on the vines to cover her ears. It hurt in a way that she couldn't describe. It was like listening to a thousand voices at once, all mixed together into a nightmarish sound that crawled under her skin and pierced through her heart. Her body rejected it, and she knew in her soul that no human was ever supposed to hear it. Her limbs moved before she could think, her body desperate to get out of the creature's presence as she stumbled to her feet, tripping over the vines as she blindly ran from the cave.

She didn't realize what she was doing until she felt the sting of cold rain across her face as the harsh winds knocked her to the ground, and she slid across the muddy plateau. Thunder rattled in her ears, lightning strobed through the darkness, and her broken nails dug into the mud and rock as she struggled to hang on and nearly fell over the edge of the large ledge. She managed to haul herself back onto the plateau in full before collapsing against the ground and sobbing out in agony.

She was going to die here, and Aiden would die alone.

She could feel herself hyperventilating as the rain grew so heavy, she thought she might choke on it. The numbness in her arm had grown so bad she could hardly even use the limb as she rolled onto her back and stared up at the sky. It flashed and rumbled, the vibrations of the thunder moving through her body as she instinctively reached for the necklace around her neck. It had somehow stayed on during the climb, and she clutched at it desperately as she shook in the cold.

Had Miku known about this creature? Did the village Elders? Was this what they had met when they climbed the path all those years ago? Where was her father now? Aiden's parents? Was Aiden still on the ledge waiting for her to return?

Her eyes stung as the tears rolled down her cheeks and blurred with the rain that tried to flood her lungs. Was this really how she was going to go out? Broken, muddy, defeated, and lying in a heap on the ground as she left Aiden to die alone?

Her eyes fell closed as her heart broke.

What would Miku think of her– coming this far only to fail and give up at the end?

She had made a promise. She had promised him that she would come back. She couldn't stop – not now, not ever – not until her heart gave out. Her eyes flicked open, and her head turned in the mud to gaze back at the warm flicker of light that came from the cave behind her head. The vines were right there, less than twenty feet from her reach, and she could see them through the curtain of water.

She could hardly feel her body in the cold, but as she gripped her necklace tighter, she felt something hot and angry surging through her chest.

Aiden was a good man. He had never caused anyone harm, he had never done anything wrong, and he didn't deserve this. All he had wanted to do was save his sister. He had blamed himself for roping Mizuki into this, but the truth was, it was his connection to her growing up that had led to his family being targeted. She knew it to her core, and while she blamed the Elders for what they did, it was still his link to *her* that had led them to this point, not the other way around.

If she died – then so be it, it seemed to be what her family was destined to do in this godforsaken world, but she would not allow Aiden to be a casualty of her great-grandmother's fight. He was waiting for her, and she would go to him. If it was the last thing that she did – she would get there. She wouldn't stop, because if she did, the Elders would have succeeded, and Miku's fight would have been for nothing.

Forcing her body to move, she rolled onto her side and groaned in pain. She didn't care about the creature. She didn't care what it was or where it had come from. It didn't matter, not anymore – not when she only had a few moments left, and she needed to see him one more time. Her feet slipped beneath her as she hauled herself from the ground with a heavy groan and staggered to her feet. Slouched and drenched in mud, she forced herself to move back toward the entrance of the cave.

She could see the outline of the creature standing by the fire. She paused before the curtain of water, then stepped back inside the cave. She could hear her soaked clothes dripping onto the cold stone beneath her feet as she crossed the threshold. The echo sounded impossibly loud as her heart thudded in her ears and her eyes remained locked to the creature's back. It didn't move, but she knew it heard her because its quills prickled and its back stiffened. Pushing down the nauseous fear that was rolling in her stomach, she stepped toward the vines, monitoring the creature as she moved. She made it three steps before its voice sliced through the air once more, and her body instinctively seized with terror.

"Outside."

She fought against the urge to cover her ears as her eyes shut in pain. It took everything that she had to ignore her body's desire to run. She slid her foot across the ground, forcing herself to take another step forward across the stone.

"I told you to go outside."

She gritted her teeth to stop herself from emptying the contents of her stomach all over the ground as she took another step and ignored the impulse to flee. All she needed was the vines. That was it. The second she had them, she would run and make for the path. She managed another two steps before the creature's quills bristled once more, and it shifted.

"Outside!"

The volume of the voice radiated down her spine like a blow to the head, and it made her body still on spot. The thing moved faster than Mizuki thought was possible, and before she could blink, she felt her body jerking from the ground as it gripped her by the neck and lifted her into the air. Her bare toes scraped across the stone as it raised her to eye level, and its blood-red gaze bore into her face. She choked, struggling to breathe as she grabbed at its scaled arm and clawed against its hold.

"Or do I need to put you out there myself?"

Tears stung the corner of her eyes as its voice grated her nerves, and she flinched at the sound.

"Please d-don't," Mizuki rasped, using the last bit of air she had left in her lungs as her vision started to blur. She tried to inhale, but the creature only gripped her tighter.

"Is that all your species can say anymore?" the creature hissed, its gaze narrowing as if in disgust.

"N-No," she wheezed. Black spots were starting to cloud her vision, and she knew she was going to pass out. "I – s-speak."

The creature stared at her for another moment before she felt the balls of her feet touch the ground once more, and the pressure on her neck lessened. She inhaled hard, still gripping at the beast's forearm as she coughed and its red gaze moved to Mizuki's left arm.

"I forgot it was a sacrifice year," the creature said. Its horrible voice was quieter this time, but the noise still ran down her spine like a sharp jolt of pain. Its eyes shifted back to her face once more, and it looked at her almost curiously. *"You're the first one in decades to make it to the top alive. Normally, they die along the way."*

She felt the flats of her feet fall level with the ground as the creature lowered her further, and the glow from its eyes seemed to lessen as it stared at the necklace that was hanging from her neck. She felt its clawed hand twitch as its eyes creased, then it let go completely, and she crumpled to the ground.

Gasping for air as her eyes blurred with tears, she looked up to see the creature staring at her with an odd expression. It was curious, if not thoughtful, though the disdain was still evident. Its feathers bristled once more as it shifted its empty red gaze back to the cut on her hand. It didn't move, and as her breathing finally started to regulate, Mizuki forced herself to sit up.

"Are you Veles?" Mizuki whispered, and she instantly regretted her words as the creature's eyes darted back to her face and the quills along its back stood up in anger.

"I am not your god." Its deep voice rumbled, and she recoiled at the sound. It took a step forward, its clawed feet scratching into the rock as it leaned down to glare into her eyes. It looked at her for a moment, then let out a sharp exhale like a scoff. *"I see nothing has changed."*

"What hasn't changed?" Mizuki asked, unable to stop the question as she leaned away from the beast.

"Humans," the creature said, and she cringed at the sound once more. It eyed her for another long moment then made a strange noise that almost sounded like a sigh. *"You're dying. You only have moments left – get out."*

"I can't," Mizuki whispered, her head shaking as she glanced at the vines. "I need those vines."

"They're not yours to take," the creature hissed, its eyes narrowing once more. *"Out, or I will throw you out."*

"My friend is out there," Mizuki said, that same desperate burning determination that she had felt on the plateau surging through her body once more. Even if this thing did throw her from the cave, she didn't care, so long as she had the vines. She groaned as she staggered to her feet and fought the urge to vomit. "I promised him I'd come back."

"Then you lied to him," the creature said, watching as she took a step toward the mess of vines to her right. *"You will not make it."*

"Yes, I will," Mizuki whispered, taking another step.

Her entire left shoulder was numb now. She could feel it starting to spread into her chest, and she knew she was going to die. She glanced at the creature as she moved. She could see the red glow continuing to fade from its large eyes, revealing a tiny sliver of green around its pupils as it watched her step toward the vines but did nothing to stop her.

"I have to."

"He is probably already dead," the creature countered, its voice making her cringe as its eyes narrowing at her once more. *"Let him go."*

"No," Mizuki said, her voice far stronger than she felt.

She glared at it. Her eyes watering in pain as the unease of its presence made her skin crawl. This *thing,* whatever it was, was heartless. It stood there like a void before her, glaring and unmoving and filled with so much rage she could feel it in the air – and the longer she looked at it, the more she hated it. It was everything wrong with this world, everything that had gone wrong in her life, and she could feel her face contorting into an angry mess as she forced her body to move and gather the vines from the ground once more.

"I'm not giving up on him," she said, tears burning at the corner of her eyes as all her emotions began to pour out of her chest.

She couldn't hold them in any longer. Her heart couldn't take it. She had been bottling everything up for ten years, and the sum total of devastation was simply too much – if she didn't let it out now, she might very well die or explode from the pain.

She had lost everything.

Everyone.

She was *not* going to lose Aiden now, too. She wouldn't, regardless of how much it hurt to breathe, and no matter what this *thing* said. She forced herself to stand once more as she lifted the vines from the ground and glared at the wretched animal before her.

"Not now. Not ever. Not even if you try to stop me," Mizuki challenged, and the words came pouring out. "It's my fault he's here – it's my fault he's alone. I promised him that I would come back. I *promised.* That means something to people, and it's not something you can walk away from."

She hauled the vines over her shoulder, trying not to collapse under the heavy weight as sweat poured down her face. She made to step toward the storm once more, planning to walk right by the beast without so much as a second glance.

"You're so much like Ren," the creature murmured.

Mizuki froze.

"How do you know my brother's name?" she whispered as cold fear snaked down her spine. She twisted back to look at the creature, barely feeling the painful shudder that coursed through her body when it spoke.

"You look like her too," the creature continued, its voice growing distant as a strange expression moved across its ugly face.

"Her?" Mizuki said, her eyes tracing over the creature in confusion as she tried to understand. Then, her whole body stiffened in realization, and she felt her mouth go dry.

It couldn't be.

It wasn't possible.

Earnan had said so, but – how?

"Miku's mother," Mizuki whispered, and she watched as the creature met her gaze. "You knew Ren Altherr?"

Its eyes were still cold and empty, but its gaze was entirely different from the angry and disgusted look that had burned into her skin when it first entered the cave. The red was nothing but a dim glow as it watched her in silence and a low whisper filled the air. It looked almost calm, its expression one of thought and reflection as it slowly inclined its head, and her mouth fell open in disbelief.

"Who are you?" Mizuki whispered as the dull clicking noise returned.

Beneath it she could hear a dull murmur like a bubbling stream in her mind. Everything around them was fading away, blurring out of focus and disappearing from her mind. She couldn't have moved even if she wanted to. Her eyes remained fixed to the creature that was starting to look more and more familiar as something cold and foreign shifted through her body. Its face was changing, and its frame was getting smaller as it took a step towards her and the clicking intensified.

"What happened?"

The murmur was getting louder. Her skin prickled as the creature stepped closer again, and the faint smell of earth, rain, and blood filled her nose. The creature's pupils were growing wider, and her heart felt like it was caught in her throat.

"Earnan said that you knew her," Mizuki murmured, the words slipping from her lips as if being pulled out by an invisible string. "He said that you did all this. That you destroyed the world and that you knew my great-great-grandmother."

She swallowed, the air catching in her lungs as her entire body started to shake. She couldn't have stopped the final word even if she tried.

"How?" she whispered as the creature took a final step, closing the distance between them to less than a foot as it towered above her.

"I'll show you."

Its voice rumbled with the thunder that echoed in the cave. Mizuki shuddered so hard the vines fell to the floor. Her arm jerked as the creature grabbed her, its clawed hand reaching toward her head as her body stiffened in terror. The low clicking noise shifted into a deep rattle as its face grew so close, she could feel its breath across her cheek. It was freezing cold. It smelled like the storm, and her skin prickled as the low whispers began to consume her mind. Then its clawed finger pressed against the center of her forehead and her body convulsed.

It hurt.

It burned.

She could feel it inside her mind. It was digging under her skin, burrowing like a bug as the dull whispers grew louder. It thrummed like a living heartbeat in her head. Loud and powerful as a great raging river. Before she could even open her mouth to scream, her vision blurred, then everything went white as the world disappeared, and the last thing she saw was three glowing red eyes.

PART TWO

Lilah

The smell of coffee filled the air in the small kitchenette, and a scowl shifted across my face as I looked at the coffee maker in annoyance and tried to focus on the low sound of the television from the corner of the room. It was constantly set to the news, and right now, the anchor was giving the latest death toll from a NORVIX outbreak several cities over while the headline below briefed on the growing tensions in the east.

I wasn't sure why the network seemed to think that the latest failed negotiations with the Sovereign Federation were *'breaking news'* since every other attempt at negotiations had been unsuccessful. It seemed like a rather obvious outcome given the most recent drought, the contaminated water that reeked of foul play, and the suspected government scandals that were almost certainly true.

I sighed and pushed my loose curls behind my ear.

"It's not hard to brew a new pot," I muttered under my breath as my glare naturally shifted toward the empty doorway, and I fought the urge to scream. I wasn't angry at anyone in particular, nor had I been surprised to find the small kitchen in disarray when I arrived. I was just annoyed with the general lack of responsibility in the office and the routine failure to clean up or refill things once they were used.

The people here were disgusting.

It seemed like every time I entered the kitchen, the coffee was gone, the tea canister was empty, the sugar was almost nonexistent, and the milk had been left out on the counter. That was assuming that there was any coffee, tea, sugar, or milk to begin with. I knew that some people were stealing the supplies to bring home to their families, and for that, I could sympathize, but given that they could still purchase tea and coffee at the grocery stores and that anyone working here was paid enough to be able to afford it, it wasn't an abundance of sympathy. It was diminished further when I looked at the mess on the counters – the often plugged and food riddled sink and the blatant disregard for sorting trash into the proper bins.

To be blunt, the behaviour that I witnessed in this office was nothing short of deplorable.

Just last week, I came in to find that someone had stolen the last of the boxes of sweetener that the office manager had gotten for our floor and drained the pot of coffee that I had made. I should have known better – it was my own fault for assuming that these people had any decency. I had slipped back to my office to finish a few emails while the coffee brewed and returned just in time to watch someone pouring the last drops from the piping hot pot into their mug.

It hadn't mattered that I had left my chipped and worn coffee mug sitting right there next to the coffee machine to stake my claim. It hadn't mattered that I was only gone for ten minutes, which was *barely* enough time for the coffee to brew, and apparently, it hadn't mattered that Bob – the guy who had taken the last bit of fresh coffee – had seen me making the pot when he walked by the kitchenette. He had known that I made it and that I had yet to have any because my cup was still empty on the counter right beside it.

Yet he had finished it off anyway.

And now today, a full week later, that memory still pissed me off. Bob had looked me straight in the eyes, shrugging his shoulders in some sort of lame, sheepish response to getting caught. He had said something stupid, I can't remember the exact words now, but it was along the lines of *'oh, looks like you missed out,'* before he left the kitchen with an amused laugh.

Out of everyone in this office, I think I hate Bob the most. I had thought about telling him off, telling him that I thought he was ignorant, inconsiderate, and unbearable as a human being. Tell him that stealing other people's food from the fridge wasn't funny, nor was his wasteful use of water and sugar acceptable when we were supposed to be rationing it.

I had wanted to do it.

But I didn't.

Instead, I had clenched my teeth in annoyance, watched him walk past, and then started another pot of coffee while I listened to the television. I had done my best to ignore the itch under my skin as my eyes looked over the mess on the counter – the spilled sugar, the splattered coffee, and the empty milk container that sat there even though the recycle bin was less than a foot away. Sadly, that day had been just like all the rest, and I had cleaned up Bob's mess in silence, just like I always did, while wondering how the hell people had become so inconsiderate.

Thinking back on that day now, I could feel my irritation flaring. I let out a sigh and closed my eyes, trying not to think about Bob as I stood guard next to the machine and waited for my coffee to brew.

It hadn't always been like this. At least, not from what I could remember, though that was a long time ago now. It almost felt like I was living on an entirely different planet, and often I found myself wishing that I had become an astronaut or an agricultural scientist so that I could have gone on the Prospect Mission and left this planet behind.

Then again, UNSA, the United National Space Association, had lost contact with the Viking Outpost a week ago after the dust storm hit. So right now, those on the Prospect had no idea what they were headed into or if the outpost was still standing. It was quite possible that they would arrive in just a few months to find nothing, but the mission had always been a one-way trip, so there wasn't anything that UNSA could do about it now except plan to send them more resources.

I shifted my gaze back to the television, watching as the lead news anchor began to cover the next hot topic of debate – the continued battle between HUANEE and the UNC – which had caused quite an uproar, not only between the people within my office but across the globe and between governments as well.

'Today marks the second week of inaction since the devastating attack on the Hippleton Mining Facility that left more than two dozen dead. We go now to Mark Wong, who is live on-site – Mark?'

'Thank you, Kasey – I'm standing outside the barrier that surrounds the remains of the Hippleton Mining Facility, a massive open-pit phosphate mine that has been in operation for just over one year and has been riddled with setbacks and problems since its inception.'

'When the Hippleton Mining company announced the location for their new operations a few years ago, they were faced with heavy opposition from local environmental groups, nearby residential communities, and municipal governments. Yet despite this, they were able to push the permits through, and they began working last May, maintaining a steady pace until two weeks ago when the global environmental group, known as HUANEE, or Humanity United Against Natural Exploits and Experimentation, attacked the facility.'

'Speaking with residents in a nearby town, they say the attack sounded like an explosion – fire could be seen more than a kilometre away as machinery was destroyed, the head office buildings were demolished, and the sides of the mines caved in. You can just see the edge of the wreckage behind me, and it looks like a warzone.'

The camera panned to the right, showing what appeared to be the wreckage of a large brick building and several destroyed pieces of industrial equipment. It was difficult to tell, since all I could make out on the small screen was a few pieces of bent metal and a melted pile of twisted plastic. My brow arched at the sight; it would take a lot of heat to melt everything like that.

'Authorities are putting the death toll at twenty-six, but due to the instability of the cave in they have yet to finish searching the mine, and it is unclear exactly how many people are still missing. They are unsure when, or if, they will ever be able to get an exact number – but one thing that is clear is that the pressure on the UNC, the United National Congress, to do something about these attacks is mounting, and the public debate is starting to get heated. Back to you, Kasey.'

'Thanks, Mark – this attack is the second this month, but it is the largest one to date in an increasing display of violence by the environmental group that claims they are "sick of waiting for the government to do something". As of right now, HUANEE has not accepted responsibility for the attacks that have been happening across the globe and targeting sites of environmental concern, even though all of the attacks have been marked with their symbol. Yet they do not deny the claims that they are associated with the violence either. Instead, they have taken the unique approach of outwardly applauding the attacks on social media while asking their members to stay safe and to stay hidden.'

Smart move, I thought, glancing at the coffee machine as the first sounds of the fresh brew hitting glass filled the air. In recent years, the UNC had developed a habit of going after and attempting to silence any organizations that opposed their administration or challenged their global bills. I knew that most would disagree with me, but this domineering behaviour was part of the reason why things with the Sovereign Federation had gotten so bad. Not that the Sovereign Federation was any better; they were unquestionably worse.

'Since the attacks started back in February of this year, pressures on the United National Congress have been mounting, with many individual country governments demanding that something be done. However, some countries have voted against taking action, claiming that this is simply humanity taking back control and that instead of spending resources to hunt down the members of HUANEE, the UNC should be passing new

global legislation to better protect the limited resources that remain.'

'At this point, it is unclear if the UNC will take any steps to hold HUANEE accountable when the country representatives are so polarized, but many are wondering if legislation could ever be effective given the nature of HUANEE's organization.'

'Aside from the recognizable and controversial symbol which decorates their online presence and marks the scenes of their attacks, they exist entirely online and leave no physical footprint. Cyber Investigation groups from multiple countries have been unable to pinpoint where the group is operating from or how they are coordinating their attacks, which has left many skeptical about what can be done. Many others are making wide-sweeping conspiracy claims about who the face behind HUANEE is and what countries may be backing the environmental group that many are now calling a terrorist faction.'

'The UNC is expected to meet on the issue next week and take another vote to determine a course of action. Up next – experts are suggesting that the world may only be a single decade away from global mass starvation; however, scientists on the UNC Agricultural Committee deny this claim and call the recent study a scare tactic by environmental groups pushing for impractical changes. Stay with us over the break for more details.'

I watched as the station switched to commercials and then forced my eyes back to the full pot of fresh coffee that sat to my right. It hardly seemed important now – though then again, *nothing* seemed important anymore. Not when the world around me was burning. At some point, life had shifted from living to existing, and within that framework, nothing that I did mattered.

And it hurt.

Always.

Constantly.

Like an itch under my skin that I couldn't scratch. Meanwhile, assholes like Bob continued to live their life with no regard for those around them and without a care in the world. The sad truth was, it wasn't just him – it was the majority of people.

It must be nice, I thought bitterly, to get up in the morning without feeling physically ill. Or without feeling like you were dying a little bit more every day while your conscience suffocates you. I wished that the rising temperatures, massive storms, and mounds of trash didn't bother me. I wished that the food shortages didn't concern me or that every time I heard about a new species going extinct, I didn't throw up in my mouth a little bit while gritting my teeth in pain. I wished I could close my eyes and feign ignorance too, but more than anything – I just wished that it was different.

At thirty-two, I shouldn't be this jaded. I shouldn't be this bitter. I shouldn't be standing here thinking about the last news report while feeling sad that more people hadn't died in that explosion. I shouldn't wish for HUANEE to attack more places, secretly hoping that they targeted my place of work next.

I shouldn't be, and yet I am.

People could say what they wanted to about HUANEE, but they were destined to happen. They were the culmination of decades worth of human anger and frustration at the lack of change. They were violent, yes, and their tactics may be cruel – but at least they were doing something.

As a small child, I was so hopeful and naive. I thought that the world could change. I thought that people were better than this, but it turns out they're not, and it turns out I'm just like everyone else. I wanted to make a difference; that's why I went into environmental engineering, but evidently, crippling student debt and the need for food, shelter, and money have a way of changing your mind. So, I took a job in the chemical manufacturing industry, working in the Health, Safety and Environmental group, and I convinced myself that it was okay because I could help to make the industry better.

I snorted at the thought, grabbing the fresh pot of coffee and pouring myself a mug.

Ten-year-old me would have been disgusted at what I have become. I had wanted to change the world. I had wanted to help – to do something that I could be proud of. Not only have I done nothing, but I have become part of the problem, silently watching the world burn like everyone else and hating myself for it.

I spend my time at work fighting with management about safety concerns and regulations. I argue about environmental protection needs, and then I'm told that I did a good job when we implemented the bare minimum requirements. I spend afternoons trying to convince my company to spend money on things to protect the land we use, while their bean counters find every excuse possible to try to get around those requirements because they're not profitable and there's no return on investment.

Just last year, a species of bird went extinct, and people actually celebrated – because now we can finally get rid of the grasslands to the east of the facility and use it as plot space for a new outbuilding. That day had been a particularly low point in my career.

Oftentimes, it feels like everyone around me knows that the world is ending, and they're all simply putting in time until the clock runs out. Or maybe they just think that they can escape it because the war hasn't hit us yet, the weather isn't *that* bad, and they have enough money to keep themselves safe and fed. Maybe they're just waiting it out. All I can wonder is – how the hell did it get this way? Was it a case of people not understanding the consequences before it was too late, or did our grandparents just truly not care about the world that they left us?

That question haunts me at night. It keeps me up, it makes me wonder what could have been, and I can't help but feel like it didn't have to be like this. People didn't have to be like this. Maybe if we all cared a little more and wanted a little less, life would be different, the planet wouldn't be dying, and humanity wouldn't be banking on the Prospect Mission succeeding – because what happens if it doesn't?

A low, dead sigh left my lips as I placed the coffee pot back on the heating pad then took out the single packet of sugar that I was allowed to have as per the rationing restrictions. I knew people broke the rule all the time, but I refused to. My existence was bad enough for the planet; I could at least manage to drink my coffee with half of the sugar that I wanted.

I did my best to swallow the sickness that was building in my stomach as I stirred my coffee and stared at my thin fingers. They looked like bone with just a little bit of skin wrapped around them, and my once tanned and healthy-looking skin was now pallid and dry. I knew I had bags under my eyes and that my once vibrant green irises were now dull in colour and filled with exhaustion. I knew that this afternoon was going to be hell and that it would take every bit of my strength not to just quit my job and throw my computer against a wall.

And I knew that the bitter, empty cold in the center of my chest would never go away. It had always been there, just below the surface, but after my sister died in one of the last NORVIX outbreaks, it was as if the feeling had dug its claws so deeply into my chest that I couldn't breathe, and I knew that a piece of me had died along with her.

Yet under my anger was the tiny little voice that told me I didn't have it that bad and that I really shouldn't be complaining about my life so much. The war in the east with the Sovereign Federation had yet to reach us, and while yes, food was being rationed, at least it was still available. I had clean water, a home, and family left alive. I had more than most. I shouldn't be so depressed, and yet regardless of this, I was plagued with desperation – like my very soul knew that there was something deeply and disturbingly wrong with the world. There was something wrong with us humans, for how could we have allowed this to happen? How could we torch our own home and do nothing about it while we exploit those around us for our own benefit and show no remorse?

I watched as the black liquid swirled in my cup, feeling sick at the thought of working another four hours in this hellhole before heading home. I forced down the wave of nausea and focused on the black coffee as I tried to clear my head. The colour reminded me of my best friend's hair – Ren's hair – and that thought made my tense shoulders relax. Without her, I wouldn't be here. After losing my sister, she became the only beacon of light in my life and the only good thing in this world. She was the reason why I got up every morning and the reason why I hadn't just taken my own life to escape this hell – because I knew if I did, it would kill her, and it would devastate my family. So, I forced myself to throw the wooden stir stick into the compost bin, and I buried my emotions, just like I did every other day.

I sighed and rubbed my temples, taking three slow, deep breaths before I grabbed my coffee off of the counter and turned to leave the room. It was time to go pretend – to pretend that I was okay and pretend that I cared about this job and the people around me.

I didn't, but that didn't matter because it was all meaningless anyway.

"Oh, great! You made coffee."

I suppressed a cringe as I heard the annoying voice, and I fought to keep my face impassive as I stared at the leech who had just walked through the door. Bob grinned widely as he made his way toward the counter, mug in hand, ready to pour himself another fresh cup, even though he had already had his ration's worth for the day.

"Well, someone had to," I said with a tight smile, shuffling past him to take my leave. I knew better than to unleash my inner rage and disgust while at work, but despite my best efforts to sound calm, there was a distinctly bitter tone to my voice.

"Uh oh," Bob said with a laugh as he quickly started to fill his cup, spilling coffee on the counter as he poured. He would leave it there, and it would sit for hours until either myself or one of the few other decent people in the office cleaned it up. "Tense week, Delilah? It's only Wednesday, you know – still two more days to go! You need to learn to lighten up."

I paused by the door, his words digging into my skin as I turned back to look at him. I watched the arrogant man greedily dumping packet after packet of sugar into his mug, spilling some into the mess of coffee that he had just made. He was laughing at his own joke. He was smiling without a care in the world. My hand gripped my mug so tightly that I couldn't feel my fingers as my eyes narrowed into slits of hatred.

The world would be so much better off without people like him in it.

"Right," I said, watching as the man continued to busy himself around the small kitchenette, completely unaware that I was glaring daggers at him.

I had heard that phrase before.

A lot.

"That's what people keep telling me," I murmured as I tasted bile at the back of my throat. I turned on my heel and left before he could say anything else, making my way down the hall toward my office as I glared at the floor. "Asshole."

Food prices are expected to soar in the coming weeks. After the most recent drought, farmers are anticipating that more than 30% of their crops have been lost, and what remains will be distributed by the federal government and rationed based on age and medical needs. Talks are ongoing as to whether or not the proposed Food Stamp Program will be approved and enforced before the end of summer – but based on reduced global trade and overall world food shortages, it is expected that this global bill will push ahead by the UNC faster than its originally anticipated date of September–'

"It's your turn."

'And now, for an update from CKPX News correspondent, Omar Sleiman, who is on-site at the military base in –'

"Lilah."

Thanks, Kasey – it seems like little has changed over the course of the last few days. The UNC had anticipated difficulties during their negotiations, but no one had predicted that the meeting would end in outright violence. Up until the meeting two days ago, the commanding officers were hopeful for a temporary cease-fire agreement. However, given the turn of events, troops have begun to mobilize once more as threats of nuclear violence hang in the air. We'll need to wait to see what happens as they head north and–'

"Lilah!"

"What?" I snapped, turning my head to look at the voice that had distracted me from the news report. I froze the second that I realized who I was yelling at, the wave of rage that had flashed through my veins petering out as I took in the annoyed expression on my best friend's small, thin frame. She was glaring at me. Her normally kind blue eyes were narrowed in irritation. Her mouth was drawn into a tight line. I could see the tension in her body as she gripped the cards she was holding tightly in her hands, and I felt my heart drop.

I hadn't been paying attention.

I hadn't even heard her speak before that moment, and I knew that she must have because Ren rarely yelled. Not unless it was absolutely necessary. My eyes traced over her angry face, and I swallowed. Her jet-black hair had been cut short just a few weeks ago to try to combat the heat in the hospital where she worked as a nurse, and it framed her face beautifully. Though, right now, it just helped to accent her irritation as she looked at me.

"I'm sorry," I said, feeling the last of my anger reducing to a low simmer at my core. "I missed what you said, Ren."

"I know," she said, her voice becoming softer as her frustration started to fade. It was replaced by a deep look of sadness until my eyes glanced at the bright red *'breaking news'* banner that flashed across the television screen, and her expression hardened once more. "Why do you always have that on? It's like having your mind scraped against a cheese grater day in and day out – it's not good for you."

I frowned as I looked at her. "It's important, Ren."

Ren and I didn't usually argue. We've always been close, and for the most part, we have always gotten along. We've been through a lot together over the years, and we have always managed to work things out, but my recent obsession with worldly disasters was one of the few things that did spark the odd disagreement between us. She seemed to favour keeping aware of what was happening but then choosing to live her life as happily as she could outside of that information. I was the opposite – I listened to the news constantly, thought about it all the time, and kept track of all the stories and their progressions.

"I never said that it wasn't important," Ren said as she grabbed the remote from the edge of the table and turned the television off. My lip twitched as a flicker of irritation sparked through my heart, and silence rang heavy through my apartment as she fixed me with a serious stare. "But your obsession with the news and everything going on is unhealthy, Lilah. You don't need to watch the latest reports every minute of every day – it doesn't help you. Missing one headline isn't going to impact your life or change things, except to maybe give you a break. Don't think I haven't noticed the permanent crease that's formed between your eyebrows or the bags that are under your eyes. Have you been sleeping at all? Or eating, for that matter?"

I frowned again, the crease she had just referenced growing deeper as her words circled my mind. I didn't usually get angry with her, but there was something about the way that she spoke that just hit a nerve. Maybe it was because deep down, I knew that she was right, and I didn't like it.

"I've been eating," I said, gripping the cards that I was still holding hard. I met her gaze straight on even though my words had been a lie, but that was beside the point, and that tiny ball of rage that seemed to permanently sit on my chest was flaring. "What am I supposed to do, Ren? Pretend as if nothing is going on like everyone else? Have you even bothered to look at what's happened today? What happened this week? One million people died in India, Ren – a *million!* Just like that because of the last outbreak, the landslide, and the flash flooding!"

"I know!" Ren said, her eyes narrowing into a glare once more before she closed them and sucked in a sharp breath. I watched as she set her cards down on the table, gripping the surface tight as if she were physically restraining herself. Then she let out a low exhale and opened her eyes. "I know, Lilah – I read the headlines in the morning as I have done for years. I'm not saying that this stuff isn't important. I'm not saying that it doesn't matter or that you shouldn't care – *everyone* should care. I'm just saying that worrying about it constantly isn't good for you, and it doesn't gain you anything."

"So you're saying that because I'm not actually doing anything about it, I'm just wasting my time and worrying my life away," I scoffed.

I knew I was out of line, but the truth was I just didn't care, because the anger in my chest was drowning me. That very thought had been festering in the back of my mind for weeks, and I couldn't stand it. I expected her to snap back at me or to get upset at my snide little outburst – but she didn't. Instead, her eyes just grew sad once more and her grip on the table loosened.

"That's not what I said," Ren whispered, and I could hear the hurt in her voice. "And you know that's not what I meant, Lilah."

"Maybe not, but it's true," I said, bitterness lacing my voice as I dropped my eyes to the table and glared at my cards. I couldn't even remember what I had been trying to do with them or why we had decided to play this game when neither one of us particularly liked it.

"It isn't true," Ren said as she reached across the table and gently took my hands in hers. "You might not be out there on the front lines, but you help in other ways, Lilah – you do more than your fair share, and that's why I'm worried about you."

She hesitated, and I felt her grip my hands more tightly.

"Ever since your sister died, you've become obsessed," Ren whispered, and my body went rigid at her words.

We hadn't talked about my sister, and Ren hadn't even dared to attempt to bring it up. Not since it happened. Not since her body was burned with a bunch of others, and the hospital sent a small container of ashes to my parents.

She had been infected with NORVIX, so we weren't able to see her before she died. The ashes were supposed to help with closure, and I suppose in some ways they did since my parents treasured them. They talked to the ashes in the container and had said their goodbyes, but I hadn't seen the point. I doubted that there was any of her in there. With how many had died in that outbreak and how many containers the hospital had needed to send out, any practical person would look at the situation and know that they were just sending out containers of generic human ash. If we were lucky, there was a gram of her in the thing, but either way, I wasn't going to say goodbye to a *jar*.

LILAH

"Lilah – you're donating all of your money to support the research for finding a cure. You give what little is left to the UNC's Global First Aid response team, and you've sold nearly all of your belongings to raise more money to donate to environmental groups. You're giving more than you have, more than you should. You don't eat, and you don't sleep – when was the last time you went to visit your parents outside of obligatory birthdays and holidays? When was the last time you did anything for yourself or enjoyed a single day of your life?" Ren asked as she gripped my hands tighter. I could feel her eyes on my face, but I refused to meet her gaze as a deep, hollow, and empty pain started to radiate in my chest. "That's not living, Lilah. That's not even surviving. You're killing yourself. Not all in one go and not all at once, but slowly – you're killing yourself, and it's killing your family and me."

I heard her shift across the table from me, and I knew that she was leaning against the worn and battered surface toward me.

"I know things are bad right now," Ren whispered, and I could hear the pleading in her voice. "But we can't give up; we have to keep living – keep fighting and believing. We have to hope that things can get better. We have to believe that and remember why life is worth living. Otherwise, what will be the point in surviving this if there is nothing left of who we are when it's over?"

I swallowed. I could feel my throat starting to burn as all the memories that I never allowed myself to think about bubbled to the surface of my mind. I could still see my sister's face. I could still hear her voice. I could still remember every cruel word that I had ever said to her as a kid, how she had broken my bike and how it had taken us so many years to get along. I could still remember the day that she told me she was accepted into nursing school and how my stomach had fluttered with a mess of rampant emotions all at once – pride, fear, respect, admiration – love.

It hurt.

I hurt.

I hated the feeling in my chest. I hated the burn that never seemed to go away, and I hated myself for ruining the one good thing that had happened all week – my dinner with Ren. I didn't want to argue with her. I didn't want to think about these things or talk about my sister. I didn't want to be angry all the time, and I especially didn't want to be angry at Ren. She was the only person I trusted. The only person who made this world bearable. The only person that I actually liked. I knew what she wanted, and I knew what she was looking for. She was trying to help me. She was trying to pull me out of the pit that I constantly sat in, and she was trying to give me hope.

But I didn't have any, and I couldn't give her that affirmation.

That had died in me a long time ago, and this was the one obstacle between us that I knew we could never resolve. It was a chasm as wide as the ocean, and it ate away at my soul. Ren had life in her. She was happy, despite the hard times. She was hopeful and kind and perfect. She sat on an island trying to pull me to shore while I drowned in the waves, but it was never going to happen, and I wasn't going to talk about this.

"I'll move twice and draw one card," I said as I slowly untangled my hand from Ren's fingers and moved to pick up my piece. From the corner of my eye, I could see her face falling as I did what I had started doing a few months ago, and I dropped the topic entirely. Then I buried it in the deep, dark pit that sat below my heart. "Then I'll build one castle."

Ren stared at me for a long moment as I shifted my pieces around the board. We had taken to using a bottle cap for one of the markers since the game was so old that nearly half the pieces were missing. As I moved my knight around and built a castle on a random plot of land, I remembered why we had decided to play this game – it was the only one I had left because I hadn't been able to sell it. I glanced up at her as I completed my turn, expecting to see the small but exasperated smile she usually gave me after one of our arguments – which seemed to be happening with increasing frequency – but it didn't come.

She just stared at me, her eyes sad, her shoulders slumped, and her jaw clenched tight. For a brief moment, when her brow creased ever so slightly and she instinctively reached for the necklace around her neck, I thought that she was going to push things. I thought that she was going to try to force me to talk about what had happened, but she didn't.

She didn't say anything, and silence began to fill the air once more.

Had I not been looking directly at her as she moved to take her turn, I would have missed the hurt that flashed across her eyes before something tight and uncomfortable filled the air between us. It was unlike anything that I had ever felt before, and a cold nervousness began to shift down my spine. Despite our differences, and no matter the argument, we always ended the night on good terms, but for the first time in the history of our relationship, I felt like a line had been drawn in the sand between us. Like something had cracked and broken, and she was either tired of me and finally admitting defeat in trying to get me to change, or she herself was finally breaking and succumbing to the hopelessness.

I wasn't sure which of the options was worse – and I didn't know how to feel about it. So, I did the only thing that I could do at that moment; I left the television off, and I finished the game with Ren, all the while ignoring the uneasy feeling that was growing in my heart.

The Accident

"Are you sure I can leave?"

"Yes, it's fine."

"But we still have to finish the paperwork for the spill – it's going to take you another three or four hours if you do it alone."

"It's fine," I repeated for the second time while trying to hide the annoyance from my voice. I gave my coworker what I hoped was a friendly smile. "Your kid is sick, Pari – go home."

"I know, but–"

"Pari, really – it's not a big deal. You've been here all week, and you've hardly been able to see your daughter. Go home, send your babysitter home, and take care of your kid. I've done these forms a dozen times. It won't take me long to finish them," I said while grabbing her light sweater from the hook and holding it out to her.

I tried to ignore the irritation that sparked in my chest at hearing the words leave my mouth. I had done these forms over a dozen times, and there was something very wrong with that because these sorts of things shouldn't happen that often. In fact, they shouldn't happen at all.

I had been working the last two months on a new project, managing the HSE aspects of the work alongside Pari Zara, Nick

Ward, Ludo Brown, and Eduardo Montiel. Today, a contractor had accidentally opened the wrong valve and released an unknown substance to grade – and some had gotten into the sewers. To say that the situation was a mess would have been an understatement. We spent the last several hours running around the office and construction site ordering testing, implementing containment protocols, and ensuring that all personnel were safe while working with operations to try to understand what the substance might have been. Pari had already interviewed the contractor to find out what the hell had gone wrong while I had overseen rounding up everyone who had been exposed and getting them to testing.

Now that we had completed the immediately required response steps, we had less than eight hours to complete our paperwork and get it submitted to the Ministry to record the incident and provide all proper documentation. What was particularly frustrating about the spill, though, was that it had happened just at the end of the day shift, which meant that even though my day had started at 6:00 am, and it was now nearing 11:00 pm – and I should have left five hours ago – I couldn't go home. I had to get the paperwork completed and filed before the deadline, or management would have my ass, and the Ministry would slap us with a non-compliance.

And there was no one else to do it.

We had been working twelve-hour shifts, rotating one day off a week between the five of us. Nick and Ludo were out in the field monitoring the night shift, and Eduardo was at home asleep. Pari had called her babysitter hours ago to ask the girl to stay late, despite it being a school night, but just a moment ago, the girl had called to inform Pari that Amrita, Pari's daughter, had woken up puking in her sleep. I could understand Pari's hesitation to leave. She was a good woman, she worked exceptionally hard, and she didn't want to leave me here to finish the reporting alone – but what was I supposed to say?

Tell Pari that she needed to get her sixteen-year-old babysitter to suck it up and stay even later while taking care of a sick kid? That hardly seemed appropriate. Besides, I was the person most familiar with the paperwork that needed to be completed, so it made sense for her to just go home and for me to complete them on my own. I fought back a sigh as I looked at the exhausted woman before me. She had been through enough in the last two years; she deserved a break. She had lost her husband in the previous outbreak, and her mother was suffering from the first stages of dementia. She worked herself to the bone to be able to afford proper care. I knew that she was struggling to keep her life together with everything going on, and her daughter meant more to her than anything in the world.

And I knew I couldn't let her stay.

"Please, Pari," I said, stepping towards her and holding the sweater out further. "I'm asking you to go. You're not leaving me. Go home and take care of your kid. Make sure that she's set for tomorrow. I'll only stay long enough to do what's mandated; you can deal with the rest tomorrow with Eduardo when he comes in. Besides – I'm the one with the day off tomorrow, so it doesn't matter if I stay late because I can sleep in."

Pari hesitated, and I could see her searching my face for signs of resentment. "Are you sure?"

"I'm sure," I said, and she finally nodded, then finally took the sweater from my hand.

"Thank you, Delilah," Pari sighed in relief as she tied her thick dark hair into a messy bun on the top of her head. "I promise that Eduardo and I will make it up to you tomorrow by taking care of the rest. Only complete the necessary forms, promise?"

"I promise," I agreed, smiling at her as I watched her quickly pack up her purse and locate her keys from her cramped desk.

"I owe you one!" she called over her shoulder as she raced towards the exit.

"No, you don't!" I hollered back even though I knew she likely wouldn't hear it because the door was already swinging closed. Silence filled the small office as the latch of the door clicked into place, and I let out a heavy sigh. I stood there for a moment, running my hand through my hair and tilting my head up toward the ceiling as I let out an exhausted breath. "Well – I guess I better get started."

It was difficult not to groan in frustration as I began the tedious task of filling out the Ministry forms. They were long, convoluted, and half of them were entirely useless – almost as useless as the small fine that the company would receive for the spill. Everyone knew that the fine did nothing to prevent these sorts of things from happening again. Worse than that, though, was that I knew the contractor who had messed up would be hung out to dry, and that wasn't fair. Even though the incident was his fault directly, the problem was so much bigger than that, and he had been set up to fail.

The company had started the twelve-hour shifts a few weeks ago when we had fallen behind schedule due to extreme heatwaves – which, in and of itself, was ridiculous. Blazing heat in August and September had become commonplace in this area over the last two years, and yet the project planners still liked to pretend it was abnormal. So now, the shifts ran seven days a week with a night crew and a day crew. Our efficiency had dropped. Our injury rates had soared – which was not only normal, but it was to be expected, especially since a lot of the crew were picking up extra shifts to try to earn more money or to cover for their buddies when someone fell ill, or a relative died of NORVIX.

The contractor who had messed up was one of those guys.

I knew him. Well, I didn't *know* him, but I knew who he was, and I knew what he had been through. His son had cancer, his wife had died two years ago, and according to Pari, today he had been covering a shift for a friend whose wife had just passed away. The man was exhausted. He was doing what he needed to do to survive, and he had been trying to do the right thing, but he hadn't been fit for work. His foreman had allowed him on the crew regardless because he knew that the guy needed the money, and he didn't have anyone else to fill the position.

I shook my head as I began inserting images and attaching the documentation required to back up my report, knowing that this would not be the last one I would fill out before this work was over. Then, as per my habit when working alone, I popped in a single earbud and used my phone to stream the latest news.

The new Food Stamp Program has been criticized for not properly taking into consideration special needs, dietary restrictions, and marginalized groups that face greater difficulties in obtaining access to approved grocery stores. These are just a few of the growing concerns associated with the new program, the disorganized rollout, and the refusal of the federal government and UNC to clarify how long the restrictions will be in place. At this point, residents have complained that many have been turned away for not providing the proper documentation to obtain their stamps, while others have allegedly managed to get double the rations by falsifying their documentation. Authorities are looking into the matter, but at this point, there is no talk of additional security checks being put in place.'

I snorted, bitterness surging through my chest as I thought about Bob and how he was probably one of the individuals cheating the system. Honestly, most of the people that I worked with were likely culprits. Why was it that the people who had the most agency were the first ones to try to take more than their fair share? I suppose it had something to do with them never having shared before or never having struggled and gone without. The idea of being short on food was probably terrifying for them.

'Yesterday the federal government confirmed that stores are allowed to continue selling unrestricted items, as per global Bill G-1345 approved last month, but they will be required to provide full and transparent documentation to log the receipt and sale of all items that fall under the Food Stamp Program restrictions and are delivered by the Federal Agricultural Reserve.'

'Local shop owners are protesting the requirements, saying that they have not been given any hard guidelines on what is required for proper documentation and that they have not been given any auxiliary funding to cover the costs of implementing the program or installing upgraded security measures. Just last week, a local shop owner in the downtown core, who wished to remain nameless, indicated that he had purchased a gun in order to protect his business after a friend of his was robbed and his products stolen. CKPX News correspondent Mark Wong is following up on the story, and we will have more for you tomorrow.'

This was going to end in violence. As if the theft, muggings, and break-ins weren't enough, now the stores were being targeted. I could hardly blame the shop owners for feeling the need to take action, but I doubted it would go over well if that man actually shot someone.

'In addition to the controversy regarding the Food Stamp Program, the UNC has faced both criticism and praise for finally taking action in their continued battle against HUANEE and the group's violent tactics. Over the last month, the alleged environmental organization has made four more attacks, devastating infrastructure, injuring hundreds, and causing a full work stoppage at several manufacturing sites across the globe as companies struggle to address security concerns. It was one such attack that finally pushed the UNC to accept a draft proposal backed by over fifty countries which would allow authorities across the globe, including the United National Armed Forces, to arrest, detain, and question, without the need for a warrant, anyone suspected of being involved with HUANEE.'

'Many, including members of the public, are praising the 'Autonomous Defence' Bill, saying that it is high time that the UNC took action to put an end to the chaos being caused by HUANEE on a daily basis, especially coming on the heels of the organization's latest online fear-mongering.'

'After an attack that left a battery manufacturing plant on the west coast devastated, the United States formally condemned the group's actions and allocated additional resources to their defence sectors to deal with the issue. The U.S. Secretary of Defence made a live announcement just thirty minutes after the attack, in which he vowed to hunt down and prosecute every person involved.'

'The response from HUANEE was not only unexpected, given the group's usual silence when called out in the media, but it was also confusing and deeply disturbing – and it has sparked outrage across the globe. Just a few short hours after the U.S. Secretary of Defence made his announcement, HUANEE issued the following statement: "All of humanity will face holy prosecution by our god, and he will show you no mercy."'

'Many conspiracy theorists claim that this statement confirms the association of HUANEE and their symbol with that of Veles, the god of the earth from Slavic mythology. However, many other religious groups have claimed provenance as well, including an extremist church from Don Haven, who just yesterday claimed that this is confirmation of the coming of the rapture and that the symbol used by HUANEE is irrelevant.'

I paused, my hands hovering over the keys as I rolled my eyes. It certainly wasn't the first time that a religious group had made proclamations about God's wrath lurking on the horizon. Those claims have been made on the daily since NORVIX broke out. HUANEE's symbol had always tied them to Slavic mythology, but for people to think it meant anything deeper was beyond ridiculous. HUANEE's statement would undoubtedly upset people.

'In general, the claim has been widely rejected and condemned by religious groups across the globe. Many are standing in unity against the environmental group, claiming that not only is HUANEE using religion as an excuse to justify their violence, but that they are also disrespecting the Slavic pagan religion by misappropriating the symbol of Veles and tarnishing it with their acts of terrorism.'

Saw that one coming.

'As always, HUANEE refuses to answer any questions issued to the group, and all attempts to contact them have been futile, so it is unclear what they were hoping to accomplish by releasing the public statement. At this point in time, the statement has only caused more people to back the UNC and the newly proposed bill. Yet despite this, there are still many countries, lawyers, and human rights activists that are speaking out against the proposal.'
'They are concerned that the Autonomous Defence Bill was drafted too quickly, that the words are too vague, and that it lacks any substantial ties to the HUANEE situation, which could

allow governments to use it for other purposes. New Zealand's Prime Minister expressed concerns, stating that the bill is being pushed through under the guise of responding to an emergency, but that the real intent is to return overarching power back to the nations, with no accountability for law enforcement and no set end date for the dangerous capabilities that would be granted under the bill.'

'Many experts agree with the Prime Minister, noting close similarities to a bill proposed nearly ten years ago which had been very narrowly defeated by majority vote. They are urging the public, national governments, and UNC council to look past the immediate stressful conditions and to examine the bill with an unbiased eye, as they believe that the bill has nothing to do with HUANEE and is instead a step that could build the foundation for oppressive dictatorships in several UNC nations. Their concern is that, if passed, the bill could lead to selective population control efforts, a larger wealth gap, and the means for countries to push their own agendas unchallenged while diminishing the authority of the UNC.'

'Regardless of the concerns, G-1348 is pushing forward for review, and it is expected that the bill will be voted on in the upcoming weeks.'

I listened as the news anchor began to discuss the most recent tsunami in Asia that had devastated several small islands. The UNC's Global First Aid response teams were deployed to help, but as of midnight, the death toll was already in the double digits with hundreds of others missing. I thought about the attack on the battery manufacturing plant that wasn't far from here and how it seemed like the attacks were working their way up the west coast in my direction. I thought about how the Food Stamp Program and its pathetic rollout had made life so much more difficult. With the extended hours I was working, most of the restricted goods were gone by the time I got to the grocery store, and I had been left picking through the bruised and nearly spoiled food remaining.

My stomach growled as if to emphasize the point. I hadn't packed dinner, so it had been over twelve hours since I had last eaten, but given the barren condition of my fridge, I knew there would be little to eat when I got home. I had some bruised peaches and a few cans of beans left that I had been hoping to stretch for another few days. I let out a sigh as I finished the final form and uploaded it to the Ministry's reporting site. It was almost 2:00 am; it would be near 3:00 am by the time I got home, and yet, despite that, I knew I needed to force myself to go to the store first thing in the morning, or those beans might very well be the only thing I have for another full week.

"And no one will care," I sighed as the website dinged to signify that the report had been successfully uploaded.

With that done, I could go home, but completing the work had hardly felt like an accomplishment. I saved a backup copy to our server, already knowing that when I returned two days from now, my boss would probably be pissed that I had been so honest in the report. He was a fan of only giving the absolute minimum information that they asked for, and he always tried to downplay things. I was the opposite, but I would deal with that when the time came.

I gathered my belongings from my desk in silence, placing my phone in my purse and continuing to listen to the news as I grabbed the sweater that I had brought in case the office was too cool. I tried to ignore the agitation that was inching through my body as the anchor started to talk about the latest forest fire that had broken out.

There weren't many forests left to burn. Just like with the Ministry fines, decades ago, the forests used to mean something, and the fines had been significant. Humanity had started to accept responsibility for its role in the planet's decline, and the UNC was formed to govern a unified effort to change. The majority of nations joined it, and those that refused united as the Sovereign Federation a few years later. Things looked brighter for a while: firm laws were passed, and money was put into research and technology – but then, things changed again, and this time it was for the worse.

Twenty years ago, the wrong person got elected, the existing laws were removed and modified, the narrative was altered, and small wars started to break out in the countries that bordered the

Sovereign Federation. Priorities shifted. Scientific research was silenced, misinformation became commonplace, and the inequality in wealth and resources had grown so large that it became an unavoidable conclusion that someone had decided only certain pockets of humanity deserved to survive.

Perhaps someone in charge had realized that the UNC's efforts weren't enough, that even though the majority of the world had unified and were attempting to change – it still wasn't sufficient to save us, and so they sought to pin the blame on our so-called 'enemy'. It grew worse as resources became more scarce and the pilot projects to improve wildlife and ocean health failed. Fear was transformed into a tool, the most effective weapon in the UNC's arsenal – once people were sufficiently afraid, they became blind to the erosion of their principles.

That – or they didn't have it in them to care anymore.

Everything was falling apart, and I could feel my body beginning to sag under the weight of the voice in my ear as I left the small office and made my way toward the gates. I tried to keep my face impassive as I waved goodnight to the new security guards and pushed my way through the turnstile. The company had hired them after the HUANEE attacks had started, and they were nice people, but as I said goodnight, I only felt the uneasy knot in my stomach grow tighter. I tried to focus on my steps, pushing down the wave of emotion that seemed to be brewing beneath the surface as I navigated my way through the cars toward the eastern lot where I had left my vehicle.

It was hot, and my clothes were already sticking to my skin as I moved. I could have just left my sweater behind because there was no way I would need it tomorrow. The air felt stagnant and dead; I could hear the thrumming noise of construction behind me and the dull buzzing of the old lights that lit up the pathway. If these changes to the weather kept up, soon autumn would no longer be a season, and we would go straight from scorching hot summers to dry, freezing cold winters in the blink of an eye.

I stared at the abandoned garden beds that lined the path and felt my heart sink further as the news anchor droned on about the war in the east and how UNSA had still not managed to regain communication with the Viking Outpost. The Prospect was growing closer, and the crew was doing everything that they could to remain optimistic, but UNSA had already started to prepare a new shuttle with additional supplies because they suspected the worst. A long time ago, the company used to plant flowers in the garden beds in the spring, and they would last throughout the summer. Now, flower gardens were a thing of the past. No one bothered with them, and I wasn't sure that I could remember what they looked like.

The grass was brown and mostly dead during the summer – and that was assuming that there was any grass at all. Most people had taken to transforming their entire yards, if they were lucky enough to have one, into crowded vegetable gardens in an attempt to provide food for their families. Often the effort was in vain; most seeds didn't grow because of their modified genes, and even if you could manage to sprout some life in the hot and barren soil, people would steal it from your yard – if the animals didn't get it first.

The number of times that I had seen people chasing ragged-looking rabbits and rats from their yards with a shovel was unbelievable. City police were swamped by calls of violence and burglary. Theft had become so common that even I had taken to placing a pole in the sliding door of my balcony after my apartment complex reported several break-ins.

People were getting desperate.

I frowned as I reached my car, my heart aching in pain as thoughts of my last encounter with Ren floated to the front of my mind. I hadn't seen her since July when we had played that stupid game. I had talked to her once on the phone since, but her schedule at the hospital was busy, and with my twelve-hour shifts, we hadn't been able to meet up. The uneasy feeling between us had remained, and while I didn't like being on bad terms with her, I had no idea how to fix it.

My car barely started when I turned it over; I needed to replace it, but I didn't have the money to do so. To be honest – I had sort of figured that the world would be over before my car died, but listening to it run now, I realized that I had been wrong. I let out a sigh as I removed the earbud from my ear and turned on the radio to listen to the news from my car. I didn't bother trying to turn on the AC – I knew it would be a death sentence for the old vehicle – and instead, I just rolled the windows down the few inches they were still capable of moving as I tried to breathe. I didn't know if it was the heat or just the exhaustion, but as I drove from the parking lot and out onto the dark road, I could feel my lungs starting to sting with pain.

Usually, I found the drive home relaxing. Being alone in my car away from work and the intense heat of the city tended to calm my soul. I liked to take the old country road that headed northwest and twisted through the last of the forest that surrounded our city. It was quiet, the road was nearly always empty, and I enjoyed the ride. Yet today, as I switched on my blinker and turned onto the dark old road, I felt my chest tighten even more.

I tried to ignore it for the first kilometre as the news anchor gave an update on the latest failed NORVIX vaccine trials. I tried to fight against the uneasy feeling that continued to grow in the pit of my stomach as my hands started to twitch against the steering wheel. I swallowed hard, clenching my teeth as the urge to vomit rushed through my body.

It didn't make any sense. There was nothing significant about today, nothing to make me feel this way, and yet the longer I drove and the farther I got into the woods, the more and more it felt like my heart was breaking in my chest. I inhaled sharply as a stabbing pain shot through my lungs and radiated down my spine. I fought to keep my hands steady as I blinked, and to my horror, I realized that I was crying.

"Stop it," I whispered, my voice quivering as my bottom lip began to tremble. I hadn't cried in years. I never allowed it, and yet the harder I tried to push it all down, the more water streamed down my face. "Stop it."

That sick and twisted feeling was growing, and along with it, a surge of fear, panic, and anger rocked through my body as everything that I had been obsessing about for the last few months flooded my mind in one single wave. I covered my mouth as a sob left my lungs, and I fought the urge to vomit as I gagged behind my hand. I hated this. I hated all of it. Everything.

Everyone. I didn't want to be here. I didn't want to live this life, and I didn't want to have to get up and do it all again tomorrow.

What was the point?

What was I waiting for?

Was I waiting to legitimately starve? Was I waiting until the Prospect Mission landed, and we found out whether the colony would be a success? Was I waiting for the war to move across the ocean, to leave no escape at all? Or was I just hoping to die in the next NORVIX outbreak? Had I truly wanted them to find a cure? I didn't know... and the answer to the question made me gag as a second sob left my body.

Or was I secretly holding on to some tiny shred of hope that Ren was right, and people still had a future?

I struggled to breathe as my vision started to blur. I could just barely see the clouded white wisps that were forming across the road, and my eyes narrowed. We don't usually get fog in this area at this time of year, though this road was notoriously bad for it in the spring. A disturbed laugh left my lips as I started to smile, and I gripped the steering wheel tight with both hands once more.

"Of course," I choked out.

Why wouldn't this happen now? Why was I even surprised anymore by the way the weather behaved? I could see the fog growing thicker, extending up into the night and making it nearly impossible to see. A part of me hoped that I might just crash and die so that I wouldn't have to deal with this anymore.

The radio began to crackle. I could feel the hairs at the base of my skull prickle as cool air washed over my skin. I forced myself to breathe, one breath in, one deep exhale out as I slowed the car and tried to navigate through the mist, but it only got worse. I switched my headlights to the fog setting to try to increase my visibility, and then it dawned on me that I was shivering and that the cool air was now cold.

My brow knitted together in confusion, my panic attack almost nearly forgotten as I squinted into the fog while trying to figure out what the hell was going on. The weather reports, while often inaccurate, had not mentioned anything about a high-pressure system moving through our area, and I felt my already rapid heart begin to beat more anxiously. I couldn't see a thing past twenty feet ahead, and I would need to stop and wait for the fog to clear. Switching on my hazard lights and hoping that they still worked, I continued to slow – then my body seized with fear as something massive darted across the road.

"*Shit!*" I slammed on the brakes, my poor old car skidding to a noisy halt as I narrowly avoided hitting the huge deer that darted into the treeline on my right.

I gripped the wheel tight, my heart in my throat as I managed to swerve onto the shoulder and avoid crashing into the ditch. It had all happened so fast that I barely took any of it in. I stared dumbfounded at the illuminated white mist before me, trying to remember to breathe as my body started to shake once more. Then a low groan came from the front of my car, and the headlights flickered.

"Oh no," I whispered, as the lights suddenly went out and my rattled mind realized what had happened. "No – no, no, no, no, no!"

Without pausing to think, I tried to restart the car. It whined once, the lights and radio briefly came to life before going out completely once more.

"Please," I groaned as desperation filled my voice. My hands shook as I tried to turn the car over again. "*Please* – please don't die. Come on – please!"

This time only a pathetic groan left the engine before I was surrounded by silence, and I knew the giant hunk of metal was finally dead.

"SHIT!" I smacked the steering wheel in frustration, knotting my hands into my hair before my safety instincts took over. I put the car in park, then reached over to the passenger side and grabbed my purse from the floor. Without hesitating, I pulled out my phone and then exited the vehicle.

In just a few short steps, I made it to the trunk of my car, and I began pulling out my roadside flares and reflectors. I knew it wouldn't do much in this thick fog, but it was better than nothing, and it might stop someone from rear-ending me in the rare chance that anyone else came down this road at two in the morning.

With the faint amber glow of my flare radiating by my back wheel, I quickly made my way to the front of the car and popped the hood open. I had no idea what I was looking for, I wasn't a mechanic, but I knew that the steam and smoke that puffed out of the engine wasn't a good thing. I groaned in annoyance as I looked at the rusty and battered innards of my now dead car. It was honestly a miracle that the thing had lasted as long as it did, and I had no idea what I was going to do to get to work now. Maybe I could pay Pari or Eduardo to pick me up. They didn't live close, but until my next paycheck came in and I could afford to buy a new beater car, I didn't have many other options.

"I can't believe this," I murmured, glaring toward the edge of the road where the deer had run off.

It was nowhere to be seen, which was to be expected. The news had reported that a small herd of whitetail deer had moved into the area after their habitat several kilometres away had been destroyed, but after the federal government had lifted several of the hunting bans this past month to try to help combat the food shortages, I hadn't been expecting to see any. I had assumed that they would all be dead by now. It wasn't like it used to be when deer were common in this area, and this road was notorious for collisions with them in the spring and autumn.

Now, most of the new generations had never even seen a deer in person.

Knowing that there was nothing I could do to fix my car, I begrudgingly closed the hood and leaned back against it before pulling my phone from my pocket and dialling Ren's number. I did it on instinct, but as the ringer started to sound, I felt my muscles grow tight with anticipation once more.

Would it be weird talking to her again, as it was the last time? She had always told me to call her if I had trouble with my car – she knew it was a wreck, and she was convinced the thing was a death trap – but that was before our last get-together. I knew she would be up because she was working night shifts at the hospital this week, but today was her day off. I clenched my jaw as the phone rang two more times, and I started to wonder if her offer still stood while our friendship felt so fragile. Just when I was debating hanging up, I heard the familiar click of her phone connecting and then her voice sounded in my ear.

"Lilah," Ren said, her voice laced with concern. "What's going on?"

"Hey, Ren," I said as I shivered in the cold breeze that grazed my body. The wind was starting to pick up, and my thin old blouse was doing little to keep me warm as it rippled against my skin. "I'm on Line 31 – I nearly hit a deer, and my car won't start. I was just wondering if you–"

I paused. I could hear the sound of my own voice echoing distortedly in the speaker as Ren's voice rang out in chopped pieces from my phone.

"Lilah? – I can't hear you – Lilah, what's going on?"

I frowned, lowering my phone to glance at it and check the signal. I still had three bars, and I knew that there was service in this area.

"I nearly hit a deer," I repeated as I pushed off my car and brought the phone back up to my ear. I started walking down the road, hoping that maybe I was just in a weird zone, but everything still sounded terrible another twenty feet away. I could barely hear her words as I began to repeat myself yet again. "I'm on the 31, and I think that my–"

My phone beeped, and the call dropped entirely.

"Seriously?" I groaned, my shoulders dropping in defeat as I looked at the old and battered phone. It was almost as useless as my car.

I knew this was probably my fault as the device was ancient, but I had put off buying a new one because it still worked, and I was trying not to be wasteful. I felt my face fall – apparently, good intentions meant nothing, and all my possessions were determined to fail me tonight. I tried redialing twice more, but the phone disconnected and dropped both calls before a 'no service' signal flashed in the corner of the screen.

"But of course," I whispered, feeling a burning sensation at the back of my throat as my eyes started to sting. I could feel myself unravelling as I grew overwhelmed. The same uneasy anxiety that had hit me before the fog was trying to take hold once more, but this time it came with a dark and deeply seated rage splitting through my chest. "I hate this."

The words came out as a hoarse whisper, and I felt the anger start to grow. My hand was gripping my phone so tightly that my knuckles were white, and I didn't even realize that the air had grown even colder until I saw my breath crystalize before my face. I jerked as the wind tugged at my clothes, and I heard something move in the forest to my right – and it was at that moment that I realized… I was alone.

Alone on an old and nearly abandoned road that no one took. Alone at two-thirty in the morning, in the dark, standing twenty feet from my car. I shivered, my skin covered with goosebumps as the fear washed through my body. The wind was still blowing through the trees, and I could barely see them moving in the thickening fog, but the air was entirely quiet, and they weren't making any sound as they swayed. Wrapping my arms around my body, I made my way back to my car as the uneasy feeling continued to grow.

I didn't want to be here.

Something wasn't right.

I couldn't explain the feeling as it shifted down my spine and sank deep into my bones. Maybe I was just overtired. Maybe Ren was right, and I was pushing myself too hard – but I had been exhausted all my life; I was familiar with the feeling, and *this* was not that. This was something else.

As I reached the front of my car, the flare at the rear flickered out, and I froze in the darkness. The hair at the base of my skull prickled, and my pulse began to quicken. That flare was company issued – it was waterproof, and it was supposed to burn for hours. A cold chill ran down my spine as suddenly it felt as if a million eyes were watching me from all directions. Then, the wind shifted, and I heard a low clicking noise drifting through the air. It sounded like a tap – as if someone or something was knocking two small pieces of wood together – but it was coming from all directions. I forced myself to look to the side, my eyes wide with fear as they scanned along the edge of the road through the fog, looking for any sign of movement.

There was nothing.

I desperately wanted to believe that there was nothing wrong. That the fear was just a manifestation of my earlier panic attack and that I was being ridiculous. I wanted to believe that everything was fine and that I shouldn't be afraid. Nothing would happen here. There were no animals or people in these woods, and everything was fine. Yet no matter how rational I tried to be, I could feel the panic taking hold.

I don't want to be here.

The thought entered my mind for a second time, and it was so deep and instinctual it was as if every bone and muscle in my body was telling me to get as far away from here as possible. My legs moved before I could think, and suddenly I was desperately grabbing at the handle of my car door. I could feel terror building in my chest, clouding my mind and my thoughts as I desperately struggled to get back inside my car – but the door wouldn't open. It was locked, and in the back of my mind, I knew that didn't make sense, but my ability to reason was nearly gone.

My eyes darted around through the darkness once more as my hands began to shake, and the low clicking noise shifted into a deep rattle.

My gaze locked to the partially opened window, and without pausing to think, I pressed myself up against the side of the car and jammed my hand inside. My muscles strained, my fingers stretched, but no matter how I turned myself, I couldn't seem to get the angle right, and my fingers could only brush against the old lock. My heart started to race dangerously fast; each breath was clouding before my face, and I knew I was on the verge of hyperventilating. I could hear something buried within the noise of the now rustling leaves, something within the deep rattle that seemed to be growing louder and louder with every violent thump of my heart.

It was a murmur. A whisper. Low, angry, and dark. I couldn't make out the words; they didn't sound like any languages that I knew, but hearing them made every muscle in my body stiffen with terror. It grated on my nerves. My face cringed in pain. I forced myself tighter against the car, my nails scratching against the fabric of the interior in another failed attempt to unlock the door.

I'm going to die here.

The thought hit me like a physical blow, and before I even knew what I was doing I yanked my arm from the window. I felt the skin tear, but my mind didn't register the pain as I took off down the road sprinting as fast as I could. My legs ached from the effort, and my lungs burned as they worked harder than they had in years. I could feel tears streaming down my face as the low whispered words grew louder and louder and louder until they were like a heart beating inside my skull, possessing my soul with dread.

My foot caught against the ground, and my arms flew out before me as I went down hard. I groaned out in pain as my face scraped across the asphalt, my thin blouse doing nothing to protect the skin on my arms as I skidded across the rough surface and shredded the material. Wheezing in pain, I struggled onto my knees. The air had grown so cold that my entire body was trembling, and my cramped muscles were starting to seize. Grunting audibly, I struggled to my feet and prepared to run again, only to stop instantly as my eyes locked onto the massive creature that was standing before me.

I couldn't move.

I couldn't breathe.

My brain failed to process the sight as my legs grew limp. I collapsed to my knees once more. Every muscle in my body screamed at me to run as a sickening wave of nausea rolled through my stomach. My head tilted back, taking in the shape of the creature. It was haloed by fog, surrounded by a dim flickering light. It was the deer that I had almost hit, but it wasn't a deer at all. It was something else entirely, and there was something wrong with it – something deeply and horribly wrong.

There were claws on its feet where there should have been hooves. Its legs were too long, and its antlers were massive, twisted and warped. I could feel the sound of every breath it took rattling through my chest like a raging storm. It was staring at me, two glowing red eyes fixed to my face, and I felt my mouth fall open in horror and awe. I couldn't speak. I couldn't do anything. This was something from a nightmare – something that could only exist in the depths of hell and something that no one should ever see. I could smell death clinging to its body, see blood dripping from its shoulder as it took a step towards me, and I saw its full face.

All of it was wrong.

Unnatural and grotesque. Its eyes were too large, its teeth were too sharp, and as it opened its mouth, I realized that the horrible whisper that was building in my mind was coming from its lungs. Every survival alarm I had went off in my head as it moved again and started to close the distance. I wanted to run. I tried to scream, but I had yet to inhale since first seeing it, and I only managed to choke out a faint, strangled noise as a distorted and ghastly sound came from the abomination's mouth.

My blood ran cold.

I could feel something turbulent and insidious growing in the pit of my stomach. Not a single coherent thought crossed my mind as the beast's hellfire gaze consumed my soul. Something was moving through me, eating into my skin and burrowing into my brain. I could feel it like a splinter, raw, infected, festering. Its head grew closer; it was leaning down now, and something was reaching out toward me. It was so close I could see a thin white scar that traced down the center of its forehead.

The thrum of its voice was inescapable, and it grew like a great raging river. I felt something hot touch the center of my forehead. A third red eye opened wide inches before my face. Then an agonizing scream left my lips.

Red.

It was all I could see.

It was all I could hear.

I could taste it in my mouth like the bitter tang of metal and blood as every nerve in my body was simultaneously set on fire.

And then... there was nothing.

Nothing at all.

Officer Wilson

OCTOBER

Warmth. It was all I could feel. It surrounded my body like a
cocoon, safe, secure and whole. I wanted to snuggle into it deeper.
I wanted to lay there forever, it was peaceful, and I was content
in a way that I had never felt before. I couldn't seem to move my
body. It was too heavy, but I didn't care; I was comfortable. I was
enjoying the feeling of floating in and out of a beautiful daze while
my soul felt lighter than air. I couldn't make anything out – no
images or dreams. Just warmth and soft colours as my heart
calmly thumped away in the depths of my chest. Then I heard
something, and it seemed to penetrate through the warmth and
reach my absent mind.

It was quiet and soft like a whisper.

'*A voice*', my brain murmured as I continued to drift.

It sounded again, somewhere off to the side and out of reach.
It was like it existed in another realm, and I didn't have proper
access to it. I couldn't quite grab onto it or understand the words
it was saying, I just knew that I liked the sound of it because it
was familiar and comforting. My mind slipped away from me
once more, and I drifted in silence until I heard voices again, but
this time they sounded louder and different. I realized that I must
be waking up, from what I wasn't sure, but my brain was starting

to function once more, and questions were filling my head. I could feel my limbs shifting against something cool, and I knew that I was partially reclined.

"You're here for Lilah–"

The voice cut out, but I didn't mind. I didn't want to listen to it. I didn't know this voice, and I wanted to go back to the quiet.

"Yes – driving down 31 – hit a deer–"

My pulse spiked.

The words pierced into my brain like fire. Red and black shapes warped through my mind and inched down my spine like poison. My throat was burning. My limbs were trembling. The beautiful calm that I had felt was gone, and I could feel panic building in my chest as something else twisted in my gut. It was hot, angry, and violent. It tasted like battery acid and smelled like burning flesh. I gagged and choked as images of the deer took shape in my mind.

Not the deer, I begged. Not that *thing* – please, no.

But my brain latched onto the word like it was an obsession, and all I could see was the creature's grotesque face. The smell of its breath was on my skin. The freezing cold air was making me shiver. Burning white-hot anger surged inside me – but it wasn't mine – it was too wild, too large, and too impossibly hot. I was going to die. It was going to consume me and burn me alive. I could feel it scorching across my lungs and cutting through my bones as my heart blackened and burned under the immense heat.

I couldn't breathe.

Angry images rolled through my head like a silent movie. Death, blood, horror, destruction, and a massive explosion – but everything was disjointed and broken as if I were glimpsing through time at random, disconnected intervals. I saw temples and forests, symbols I didn't recognize and things that no longer existed. I saw fires and tall buildings, darkness and the sky – then two bright flashing lights. I instantly knew it was a car, and as it came hurtling into view, I saw my own terrified face behind the wheel, and my heart stuttered violently in my chest. My body convulsed; I shot up in bed, reaching out for something to grab onto as my eyes flew open. I hissed out in pain at the bright offending lights, and a ragged gasp left my lungs. It felt like something had just punched me in the gut and broken all my ribs.

"Is that normal?" A deep and unfamiliar voice sounded to my left. "Is she alright?"

"Sir, please wait outside the door."

The sound of moving feet echoed in my ears as I continued to wheeze and tried to cover my eyes.

"Should I call the doctor?"

"Just let the nurse at the front desk know she's awake – Ms. Eldritch?" The unfamiliar voice sounded close to my left. "Ms. Eldritch – just breathe, it's okay. You're okay."

The bright lights dimmed, the dull murmur of noise to my left disappeared, and I felt my body fall back against something soft as my bleary eyes cracked open once more. Everything hurt. My body ached. I panted as I desperately looked around and tried to figure out what the hell was going on, but I couldn't seem to get my eyes to work properly.

"Where am I?" The words instinctively fell from my mouth, but even I knew that they sounded wrong. Everything was distorted, deeper, and ragged. It wasn't my voice, and I cringed at the noise. I sounded like I had not spoken in years and like I had aged several decades on top of that.

"You're at the hospital." The same voice that had spoken my name answered calmly, and I felt someone moving at my side. My head jerked to the left as something touched me and the contact burned against my skin. "Slow down; you're okay."

My stomach rolled, and I closed my eyes tight, forcing myself to inhale several times before I finally tried cracking my eyes open once more. I could see white in the dull light, lots of it. The walls were white, the ceiling was white, the sheets wrapped around my body were white, but standing just to the left and blocking my view of the glass door was a woman wearing soft pink scrubs.

"Ms. Eldritch," she said, her voice soft as she gently touched my arm once more. I resisted the urge to hiss out in pain as I pulled my arm away and slowly lifted my head to meet the woman's gaze. "Can you hear me?"

"Yes," I breathed, nodding my head.

"Ms. Eldritch," the woman said deliberately slowly. "You were in an accident. Do you remember your full name?"

I stared at her, my narrowed gaze taking in the calm and professional look on her face. She was short and thin. Her skin was tanned, her hair was dark, and her eyes were a deep warm brown that radiated kindness. She was holding a clipboard and looking at me expectantly, but every so often, her eyes would shift to the information showing on the screen to my left. I could just now hear the faint beeping as my pulse finally started to level out.

"Delilah Danya Eldritch," I said, inhaling once more and forcing the air out more slowly. "I remember."

"Very good." The woman smiled, and it appeared to be genuine as she ticked something on her chart.

She told me that her name was Maggy Gill and that my NORVIX test had come back clean, so I was on the secure side of the hospital. Then she quickly rechecked my vitals and did something to the machine to stop the annoying beeping noise before she turned her attention back to me and helped me sit up more comfortably. I fought against the pain of her touch and breathed a quiet sigh of relief as she finally removed her hands from my body. Then she asked me to recite my birthday and home address, running through a string of questions as I insisted to her that I was fine and knew exactly who I was.

I waited patiently as she looked at my eyes, then moved her finger back and forth and told me to follow it. I did it, but I could feel a dull headache forming at the base of my skull as I concentrated on completing the task. Then I complied when she asked me to look at a marker on the wall for thirty seconds before returning my gaze to her finger.

She asked me a few more simple questions, then shone a penlight in my eyes to check for pupil dilation. I hissed in pain as she did it, the dull ache at the back of my mind flaring angrily as the light scorched my retinas – but thankfully, she reported that my eyes were working normally. Though that didn't rule out having a mild concussion. I nodded in understanding, letting out another sigh of relief as she switched off the light then asked me a few more questions about the date and the year. When she was finally done and had captured her notes on the chart, she paused and met my gaze with another warm and caring stare.

"Ms. Eldritch," Maggy said, her voice calm. "Do you remember what happened before you got here?"

"I – I was driving, and I–," I faltered as my head throbbed and my eyes pinched in pain.

I could still taste the battery acid in my mouth; I could still feel the heated anger burning in my chest like a wildfire. My heart was starting to race again, and Nurse Maggy was watching me as she patiently waited for me to continue – but I didn't. I just sat there staring at her.

"It's okay, take your time," she said, giving me a reassuring smile. "Just tell me what you remember."

I swallowed hard, struggling to get my brain to work and figure out what to do. Remembering wasn't the problem. I knew *exactly* what had happened, or at least I thought I did, but I wasn't about to say it. Even now, with my head pounding, my chest on fire, and my mind spinning, I knew that if I told this woman what I thought had happened to me, she would think that I was crazy. She would order a psych evaluation, and I would be stuck here while they ran a bunch of tests. No one would ever believe me, and I wasn't sure that I believed myself, but I knew that I didn't want to say anything that would extend my stay in this hospital any longer than necessary. So, I did the only thing I could do.

I lied.

"I remember driving," I repeated, watching her face carefully as I spoke. "It was dark – and late. I took the old highway, Line 31, like I always do, and a deer ran out in front of my car. I – I think I almost hit it. I don't remember anything after that."

I tried to ignore the cold shudder that ran through my body as memories of red glowing eyes floated through my head. I tried to ignore the sickening pull through my gut as the murmur that I had heard in the dark started to fill my mind like a low whisper.

"Very good," Nurse Maggy said, looking almost proud that I could remember so much. "Things might be a bit fuzzy over the next few days, so don't try to force anything, okay? That said, your eyes, verbal, and motor responses are excellent. They did a CT scan when you first came in and everything looked normal, but the doctor will be in shortly to go over it with you and ask you some questions. You were very lucky, Ms. Eldritch. The team that brought you in said that it was quite a crash, but most of the mess belonged to the deer, so aside from the minor laceration on your head, you're completely uninjured."

My hand reflexively reached up to my head as she uttered the words, and I felt the soft cotton bandages that were wrapped around my forehead.

"Don't worry." Nurse Maggy nodded toward my head. "It only needed four stitches, and it should heal up nicely with minimal scarring."

"Okay," I said, my hand dropping back to the bed. "Thank you."

"Of course," she said, smiling at me.

The dull whispers in my mind were growing louder, but I fought to keep my face calm and my heart steady as I stared at Nurse Maggy. She was writing something on my chart, but at a soft knock on the door, she glanced behind her and then let out a barely audible sigh of annoyance.

"Ms. Eldritch, there is a police officer here who will need to ask you a few questions," she said, turning back to face me once more. I tensed at her words, and she must have noticed because she gave me a reassuring look. "Don't worry; your toxicology came back clean as a whistle. This is just routine. He needs to get your statement so he can fill out his paperwork regarding your accident, and he will let you know about your car and the deer. It shouldn't take more than a minute, but I won't let him in here until the doctor clears you, no matter how many times he knocks."

There was another soft knock before the faint sound of footsteps echoed outside the door, and Maggy shook her head.

"Ignore him," she said as she double-checked her chart. "I miss the days where they weren't allowed to be in here. This is a hospital, not a precinct. He's probably just annoyed that he decided to stay and wait for you to wake up, but that's his own fault. Usually, they just have us call them in situations like this to let them know when the patient is conscious and ready to answer questions – but I think he may have flagged you. Don't worry, I'll tighten up the ties on the back of your gown before he gets in here to hide that tattoo, or I'm sure he'll be a real prick and try to use it as grounds to yank you out of here for questioning. Okay, I'll go see what's keeping the doctor – sit tight."

"Tattoo?" I whispered, watching as she closed the door behind her.

I didn't have any tattoos. I had always wanted one as a teen, but that interest fell by the wayside when the world started falling apart. It hardly seemed like an important thing on which to spend money when people were dying left, right, and center. I had long since stopped thinking about it. I stared at the door for a long moment, my brain trying and failing to work out why she would think that I had a tattoo. My gaze dropped down to my lap, and I stared at my hands. They looked like mine, mostly, but there was something about them that was off. Yet I couldn't put my finger on it. I moved them slowly and watched the way that they shifted as my heart began to beat more quickly.

I could hear the dull whisper in my mind getting louder again as my gaze narrowed further at the long thin digits, and then it hit me – they were longer, much longer, and they were not skeletal thin as they had been the previous day. I swallowed nervously, twitching each finger and frowning at the unfamiliar appendages. I wasn't sure what to make of it. Was my memory of my body wrong, or had they truly changed?

I had just reached for the neck of my gown, intending to try to find this alleged tattoo, when the door to the room opened, and my head snapped toward the sound. A tall, handsome man walked in with Nurse Maggy and quickly closed the door behind them, probably to keep the officer who was waiting outside at bay. I wasn't sure what I had done to get flagged, given that my toxicology was apparently clean, but I wasn't stupid; I knew that being flagged wasn't a good thing.

I pushed the thoughts away, forcing my addled mind to focus on the man before me. I needed to pass whatever tests he gave me so I could get out of here as quickly as possible and figure out what the hell was going on. My gaze trailed over his body, he was wearing a white coat, and the smile on his face was kind despite the dark bags under his eyes. He probably worked a ridiculous number of hours here at this hospital, and yet, like Ren, he still looked happy.

"Ms. Eldritch," he said, his voice warm as he picked up my chart and quickly scanned over the information. "I'm Doctor Davis. I've been your attending physician since you came in. It seems like you had quite the night – you're very lucky that your injuries are so minor. Maggy says that you remember everything up until hitting the deer and all of your personal information, which is excellent. It can take a bit of time for memories to come back into focus, and sometimes people don't remember anything about their accidents or the day surrounding the event, so this is great news. Does your head hurt, or is anything else foggy?"

"No," I answered, watching as he nodded and put the chart back in the holder at the end of my bed. "I'm fine."

I remained motionless as he pulled out his stethoscope and slid the cold metal against my skin under the thin medical gown. Then I did exactly as he asked when he asked it, taking deep breaths and answering his questions as he slowly checked me over. I tried to ignore the continued tightness across my chest and the dull whisper in my mind as he ran through everything that Nurse Maggy had already asked – but in a different order – and I answered the new questions he added to try and trip me up. His attempts didn't work. I was fully conscious and entirely lucid. Thus I understood perfectly that the strange feelings I was experiencing were all in my head, because my vitals were fine, and he didn't mention there being signs of anything wrong.

"A bit of light sensitivity," Dr. Davis murmured after I had flinched at the light that he shone into my eyes. His gaze traced over my face for a moment before he took a step back. "You could have a mild concussion. Your CT scan was normal, there was no major trauma, just the minor laceration and some bruising, which should heal in a few days. Given the state that you came in, I'm surprised at how well you're doing now and how much you remember. I wasn't expecting you to wake up so quickly or be completely coherent."

"I really am fine, Dr. Davis," I said, sitting up a little straighter. "I feel great."

He smiled, shaking his head as if something about my words was amusing. Then he stared at me a moment longer before continuing.

"That may be, but I'll order some additional testing just to be safe," he said, and I fought the urge to frown. "But in the meantime, no screen time and lots of sleep. If you experience any dizziness, nausea, slurred speech, vomiting, fatigue, double vision, headaches, or memory loss over the next few weeks, make sure that you come back in right away. I'll have you stay overnight just in case, but we should be able to discharge you tomorrow morning. I'm going to recommend that you take the next week off work and I'll write you a note to cover it. Technically, based on your current status and our new procedures, I'm supposed to clear you to speak to the officer outside – but I can ask him to come back tomorrow instead."

"No," I said, shaking my head. "I feel fine, and I'd rather just get it out of the way."

"Alright," Dr. Davis said, though he sounded a bit hesitant. "Then I recommend that you have either myself, Nurse Maggy, or your emergency contact present with you for the conversation. I suspect she wouldn't want it any other way; she's been lingering here all night waiting to make sure that you're alright."

"Wait," I said, disbelief crawling into my voice as I fought the urge to squirm in discomfort at the heat growing in my body. "Ren is here?"

"Yes." He smiled, his eyes warming as he watched the realization form across my face. "She followed the ambulance in – I'll let her explain it to you, but she's been here all night helping out around the station and waiting by your bed for you to wake up. I had to all but drag her away this afternoon to go eat. Otherwise, she would have been here when you woke up."

"That sounds like her," I murmured, a small breath leaving my lips. With the strain that surrounded our relationship, a part of me had thought that she might not come, but evidently, I was wrong, and Ren was even more forgiving and compassionate than I had given her credit for.

"She's in the lunchroom right now," Nurse Maggy said. "I'll take out your IV, then go get her."

"I can do that," Dr. Davis offered, picking up the clipboard once more to add a few final notes. "I'm about to go on break anyway. I'll make sure she gets in here before I give the officer the all-clear."

I watched him initial the bottom of the chart as Nurse Maggy began to remove the IV from my arm. He paused after he put the clipboard back into the holder and turned around to look at me again.

"It's nice to finally meet you, Ms. Eldritch," Dr. Davis said after he seemed to hesitate for a moment. "Ren has told me a lot about you, though I wish I could have met you for the first time under better circumstances. Well – I'll go let her know you're okay."

"It's nice to meet you, too," I said, and he smiled warmly before leaving the room.

My brow creased as I watched him close the door, and I fought not to hiss in pain as Nurse Maggy touched my skin. Ren had never mentioned a doctor to me, and I had never heard the name Davis before – at least not that I could recall. I frowned, the uneasy feeling in my chest expanding as I tried to figure out why the interaction had felt so odd. It hadn't been unprofessional by any means, but it had almost felt personal. As if he knew Ren as more than a coworker, and for some reason that just made my discomfort grow. We told each other everything, or at least we used to, so if he was close enough to her to know about me and to feel the need to greet me in such a way – then why hadn't she said anything?

"There, all set." Nurse Maggy's words jolted me from my thoughts, and I turned to see that she was reaching up to adjust the ties of my hospital gown. She met my gaze with a careful look, then dropped her voice low as she pulled the gown up higher and tied the ties tighter. "I never ask questions about people's personal lives or what they do with their time. Not only is it against hospital protocol, but it's none of my business. My job is to treat the people who come in here regardless of who they are or what they do – I don't care what laws the UNC has passed or plans to pass; that's the oath that I took as a health care provider, and I plan to uphold that. I know that Dr. Davis and the other staff in this hospital feel the same way, so you don't need to worry. No one here will say anything, and nothing has been documented in your file because it is irrelevant to your medical history."

Nurse Maggy paused as she finished tying the last string, and then her voice dropped even lower.

"Don't let that officer intimidate you," Nurse Maggy said as she met my gaze with a serious stare. "The bill hasn't been passed yet, and he has no grounds to question you on anything. He is here to take your statement and talk to you about the accident only. You're not obligated to tell him anything else, and I suggest that you don't. As Dr. Davis said, we'll make sure he doesn't come in until Ren gets here, and she'll make sure that he sticks to protocol. She's been through this before with other patients, so she'll know if he is fishing."

"Okay," I said, nodding to the kind woman. I didn't understand what she was driving at, and I had no idea what she was referring to with something not being noted in my file, but from the intensity of her tone, I knew to take it seriously. "Can I go to the washroom?"

"Of course." Nurse Maggy smiled at me and took a step back to help me from the bed.

It was all I could do not to scream out in pain as I let the woman help me from the bed and lead me to the small adjoining room. I waited, my body tense with anticipation as she showed me where the panic button was in case I needed help. Then she made sure that I was standing steady before she finally left, and I was able to close the door. The second it clicked shut, I locked it and sucked in a sharp and ragged inhale of pain – but it wasn't just from her touch.

Moving hurt, but not with any sort of normal pain that I could describe. Instead, it was as if my body felt wrong. As if it wasn't truly mine, and my brain was driving an unfamiliar rental corpse. I stumbled my way to the sink, my hands immediately going to the taps and cranking on the cold water as my urge to cool the burning heat that was surging through my body became unbearable. I dropped my head and drank directly from the faucet, but no matter how much I drank, the burning heat in the center of my body remained. I gave up when I couldn't drink anymore and resolved to just ignore the awful sensation that seemed to be a permanent feature of this strange body. Then I finally raised my head to look at my reflection in the mirror, and what I saw made my heart stutter in my chest.

It was me, and yet it wasn't.

I looked less thin and less pallid. Yet there was a distinctly ashen undertone to my skin that left me looking sickly. I stared at my reflection, wondering if my irises had always been that large and if my ears had always been that pointed. Why did I look like myself while I simultaneously looked and felt like an entirely different person?

The bandages wrapped around my head didn't help, and it made me wonder where the injury was. Was it on the side or on my forehead? I frowned, watching my oddly unfamiliar face shift. It was hard not to stare at it, but I forced myself to look away. I would deal with my bizarre appearance and the head wound later. Right now, there was something much more pressing. I didn't need to use the washroom; I came in here because I needed to figure out why Nurse Maggy was worried about my gown. Without hesitating, I undid the top tie and ripped the long fabric over my head until I was left shirtless before the mirror, staring in disbelief.

"How did this happen?"

The words were barely a whisper from my lips as I stared at the vivid black ink that marked my skin, and I instantly understood *exactly* why the nurse had told me she would help me hide it. There, on my chest, spanning across my sternum, was the symbol of HUANEE. The shape was unmistakable, and it would be recognizable by anyone who saw it – and hiding it would be difficult given that the points extended up past my collarbones.

My legs started to shake as my vision blurred with tears of panic, and I gripped the sink to prevent myself from falling over.

How had this gotten there? Who did this to me? The whispers in my mind grew louder as I stared at it, unable to look away. Had I still been wearing the heart monitor, Nurse Maggy would have been rushing into the bathroom in a panic because my heart was beating so hard and fast that I could see it pulsing through my skin in the mirror. I tore my eyes away from the ink marking my skin, forcing myself to meet my own gaze once more as I leaned my hips against the cool porcelain sink and then raised both trembling hands to my head. My fingers ghosted against the soft fabric of the bandage, and then before I could stop myself, I peeled it away and felt my body grow stiff.

There, in the center of my forehead, exactly where that *thing* had touched me, was a thin white scar. I could see the stitches that they had added, but the wound was already completely healed. My hand shook as I reached toward it and gently brushed my finger over the new skin. It was smooth and cool, and it looked as if it had been there for a lifetime. I struggled to inhale as the whispers grew so loud, they were like a heart thrumming in my mind, and I stared transfixed at the white scar that ran down my head.

It was exactly like the deer's – exactly where that abomination's third eye had opened. My stomach lurched, and I tasted bile at the back of my throat as my gaze slowly trailed down over my body, and I didn't see a single mark or bruise across my skin.

It didn't make sense.

Nothing about any of this made sense, and I started to shake violently as my lungs refused to breathe. Then a keen knock on the door made me jump.

"Ms. Eldritch?" a deep voice called. "Is everything okay?"

"I'll be right out!" I called back reflexively even though I didn't recognize the voice.

I could hear someone else speaking softly, and I knew it was Ren, which only made my panic double. They must both be waiting for me, and I couldn't stay in this room much longer. I needed to talk to this officer. I needed to get this over with so I could be alone again and figure out what had happened. My hands continued to shake as I quickly pulled the bandage down around my forehead to hide the already healed wound. That was yet another problem I would need to sort out. They would probably want to check it before I left tomorrow, and there was no reasonable explanation for the lack of injuries on my body, given what had apparently happened to me.

I struggled back into my gown, doing my best to shut out and ignore the dull murmur in my mind as I carefully re-tied the top so that the symbol on my chest was completely covered. I did my best to force down the panic as I smoothed out the wrinkles. I tried to focus my mind as my head started to throb. I didn't want to be here, and I didn't want to do this, but I knew if I didn't find a way to push the spinning chaos in my gut to the side, I would end up making things even worse.

I took the time to flush the toilet and run the tap, so it sounded like I had properly used the facilities before I washed my hands and splashed some cold water over my face. Then, I inhaled slowly, twisted my face into one of discomfort and opened the door.

"Sorry," I said, my voice coming out hoarse as I shuffled out of the washroom and tried to make it look like walking was even more difficult than I already found it to be.

I looked up into the dimly lit room to find that Ren was standing just a few feet before me, waiting, while the officer was standing next to the chair along the far wall. He was tall and lean, with fair skin and lighter hair. There was a shadow across his lower jaw, early morning scruff that he had yet to shave since he had been at the hospital all night waiting for me to wake up, and I now understood the reason why. If that officer had seen HUANEE's symbol tattooed on my body at the crash site, not only would I have been flagged, but I would have just become his new *favourite* person. He would be keeping tabs on me and trying to find any excuse in the books to legally bring me in – but there was nothing I could do about that now, so my eyes shifted back to Ren, and I gave her a weak smile.

"I guess I'm moving a little slower than normal," I said, shrugging sheepishly. "I'm feeling a bit stiff."

"Of course you're feeling a bit stiff," Ren said as she looked at me in disbelief. "You idiot – you could have died."

Before I could say anything back, she had closed the distance toward me and pulled me into a tight but careful hug. I could hear her muttering in Japanese – calling me an idiot over and over in between expressing her relief. I held her in return, trying my best not to flinch while biting my lip to fight against the pain her touch brought across my body. When she finally pulled back, I let out a sigh of relief and allowed her to help me back in bed, where she took a seat on the edge protectively by my side.

I could tell just by looking at her that she was nearly bursting at the seams with unspoken questions. She glanced at me in concern, but she didn't say anything and instead turned to watch in silence as the officer stepped closer. I looked up at his movements, half expecting him to appear annoyed and threatening, or perhaps even excited about getting a new lead – but that wasn't the case at all, and to my surprise, he gave me a warm and friendly smile.

"Don't worry about taking your time," the officer said, pausing his approach just before the bed. "I didn't mean to rush you. I know Dr. Davis said that you're fine, but I've been in this job long enough and seen enough crash victims to know that sometimes reactions are delayed – I just wanted to make sure that you hadn't lost your balance in there or gone into shock."

"Oh." I faltered, trying to hide my skepticism toward the kindness of his words. "Thank you, sir – but no, I'm alright."

"Good." He smiled again; then he outstretched his hand toward me. "I'm Theron Wilson; I responded to the emergency call that Ms. Altherr placed."

"Delilah Eldritch," I said, quickly shaking his hand. I didn't manage to contain my wince as his touch burned my skin, and I knew that he felt it.

"I'm sure the nurse has already told you, but your toxicology came back clean, so there won't be any charges. I just need your statement for the record," Officer Wilson said as he stepped back and pulled out his notebook.

"Yes, she did," I confirmed, nodding at his words.

He hadn't been what I was expecting. He looked nice enough, but there was something about him that I didn't like.

"Great," Officer Wilson said as he pulled out his pen and flipped open the notebook. "Then I'll just ask you a few questions."

He asked me for my name and address, then asked me a bunch of other questions that both Nurse Maggy and Dr. Davis had already gone over. I answered them all carefully, being sure to only provide the information that I knew he needed without allowing him to turn the exercise into a friendly and open conversation – which he was clearly trying to do. The entire time Ren sat there rigid and alert, her sharp gaze watching the man as he took notes. Yet he continued chatting in his friendly manner, seemingly unphased by her presence, and she didn't speak until Officer Wilson started asking me questions about what I remembered from the night before.

"Do you remember having anything to drink or ingesting any substances before getting into your car?" Officer Wilson asked me; his pen paused over his notebook in wait. "Perhaps a birthday drink?"

"Lilah's tox screen came back negative," Ren said, and though her voice was calm it, had a distinct edge to it. "You know that. The hospital already released the records to the police department as per protocol."

"I know," Officer Wilson agreed, his warm eyes crinkling as he gave Ren a small smile. "But I'm just following procedure – these are standard questions."

I frowned, my gaze shifting from Ren back to the officer. "A birthday drink?"

"Your birthday is September 30th, is it not?" Officer Wilson turned to look at me. "Which was yesterday. Today is October 1st."

"Oh, right." I saw something sad shift behind Ren's eyes as she turned to glance at me. I had entirely forgotten that it was my birthday. It hadn't even crossed my mind with how busy everything was. I cleared my throat and shook my head, ignoring the scorching heat that continued to burn in my stomach. "No, I didn't have anything to drink – I was working last night. My coworker Pari Zara can attest to that."

"I'll follow up with her." Officer Wilson nodded, writing down the name. "Happy belated birthday – I'm sorry that your night ended as it did. Not exactly the best way to turn thirty-three."

"Thanks," I said uncomfortably, not really sure what to make of that.

"So, I already reached out to your employer, and they said that you were supposed to leave work at 6:00 pm last night – but you were delayed. What time did you leave?"

"Just after 2:00 am," I said, and I felt Ren tense at my side.

"They use swipe cards at the office," Ren added, her eyes narrowing as she watched the man take another note. "They can verify that, and security would have seen her leave."

Officer Wilson nodded, adding something else to his little booklet.

"Were you tired when you got behind the wheel of the car?" he asked, meeting my gaze once more. "You've been working a lot this past month from the sounds of it – enough to forget your own birthday."

"She forgets her birthday every year," Ren said as her fingers curled into the edge of the bed.

"A diligent worker, no doubt," Wilson replied. He kept his voice calm as his eyes shifted back to Ren. "I wasn't implying anything, Ms. Altherr; I'm just doing my due diligence."

"No," I said firmly, and both of them turned to look at me. "I wasn't tired. I was awake and alert when I left, and the security guards at the gate can confirm that. I stayed late because there was an incident, and we needed to file some paperwork, but I was fine when I left. I took the same road that I always take – I just got unlucky."

"So you don't think that you might have fallen asleep behind the wheel?" Officer Wilson pressed though his tone remained friendly.

"No," I said, my voice growing clipped as annoyance flooded my veins. "Not a chance. I work in Health and Safety, Officer Wilson, and I take it very seriously. Had I been too tired to drive, I simply would have slept in the office."

"Alright," Officer Wilson said, accepting my words.

He jotted something else down, then he slowly lowered his notepad to look at me more closely. I sat there rigid as a board as he stared at me, his gaze shifting over my body and twice lingering on the collar of my medical gown. It was all the confirmation that I needed to know that he had seen the symbol, and he knew exactly what it was. I felt my skin prickle as he met my gaze once more, noting the lack of warmth behind his grey eyes.

"You saw the deer run before your car?" he asked, and this time his voice was quieter.

"Yes," I replied stiffly.

"And then what happened?"

I hesitated as the ache in my mind started to throb once more.

"I don't remember," I lied, watching the way his lips twitched ever so slightly. Was it a frown or a smile? I wasn't sure, but he didn't take any more notes as he continued to speak.

"So you don't remember calling Ms. Altherr for help?"

"No." I shook my head, swallowing hard. "I'm sorry I don't."

"Any idea why you might call her after an accident?" Officer Wilson asked, his brow arching in question as he took a small step forward. "Why not call emergency services yourself?"

"I don't know," I said, fighting to keep my voice level as Ren watched the exchange unfold between us. "I don't remember. I have her on speed dial, so I probably did it reflexively."

"I see," he said, then his eyes shifted to Ren. "Do you remember what Ms. Eldritch said when she called you?"

"I couldn't understand most of what she said," Ren said, her chin rising as she met the man's gaze almost defiantly. "The call kept cutting in and out, and Lilah didn't sound right – she sounded disoriented. All I heard were the words: deer and 31, and that was enough for me to know that something was wrong. As Lilah has already said, she takes safety very seriously, Officer Wilson, and she would not call me in the middle of the night unless she was hurt."

"So you called for emergency services?"

"Yes." Ren nodded at his words.

"But then you got into your car and drove out there too?"

"Yes," Ren said again, not blinking as she stared at him hard. "With all due respect, sir – emergency response times have been a bit slow in the last few months. Between all the robbery calls and issues going on in the city, and with police and ambulatory care budgets being cut, I know that you're all overworked and stretched thin. I'm familiar with the route that Lilah takes home from work. I figured I might get there before anyone else, and given that I'm a trauma nurse, I thought it was in her best interests if I went to find her in case the ambulance was delayed."

"Well, you weren't wrong," Officer Wilson said as he looked between Ren and me. "You did get there first. You're very lucky to have such a good friend, Ms. Eldritch – Ms. Altherr arrived a full two minutes before the ambulance and just a few seconds before me – she made sure that they took good care of you."

I knew that he wasn't satisfied, but he repocketed his notebook just the same before he gave us another warm smile that made my stomach curl.

"The deer that you hit has been taken to the local butchers on 8th Street, and you reserve first claim on it until 6:00 pm tomorrow. After that, it will be distributed to the waitlist as per the Food Stamp Program regulations, so I suggest that you head on over there first thing tomorrow morning if you want a good opportunity for extra food," Officer Wilson said as he straightened to his full height and rhymed off the information with ease. "Your car, on the other hand, was unfortunately totalled in the crash. The MVD should be done processing it later today, though based on the initial report and seeing it myself last night, I doubt that it will be salvageable."

"Alright," I said in acceptance, not bothering to question or comment on the car. I wanted this to be over, and I already knew my car was ruined even if I didn't believe that I had hit the deer.

"The paperwork for the car and the final report will be dropped off later tonight by one of the other officers, and you can decide what you want to do with the car then. In the meantime – that's all my questions, and I have everything that I need. Ms. Altherr?" Officer Wilson turned to look at Ren, and his expression remained warm and friendly. "Could you do me a favour and just let the head nurse at the station know that someone will be by to drop off some forms later today? I also need you to get the attending doctor to sign this release confirming that the patient was coherent and of sound mind during our conversation. Once I have that, we're good to go – I'll just get Ms. Eldritch to quickly sign these forms and then I can meet you back up at the station."

Ren hesitated, her gaze flicking between the officer and me as her body remained tense. I knew she didn't want to leave my side, and I knew she didn't like the idea of leaving me alone with Officer Wilson, but she didn't have a valid reason to refuse. He had been perfectly polite to us, and his request wasn't unreasonable.

"It's okay," I reassured her, giving her a small smile as I sat up straighter. "It'll just be a second."

She nodded, but I could see her mouth pressing into a tight line of disapproval as she slowly slid from the bed.

"I'll be right back," Ren said as she took the forms that Officer Wilson held out, and she hesitated by the door again. "If you feel dizzy, Lilah, just press the call button – okay?"

"I will," I said, knowing what she truly meant.

Officer Wilson thanked her as she left and closed the door behind her before turning around to face me once more. Then, he surprised me yet again. I had expected the facade to drop with Ren out of the room. I had expected his entire demeanour to change, but it didn't, and somehow that just made me even more uncomfortable as he took a step forward and pulled several forms from his pocket before handing them to me with a warm smile.

"I just need four signatures," he said as I took the pages that he offered and unfolded the forms. He pointed to the bottom of the first page. "First page is just acknowledgement that we spoke today regarding the accident and that you have given me your statement in full. The second page is for the deer; sign both spots at the bottom, and we each get a copy. You'll need it at the butchers to pick up the meat. The last page simply states that I returned your belongings to you."

He turned and pointed toward the chair, and I noticed a small bag on the floor by its side.

"If you think anything is missing, just let us know – but we're pretty sure that we got it all," Officer Wilson explained as I quickly scanned the first sheet.

I nodded in understanding, then took the pen that he offered me and signed each page in turn. They were exactly what he said they were, which only made me more nervous as I returned the papers to him, and he tore off the ticket for the butchers.

"So, how's the head?" he asked, gesturing toward my forehead as he handed me my copy of the receipt.

"It's fine," I said cautiously, taking the butcher's ticket and fighting against the urge to glance at the door. I didn't like that he had closed it, and I didn't like that Ren had yet to return. "The nurse says it should heal with minimal scarring."

"That's good," Officer Wilson said, taking his pen back and sliding it into one of his many pockets. "I'm amazed that it was the only injury you had. I'm sure that your friend will tell you, but the scene was pretty rough."

"I guess it's a good thing that I don't remember much of it then," I said, watching as his eyes creased.

"I guess so," he murmured, and I nearly shuddered under his gaze as his eyes once again dropped to the neckline of my gown.

I swallowed, feeling my panic start to grow as the seemingly constant whisper in my mind intensified once more. I glanced at the door, hoping to see Ren returning, but there was no one in sight, and Officer Wilson didn't appear to want to leave. He stared at me for a long moment, and I could feel sweat forming across my skin as the heat that continued to surge through my body grew uncomfortable. I needed another drink. Better yet, I needed to go take an ice bath before I was burned alive.

"You're sure you don't remember anything?" he finally asked as he held my gaze. "Nothing after the crash?"

"No." My voice cracked, and I fought to keep my hands from shaking as I looked at him. "I'm sorry – I don't. After the deer, everything just goes black."

"I see," he said, then he took another step forward, and his voice dropped lower. "What I find fascinating about the whole thing is that I found a recently used road flare in the ditch by the end of your car."

I stared at him, my entire body rigid as I fought against the burn that was inching up my throat.

"Maybe someone stopped there," I said, forcing the words out. "I've run into cars with flats on that line before."

"So have I," he noted, and I didn't miss the way that his lips twitched again. "But what was particularly interesting about it was that it matched the ones in your trunk."

"That is interesting," I whispered as I fought to keep my face indifferent. "It must be a popular brand of flare."

"Must be," he murmured, his eyes darkening as he watched me try not to squirm. Then he took a final step closer. "But that's not even the best part."

My jaw locked tight. I refused to ask him what the best part was, and I refused to say anything else, but he only smiled and leaned down toward my face.

"The best part is the blood and skin that we found on the road about twenty feet behind your vehicle," Officer Wilson whispered, and I felt the burning terror in my heart double as images of that night flashed through my mind once more. "That – and the fact that your cell phone was on the ground beside your car, even though your windows were rolled up and your doors were locked. Truth be told, Ms. Eldritch – normally, I wouldn't care. An accident like that isn't a priority for us. They happen all the time, and they're not worth investigating, so no matter how odd the circumstances might be, we write them off, provided that the tox screen comes back clean. But given the supplemental details of your person–"

His eyes dropped to the neckline of my gown again, and my lungs ceased to function.

"I ordered forensics to take prints off the road flare, and I had them log the blood and run comparison tests against your DNA, and guess what?" Officer Wilson paused, then dark smile crossed his lips as he looked at me. "They match."

I heard voices behind the door and the sound of approaching footsteps, but Officer Wilson's smile only grew more unsettling as he leaned even closer.

"Now lucky for you," he said slowly, his voice all but vibrating in the air. "I can't do anything with that information right now, so it will simply sit in our database."

A sharp pain started to shoot across my chest. The voices were getting closer, Ren was coming back, but I couldn't look away from Officer Wilson as his voice took on a dangerous tone.

"But the second that the UNC passes that bill," Officer Wilson murmured as the footsteps reached the door. "I'll be seeing you again real soon."

The Elk

OCTOBER

"What the hell were you thinking, Lilah?!"

Ren's whispered yell echoed through the small room as I sat there staring at her, fighting to ignore the burning sensation that permeated my body. I had already had another two glasses of water. I had already calmly and innocently asked Nurse Maggy to check my temperature. It was precisely 37 degrees Celsius – and there was nothing physically wrong with me, even though I was nearly certain that I was being burned alive from the inside out.

When Ren returned to my room with Dr. Davis and Nurse Maggy, Officer Wilson had politely taken his leave. After which, I sat there quietly as Ren talked to my medical care providers, and the three of them looked over some forms and charts. I didn't bother asking what they were – I knew that Ren would act in my best interest, and the truth was I didn't care. I had other things on my mind – things that I needed to deal with and things that desperately needed my attention. Like for starters, figuring out how the hell I had a perfectly healed tattoo on my chest after only being unconscious for ten hours and secondly, how on earth I was going to get out of this hospital without someone noticing that I didn't have a single bruise, mark, or injury that came from my accident.

However, it seemed that Ren had different plans. The second that Dr. Davis and Nurse Maggy left the room and securely closed the door behind them, Ren had all but exploded at me in rage. I had never seen anything like it – half of it came out in Japanese, and I had to rely on my rusty skills to try to translate it.

Ren didn't yell – not even this weird whisper yelling thing that she was doing, especially never at me. I had heard her swear on occasion in frustration, but not like this, and looking up at her now as I sat there in my uncomfortable hospital gown, I could barely recognize her. There was a terrible mix of emotions showing on her face, and all of it was wrapped up in a blanket of stress and anguish. If not for the fact that she was still wearing the necklace that I had given to her three years ago, I would have assumed she was so furious that she was done with me.

"Why on earth would you get that symbol tattooed on your chest?!" Ren hissed in her tight, angry whisper as she stepped closer to the bed. A few more choice words left her lips in Japanese before she fixed me with a firm stare and continued her rant. "That officer saw it after he helped me break open your car door because the ambulance hadn't arrived yet, and I thought you might be bleeding out! Why would you get it?! Are you trying to get arrested? Do you realize what will happen if they pass that bill? You'll be picked up, brought in for questioning, and no one will ever see you again!"

"Do you honestly think I'm that stupid, Ren?" I asked, the burning anger in my chest starting to flare as my eyes widened at her in disbelief. "You seriously think that I went out and got this tattoo? That I would get HUANEE's symbol on my chest, with everything that's been going on?!"

"Well, it's there, isn't it?" Ren said as she gestured to my sternum.

"Well, *I* didn't put it there!" I snapped, glaring at her as I slid from the bed and stood with my bare feet on the cold ground. I watched her face contort in confusion as she let out an almost exhausted sigh.

"Lilah – what the hell are you talking about?" she asked as she shook her head, then suddenly her demeanour changed, and she looked at me with concern. "Do you not remember getting it?"

"No, I don't remember getting it," I said as I snagged the spare hospital scrubs that Nurse Maggy had brought in for me off the chair. I didn't want to wear this stupid, uncomfortable gown anymore, though I suspected that the scrubs wouldn't be much better. "Because I didn't get it! I never got this tattoo, Ren. It just appeared when I woke up!"

"Lilah," Ren murmured, her voice growing softer as her eyes filled with even more concern. "That's not possible. That tattoo is completely healed. You couldn't have—"

"I know I couldn't have gotten it last night." I cut her off, holding the scrubs tightly in my hand as my voice dropped low. "I know that's impossible – but I'm telling you that's what happened."

Silence stretched between us as I continued to glare at my friend, and she looked at me cautiously.

"Lilah, you split your head open on your steering wheel," Ren whispered, and I stiffened at her desperate tone. "When I got there – when I saw you slumped against it. Lilah, I thought you might be dead."

She took a slow step forward.

"The deer you hit was huge, Lilah," Ren said, her voice almost cautious. "It totaled the front end of your car, entirely crushed it – it was almost torn in half and splattered across the windshield. And you... you were draped over the steering wheel. The airbag didn't go off, you were covered in so much blood that I couldn't even tell what was injured until Officer Wilson and I got inside your car. Seeing you there like that... Lilah, I don't even know how you managed to call me. You should have died. You should have been dead. Your neck would have broken, and your ribs would have been crushed, but somehow – you were breathing. I know that Dr. Davis cleared you, and I know that you don't remember what happened, but you hit your head really hard. You were *completely* unresponsive when I found you. There might be things that you don't fully remember. Memories that you don't even know are missing—"

"I didn't get this tattoo," I said, and I watched her face fall.

"Lilah—"

"No, you don't understand." I cut her off, shaking my head as my legs started to tremble. "I know I didn't get this tattoo because I know I didn't hit that deer."

Her brow furrowed, but I continued on before she could say anything else.

"I *almost* hit it," I whispered, hearing the dull voices in my head begin to grow. "I swerved, and I missed it. That's why Officer Wilson wanted to talk to me. He found my road flare behind my car because I had stopped and gotten out – I put it there. I called you while I walked down the road trying to get a better cell signal, Ren. He found my phone outside of my vehicle, so he knows it too. I know this sounds crazy, and I'm not even going to ask you to believe me, but I need you to know that I didn't hit that deer, and I did not get this tattoo."

"Lilah," Ren said, taking a step forward. I could see curiosity and concern shifting behind her gaze. "What happened?"

"I don't know," I said, fighting against the urge to shudder as the fire in my bones grew hotter. I dropped the scrubs I was holding back on the chair and slowly reached my hands up to the bandages on my head. I pushed them up to reveal my fully healed forehead, and I saw her eyes grow wide as her mouth fell open. "But I'm not lying to you, Ren – and I need your help."

I hadn't wanted to involve Ren in whatever this bizarre mess was, but I didn't have any other choice. In a lot of ways, she had become involved the second that I called her, and she became an accomplice in Officer Wilson's eyes the second that she got into her car and drove out into the darkness to find me on Line 31. If I could have avoided showing her my forehead or telling her anything about that night, I would have. If I could have gone back in time and stopped myself from making that phone call – I would have done that, too. Though honestly, if I was able to go back in time, I would have just changed that entire night. I wouldn't have gotten into my car to drive home, I wouldn't have taken Line 31, and I definitely wouldn't have gotten out of my vehicle and ran down the road through the fog.

But I had – and there was nothing that I could do about that now.

Showing Ren my forehead was the only way that I could get out of this hospital without becoming a lab rat. As much as it made me sick to my stomach to ask for her help, I trusted her not to say anything. I trusted her to help me. I could tell that she didn't like this, but then again, neither did I, because nothing about this situation was normal.

I let her examine my head. I let her examine the rest of my body in the dull light of the small room, and I sat there with her as both she and I struggled to understand what was going on. She had no explanation for the healed gash across my head. She had no explanation for the lack of bruises across my chest when only hours ago, according to her, I had been black and blue – and she could not explain the small anatomical changes that seemed to span across my body.

I didn't tell her about what happened with the deer.

I didn't tell her about the whispers.

I knew that she knew that I was holding things back, but she didn't push me, and she agreed to tell Nurse Maggy that she would redress my head wound before I left so that no one would know that it had miraculously healed. She left me briefly before dinner to go home and change, and she even used her spare key to stop by my apartment and grab me some clothes. I thanked her. We ate dinner together. Then she refused to leave my side and slept next to me on the tiny hospital bed while I tried to avoid physically touching her.

That night, my mind was filled with things that no person should ever have to see. The low clicking noise echoed in my ears. The cold air bit my skin as my bones burned to ash. There was a mountain in the distance and a violent tug through my chest as I was dragged across the jagged ground toward it. It was covered in symbols; they were scratched into the stone as if clawed by nails or etched with a knife, and each of them made my stomach roll.

I woke sweating and panting, a scream on the verge of leaving my lips as I sat up in the darkness clutching at my chest. It was a miracle that I didn't wake Ren, and it took me a long time to make sense of what had happened as I sat there shaking in the dark, haunted by the red glowing eyes that were burned into my mind.

Death.

Darkness.

Fire.

I could taste it all in my mouth. I could hear it in my head as the dull whispers that didn't seem to go away grew louder and louder until I finally hauled myself from the small hospital bed and quietly staggered my way into the bathroom. I ripped the completely unnecessary bandages off my head. I stood there for what felt like forever, my head stuffed under the tap, cold water running down my face and soaking my hair as I desperately tried to cool off. Yet the burning would not subside. Giving up, I shut off the water and grabbed a towel to dry my face, then looked in the mirror at my exhausted and ashen expression – and that was when I noticed it.

The tiny hint of red.

It was nearly invisible, but as I leaned in less than an inch away from the mirror, with the dull grey glow of light from the window, I could see it. A ring – circling my irises like a crimson halo. I stared at it. Unable to look away as my heart started to race. It hadn't been there the day before, and as I forced my gaze to shift over the rest of the features on my face, I felt my stomach knot with fear.

Something was wrong with me.

I didn't move until a car alarm went off outside and jolted me from my thoughts. When I glanced back at the mirror once more the red ring around my eyes was gone, and my face looked unchanged. Knowing that I couldn't stand in the small bathroom forever, I carefully re-wrapped my head, then quietly crawled back into bed. I didn't sleep the rest of the night, and when morning finally came, I knew that I would never be the same again... everything was going to be different.

Dr. Davis discharged me that morning, and Ren waited in my room with him while I changed in the bathroom. I could hear them talking quietly through the door; I couldn't make out the words, but I couldn't help but feel like Dr. Davis was lingering and spending more time with Ren and me than necessary. This hospital was busy; surely he had better things to do and patients to see – but I pushed the thoughts aside and tugged on my clothes.

When I finally emerged from the tiny bathroom wearing the long pants and the long shirt that Ren had brought me, in favour of the shorts and t-shirt she had packed, I could see them both glancing at me with concern. I ignored it, just like I ignored the way that the clothes made my skin uncomfortable. I was already too hot, and the long sleeves weren't helping, but the idea of going out into the blazing sunlight with exposed skin made my gut wrench. So this felt like the better choice.

I put on the sunglasses that she brought me because the lights still bothered my eyes, and Dr. Davis informed me that the light sensitivity could continue for a few more days. I nodded in understanding, already knowing that the symptom would never go away. Then Ren assured him that she had cleaned and re-bandaged my head that morning and signed off on the charts and paperwork.

Technically, he was breaking the rules by allowing Ren to care for me when she was not on the clock, but Nurse Maggy had more than a dozen other patients to attend to, and she was more than happy to leave the task to Ren. I waited uncomfortably as Dr. Davis told me how to properly care for the cut and when to come back to get the stitches removed. I didn't say anything as Ren informed him that she would take care of it at home, and I nodded when he mentioned that I should come back in for additional testing the following day.

I wouldn't be coming back.

There was nothing that these people could do to help me, and I knew that even Ren knew that. I gathered the paperwork that the officer had dropped off the night before at the nurses' station and quickly filled it out. As suspected, the report indicated that the car was totalled, and I could either arrange to pick up the remains or scrap it through the MVD and get a small payment in return. Without even pausing to think, I checked the box to scrap the car and signed the papers.

We left shortly afterwards. Ren had swapped shifts to take the day off so that she could drive me around and ensure I was okay

– even though I had told her not to bother. As we walked toward the east exit that would take us to the employee parking lot, I felt my heart start to race with nervousness. I couldn't explain why, and I couldn't rationalize how I knew what was about to happen, but the second we exited the building and shifted across the hot pavement, it felt like someone had just rammed my head into an oven.

"I spoke to your boss yesterday," Ren said as I fought to keep my face composed. "He said that you could take as much time as you need."

"That's surprising," I said as I squinted behind my sunglasses. They were not as effective as I wanted them to be. "I figured he would be pissed."

"Actually, he sounded worried," Ren said as we reached her car, and she unlocked the doors. I grimaced at the idea of getting inside the hot metal box but forced myself to do it. "He said he would cover your shifts until you're cleared to come back to work."

"I'm sure he will," I said doubtfully, already knowing that he had probably just asked the rest of my coworkers to work doubles. Guilt twisted through my gut as I thought about Pari and how she would manage with her daughter. "I'm sure I can go back next week."

"Lilah." Ren hesitated as she buckled her seatbelt and started the car. The second the engine sparked to life, I cracked the window open and let out a tight breath. "Dr. Davis and I think it might be a good idea to see how things go this week before you set a timeline for going back."

I froze, the agonizing burn in my body being pushed aside as dread filled my mind.

"What did you say to him?" I snapped, gripping the door tight as I turned to glare at Ren. She was staring at me with that same concerned expression that I had seen the day before, but this time it was laced with hurt.

"Nothing," Ren said as she put the car in drive and shook her head. "I didn't tell him a thing, Lilah – I promised you that I would help, and I promised you that I would keep this secret. He would have made that suggestion for any crash victim."

My heart dropped at the look on her face.

"Ren," I faltered, letting out a breath and closing my eyes. I didn't want to be frustrated with Ren. She hadn't done anything wrong; she had done nothing but help me since the moment that I called her, and yet this burning hellfire in my chest was making it impossible to stay calm. "I'm sorry – I didn't think that you did. I'm just – I'm struggling right now."

"I know you are," Ren said, and I heard her shift beside me. "Lilah – what aren't you telling me?"

"Nothing," I whispered, opening my eyes to look at her from behind my tinted lenses once more. "I'm fine."

"You're not fine," Ren said, and I heard a tone of frustration in her voice. "You haven't been fine for years – but right now, you're beyond not being *fine*, Lilah. I just lied to my coworkers for you. I just signed off on your forms and convinced Von to discharge you even though he didn't think it was a good idea until after your additional tests, so the least you can do is tell me what the hell happened to you last night!"

"Who's Von?" I asked, and Ren rolled her eyes.

"Von is Dr. Davis – his name is Von Davis, but stop trying to ignore my question," Ren said as she put the car back into park and fixed me with a hard look. "I didn't ask you anything in the hospital. I didn't ask you for anything when I said that I'd help you – I'm not asking you for anything now; I just want to know what happened."

"And I already told you that I don't know," I protested, reaching forward to crank the air conditioning as my skin began to burn.

"Bullshit!" Ren spat, and my eyes widened in disbelief at her tone as she snapped. She hadn't truly said 'bullshit'. She had instead said a very particular Japanese phrase that I had never heard her utter before, and hearing it made the burning anger in my chest flare as she turned to glare at me. "Tell me what happened."

"Or what, you'll bring me back in and show them my head?" I snapped, my voice far more vicious than I meant it to be. I watched her expression crumple, and I instantly regretted my words.

"Or nothing," Ren said, and the painful hurt behind her eyes was unmistakable. "I'm just asking as your friend, Lilah – please, tell me what happened so I can help you."

I stared at her in silence for a long moment as the air conditioning whined and struggled to force cool air into the hot car.

"I honestly don't know what happened to me, Ren," I said, forcing the words out as I continued to grip the door like death.

"Then just tell me what you remember," Ren whispered, and I winced as her hand touched my arm.

I swallowed hard, fighting to quell the panic surging in my chest as I let out a deep breath.

"It wasn't a deer," I finally said, and I watched as her eyes narrowed in confusion.

"What do you mean it wasn't a deer?"

"The thing that I hit – or didn't hit – whatever happened, that thing – it wasn't a deer," I said. I forced myself to let go of the door and turned in my seat to face my best friend directly. "After I got out of my car and called you, I heard noises in the woods, and I panicked. I ran down the road trying to get away from it, and I ran right into whatever that thing was. I don't know how to describe it, Ren, and I can't even begin to put it into words, but it wasn't a deer. It was something from a nightmare, and it touched my forehead, right where this scar is."

I touched the center of my head as a tight silence filled the vehicle.

"After that, I don't remember anything. That's the truth," I said as I held her gaze. "I woke up in the hospital. My head is filled with images and memories that aren't mine. This mark is on my chest, my bruises are gone, my body feels different, and I don't even recognize my own hands. I don't know what's happening to me, but I feel like I'm being burned alive, and I can hear that noise from the woods in my mind like a bug eating through my brain. So if you know what that means, if you can figure this out, then please, Ren, I beg of you – tell me. Because I am scared shitless right now."

"I don't know what that means," Ren whispered after a long pause hung heavily between us. Her eyes traced over my face, and

I could see an endless stream of thoughts racing behind her eyes. "But we're going to figure it out, I promise. We'll go take care of your car first – then will go to the butchers and see that deer."

"So, you're agreeing to scrap the car?"

I stared at the man behind the bulletproof glass and tried to ignore the discomfort in my bones. I had already told him that I wanted to scrap the car, and I had already given him the signed paperwork through the tiny slot at the bottom of the glass that indicated as such. I gritted my teeth and forced myself to smile.

We had arrived at the Police Headquarters a few minutes ago, parking in the back lot near the exit before quickly making our way toward the front of the building. I had never liked this part of the city. It was in the downtown core and surrounded by nothing but concrete, pavement, and tall buildings that blocked the wind and retained so much heat it was unbearable. There had been a small altercation ongoing near the side of the building between an older gentleman and three officers – but we didn't pay them any mind and rapidly made our way inside to get out of the heat. Now, standing here with sweat dripping down my back and whispers echoing in my head, I was struggling to remain calm.

"Yes," I said, as my hands began to tremble at my sides. I didn't want to be in here, but this man was moving about as fast as molasses. I could feel Ren shifting by my side, and I knew that even she was uncomfortable. "I would like to scrap the car."

"Alright," the man said, grabbing a stamp from his right and marking the front page of the form in red ink to signify receipt. He initialled next to the stamp then slid the papers into a pile on his left. "The car will be scrapped this week, and a cheque will be sent in the mail to your home address for the sum of $500.00. Please confirm that you are still located at 603 Newberry Avenue, apartment 696?"

"That's correct." I nodded, gripping the side of my pants to stop my hand from outright shaking.

"Alright, just initial this," the man said as he slid a small piece of paper through the tiny slot.

I wiped my sweaty palms on my pants, grabbing the form and quickly scanning it over. It was a secondary release confirming that I wanted the cheque mailed. I bit back a sigh, signing the sheet and shoving the paper back through the hole. This whole process was so inefficient it was unbelievable, but there was no way around it.

"You're all set then," the man finally said as he took the signed paper. "I'll just print you your receipt. Make sure that you keep it in case the cheque doesn't show up in the next three weeks; otherwise, there is nothing that we can do for you. You received your personal items, right? You don't need access to the vehicle?"

"Access to the vehicle?" I repeated, my brow furrowing as the man began tapping on his keyboard to print the receipt. "You mean I'm allowed to see my car?"

The man let out a heavy sigh as if my question physically pained him because he had to expend energy to answer it.

"Yes," he said, a hint of irritation lacing his voice. "Legally speaking, we have to give you access to your vehicle, regardless of its physical state. Even if only a scrap of metal remained – you could technically request to see it."

"I want to see it," I said. It came out so quickly that I surprised myself, and the officer behind the front desk gave me a deadpan look as I heard the creak of a door, and noise broke out behind me. I could feel Ren shifting closer to my side, and her hand tugged my sleeve as if to get my attention, but I ignored it. I needed to see the car. I needed to know what happened. "I would like to see it – I think I got all my stuff back, but I would like to double-check."

"Lilah." Ren's tight whisper sounded by my ear as the police officer behind the glass let out a sigh.

"Fine," the officer said as the noise behind us started to grow louder. "I'll have to see when we can arrange it – believe it or not, this place isn't a tourist attraction, and we don't just let people wander around."

"Sir – Sir – you need to calm down!" a deep voice echoed behind me, but I tuned it out and ignored the tug Ren made on my arm once more.

"Alright – then how does it work? Do I have to come back?" I asked, watching as the officer just frowned deeper, and he tugged the newly printed receipt from the tray.

"Lilah!" Ren said sharply, jerking my arm so hard I turned to glare at her.

"What?" I hissed, but before I could even open my mouth to say another word, a second deep baritone sounded behind me, and I stiffened.

"Ms. Eldritch."

I instantly regretted not listening to her warning earlier. I closed my eyes briefly, letting out a silent breath before I forced myself to turn toward the voice, already knowing exactly what I would see as I looked across the sparse foyer. There, standing in his full uniform, was Officer Wilson, and he was moving right toward us.

"It's good to see you up and walking around," the tall man said as he crossed the old stone floors and gave us a small smile. It didn't reach his eyes, and though he genuinely did seem pleased to see me, I knew it wasn't out of compassion. "Here to drop off your forms?"

"Yes," I answered, forcing myself to smile at the man as Ren stepped closer to my side and continued to grip my sleeve tight.

She seemed to know that touching my skin hurt me, even though I hadn't said anything, and she had stopped doing it in favour of grabbing at my clothes. I glanced around the foyer quickly, spotting the elderly man who had been causing a scene outside being escorted through the swipe card access door into the main building. Apparently, Officer Wilson had gotten involved in the scene, and then he had spotted me at the front.

"Decided to scrap it," I said, resisting the urge to grimace at my own stupidity for lingering here longer than necessary. "I was just getting my receipt, and then we'll be on our way."

"I thought you wanted to see the vehicle?" The officer behind the glass said with confused irritation, and I nearly groaned.

"Oh no – that's okay," I said quickly, turning to glance back at the man and shaking my head. "I'm sure that I got everything – just the receipt is fine."

"You wanted to see the car?" Officer Wilson asked, reaching the front desk and stopping just a foot to my left. It was much closer than I wanted to be to him, and I unconsciously stepped back.

"It's really not necessary," I said, turning back to the officer behind the glass and mentally pleading with him not to make this into a scene. "Really – I'll just take my receipt and go."

"I'll take you," Officer Wilson said, giving us a warm smile as he leaned against the front desk.

"Oh, no – that's okay." I waved my hand as if to push the idea away. I could feel my heart starting to race, and I desperately wanted to leave. "I wouldn't want to waste your time. You have much more important things to do."

"It's not a problem," Officer Wilson said, and the light and friendly tone of his voice made my stomach knot.

"Are you sure, Inspector Wilson?" the man behind the glass asked as he nodded politely to his superior. "I can just log her in the books or see if one of the guys is free later today to take her down."

I stiffened, my eyes involuntarily growing wide. I watched as a slow smile crept across Wilson's face, and I instantly understood just how much worse my situation had become. He had never identified himself as an inspector, so I had wrongfully assumed that he was highway patrol.

"No – don't bother. I was just about to go for lunch anyway," Inspector Wilson said, and my skin prickled as his gaze slowly trailed over my body, then locked to my eyes. "Besides, I insist."

"Alright, I'll note it down," the man behind the glass said, finally slipping my receipt through the small slot.

Wilson arched a brow, gesturing his head toward the tray as I stood there unmoving. "Anything else you need?"

"No," I whispered, swallowing hard and forcing my hand to take the paper from the tray.

"Good." He smiled again, pushing off from the small counter and gesturing toward the swipe card access door. "Then let's go."

"Okay," I said, unable to come up with anything else to say or any reasonable excuse that could get us out of this without causing any more problems. I glanced at Ren, but she looked just as lost as I did as we moved across the foyer, and Inspector Wilson fell into step by my side.

"So, was there anything specific you thought was missing from your belongings?" Inspector Wilson asked, his tone casual as he swiped his keycard and granted us access to the building.

I fought to keep from shaking as he ushered us inside then proceeded to walk us past the sign-in desk without bothering to give us visitors badges.

"I don't think so," I answered, watching as several people nodded to him, and he continued to guide us down the hall. "But I was having a hard time remembering, so I thought it might not be a bad idea. I didn't realize it would be so inconvenient, though, or I wouldn't have asked the officer at the desk."

"It's not inconvenient," Inspector Wilson said as he led us toward a bank of elevators and pressed the call button. "I really don't mind. I was planning to check up on you and make sure that you were okay anyway. How did the additional testing go?"

"It's not scheduled until tomorrow," Ren said, still holding my sleeve as the elevator dinged and we followed Wilson on board.

"Ah, I see," Wilson said, pressing the B2 button before casually leaning back against the wall. Even though he was on the opposite side of the elevator, he seemed to take up so much space that it felt claustrophobic. "Well, I hope it goes well for you."

"Thank you," I murmured as I fought to swallow my nervousness.

We stood in complete silence. I refused to meet his gaze and stared at the opposite wall, but I could feel his eyes tracing over my skin. I knew his gaze was lingering at the neckline of my shirt and that he was itching for a glimpse at that symbol. When the doors to the basement parking garage finally opened, I thought I would feel relief, but the only thing that rushed through my body was further discomfort as we were blasted by a wave of heat and the strong smell of gasoline. I covered my nose and mouth, unable to stop myself from physically gagging as we stepped off the elevator and into the dimly lit parking garage. I knew Wilson saw it, and I could feel his eyes on me for the rest of the journey as he led us through countless rows of cars.

Some were dented. Others were perfect. A few were barely recognizable as vehicles, but when we turned down a row on the left and Wilson raised his hand to point to a mangled mess of blue – I knew it was mine before he even spoke.

I froze at the sight, my eyes tracing over the bent and twisted metal that used to be the front end. It was buckled right down the middle – as if I had driven full speed into a tree or some other immovable object. The driver's door was entirely missing, and one of the tires looked ready to fall off. Dried blood covered everything, the windshield was shattered with a giant hole, and blood was soaked into the interior like a sponge. Seeing it now, I instantly understood Ren's concerns regarding my injuries and Wilson's suspicions about the accident itself.

No one should have walked away from this wreck – especially not if the airbag didn't go off.

"Here it is," Inspector Wilson announced.

I continued to stare at the car, utterly dumbfounded and lost for words. He didn't say anything as I stepped towards it, but when I finally forced myself to meet his gaze, he was staring at me intently. His eyes were practically burning with anticipation – as if he was hoping that I would admit something. As if he thought that maybe there was something on or within the vehicle that he and his team had missed, and I would reveal it to him.

"Remember anything?" he asked, and his low voice made me shudder.

The heat of the garage stifled my lungs. The smell of gasoline sunk into my skin. I could hear the dull whisper growing in my skull like a chant as I stared at him.

"No," I whispered, the word breaking on my lips. Neither one of us blinked as the destroyed remains of my car sat like an unsolvable enigma before us. "I'm sorry, I don't."

"That was stupid."

"I know, I'm sorry."

"So incredibly stupid."

"I know, Ren – I said I was sorry."

"He didn't even sign us in – there's no record of us being there, Lilah. What if he hadn't let us leave? What if he tried to plant evidence in your car, or on you? It wouldn't be the first time that something like that has happened. Do you understand what he would do if–"

"Ren – I know." I cut her off, turning to look at her as I continued to all but lean my head out the window. Sitting in the small metal box was making me nauseous; I was already on the verge of throwing up, and her lecture was not helping. "I know it was stupid."

"Why did you even want to see your car?" Ren asked almost desperately, glancing at me as she navigated down the busy road.

"I don't know," I said, threading my fingers further into my hair as my eyes narrowed in annoyance. "It's not like I knew Officer Wilson was there."

"Except he's not just an officer, Lilah – he's a bloody inspector!"

"I know!" I snapped, sitting up from my slouched position to glare at her. "I know he's an inspector, and although you seem to think that I've become a complete idiot over the last twenty-four hours, I actually do understand that that makes this worse, alright? I know how bad this is – but I didn't know he was there! I just thought seeing the car might help. That maybe it would jog something in my memory or make things more clear."

"And did it?" Ren asked, glancing at me once more as she changed lanes and slowed for the next light.

"No," I said bitterly, ripping my eyes away from her to glare out at the concrete around me as the vehicle came to a stop at the red light and I could feel her gaze on my temple. "It didn't help. I don't remember anything else, and I don't know how my car got like that."

"Lilah–"

"I don't want to talk about it."

"Yeah? Well, I do!" Ren snapped, turning to look at me fully. She kept her hands tightly on the wheel of her car, but her gaze was tracing over my face. "I just want you to be careful."

"I know, Ren. I just–"

"No, you don't know." Ren cut me off. "You don't know how important you are to those around you. You never think about yourself or how people might feel if something were to happen to you. I know you didn't see him there – I didn't either, not until it was too late. I just want you to be careful. You need to pay more attention to what's going on around you – we both do, because Inspector Wilson is going to be on your ass until that bill is passed. And even if it doesn't pass, he's going to stalk you and try to find any other reason to bring you in. Lilah, Maggy's brother-in-law is a police officer. Our city's department helped respond to that battery manufacturing explosion – they're involved in the investigation. They're actively looking for any and all leads. They're under a huge amount of pressure from the government and UNAF to make credible arrests and find some answers – but they haven't found any leads.

"It's been eight months, and no one has been able to dig up *anything* on HUANEE. No one knows how they operate, who they're working with, or how they're picking their targets. Then you come along and fall into Wilson's lap with their logo tattooed to your chest like a damn godsend," Ren said, her voice lacing with worry. "Lilah, the second that bill passes, he will come for you. The second that you do *anything* wrong – even if you cross the street outside of a crosswalk, he will be there waiting to write the ticket and take you in. You are the first thing that his department has found that can tangibly be linked to HUANEE, and he is going to use it."

"Because of a tattoo?" I said, my voice hollow. "What does he think, HUANEE marks their members?"

"I don't think that he or most of the other officers looking for leads are *thinking*, Lilah," Ren said as the light changed and the traffic began to move once more. "I think they're desperate – and that makes them even more dangerous."

We drove the rest of the way to the butchers in silence as I pondered her words. I hadn't known that she was so aware of what was happening. I didn't realize that she had inside knowledge of the police force and their involvement with investigating the nearby explosion. Then again, I hadn't seen her in weeks. Regardless, I knew what she was driving at. Everyone from the local authorities to UNAF were itching to make arrests, to find a lead, and to start pinning these acts of violence on someone. Even though I had no priors, even though I had nothing to do with them – I would likely be treated as guilty regardless simply by association and for allegedly showing support toward the group.

The butcher shop on 8th Street was one of many small operations within the city. They specialized in roadkill, like many of the butcher shops seemed to these days, and they operated under the Food Stamp Program guidelines. As such, when we arrived, I knew that Ren would not be able to go inside with me. These stores had strict protocols, and even before the shortages, robberies had been an issue. I wasn't exactly looking forward to going in alone, but that was what I did as I walked around the small brick building, sweating in the sun while Ren waited in the car.

I was surprised to see that the store appeared empty through the glass window when I approached, and for a moment, I thought it might be closed – but when I pushed the barred door, it opened, and I was met with relief as cool air brushed over my skin and a small bell chimed.

"We don't have anything left!"

The deep male baritone sounded through the empty space, and I froze on the spot just inside the door.

"Dammit, Scott – didn't you lock the door? How many times have I told you, when we sell out, you need to lock the front door, or we're going to have a fiasco like May 2nd all over again!"

It was the same deep baritone, and it came from a large and weary-looking man who came out from the backroom. My eyes tracked his movements, watching the deep sigh that left his lungs as he looked up at me from behind refrigeration units that were indeed completely void of any cuts of meat.

"Actually," I said, pulling the small ticket that Inspector Wilson had given me from my pocket and holding it up for him to see. "I have a ticket. A deer was brought in two nights ago – I'm the one that hit it."

"Oh." The man looked both surprised and relieved as he leaned against the counter and motioned for me to come closer. "You must be Ms. Eldritch, sorry about that – I didn't mean to be rude. I'm glad to see that you're okay and up walking about. We never know with these things what kind of condition the ticketer will be in. We had one just last month, and the poor fellow who hit it didn't make it. His wife had to come to claim the meat – it was just awful – even knowing that she and the family would have food for the next while didn't make it any better."

"Thank you," I said, handing him my ticket and watching as he pulled out a small tablet.

My eyes skimmed over the empty cabinets once more. It was a depressing sight, and I knew that working in this industry must be truly challenging. Butchers and other people like them who had access to food weren't just harassed at work. Sometimes they were harassed at home.

"What happened on May 2nd?" I asked as he handed me back my ticket, and I gave him my ID.

"Trust me, you don't want to know," the man grumbled as he glanced up at me while making a small note on his tablet. His eyes lingered on the bandage that was still unnecessarily wrapped around my head, and I saw his eyes soften. "Just that desperate people go to desperate lengths when their family is starving. We had to get the police involved, and frankly, we're lucky we didn't lose more than we did."

"I'm sorry to hear that," I said, and the man gave me a small nod.

"I'm sorry, dad!" A young male voice broke through the room as a thin, lanky boy came rushing out from the backroom toward the front door. He was moving so quickly he didn't even see me, and it wasn't until after he had bolted the front door that he turned around, and his face faltered. "Oh, crap – I'm sorry Miss, but you can't be here we–"

"It's fine, Scott," the older man said, waving his hand at his son. "She's here for the elk."

"Oh," Scott said, his shoulders dropping as he let out a sigh of relief. He couldn't have been much older than nineteen, but already there were stress lines around his eyes, and he looked exhausted beyond his years. "I'm sorry about your accident – I'm glad you're okay."

"Thanks," I murmured, watching as he began to make his way to the backroom once more. He nodded as he passed, and I felt myself still as I heard his muttered words, *'Thank God for that – don't have to get stabbed again.'*

"Well, everything checks out with the ticket," the older man said, letting out another low sigh as he handed me back my ID. "I have to apologize though – usually we would already have it processed, but this past week we have been swamped with several drop-offs because the Jefferson butchers had to temporarily close. We should be able to have it ready by tomorrow, though. Are you planning to take the whole thing, or were you going to be selling any of it?"

"Wait," I said, my brow furrowing in confusion. "Did you call it an elk?"

"I did," the man confirmed, and his lips twisted into a smile. "The MVD reps who dropped it off thought that it was a deer, but I've been doing this long enough to know the difference, and I have to say – this one is impressive. I've not seen an elk in these parts, let alone one this big, in decades. You hit quite the animal, Ms. Eldritch."

"Oh – really?" I asked, my eyes widening in surprise. "I've never seen an elk before."

"Most haven't." The man grinned. He stared at me for a moment, an odd look crossing his face before he spoke again. "Would you like to? It's a bit of a mess, I warn you. We've cleaned it up a bit, so it doesn't look as bad, but it's quite the creature – worth the look."

"Yes," I said, the word falling out of my mouth before I even truly processed it as I gripped the counter tight. "I want to see it."

"Alright." The man nodded, gesturing with his head for me to come around the counter. "It's the antlers on this one that are truly impressive – not seen anything like it since I was a boy."

I followed him into the backroom, the burning itch under my skin finally starting to lessen as we stepped into the freezer, and the frigid air encompassed my body. I had never seen a dead animal before – well, at least not one of this size. Dead cats, dogs, squirrels, and even rats or foxes were common in the city, but I had never seen an elk. I doubted that anyone under the age of forty had.

He led me down a small row toward the back, and I could already see the massive remains as we approached the table. My feet started to slow, and my heart started to race. He led me directly before the table, then paused, and I couldn't breathe. There, nearly broken in two pieces, was the largest creature that I had ever seen in my life. It must have weighed a thousand pounds, and its antlers were so large they didn't even fit across the table. I stared at it in disbelief, finding myself speechless for the second time that day.

"It's incredible, isn't it?" the butcher asked, and I found myself nodding.

"Yes," I whispered, taking a step forward as if mesmerized by the sight.

I stared at its face, which was undamaged and unmarked – except for the thin white scar that traced down the center of its forehead. I stiffened, and the uneasy feeling in my chest grew.

"We don't ever bring people back here. Technically, I'm breaking the rules, but this is a once-in-a-lifetime chance to see a feat of nature, so I couldn't resist. I'll be honest, I almost feel bad about having to butcher it," the man said, then he turned to look at me, and I could feel his gaze on my temple. "I would appreciate it if you didn't tell anyone that I brought you back here."

"I won't say anything," I murmured, still unable to look away from that thin silver line. "I promise."

"Thank you," the man said, and I heard him shift near my side. "So – do you have any preference on cuts? Some people take it all, and others leave the organs. If you have any special requests, I can try to squeeze them in, but if you do decide to take it all, you will want to make sure that you have a big enough car to transport it."

"I don't want any," I whispered, swallowing hard as I forced my eyes to leave the elk's face.

"What?" the man asked, his face twisting with confusion as I met his gaze once more, and he looked down at me in concern.

"Thank you," I said, forcing my lips into a smile. "For letting me see it – it really is incredible, but I don't want any of the meat. I don't need it."

The man hesitated, his eyes shifting up to the bandages on my head.

"Are you sure, Ms. Eldritch?" he asked warily. "That is a *lot* of food – you could give it out to family or friends if you don't need it. You could freeze it – it will keep for a long time, or you could at least take *some* of it."

"I'm sure," I said, a true smile crossing my lips as I gestured up to the bandage on my head. "I didn't hit my head that hard; I promise – I genuinely don't need the food. My parents are already well taken care of under their pension, and my friend is covered through the hospital mandate. I would rather that you give it to people who truly need it."

"Okay," he said, though he was clearly unsure if he should be accepting my words. "I'll write out a slip for the payout then and–"

"I don't want any money." I cut him off, shaking my head as I looked up at him and the freezing cold air continued to soothe my skin. "I meant what I said – *give* it to those who need it. Keep some for yourself as well. I'm fine."

"Ms. Eldritch–," he faltered, his mouth falling open as he stared at me in disbelief.

"My name is Lilah," I said, smiling again as some of the pain in my spine eased. "I insist. If you need me to sign any forms to document it, then I'll sign them, but I don't want anything, I promise."

"That is – incredibly kind of you, Lilah," the man said, and I could see something shining behind his eyes as he struggled to find his words. He cleared his throat, blinking twice before he gave me a soft and heartfelt smile. "You've just helped a lot of people – I'll make sure that it's distributed to those who truly need it, as you asked. I promise, and if you should ever be in a tough spot in the future and need any help – know that my door is always open to you. We usually have some scraps laying around."

"Thank you, sir," I said as I nodded. "I appreciate that."

"It's Kade," the man said softly, the smile still lingering on his lips as he stared down at me. "My name is Oliver Kade. Now let's get out of the cold before we freeze."

I followed him back out of the freezer and signed a 'for distribution' slip before he unlocked the front door, and I stepped back into the heat. It hit me like a wave, eating at my nerves and burning through my skin. By the time I reached the car where Ren was waiting, I was panting, covered in a thick layer of sweat, and gritting my teeth so tightly I was afraid they might crack. It had been bad before, but after being in the cold, it felt ten times worse.

"How did it go?" Ren asked as she started the car.

"Fine," I said, not meeting her gaze as I immediately opened the window and leaned my head against the frame. I sat like that for a long moment, waiting until the air conditioning was blasting and the car was moving before I spoke once more. "I saw it."

"You saw it?"

I could feel her eyes on me as she glanced in my direction.

"Yes," I muttered, still not meeting her gaze as I watched the endless buildings soaring by the open window.

"And?" Ren pressed.

"It wasn't a deer," I whispered, knowing she could still hear me. "It was an elk."

Incurable Changes

November

'*Experts are unable to explain the cold weather that has swept across the nation and left millions of people scrambling for food, resources, and heat. The bizarre cold front caused temperatures to drop below ten degrees and snow to fall from the sky. Children can be seen outside playing as officials and law enforcement struggle to keep things under control. It's been over a decade since snow was last seen in this area, and now local natural gas and electric companies have been struggling to meet the early demand as thousands of residents turned on their heat yesterday in an effort to cut the chill.*'

'*Experts, police, and medical staff at local hospitals are urging the public to stay home and avoid travel at all costs. Employees are advised to work from home if possible, at least until the municipal government manages to get the streets cleared. As a result of the strange weather, motor vehicle accident rates have increased by over 200% and several dozen people have ended up in the hospital in critical condition. Our meteorologists at CKPX News have been working around the clock with the National Weather Institute to try to gain a better understanding as to what may have caused the unlikely phenomenon and when it will end. We will have an update later tonight with the 11:00 pm news.*'

312

I frowned. The injuries and accidents weren't limited to strictly car crashes. Ren's hospital had been bombarded with people who were injured from slipping on ice or shovelling their driveways. Yet even knowing the strain that it was putting on her and the other hospital staff – I would be lying if I said that I wanted the cold to end, because I could finally breathe again.

'Global outrage was sparked when the Autonomous Defence Bill G-1348 was tossed out last night right before the vote. Three days ago, an email thread was leaked showing that close to a dozen countries were paid to support and promote the bill when it was presented to the UNC – violating lobbying legislation and leaving the bill void in the eyes of the UNC council.'

'Advocates for civil rights are praising the whistleblower who released the email chain, while others have grown concerned that now nothing will be done. Frustration with the UNC's inaction and their inability to put a stop to the ongoing HUANEE attacks has led to protests outside the UNC Chambers in Zurich and in capitals around the world as people demand that a global state of emergency be declared.'

'Declaration of emergency status would give the UNAF additional resources and abilities to make arrests. It would also allow governments to implement widespread lockdowns, curfews, and strict protocols for travel. As of 6:00 pm tonight, the UNC has indicated that they will be holding a vote on Sunday morning to determine if a global state of emergency should be declared, and in the meantime, they are deploying additional troops to suspected potential targeted locations and encouraging all industries that may be threatened to tighten their security measures.'

Based on the severity of the most recent attacks, that was much like asking a small fish to defend itself against a bull shark; or telling a town to protect itself against a tornado by hiring more rent-a-cops. While I was grateful that Bill G-1348 had been tossed out, it was clear the UNC knew that dealing with HUANEE was beyond their current capacity when they were already dealing with the Sovereign Federation. They had probably hoped that the problem would go away by now and that an individual country would have made an arrest to stop the attacks or help pinpoint the group.

'Despite the UNC's confirmation that a new bill to replace G-1348 is in progress and will be processed and put into action within the next two weeks, experts are saying that it won't be enough. They are claiming that the UNC has been purposefully avoiding dealing with the HUANEE attacks because their resources are stretched thin with the ongoing war. The U.S. Secretary of Defence supported the claim, stating that there simply are not enough troops to manage the ongoing fight overseas while trying to track and prevent the increasing number of HUANEE attacks on American soil. The Canadian Prime Minister is expected to make a statement later tonight, while the United Kingdom, Japan, Australia, and South America are allegedly considering pulling out some of their troops as the threat of nuclear war grows.'

"Unsurprising," I muttered as I quickly grabbed my warped colander and placed it in the sink.

'Yesterday marked the nine-month anniversary of the first HUANEE attack, which occurred in India in February. Since then, incidents have spread across the globe, with over fifty confirmed attacks linked to the environmental organization and dozens of others suspected to be related to HUANEE's actions. At this point, the total death count is unclear, but the UNC has confirmed that HUANEE is responsible for at least three hundred dead or missing people. The body count is still being tallied after three more catastrophic attacks took place this month along the Western Coast of North America.'

'When questioned on their progress, UNC Officials have stated that tracing HUANEE is like looking for a single needle in thousands of haystacks. Last month the Indian government made two arrests, and the individuals have remained in questioning since, but it is still unclear if any charges will be laid or if the arrests have revealed any details about the main organization –

which seems to be a common theme and highlights the struggle that the authorities are having with trying to dismantle the group as a whole. Individuals arrested near any crime scenes often turn out to simply be witnesses. They have no prior convictions, no history of extremist behaviours, no knowledge of HUANEE, and are, in many cases, simply people in the wrong place at the wrong time.'

I couldn't help but roll my eyes as I dumped the boiled penne into the colander and began to rinse it with water. HUANEE had been active for nine months that the UNC was aware of – they didn't seriously think that the group would be stupid enough to linger around crime scenes, did they?

Ren had been right; authorities were getting desperate, and they were questioning anyone they could justify by current law. Just last week I read an article from the U.K. Journal, which reported that a ninety-two-year-old man was brought in for questioning because security footage placed him near an attack. After it was revealed that the man was homeless and that he knew nothing about what had happened, they quickly released him, and police refused to answer any additional questions.

'There are countless websites online that track HUANEE's movements and try to predict future attack dates and possible locations, but those websites have only caused country-specific governments more problems as it draws extremist crowds, content creators, and religious fanatics to potential attack sites. Several refining and manufacturing facilities have had to bring in additional private security to keep people away from the fence lines and off company property since they are unable to get the support that they need from UNAF or their local governments. This has ultimately only made identifying members of HUANEE more difficult, and it has increased the security risks and safety concerns around potential attack sites.'

Ah yes, the fanatics. They were the other half of the problem.

The UNC has stepped in to try to get the websites identifying these potential attack locations taken down, but so far, the effort has been futile. As one site comes down, three more are generated, and those being removed have filed lawsuits citing freedom of speech violations. The developers claim that their websites are not promoting HUANEE, nor are they instructing people to swarm the potential attack locations.'

'One website developer we spoke to, who asked to remain nameless, insisted that his website was intended to be used for good. With a master's degree in mathematics, he had worked closely with several colleagues to create algorithms to track and pattern HUANEE attacks in an effort to save lives. He hoped that by identifying potential attack locations, people could prepare, take precautions, or potentially leave the area. He has insisted that he has nothing to do with the organization, that he does not condone their attacks, and that by shutting down his website, the UNC is putting the public in danger.'

'He claims that these shutdowns are being implemented to try to minimize the negative effects that the attacks have had on several industries and that the UNC is caving to corporate pressure by strong-arming small websites. This theory has been widely supported after three corporations recently reported record losses, then indicated that they had mass walk-offs and difficulties getting employees to stay and work after their locations were listed on his website as a potential at-risk zone.'

"Which is no doubt true," I muttered, absently dumping the penne back into my only pot before grabbing a jar of sauce. It had expired several months ago – but that was normal. Everyone ate food that was past its expiration date now.

'Additionally, the website creator claims that based on his research, HUANEE attacks started before February of this year and that they have been ongoing for a number of years. He and his colleagues have dedicated hundreds of hours to researching the attacks and looking for similarities, and they are convinced there are more than two hundred and fifty events that can be linked – but no one had noticed the pattern to date. Up until

HUANEE began to claim responsibility for the attacks, which drew global attention, these events were previously blamed on weather, equipment failure, and a number of other independent factors.'

'Our source remained adamant that he does not necessarily believe that HUANEE is behind the attacks and that instead, it could be something else or some other organization. He believes that the UNC is trying to downplay the extent of the attacks as they struggle to manage the ongoing war while fighting internally against several countries that are calling for the UNC to disband.'

I raised a brow, my hand pausing mid-stir as I stared at the television. I knew that the infighting was ongoing, but his theory about HUANEE was certainly a new one.

'Regardless of what our source's intentions may be, it is undeniable that his website has led to dozens, and in some cases hundreds, of people flocking to these potential locations, which is putting strains on local resources and overwhelming authorities already desperate to keep up with their everyday demands while hunting down HUANEE. The UNC and local authorities have urged people to stay home and have even gone so far as to hand out fines and authorize arrests of people who refuse to leave – though this effort has done little to stop the flood of the curious.'

'Reporter Mark Wong spoke to three such individuals who had been lingering near the battery manufacturing facility that was targeted last month, and when asked why they had been there, they indicated that they came because they wanted to see Veles. The three teens were not charged in the incident as they had been escorted home by security two days prior to the attack, but they stated that they regret not fighting back against the security. They said they wished that they would have stayed for another two days because then they, "would have seen Veles in all his glory, and gotten pictures."'

'At this point, these crowds have caused nothing but problems, and several national governments have declared that they will not wait for the UNC any longer, vowing to take actions into their

own hands over the coming days. Others have conceded that they will not be able to remove the crowds completely, so they are requesting that anyone who does attend potential site rallies be vigilant and report any suspicious behaviour. They are hoping that with so many cameras and social media streams rolling, they might be able to use the additional footage to find the perpetrators of the next attack.'

"Oh, *shit!*" I reached for the pot on the stove that was burning and quickly turned off the heat.

It had been a while since I had cooked anything, and I had gotten completely lost in the news report. I glanced up at the clock that sat next to the few family photos that I had, and I frowned at the time, wondering if the pasta was still salvageable. It wasn't for me, it was for Ren, and she would be here in the next half hour.

After my accident, Ren had made a point of stopping by once a week to check up on me. It was probably related to the fact that I had refused to go back in for the additional testing that Dr. Davis had ordered. Initially, she had attempted to argue with me about it, but I had point-blank refused, and she eventually gave up. Looking back on it in hindsight, I should have just gone in for the stupid testing. It might have prevented her from starting these mandatory weekly meals and saved her from being subjected to my terrible cooking.

It wasn't that I didn't enjoy spending time with Ren or seeing her more often; it just stressed me out. I was worried that she was taking too much time off work, and I was concerned that she was wasting all of her time trying to take care of me. Even without having any family, I knew she must have better things to do with her time. On top of that, I was struggling to find answers to the questions she asked each time she came by.

Why is your hair so much longer?
I don't know; maybe it's my vitamins.
Why do you look taller?
I don't know; maybe I'm just standing
straighter.

Why are you always sweating?
I don't know; maybe it's a thyroid issue – I booked
an appointment to get it checked out.

All of those were lies.

I hadn't booked any appointments, and I certainly wasn't taking any vitamins. In fact, I hadn't eaten in the last three days because I wasn't hungry – I never was. I knew she meant well, but she wasn't helping. Her badgering did nothing but get under my skin and I couldn't tell her the things that she wanted to know.

I couldn't explain why I was constantly in pain or why sometimes there was a thick red ring outlining my irises. I couldn't explain why there were massive claw marks on my bedroom walls and small flowers starting to sprout from the cracks by my window. I couldn't explain why there was a second faint outline forming on my back between my shoulder blades – or rationalize why, when I looked it up, it seemed to resemble the symbol of another Slavic god. I couldn't explain why huge sections of time were missing from my life over the last month and a half or why sometimes I would wake up not remembering where I had been or what I had done for the last twenty-four hours.

I had tried to go back to work a week after my accident, but I was sent home only three days later because I couldn't stop sweating in the heat of the small office. My eyes had physically burned under the light of the fluorescent bulbs, and I'd nearly passed out at my desk multiple times while trying to finish a report. My boss saw me as a liability; I was useless to him because I couldn't go outside for very long before I collapsed onto the ground, panting and gasping for air. As a result, I had spent the last five weeks at home on an extended medical leave.

Every morning I got up to look outside the window and see if the undercover cop car that was staking out my apartment building was still there, watching my every move. I spent the day watching the news, reading things online, and trying to keep track of the bizarre changes to my body. Then, every night, I went to sleep for a few hours only to wake up screaming and thrashing in my bed, covered in sweat as horrid images filled my mind. To say that I had not been handling it well was probably an understatement.

I was obsessing over it, and it was impacting everything that I did.

I had gone to visit my mother for her birthday last Saturday because I caved under Ren's incessant nagging, but the experience had been awful. I took the public transit because I still didn't have a new car, and I hadn't wanted Ren to take yet *another* day off work to drive me around. The train was cramped, hot, and stuffy. I couldn't breathe. I passed out briefly, missed my stop and then had to wait for the next train to double back. The entire time an undercover police officer followed me; he even waited outside my parents' home while I completed my Ren-mandated and extremely uncomfortable visit.

A part of me was pissed that he hadn't woken me up when I passed out on the train. It wasn't like he didn't know where I was going, and if he was going to constantly follow me around, he could at least be useful.

I let out a sigh as I stared at the half-burnt mess of food. I loved my parents but seeing them hurt. I reminded them of Elizabeth, my sister. We had always looked alike, and every time that they laid eyes on me, I could see the pain.

Ren was wrong.

She thought that I avoided them because I hadn't dealt with what had happened – and maybe a part of that was true – but it wasn't the real reason. The reason I only went over two or three times a year, and why I contained our limited communication to text messages, was because I knew it hurt them. I hurt them. My mother could barely look at me. My father struggled to speak to me. It was tense and awkward, and I knew that underneath their pain, they silently wished that it had been me instead.

I didn't fault them for that – because I thought the exact same thing.

Elizabeth was their favourite for good reason. She was my favourite, too. She was kind, caring, and selfless. She lit up every room she walked into. Losing her had permanently damaged my family, and my parents did better when I wasn't around. I had been happy to see them that day and confirm that they were doing well, that my father's pension was still taking care of their needs and that my mother had been volunteering at a local hospice. Otherwise, I had nothing to say. So, I finished my tea, wished my mother a happy birthday and left. I smiled and waved to the officer who tailed me home, because we both knew why he was there, and I was tired of pretending like it wasn't going on.

Then I cried myself to sleep.

Yet that wasn't even the worst night after my accident, and there were so many it was hard to pick. Was it the night that Ren had come by with a belated birthday cake the second week after my accident, and I got angry at her for wasting her money on useless things? Was it the time that I woke up screaming so loudly my neighbours called property management to complain, and I ended up standing there in my doorway, letting my landlord yell at me as blood dripped down my throat? Was it the night I was convinced I was hearing voices and going insane? Was it the time that I told Ren that people having kids in this broken world was irresponsible, selfish, and stupid – and she had looked entirely gutted? Was it the time that I woke up inexplicably covered in mud? Or was it the time that I woke up drenched in so much water, I must have been in a pool because it would have been physically impossible to sweat that much?

It was so hard to tell.

Most of my days and nights blurred together. I couldn't keep track of them, and the missing sections of time only made it worse because they were starting to make me uncomfortably suspicious.

I jerked when I heard a knock on the door, my eyes quickly glancing toward it as my brow furrowed in confusion. Ren wasn't usually early – she was typically right on time, but with the way that the weather had been, I figured it was possible that she may have left early to avoid road closures. Letting out a sigh and putting the pot of questionable pasta down on the counter, I made my way to the door.

"You're early, Ren. I thought–"

My voice cut off, and I froze as my eyes went wide.

"Ms. Eldritch."

It was Inspector Wilson's deep voice that greeted me as he stood there before the door in a set of casual clothing. My eyes quickly swept over his body and flicked to each side. If he wasn't in uniform and no one else was here, it was unlikely that he was going to arrest me. As far as I knew, our local government hadn't done anything that would allow him to do so – a strange car accident nowhere near an attack site was hardly grounds for arrest – but I wasn't going to put it past him to try. He seemed to know what I was thinking, though, because he smiled at me, and a small chuckle left his lips.

"Lucky for you, Bill G-1348 just got thrown out," Inspector Wilson said, his eyes tracing over my frame before they lingered at my high neckline. I fought the urge to pull it higher as I stared at him apprehensively. "And so far, the remainder of your record is clean."

His eyes shifted to glance over my shoulder into my apartment. I moved, closing the door slightly and blocking the space to obstruct his view as I forced myself to meet his gaze, but I didn't say a word.

"Am I interrupting?" Wilson asked, his brow arching in question.

"No," I said, fighting to keep my voice calm. "Why are you here?"

"Just coming to check up and see how you're doing," he said as he placed his hand on the wall beside my doorframe and casually gave me a smile.

"On a Friday night?" I asked, scoffing in disbelief. "You don't have better things to do?"

"Nope," he said, his eyes creasing as I frowned. Then his gaze shifted to my forehead, and he nodded towards it. "Your forehead has healed up nicely. Can barely even see the line."

"Thank you," I responded instinctively, even though doing it made me want to cringe.

"I dropped by three days ago," he continued as if we were old friends catching up. "But you weren't here."

"It's too bad I missed you then," I said, barely managing to keep the sarcasm from my voice. I fought the itch that slid down my spine at his words. Three days ago was one of the days that I couldn't remember, and I knew exactly why he was bringing it up.

"Funny thing about that is," Inspector Wilson said as his voice dropped low and he met my gaze with an intense stare. "My officer doesn't recall seeing you leave that day."

I refused to say anything in response to his prompt. By all legal rights, I could close the door on his face because he had no grounds to be here – but I didn't want to make things worse. Especially not for Ren, because I knew they were watching her too.

"Do you know what happened three days ago?" Wilson asked, and I stiffened under his gaze. "A refining facility was attacked."

"So I heard," I whispered, my stomach twisting into a knot. "It's been on the news."

"It has," he said, nodding in agreement. He took a step forward, and my hand tightened on the door. "Don't you find that odd? Especially since you seemed to disappear for twenty-four hours when it happened."

"Not particularly," I said, and I had to fight to keep my voice level because my lungs were starting to seize in my chest. Wilson wasn't the only one who was suspicious. I had also noticed that all my blocks of missing time seemed to center around recent HUANEE attacks, but I legitimately had no recollection of those days and thus no explanation for it. "I'm sure that lots of people weren't at home when it happened – but I *was* at home. I just wasn't feeling well, so I slept the full day. I must not have heard you knock."

"I see," Inspector Wilson said, but he didn't move away. "Where were you on the 12th?"

"Visiting my mother for her birthday," I responded, my voice dry as my eyes narrowed at him. "But you already know that – your officer followed me there and sat outside the house."

"You didn't stay for very long."

"I never visit for very long," I whispered as my voice began to shake. "Anyone who knows me can confirm that."

"So why did you fall asleep on the train?" Wilson pressed, his eyes briefly sliding over my face before his gaze shifted to try to see into my apartment once more. "What has you so tired? Or were you just trying to throw my officer off?"

"I already told you that I haven't been feeling well," I answered as I felt my nails cracking against the wood of the door. "I didn't mean to fall asleep or miss my stop; it just happened. Maybe next time, you could tell your officer to be more considerate. He could have woken me up. I was lucky I wasn't mugged. Look – I have shit to do, so either arrest me or tell me what you want – but don't waste my time."

"You already know what I want," Inspector Wilson whispered as he took another small step forward. "And when I get it, you're going to tell me everything."

"And you're going to be disappointed," I whispered back as I glared at him. "Because I already told you that I don't know a damn thing."

He stared at me, neither of us moving for a long moment until his eyes narrowed critically. I could practically feel his gaze burning over my face as he seemed to analyze every little detail.

"You look different," he murmured, almost to himself more than to me. I heard a door open down the hall, and the noise seemed to pull Inspector Wilson from his thoughts as he took a step back. "I'll see you soon, Ms. Eldritch."

I glared at him, watching as he turned and started to step away.

"Tell your officer that he shouldn't smoke so much," I called after him, irritation flooding through my body as Wilson turned back to glance at me over his shoulder, and he smirked. "And tell him that his disguises look ridiculous, I know he's there – and so does everyone else on this block!"

He waved his hand in the air as if to acknowledge the feedback, the smug look on his face making my anger flare. I tried to control it, but I was unable to stop myself from slamming my door as I went back into the kitchen and grabbed the pot of pasta in frustration. I managed to pick out enough non-burnt bits to make up a plate and had just placed it on the table when I heard a second knock on the door. Gritting my teeth and desperately trying to push down the lingering rage, I checked the peephole before I opened it this time.

"Hey, Lilah, I saw Inspector Wilson leaving the lobby, did he – oh my gosh, it's cold in here," Ren said as she wrapped her open jacket around herself. She dropped her purse on the floor by the door where she always left it and turned to look at me in concern. "Why is your balcony door open? It's below zero outside."

"Sorry," I said, side-stepping her small frame and making my way across the room. I had completely forgotten that the balcony door and all my windows were open. I had done it the second that the temperature dropped and the cold front rolled in, and while it didn't entirely remove the burning sensation inside my body, it did at least make my days more tolerable. "I forgot I opened them – it was hot while I was cooking."

"Right," Ren said, but I knew she didn't believe a word I had just said. She never questioned the fact that I kept nearly all the lights off, but being suspicious of below zero temperatures while I was wearing a pair of shorts and a t-shirt seemed fair. I quickly closed the balcony door and the main window as she continued to watch me closely. "I'll just leave my coat on."

I didn't say anything when she turned the volume down on my television, and I joined her at the table as she rubbed her hands together to keep warm.

"You're not going to eat?" she asked, pausing as her hand reached for the single bent fork I had left in my possession.

"I already ate," I replied, giving her a tight smile. My skin was already starting to itch and burn without the frigid cold air drafting through the room, and I wasn't sure I could handle her questioning after seeing Inspector Wilson.

"Alright," Ren said, and I could see the concern shifting behind her eyes. She didn't argue with me, but she watched me almost cautiously as she took her first bite. "How did the visit with your parents go?"

"The same as usual," I said, averting my eyes and clearing my throat. "They're still safe and managing under my father's pension."

"Well, that's good," she replied as she took another few bites of the pasta, and the tension between us continued to grow. I could see her toying with her necklace from the corner of my gaze, and her next question was unsurprising. "What did Inspector Wilson want?"

"Nothing," I said, continuing to avoid looking at her.

"Really?" Ren pressed, her hand dropping back to the table as she fixed me with a look. "He came all the way here from the Headquarters just to say hello?"

"What do you want me to say, Ren?" I asked, finally meeting her eyes. "He wants to arrest me. He wants to charge me for a bunch of things that I didn't do because he's convinced that I know something about HUANEE, but he can't – so he's just harassing me."

"Do you know anything?" Ren asked bluntly, and I stiffened in my chair.

"What?" I said, the word coming out like a hoarse whisper. I could feel my heart clenching in my chest as I stared at my best friend in disbelief. I knew she had her doubts about what I claimed happened that night, but this was a whole new level of distrust. "You actually think that I'm part of HUANEE? That I'm involved in these attacks because of that stupid tattoo?"

"I didn't say that," Ren said. "I asked if you *knew* anything about them."

"How the hell would I know anything about them?!" I hissed, my hands curling into tight balls on the table. "Why would you even think that?!"

I couldn't believe this. I couldn't believe that she would doubt me. Anger exploded in my chest, but apparently, I wasn't the only one struggling to keep my frustration at bay because Ren's face suddenly twisted into a mess of emotions.

"Because after your accident, you've been acting like a completely different person!" Ren burst out, jamming her fork straight up into the bowl as her eyes traced over my face. "The world is falling apart, and you seem to be *enjoying* it! I came by here three days ago to drop off some food – I knocked, but you didn't answer. I got worried, I thought maybe you had fallen, or God forbid that you had killed yourself, so I let myself in, but you weren't home. Your room was *trashed*, Lilah – there were claw marks down the wall like a wild animal had been let loose, and plants were growing from your window! Then – I found out that a refinery was attacked not even one hour after I left! But that officer who's been tailing you this past month was still lurking across the street watching your apartment as if he thought you were home. He didn't move the entire time that I was here!

"You don't eat! You don't sleep! The tattoo on your chest has gotten darker since the last time that I saw it – don't even bother trying to pretend that it hasn't. You look like you've grown four inches taller, your skin is ashen, your hair is basically on steroids, and there's always this angry burning look in your eyes!" Ren yelled as her hands gripped the table tight. "That's why I'm asking, Lilah – because I'm terrified! I'm terrified of what's happened to you – I'm terrified that I'm going to find out you're somehow involved in all this, and I'm going to lose you forever!"

I sat there, dumbfounded and speechless as the pain in my heart seemed to splinter, and I could feel it splitting in two. The anger that was always there under the surface had been ignited by Inspector Wilson, but now it began to rise at Ren's words, and I could taste it like bile at the back of my throat.

How could she think that I knew anything about this? How could she possibly think that I was involved in these attacks? But worse than the pain of my breaking heart was the sinking feeling in my chest and the nauseous twist in my stomach – because I had already thought the same thing.

I couldn't explain why. I couldn't prove it with any certainty, except for the chunks of missing time that lined up with *every* single attack, one of the many oddities that now surrounded my messed-up life. The day that I had woken up soaking wet was the day after there was an attack on a fishing facility along the coast. The day that I had woken up covered in mud was three days ago – the day immediately following the attack on the refinery – and it had been a muddy, rainy mess the day before. The burning anger that Ren spoke of – I knew what it was. It was the rage that scalded my skin and made breathing the most painful thing in the world before the cold had come. It was the fire that had been injected into my soul the very second that elk abomination had touched my skin.

She wasn't wrong. I didn't care about the attacks, but she was wrong about when that had started. I had *never* cared. I had always supported them, and I had always secretly wanted them to get worse. Not because I wanted people to die, but because I didn't think that we deserved to live. We were dancing on the edge of extinction, and we were taking the planet with us. I had always thought it would be best if people just disappeared because I no longer believed that we could learn. But before I could open my mouth to say anything in return, a bright breaking news banner flashed across the television, and both our gazes shifted toward the screen.

'We interrupt our regularly scheduled coverage to bring you a breaking news update surrounding the refinery attack three days ago. Recovered security footage has been leaked online. Local officials are claiming that the footage was only just now recovered. However, the UNC is facing allegations from several internal whistleblowers that they have similar footage on file from other attacks that have been kept from the public eye and withheld even from national government officials. CKPX forensic video analysis specialists have completed a cursory review of the files, and they believe that the videos are legitimate.'

'Over the next few days, we will be investigating further and pressing the UNC for updates to determine if there is additional footage. We caution viewers that while this footage is brief and blurry, it is disturbing, so viewer discretion is advised.'

I watched the tense expression on the lead anchor's face as the program switched over to the security footage. I had been watching this channel for years, and I could tell just by her expression that whatever was coming wasn't going to be good. My eyes stared at the dark and seemingly uneventful image. It was of a roadway outside the facility near where the main gatehouse had been. Streetlights lined the walkway, and dull shadows shifted in the background as faint lights glimmered and flares lit up the sky. It was silent, almost eerily so, and just as my eyes started to narrow in confusion as to why they were showing it, I heard it. The dull whispers that were constantly in my head.

Except the noise wasn't coming from my head – it was coming from the television, and it was getting louder.

I sat rigid as a board in my chair, watching as shadows began to shift in the sky and a god-awful noise broke out. I heard the refinery alarms go off, but the loud wail from the multiple horns was drowned out by the horrendous noise that seemed to be coming from the very earth itself. There was a crack, accompanied by a groan; then a massive fireball shot up into the air on the right side of the screen as something in the refinery exploded. The light nearly blinded the camera, but not before it lit up something massive, and the news station slowed the video.

My heart caught in my chest. My throat went dry. I stared fixated and horrified at the massive moving object that seemed to stand taller than the refinery itself. It was impossible to make out in full because of the poor footage quality, but the shape of a jagged-looking wing was unmistakable. Three red glowing orbs flashed through the darkness as a roar split through the air. The security camera rattled so violently that the image began to stutter and blur. The whispers grew louder, darker, violent like the hiss of a kettle about to boil until another massive explosion went off and the camera turned to static.

The anchor came back on as headlines scrolled along the bottom of the screen. I could hear the low drone of her voice in the back of my mind, but I couldn't make out the sounds because my heart was racing in my chest, and my body had gone numb. The whispers in my head were thrumming like a heartbeat, filling the air around me. Surely Ren could hear them, and if she did, she would know.

Images flicked through my mind – the sound of fire, the smell of burning gas, screaming, hissing, yelling, alarms, the slick feel of mud as it covered my skin while the rain began to pour. The anger in my chest was starting to grow. I could feel it inching through my skin all the way down to the tips of my toes as every muscle in my body contracted.

I couldn't breathe.

I was suffocating.

I could feel the burn of heat against my skin as something painful shifted down my spine and split from my back.

"LILAH!!"

I hissed out in pain, my body convulsing violently as Ren's fingers burned against my already hot skin. I glared up at her and made to pull my arm away. She was going to let me until her eyes locked on mine, and then her grip tightened. I could feel her nails sinking into my wrists as sweat began to gather across my skin. Her bright blue eyes narrowed with scrutiny, and suddenly she was tugging me closer, all but climbing across the table as she reached out and grabbed at my face.

"Red," Ren whispered, her eyes growing wide with terror as they shifted between mine so rapidly, I could barely track it. "You have red rings around your eyes, Lilah."

The anger in my chest exploded, and I tore away from her grasp, pushing back from the table so hard the chair toppled over behind me. My vision was starting to blur. My hands were starting to shake. I could taste bile at the back of my throat again as my heart was squeezed so tightly, I was sure it would burst. I staggered away from Ren as fear ripped through my chest. Those images. Those sounds. I remembered. I was there. She needed to leave – it wasn't safe.

I wasn't safe.

"I have a headache," I hissed, desperate to get away from her and terrified of what might happen if I didn't. "You should go – go."

I stumbled down the hall, covering my mouth with my hand to stop the vomit from pouring out as I raced to the bathroom, wrenched the door open, and slammed it shut behind me. I could barely hear as the whispers grew louder and my pulse tripled. I threw up in the tub, coughing and gagging as my sweaty hands slid across the cold porcelain. I could hear Ren banging on the door behind me, the sound barely audible under the noise in my skull as I vomited once more and groaned out in pain. An ungodly sound rattled the room before my head snapped back to glare at the door.

 "GET OUT!!"

The words tore my lips like a snarl – deep, dark, and violent. I didn't recognize my own voice – because it wasn't mine. It sounded like a thousand different voices melded into one, and I cringed at the noise of it. I started to hyperventilate. It was hot – too hot. I scrambled from the edge of the tub, slipping on the floor and colliding with the wall as I fought to wrench open the window.

I ended up breaking the glass. I could feel the burning blood dripping down my forearms as I thrust my head outside and inhaled the frigid cold air. I shuddered, my eyes falling closed as my legs began to shake.

I couldn't feel my limbs.

I couldn't stop the tears that burned in my eyes as more flashes of fragmented memories broke through my mind, and I knew with absolute certainty that it had been me.

My grip on the edge of the window weakened as I tried to calm my racing heart, but the agony within it only seemed to grow more unbearable. I gagged again, slipping down the wall as my legs finally gave out beneath me, my blood-coated hands too slick to hang on as I crumpled into a pile against the wall. I clawed at my chest as it began to burn beneath the symbol that marked my skin and a sharp shooting pain cut between my shoulder blades. My nails scratched at the cold floor tiles as I curled into a ball and wheezed for air.

Heat.

Fire.

So much pain it consumed my vision. I forced myself to inhale as I continued to shake, but when I finally managed to pry my bleary eyes open and my gaze shifted across the dark bathroom tiles, I froze. There, beneath my fingers, sticking out of the old dull ceramic squares, was a flower and seven blades of grass. They were small and fragile. They looked weak, as if they hadn't been watered in days, and the grey flower drooped next to my finger.

A ragged exhale left my lungs, and I forced myself up from the floor. The whispers in my mind continued to thrum, but this time they beat in sync with my racing heart as I staggered to my feet. I stared at the tiny patch of green, mesmerized as the murmur began to form words in my mind, and this time, I could hear it.

And I started to cry, because it was a plea for help that cut through my soul.

I stumbled to the sink, my eyes distant and unfocused as I listened to the words in my head. My gaze shifted to the person in the mirror – but I didn't know them. Their hair was too dark. Their skin was too ashen. Flecks like freckles covered their skin, and I could see the faint glow of red that radiated from the shadow's eyes. The green was barely there in the center, nearly entirely consumed by the hellfire that was encompassing my body.

As I stood there, sickness churned in my gut and, without understanding why I was doing it, I raised my hand to the wall and dragged it down the cream-coloured paint. Blood smeared against the surface as the intense heat surged within my chest. I watched, emotionless and heartbroken as green began to sprout. Images started to flick through my mind again as I fell against the door, and my bloodied hand slipped on the handle. They were the same memories as before, but this time they were slower. The first time I hadn't understood. It had been too chaotic, too disjointed, and too blurry for me to see – but not anymore.

I could see it all.

I could *feel* it all.

I tumbled out into the hallway, cracking my head against the opposite wall as I struggled to find my balance. The shake in my legs was so violent that I could barely walk toward the living room. Ren was gone. Thank God Ren was gone. Her half-eaten pasta remained on the table with the fork still standing straight up in the bowl. My red gaze shifted over the worn and battered wood as I clutched my stomach and gritted my teeth in pain. My vision blurred, but I forced myself toward the table as my bleary eyes locked to a small square card that sat in the center. I could barely pick it up as I struggled to control my fingers, and my heart dropped as I realized what it was.

It was a printed photograph, a copy of the picture that Ren had taken when she had brought me a cake for my birthday five weeks ago. Our smiles were forced, our expressions were tight, and everything about the photo made my body ache in heartbreak.

I didn't recognize this person either.

She was nothing but a shell – a hollow, empty version of what she had once been. In truth, she had died long ago, and all that was left was the bitter and broken remains. I tucked the photo into my pocket as the scorching heat in my body surged, and I doubled over in pain. An agonized cry left my lips as it felt like someone shoved a hot knife down my throat.

Too hot.

Too hot.

I couldn't breathe.

I wheezed for air and stumbled toward the balcony door, my hand dragging across the wall and leaving a trail of green behind it as the whispers in my mind became a low chant. I barely made it to the glass as another reel of memories flooded my head. It was all I could do to pull the door open before I collapsed into the snow that covered my balcony and another ear-splitting cry left my lips. My vision blurred as I rolled to look up at the sky, but I was unable to see the stars through the thick smog that concealed the night.

It hadn't always been like this.

I hadn't always been like this. There had been a time when I believed that things could change. When I believed that *I* could change – but not anymore.

I was burning alive.

And the world would burn with me.

The Great Destruction

'*Voting on the 'HUANEE Response' Bill G-1349 closed less than ten minutes ago, with several last-second amendments being added to the table. The UNC is expected to make an announcement within the next hour regarding an extension of the global emergency, which was declared last Sunday. Additionally, they will be providing more details related to G-1349, which is currently expected to pass with more than 70% of the ballots.*'

'*Regardless of the bill's quick development and the UNC's immense efforts to push it through in record time to appease the public, confidence in the global authority has reached an all-time low, with several countries pulling their representatives out of Zurich immediately following the vote and stating that they will no longer abide by UNC laws.*'

My dull red gaze lingered on the screen as my fingers gripped the back of the chair I stood behind. I had expected the bill to pass. However, I had not anticipated other nations pulling out from the UNC so quickly. It had always been inevitable – but watching nearly a dozen council members being rushed from the grounds seconds after they cast their ballot was quite the sight.

The UNC has declared that any countries that refuse to abide by the global laws or that attempt to circumvent their obligations under the Global Unified Efforts Bill will be hit with heavy sanctions and treated as threats to global peace – joining the same league as the Sovereign Federation. Already, an increased number of UNAF officers can be seen stationed outside of the UNC Chambers in Zurich in anticipation of escalating protests and violence. Several UNC officials have gone off the record to state that they are concerned the recently revealed information, which they insist they knew nothing about, will result in a military coup and the dismantling of the UNC in its entirety.'

The unrest, which has been steadily building for months, exploded last Friday when security footage was leaked showing something destroying a refining facility in Western Canada. Since then, over the last eight days, four more attacks have occurred, and additional footage has been exposed confirming that not only has the UNC been aware of the links between the destructive events – but also that they have been actively hiding its existence as they struggle to maintain control and manage the ongoing war.'

In the past five days, more than fifteen different videos from as early as ten years ago have been released online. Following the string of recent attacks, new cellphone footage has been posted, and mass panic has ensued. Crime rates have skyrocketed, religious factions have called this "the end of days", and authorities are struggling to maintain peace as looting and chaos have broken out.'

My eyes shifted to the open hole where my balcony door used to be. I could see the riots from here – the flicker of lights as sirens rang in the distance, the trails of smoke from fires as people panicked and looted. They were afraid.

And they should be.

Experts have been unable to explain what can be seen in the video footage, but online, millions of people have drawn their own conclusions. Many remain adamant that the videos prove the existence of a greater being and that we are beholden to its wrath. The UNC has refused to issue a statement, but the outline of a

VELES

large black creature with three red glowing eyes, clawed feather wings, and a supernatural sound has been impossible to deny, no matter how impossible it may seem.'

'Reporter Mark Wong interviewed a man who supposedly witnessed the most recent attack at the Don Haven Dam yesterday, and the man described the sight as 'otherworldly', 'horrifying', and the 'most overwhelmingly traumatic experience of his life'. He refused to speak on it further, and he became immensely ill when we asked him for additional details.'

My brow arched as my gaze returned to the television, and I felt vines intertwining my fingers as they twisted around the back of the chair. His description wasn't entirely inaccurate – but I couldn't help but feel like he was being overdramatic. Don Haven Dam had not even been that bad.

'Yet this recently revealed footage is not the only matter that has the world breaking into disarray. Two hours ago, the U.S. President announced that they would be pulling back 90% of their troops from the war amid recent losses. The President claims that the battle in the east has come to a standstill. He stated that drone and missile attacks on the western shore of North America are inevitable and that the United States could not wait for the UNC to approve the use of nuclear weapons and full-scale airstrikes when the war is only moments away from crossing the Pacific Ocean and threatening the safety of billions of additional people.'

'At this point, the U.S. has not given a timeline as to when they plan to extract their troops or what countermeasures they intend to independently launch against the Sovereign Federation – but the UNC has formally condemned the President's actions, citing a breach of the Global Unified Efforts Bill, which requires all UNC nations to abide by the UNC's direction during war.'

I snorted, the harsh sound coming out cold and detached as I stared at the flashing colours that flickered across the screen. A piece of legislation would not stop the United States from pulling out its troops. Nor would it prevent the other nations from following suit. I had no doubts that the talks were already in progress, and it was only a matter of time – not that it would make any difference.

> *'Currently, there has been no evacuation ordered by any North or South American governments, but that has not stopped people from fleeing the western coast as fears of an attack grow. Within the chaos, countless places of worship have opened their doors around the world and are encouraging people of all backgrounds and affiliations to come and join them. Most are calling for world peace and praying for deliverance as they repent and ask for forgiveness.'*
>
> *'On the other hand, some have welcomed the war and have started to breach existing NORVIX and travel restrictions in order to gather. A few have issued formal statements declaring that the world's time is up and that this is the Rapture or the beginning of the Book of Revelation. The divide among religious communities has caused worldwide outrage and condemnation, with groups accusing one another of using these arduous moments as a method to sow more fear, spread hate, and generate profit.'*

I let go of the chair, rolling my stiff shoulders back as I let out a breath. Praying wasn't going to save anyone, and bringing religion into this only caused more confusion. My inhale rattled like the wind through the trees as I felt another explosion go off somewhere in the east. My eyes narrowed, and I could feel my muscles tense with pain. It wasn't as bad as the airstrike had been, but the anger in my chest was swelling regardless.

> *'At this time, we do not have an update on the situation in the east after an airstrike decimated the UNAF airbase in Kyiv two days ago, but military officials have stated that the ground has been lost and that they will not be able to go in to complete a search and rescue until the area is secured. It's unclear when that may be due to an unorthodox strike by the Sovereign Federation, which took out dozens of satellites and left UNAF partially blind. Though we are hopeful that there will be more information within the next twelve hours.'*

'Our network would like to remind viewers that CKPX News remains dedicated to bringing you updates as soon as they are available. We understand your concern, and we feel it too, but at this time, we would like to urge the public to please stay at home. Follow the directions of your local authorities, keep your radios, on and charge your electronic devices in preparation for unexpected power outages.'

'If an airstrike is inbound, the emergency sirens will go off, and evacuation directions will be provided. However, as of this moment, no attack is expected and attempting to leave the city will cause more harm than good. With the continued snowfall, city workers are struggling to clear the roads and—'

A knock sounded to my left, tearing my attention away from the television screen as the news began to cover the latest update on the looting and crime that was happening less than twenty kilometres from my apartment. My eyes shifted to the dark wooden door almost lazily as a deep sigh left my body. I knew who it was, and I didn't want to answer the door, so I turned away to gaze at my balcony once more.

The snow was getting thicker.

I could barely see the trails of smoke from the riots anymore through the intense flurries. Yet it still didn't feel cold enough. I was able to breathe more easily, but the constant burn that scalded my throat continued to smoulder. It was getting uncomfortable, so I urged the temperatures lower. Colder. Freezing.

I wondered how low I could make it drop.

After last Friday, when I realized what I had become, it had only taken me a day to figure out how to do it. It wasn't difficult, all I had to do was desire it, and it would happen. So I had dropped the temperature another ten degrees and broke the hole in my wall. It took one more day to figure out how to control the snow. Another to figure out how to control the change of my body, and a fourth to be able to shift the ground beneath my feet at my will.

And, as I figured it out, I had begun to systematically remove the problems that plagued my mind and caused my body to burn.

Yet it still wasn't enough.

I could feel it.

Each living creature's movement felt like ants crawling over my skin, and I wasn't sure how much longer I could take it as every sensation in my body was replaced with nothing but pain. My emotions were all but gone, buried beneath a vast sea of rage. Smothered by a boiling blanket of tar, and it was getting difficult to remember what it felt like to know anything other than hatred. There was only a sliver of green left in my eyes now, and I could see and feel it fading with each breath that I took.

It was only a matter of time before I broke beneath the crushing pressure. It was building like a wave in the ocean – roiling, pulsing – hurtling toward the coast. I still didn't know what this thing was. Even though I could use it, I didn't truly understand how. I was barely in control, and I knew it wouldn't take much for me to lose it.

"Lilah."

I blinked as the knocking on my door intensified, and the familiar voice rang out.

"Lilah – open the door!"

More pounding against the wood.

I didn't understand why she was here.

"*Lilah!!* I'm not going anywhere, so open this door!"

We hadn't spoken in eight days, not since I had screamed at her to leave. That was probably for the best because I couldn't even begin to imagine what she must be thinking right now or what I would have said to her if she had come back sooner. She had to know. In my heart, what little remained of it, I knew that she did, and I didn't understand why she would return here willingly.

"LILAH!!" she screeched, smacking the door even harder than before. "If you don't open this goddamn door right now, I'm going to break it down!"

Ren's scream of frustration echoed into my apartment as her knocking became violent and desperate. There was a loud thump as if she had kicked the wooden surface. Then I heard the sound of a key scratching in the lock before the handle twisted and the door opened the width of the security chain.

"Lilah!" Ren yelled, shoving against the door again. "I know you're in there – open this fucking door!!"

Shifting across the floor in three rapid steps, I shoved the door closed, unhooked the chain, and then wrenched it back open in full. I stared down at her, my glowing red gaze scanning over her tiny frame. She was wearing a thick winter jacket, two sweaters, and what appeared to be thermal hiking boots. She was clutching mittens in her hands; her hair was a dishevelled mess and coated in snow – but she looked up at me defiantly, her eyes like a raging storm of water.

"What do you want?" I asked, my unnatural voice making her physically flinch.

I stepped back from the door, feeling entirely indifferent. There was no point in hiding anything now, it wasn't like she or anyone else could do anything to stop me. I watched the way that her eyes shifted around my apartment as she hesitantly stepped inside. Her gaze lingered on the pile of snow near the hole to my balcony, then on the endless streams of vines and flowers that sprouted from the walls, floor, ceiling, and chair.

She looked uncomfortable; I could see her swallowing as she slowly took another step forward then stiffened as her gaze latched to the smears of blood on the wall. She stared at them, then her eyes dropped to the large black feathers that littered the floor. I was fairly certain that she was going to turn around and leave, but to my surprise, she straightened, determination flashing across her face before she forced herself to look at me.

"I'm leaving town," she said. There wasn't an ounce of fear in her gaze as she looked at me, but there was something else lingering beneath the surface.

"Good," I said, and she cringed at the sound of my voice again. *"You should go."*

"Von's friend Aleksander Kozak has a cabin in the mountains," Ren said, clutching her mittens tightly. "So we're heading there tonight before it's too late. Before we get stuck in the city."

I stared at her, not understanding why she was telling me this or why the hell she was here. It had been eight days, and I was sure that she would have already left town or called Inspector

Wilson to turn me in – and yet she hadn't. I remained silent as she shifted on her feet. I could see that she was hesitating, weighing her words and trying to decide how to say whatever it was that she was thinking as I stood rigid and uninviting before her like the demon that I was. She swallowed again, her hand coming up to toy with the necklace beneath her sweaters, and I stiffened as tears started to fill her eyes. Then she took a step toward me and stared up into my red eyes with the most devastating look I had ever seen.

"Why?"

The word was so hoarse and broken that I could barely hear it above the whispers in my mind. Ever since the airstrike in Kyiv, they were significantly louder, and I had been barely managing to ignore the heat.

"Why what?" I asked, my eyes narrowing at the harrowing look on her face.

"Why did you do it, Lilah?" she whispered, her voice breaking as her head started to shake. "All those people – you killed all those people."

"Those people killed themselves," I said, finally understanding what she wanted as her eyes squinted in pain. She came for answers. She came because she needed to understand, and she couldn't accept the truth.

"It's not you," she whispered, still shaking her head. "What happened to you is making you do this – it's not you, Lilah."

She was wrong, but telling her that was a waste of time. I could feel her heart racing as her eyes started to shine. I could tell that she was struggling not to fall apart. She came here looking for something that no longer existed, and she needed to leave.

"You should go," I said, and a single tear broke loose and fell from her eye.

"Come with me," she breathed, a sob nearly leaving her lips as she took a shaky step forward.

I could hear the news anchor on the television announcing that UNSA had just received a ping from the Viking Outpost and Bill G-1349 had passed with 80% approval. They were beginning to rhyme off the new capabilities of UNAF and national law enforcement, as well as the approved bill amendments. Ren's eyes shot to the screen, and she swallowed hard before urgently meeting my gaze.

"Maggy is waiting downstairs in my car with her son, and we're leaving now," Ren whispered as she raised a shaking hand to reach for my arm. "Aleksander already left to make sure the roads are clear. Von is meeting us there – I want you to come with us, please."

I nearly snorted at her words, but to my surprise, I felt them stir something within my chest. I stared at her for a long moment, struggling between the urge to be cruel under the heat that burned my body and my desire to keep Ren safe.

"You know I can't do that, Ren," I said finally, as a dull, empty ache tugged within my hollow chest. Her fingers brushed my ashen skin, and my eyes cringed in pain as I took a step back.

"Yes, you can," Ren pressed as she followed my step. "You don't even have to pack anything. We have enough stuff. Just grab your jacket, and we can go – we can leave right now."

Had she lost her mind? Had she not seen the news? Aside from my inexplainable appearance, which would most certainly terrify her friends, the idea was terrible and impossible for a multitude of other reasons. The most prominent being that I just couldn't.

"Ren," I said, shaking my head as the ache in my chest started to grow.

Why were her words affecting me like this? Why was this so hard? I'd spent the last week in an emotionless void, without an ounce of remorse for what I had done, and yet somehow seeing Ren was making my heart break.

"I don't have a choice," I said finally, but she shook her head in denial.

"Yes, you do!" Ren retorted, her voice growing louder as tears flooded her eyes completely. Her hands clenched into fists, and I could hear the heartbreak in her voice as she stepped forward again and glared up into my unfamiliar eyes. "You have *always* had a choice, Lilah. Just because you started down this road doesn't mean that you have to stay on it. I am asking you; I'm *begging* you – please, don't do this. Whatever this is, whatever has happened to you, whatever is hurting you – we can figure this out! You can leave now and come with me, and we can make this right! There is still hope, Lilah."

She reached for my hand, tugging at my humanity and urging it to break free from the dark and impenetrable box that I had stuffed it in when the burning had taken over my body.

"I can't," I said as bile began to bubble at the back of my throat.

It hurt.

I could feel her ferocity eating at my soul, but it wasn't enough to drown out the whispers – or maybe I was choosing to listen to the constant murmur over her words. I didn't know. I couldn't tell anymore, but I could feel my discomfort growing as the hatred in my chest raged.

"Can't?" Ren challenged as her face crumpled with pain. "Or won't?"

"They're one and the same now, Ren," I muttered as unease flooded my veins. *"You don't understand the hold that it has on me – what it is. You don't understand the pain. This has happened before, and it will happen again – over and over until the end of time because people are never going to change."*

"You're wrong," she whispered, her eyes growing hard as she raised her head higher. "You've always been wrong. You have and will always have a choice, Lilah."

Her eyes narrowed at me, and I realized what it was that had been lingering behind her gaze. It was disgust. It was pouring from her gaze like smoke from a fire, and it stabbed through my already broken heart.

"Elizabeth would be ashamed of you," she whispered, and I stiffened at her words as her eyes traced over my tall frame with contempt. *"I* am ashamed of you. You have a gift. You have the chance to make a true difference in this world – the ability to undo the damage. You could teach people how to change, and you're squandering it. And not only are you squandering it, but you're actively making it worse by *choice* because you're too angry to see this any other way."

I stared at her for a long moment as the news report continued to drone on. A thousand thoughts and scenarios raced through my head, but all of them concluded the same way, and I knew that Ren would never understand. She didn't know about the burn, the whispers, and the darkness. She didn't know what had happened before, and she didn't know that this was inescapable. There was nothing I could do, and there was nothing left for me to say. The world was falling apart. Inspector Wilson would be here soon now that Bill G-1349 had finally passed, and I had no intention of going anywhere with him, but she didn't need to be here for that.

"You should go," I said finally, as the brief flicker of emotion that had been budding in my chest was snuffed out and burned to ash by the unyielding rage in my core. *"Get out of town while you still can, and stay away from the coast."*

She stared at me hard, something cold shifting behind her eyes as she reached into her pocket and pulled out a scrap piece of paper. Then she all but shoved it into my hands.

"What's this?" I asked, my eyes dropping down to glance at the crumpled note.

"It's an address," she said, her eyes raking over my form once more. "It's where we're going, and it's where I hope to find you again. Because even though you've entirely given up – I refuse to. There are still good people in this world, Lilah, and they are desperate to make things right. So I won't stop believing. Not now. Not ever. Not even in you – because I can't."

Her voice broke, and her right hand grabbed the fabric over her stomach tight as her left gripped the necklace that lay beneath her sweaters.

"I have to believe," she whispered as more tears began to roll down her face. "You still have the opportunity to change this, Lilah. The world would understand."

I watched as she forced herself to leave. Her face was pinched in pain, her shoulders had dropped in defeat, and it looked like she was carrying the weight of the world on her back as she stepped toward the door. She paused when she reached it and lingered there for a moment as she turned back to face me with an agonized look.

"Please come back to me, Lilah. The world needs you. I need you."

Then, for only the second time in my life, she left me.

I stood there staring at the wooden door, unable to move as the image of Ren's broken face lingered in my mind. I had never seen her look like that. In all the years that we had known each other, and with all the things that we had been through – after her parent's deaths and the bout of illness that had nearly claimed her life as a teen – she had never broken, not once.

Until now.

Until I broke her.

My eyes shifted away from the door as a sharp shooting pain ached through my heart. How did this happen? How had we gotten here? When had I become the source of Ren's pain? Was it now, or had it always been me?

The questions spun as I stared at the wall, and my eyes landed on the pictures that sat next to my old, barely functional clock. I moved toward them, unable to breathe as the muscles in my chest seized. I gathered them both in my hands, my bleary eyes shifting over the familiar faces as the pain grew worse and morphed into a dull ache.

I never let myself look at these anymore because it hurt too much to bear.

The first photo was from a family dinner. It hadn't been a significant night, but my mother had insisted that we take it. All four of us were seated around the table, laughing at the joke that my father had just told us as we all teased my mom for her failed attempt at risotto that evening. The second was of my sister and me. She was smiling wide, her eyes nearly sparkling with joy as we celebrated my twenty-first birthday.

That felt like a lifetime ago now, but the memory was still fresh as ever.

I hadn't wanted to wear that stupid crown – but Elizabeth had made it by hand, so of course, I had worn it without complaint. She had baked me a cake that day too. She had spent hours decorating it, adding sprinkles and flowers and going all out. I remember that it tasted terrible. For all my sister's talents, she was an awful cook, but my parents and I hadn't had the heart to tell her after she had worked so hard on it. So we ate our pieces with vigour, insisting that the cake was delicious, even though she was incredibly skeptical of our praise. She hadn't been able to eat it herself to confirm, though, because she had been allergic to wheat.

My heart dropped.

When had I grown so cold?

Was it after her death – or was it before? It felt like it had always been there, a splinter in my heart festering like an infected wound, and her death had simply exposed it. I had always been ugly on the inside. Perhaps she had been what was keeping it at bay all those years because I couldn't remember a time when it didn't exist.

I don't know how long I stood there, motionless, unbreathing, and paralyzed with conflicting thoughts, but I could see the sun setting behind me from the corner of my gaze. I could feel my emotions dancing below the rage that was consuming my soul, and they were screaming at me in pain, begging me to listen. I didn't want to do this – or did I? I couldn't answer that question with confidence anymore, but I knew that Ren was right.

Elizabeth would be ashamed of me.

If it had been me and not her, this never would have happened.

If she had been the one in that accident, she could have found a way to soothe the burn.

My hand clenched around the small bit of paper that Ren had given me as my heart started to race. I could still grab my jacket. What I had done was unforgivable, but maybe Ren was right; maybe there was still time? My feet moved despite the resistance that I felt in my bones, and I grabbed my thin spring jacket from the hook by the door. I pulled it on, wondering what the hell I was doing and how on earth I would be able to change this. I tucked the two photos into my coat pocket before grabbing the one of Ren and me from off the table and securing it as well. I fought against the instant flare of heat that encompassed my body as I buttoned the extra layer of clothing.

It didn't have to be like this. *I* didn't have to be like this.

Maybe.

If I could just resist the pull.

The blaring sound of emergency sirens split through the air, startling me from my thoughts as a sharp pain shot down my spine. My head jerked up to look at the television as bright banded colours flashed across the screen.

'EMERGENCY ALERT'
The Sovereign Federation has launched an airstrike against the western coast of North America. GMD interceptor missiles have been launched, but if the defence system fails, the blast radius is expected to reach the bay area and extend along the coast.'
'Residents are instructed to shelter in place underground, and if possible, to leave the city in a safe and orderly fashion. Police will be guiding traffic and opening all highways unidirectionally out of the city.'

I could feel my chest start to tighten.

'UPDATE: Sovereign Federation missiles have been launched toward Zurich, Sydney, and Tokyo.'

Sweat began to pour from every inch of my body as the heat became insufferable and the rage burned in my core. I couldn't move.

'UPDATE: the U.S. has launched a counterattack and—'

A scream tore through my lips, and my body crumpled inward as the most agonizing pain that I had ever felt split through my chest. It was worse than the airstrike in Kyiv. Worse than the pain of the heat. Worse than the pain of the rage.

It was toxic, noxious – choking me with excruciating agony. I knew what it was without even understanding how as my skin began to bubble and burn, and my eyes grew wide with terror. Radiation, and it was going to kill me. It was burning through my limbs and dissolving my bones. Any thoughts I had of my own vanished as the second wave hit, and the scalding hellfire in my center exploded from my chest in a wave of rage and death.

I was lost in the current.

The flesh of my body was nothing but a tool for the immense power that surged within me. Everything faded away – all I could see was red and black as my lungs inhaled and a god-awful noise split from my mouth.

Burning. Burning. Burning.

It was all burning.

The smell of seared flesh filled my nose as water began to rise. I could taste it in my mouth, the ash of the bodies that were melted beneath the lava drawn from the earth. Rock crumbled as the air scorched with heat. I was the land. I was the air. I was the sea. I was all of it – everywhere – and as I inhaled then let the tormented sorrow screech from my lungs, the world buckled and broke beneath my feet.

Land vanished.

Mountains rose.

The earth was reshaped, and I could feel it all as the broken remains of my heart shattered into pieces, and I drowned beneath the rage. I couldn't see, I couldn't breathe, I couldn't hear as the blazing red encircled my body, and I vanished from existence while destruction reigned over the earth.

PART THREE

The Truth

Fire. Burning. Pain. Death.

Mizuki gasped for air, collapsing to her knees as a wash of white flooded her vision and the world twisted back into view. It was like being hit in the gut, like having her insides pulled outward through her ears as her body burned and her mind split in two. She gagged, an intense wave of nausea twisting her stomach as if it was trying to ring it dry. Bile filled her mouth, she could feel it in her nose as every scream and every desperate cry for help echoed in her mind, and then the sickness burst from her body as her nails bit into the cold stone.

She retched, blood and bile splattering across the ground as her eyes burned with tears.

"All those people," she wheezed, gagging again as tears poured down her face.

It was in her head.

Under her skin.

She could taste the ash in her mouth and smell the burnt flesh as if it were inches from her nose. She had never seen such destruction. She had never felt such heat, such anger, such violence, and such scorching hatred before in her life. How had that woman survived it? How had she lived it?

Mizuki felt like her heart was being ripped into tiny pieces as a broken sob left her lungs, and she collapsed against the ground completely. She couldn't breathe. She couldn't handle it. *Billions* of lives were gone in an instant as this *thing* reigned terror and destruction across the globe on a scale that the world had never seen – but this thing wasn't a thing at all, and it wasn't a god.

It was human.

It was Lilah.

A woman who not only allowed the world to end; she had wanted it to.

"You killed them," Mizuki whispered, her arms shaking beneath her battered body as she pushed herself up to her knees and looked at the deformed creature. It was standing there in silence, watching her while its dull red eyes continued to show no emotion whatsoever. "You killed all those people."

"That much is obvious," the creature replied, its low voice making Mizuki cringe.

"All of them." Mizuki agonized, bile burning the back of her throat again as her eyes pinched in pain.

She could feel more hot tears streaking down her face as she glared up at the creature. She knew that she would never be able to unsee the horrors in her mind. She would never be able to unhear it or to rid the smell from her nose as she watched thousands upon thousands of people burn beneath a volcanic eruption while millions more drowned when their country was obliterated by a colossal wave of water.

"Even t-the children," Mizuki stammered. "How – *how* could you do it?"

"I showed you how I did it," the creature answered, and Mizuki felt her stomach lurch at the emptiness that radiated from the beast's eyes.

How could it not care?

How could she feel nothing after everything that she had done?

"Your family," Mizuki whispered, her breath catching as a new wave of nausea hit. "You killed your *family* – how could you do that? Your mother and father – how?"

"It was what was necessary."

Mizuki shook her head and clenched her eyes shut tight.

No.

It wasn't.

It hadn't been, and even Lilah had realized that at the end.

Another sob left her lips as she opened her bleary eyes and resisted the urge to gag. She felt like she was covered in a layer of death, dirt, and grime – and she knew she would never feel clean again. How had that woman become this heartless and cruel? The cold calculation had always been there, but what she had done was unforgivable in a vastly different way. The magnitude of it had been like nothing the world had ever seen. It was mass annihilation on a global scale, and she refused to believe that this creature could be so indifferent.

"You didn't even give them a chance," Mizuki countered, and she saw the creature's quills bristle.

"They had their chance."

"No." Mizuki shook her head more firmly, her disgust and anguish morphing into a flicker of rage as she hauled herself up from the ground. "That's deerspit, and you know it. You could have helped them. You could have shown them – you could have done *anything* other than what you did, but instead, you killed them all! *Billions* of lives in the blink of an eye!"

Mizuki swayed on her feet, a wave of dizziness washing over her body from the effort as her left shoulder sagged. She met the creature's eyes once more, but this time her fear dissolved away as she stared up at the abomination, utterly repulsed.

"You were right," Mizuki whispered, a cold tone seeping into her voice. "You're not a god – you're a monster."

Its quills prickled again, and its eyes narrowed.

"I'm a monster?" it growled, its voice shaking the ground beneath her feet. It stalked toward her, stopping less than a foot away and towering above her small frame as the red glow from its eyes intensified. *"You humans destroy everything that you touch – you have no regard for any other living thing and no respect for this planet. There was no hope for your kind. There has never been any hope for your kind. That's why this happens again and again. Had I not acted, they would have decimated the earth along with everything else that lives on it."*

"*You* were human once, too, Lilah," Mizuki whispered as she raised her head to look the creature straight in the eyes. "And *you* were the one that destroyed this planet. Not them."

The feathers around its neck flared, and its eyes narrowed into slits of anger – but she wasn't afraid, because beneath the creature's burning rage, she had felt an endless sea of agony. A deep sadness started to fill Mizuki's heart. This thing had single-handedly destroyed the world. It'd had the strength and will to sink continents into the ocean and nearly break the earth in two, and while it made her sick with disgust, she felt bad for this woman, and she felt pity for this creature. Even if only fleeting, Lilah had wanted to change, and her inability to do so broke something deep within Mizuki's heart.

How tormented and broken must she have been to harbour such anger? How long had this thing existed in darkness and hatred to be in such pain? How lonely and how utterly lost must Lilah have been to see this as the only way out?

"I pity you," Mizuki murmured, fresh tears springing to her eyes. "That you could see no other way except for the one that you chose. That you couldn't see the love that was there; you were surrounded by it – but blind to it. They didn't all deserve to die."

"They didn't all deserve to live," the creature growled.

"Maybe not," Mizuki whispered as she swallowed hard. "But you didn't bother to sort them out, did you? You didn't even try. You had all that power at your fingertips. You had every chance to make a change, to *help* them, and you didn't. You saw them as a lost cause because you saw exactly what you wanted to see, what you had *always* seen. You had already decided long ago that the earth wasn't worth saving, so you gave up. You did this, Lilah – not them."

Mizuki stepped back from the creature, staggering across the stone floor toward the mess of vines that lay just a few feet away.

"What are you doing?"

The low growl made her skin crawl, but Mizuki ignored the uncomfortable feeling. It was nothing compared to the agony that now sat on her heart, and there was nothing that this creature could do to hurt her more than she already was.

"I'm taking these vines," Mizuki grunted as she looped the green strands and then attempted to lift them from the ground.

Her legs shook beneath her as she stood. The wolf bite on her calf was starting to ache something terrible, and she knew it was probably infected and covered with mud, but that didn't matter. None of that mattered. Her heart was beyond broken, and under the weight of the horrors that she had seen, she wasn't sure it would ever heal.

But there was still one thing left that she could do.

"I'm going to save my friend," Mizuki murmured, not speaking to anyone in particular.

"Your friend is already dead," the creature said. Its voice was cold, and it shifted across the stone out of her way as she forced her legs to move.

"You don't know that," Mizuki said, staggering forward under the weight of the vines as sweat began to pour down her face.

She knew she was crying. She could feel the steady stream of tears trailing down her face with each step she took, and she knew that the poison had likely reached her heart. It wouldn't be long now before it gave out, and it was unlikely that she would make it back down the path to him.

"You're going to die," the creature said, and Mizuki simply nodded in agreement to its blunt words. *"You'll die before you even get to him."*

"Probably," Mizuki admitted, pausing before the curtain of water that ran over the entrance of the cave.

She turned back to look at the creature as her heart ached in pain. It hurt. So much more than she could explain, and the sorrow was like an endless pit in her chest as her bones threatened to give out.

"But I won't know that unless I try," Mizuki whispered, watching as the creature shifted at her words. "I'm not going to give up. Not now, not ever – not even if you think it's pointless. I'll fight until I take my last breath because I will not leave my friend to die alone. I'm dead either way, Lilah, so I might as well die doing what I know is right."

Mizuki saw something flicker behind the creature's eyes before she turned and marched into the darkness. She wasn't sure what it was. It was too fast for her to place it, but the creature had gone impossibly still at her words and remained unmoving inside the cave as she crossed the threshold into the night. It didn't follow her through the water, but she could feel its gaze boring a hole into the back of her head as she gripped the vines tighter and moved across the plateau.

The descent was so much worse than the climb. She had assumed that it would be the other way around since gravity would be working in her favour – but it wasn't. Her feet slipped on the mud and rocks. Rushes of water threatened to carry her off the edge as the cold wind tugged at her body. The rain stung like needles as it collided against her burnt and weather-worn skin. The lightning that flickered through the sky felt closer than ever as she fought her way down the ledges in a tangle of thick vines.

Her lungs burned, her chest ached, her pulse continued to race, and sharp pains stretched across her sternum. She sliced her knee open on a rock, nearly falling over the edge as she was blasted from her feet by a massive gust of wind. She couldn't see the cut in the darkness, but as her fingers quickly brushed over the torn hide of her pants, she could feel the warmth of her blood and the shredded fragments of skin.

Her body grew hotter from the poison, and the sweat continued to pour. She knew that it must be freezing outside, and yet she felt like she was boiling alive as she staggered around the bend and made her way toward the place where Aiden had fallen.

"AIDEN!" Mizuki screamed, her voice barely audible over the wind as she stumbled toward the broken edge and dropped the vines to the ground. Her stomach lurched as she collapsed against the ground, laying in the mud as she inched closer to the edge. Her broken nails dug into the dirt and stone as she leaned her head over and scanned her eyes through the darkness. "AIDEN! AIDEN – I'm back! Are you there?!"

It was getting harder and harder to breathe. She could feel her heart starting to slow as it struggled to beat. She peered through the rain and willed her eyes to find the small ledge again.

"AIDEN!!" she screamed, her throat tearing as she shuffled along the broken edge. She could taste the bile at the back of her throat as fresh tears burned in her eyes. She couldn't lose him. She couldn't bear the thought of having left him here to die. "AIDEN!"

"Mizuki."

"Aiden!!"

His voice had been so weak she barely heard it, and it wasn't until the next flash of lightning that she managed to find him in the night. He was curled against the edge of the crevasse, still sitting on the small ledge that had stopped his fall. She shuffled another ten feet along the edge, so she was above him and caught sight of his face as another massive roll of thunder shook the ground.

"Aiden!" she yelled, a choked sob leaving her lips. "I'm here."

"Thank Veles, I thought you had died," he said, and she couldn't stop herself from smiling down at him.

"Not yet," she sniffed, wiping the water and tears from her eyes. "I found some vines! I'm going to drop them down and pull you up!"

She didn't wait for him to respond because she didn't care if he thought this was a good idea. She didn't care if he was worried that he might pull her over or that it might end in tragedy. She shoved herself up from the ground, groaning out in pain as she crawled through the mud toward the vines. She grabbed the one end, dragging the thick green strand across the path toward the nearest jagged rock that stuck up from the edge. Giving it a shove with her shoulder to make sure that it wouldn't break, she then wrapped the vine around the stone and hoped that the thing would hold.

Her hands slipped as she tied the knots, she had to use her knee and her body to get them tight enough before she staggered across the stone dragging the rest of the bundle with her. She made a small loop at the other end, then threw it over the edge toward Aiden as she laid back down in the mud.

"Can you grab it?!" Mizuki yelled, watching through the flashes of light as the vine whipped through the air.

"I don't know!" Aiden struggled to reach it, and as a giant flash of lightning cracked across the sky, she realized that the ledge he was sitting on was even smaller than before. The right half of it had cracked away, and she didn't doubt that the rest would be soon to follow. She watched as he failed three more times, then finally managed to grab hold of the vine. "GOT IT!"

A deep sigh left her lungs. She closed her eyes tight, then forced herself to continue knowing that even with her plan, Aiden might not have the strength to climb up the rock wall.

"Stick your good foot in the loop!" Mizuki yelled down to him, hoping that he would be able to hear her over the howl of the wind as it ripped over the path above her. "Climb the rocks using your arms! I'll pull the vine up as you go and loop it around the rock so you can use it as a foothold!"

She heard him yell back in agreement then watched with bated breath as he struggled to his feet. She let out another sigh of relief as it became clear that his broken leg was the same one that had been shot with the poisoned arrow, and she felt her heart surge with hope that he could still at least partially move his left arm. When he was finally gripping the rock wall with both hands and appeared ready to climb, Mizuki got back to her knees and shortened the vines, wrapping them around the jagged rock as many times as she could until the makeshift rope was tight. Then she struggled through the wind across the path to look back over the edge and signal for him to start.

The climb was slow and painful. Twice Aiden nearly lost his hold and collapsed back to the ledge below when his poisoned arm gave out and he lost his balance. She could hear him groaning out through the storm as he struggled to keep going, and she continuously called down to him in reassurance. She didn't know why she was doing it. She had never been particularly good at giving encouragement, yet she found herself unable to stop talking and the ramble poured out uncontrolled.

Maybe it was the guilt of having left him there alone. Or maybe after spending seven days by his side and finally opening up to him, her discomfort had fallen away, and the flood of feelings she once kept tightly dammed was now rushing forth with a current too strong to be stopped. She wasn't sure, but each time he inched himself closer to the top, she called out to him then forced herself to crawl across the path to pull the vine tighter.

As he grew nearer to the top, the green strands groaned in protest under his weight. She didn't know how much longer it would hold, but after wrapping the thick vines around the jagged rock for the fifth time while Aiden clung to the cliff face to keep his weight off the line, she wasn't sure that she wanted to trust it. Stumbling across the path once more, she saw the first hint of light in the distance. Morning was coming, but the storm had yet to let up. She dropped to her knees in the mud and pulled herself toward the edge, then leaned over once more.

"Aiden, grab my hand!" Mizuki yelled as she kicked her toes into the mud and extended her right arm as far as it could reach. He was just a foot below her now, and she could see the strain on his face as he squinted up through the rain. "I don't think the vine will hold!"

"Mizuki," Aiden panted, his face grimacing as he forced himself to grab the next rock and haul himself up. "I'm not sure I can make it."

"Yes, you can," Mizuki said, stretching her arm out as a sharp jolting sensation cut across her chest. "You're almost there – you can do this."

An agonizing groan came from his lips as he pushed off the vine hard, hauling himself up the rock face as he reached for her hand. She heard the sound of a snap as she grabbed his forearm, and the vine slid over the edge. Aiden's weight tugged on her arm, and she skidded across the path before his foot caught a rock along the face of the ledge.

"Don't let go," Mizuki grunted, her nails sinking into his forearm. The throbbing sensation in her chest was making it hard to breathe. It was radiating through her entire body now, and it was everything she could do to keep her hold on him as her muscles threatened to give out. "We're almost there."

His nails cut into her arm as he struggled to keep his footing on the slippery rocks. She could see the sweat on his face as he looked up to meet her gaze through the rain. Their eyes locked as a flash of lightning lit the sky, and then a gust of wind tugged his body, and she felt her shoulder strain as his left arm slipped from the wall.

"Aiden!" She gripped him tighter, her eyes closing as she slid through the mud closer to the edge. She could feel the rocks scraping against her feet and legs as her shoulder nearly slipped over the edge.

"Mizuki."

She opened her eyes at the soft sound of Aiden's voice, and when she met his gaze once more, her heart caught in her throat. He was looking at her in a way she had never seen before, and it made her stomach twist. The narrow rock shelf beneath his good leg broke, and he slipped another half foot down before it caught another lip.

"Mizuki," Aiden said softly as he strained from the effort of clinging to the vertical wall. "You have to let go."

"No," Mizuki whispered, and she fought to dig her feet into the mud and spread herself wider against the surface of the path. She could feel her body slowly sliding through the mud closer and closer to the edge as Aiden's feet continued to slip. "I can't – I won't – I'll pull you up."

"Mizuki–"

"No!" Mizuki's vision blurred with tears as a sob cut from her lungs. They were burning so badly that she could barely breathe, and when she blinked her eyes so she could look down at Aiden, she felt her broken heart shatter as a dark red glow crept over the horizon behind him. "I can't."

"If you don't let go, I'm going to pull you over this cliff," Aiden said, but she shook her head and gripped him tighter. She slid another inch through the mud. The wind ripped at her body, and she winced against the sting. Then she felt his grip on her forearm start to loosen, and panic surged through her veins. "You have to let go."

"No." She shook her head again, her nails scratching through his skin as his muddy arm started to slide through her grip. "Aiden, don't! Please don't do this. I can still pull you up!"

"Mizuki," he whispered, his tone so soft it was nearly inaudible as a massive clap of thunder rocked the earth. "I'm sorry – I'm sorry that we're here."

"Aiden, stop," she whispered, staring at him through the tears. "I already told you – there's nowhere else I'd rather be."

"I'm going to let go now, Mizuki," Aiden said, his eye fixed to hers as his fingers continued to slacken.

"Aiden, please," Mizuki pleaded, clutching him tighter as she slid through the mud. "Please don't."

"I never told you," Aiden murmured, his gaze searching her face as she heard the stones beneath his feet crack. He clung to the rocks with his left hand, but she could see his fingers slipping and his arm shaking with the effort. "All these years, and I never told you."

"Don't," she whispered, unable to look away from his face even though it felt like he was ripping out her heart. She knew what he was going to do. She knew what he was going to say, and the second that he uttered those words, he would let go, and she would have to watch him fall. *"Please don't."*

"Mizuki."

She felt tears stream down her face as she held his gaze. She didn't want this. Not like this.

"I lov—"

His words were lost on the wind as it rushed over her body and tugged at his frame. The fragile stone beneath his feet shattered, and she watched in horror as his arm slipped through her muddy fingers.

"AIDEN!!"

She shrieked as her hand outstretched into the darkness, and the wind tore his body away. She screamed again, watching as he fell further and further into the abyss as lightning cracked through the sky and thunder rattled her bones.

The wind caught her side, dragging her from the edge across the path through the mud. It filled her nose and mouth. Her nails scratched at the rock as she struggled to get her bearings until she rolled to a stop in a pool of water, and the rain began to pour from the sky in sheets. She forced herself to her knees, choking and gagging on the grime that coated her face as she scrambled across the ground. She dragged herself to the edge peering over it into the darkness as the erratic beat of her heart started to stutter once more.

"Aiden!" Mizuki choked out, desperately staring into the darkness and urging her eyes to see. The ledge he had fallen on was still there, but there was no sign of him or the vine. Any traces of his existence seemed to have been washed away by the mud and water that slid down the path. "Aiden."

Her voice broke, and her arms collapsed beneath her.

"No," she whimpered, struggling to turn herself over so she wouldn't drown face first in the mud. "No, no, no, no, no."

Her vision blurred with more tears as she rolled onto her back. She stared up into the sky through the rain that tried to flood her lungs as lightning flickered through the air. Her throat burned. She couldn't feel her left side anymore, and she could feel herself sinking into the mud.

Why?

Why did it have to be him?

Why was it everyone surrounding her family?

Why did the Altherrs always fail in the end?

Ren had been unable to sway Lilah, Miku had been unable to sway the village, and now she had been unable to save the most important person in her life. Her family's history contained nothing but failures – and she would die here alone, drowned in the rain and mud as she sobbed, and her body grew numb. She couldn't even make it back to the cave or the village. If she had the strength, she would try. She would crawl back to the gate to try to find a way to tell the village what she had learned, but when she attempted to move her arm, and it remained motionless at her side – she knew it would never work.

She wasn't going anywhere. Besides, even if she somehow managed it, they would never let her in. The Elders would have the Village Guard kill her on sight, and for all she knew, anyone who would have listened to her was dead. She watched as another flash of white streaked across the sky, and the beat of her heart began to slow as her body went limp.

"I'm sorry," she whispered as the rain filled her nose and her vision began to wane.

She didn't know who she was saying it to, but she meant it from the bottom of her heart. She was sorry that she wasn't enough. Sorry that she had failed despite her best efforts. Sorry that her family had been tangled in this from the start and sorry that she had somehow managed to make it all worse. This wasn't how she thought things would end. She hadn't been lying to Aiden before, she had never expected to live very long, and she had always assumed that she would die outside of the village.

But not like this.

Numbness shifted through her chest as the pain that radiated down her spine lessened. It wouldn't be long now. She could feel it coming as her vision started to speckle with black. She hoped that her father was okay and that her mother was safe. She hoped that the O'Kanes hadn't faced any backlash, that Maebh got to grow old and be happy and that the girl didn't blame herself for what happened to Aiden. She hoped that the Elders lost their power – that maybe when they died, the next leaders would be more caring.

She hoped that her brother's death hadn't been this painful, that maybe he had passed in his sleep and that he hadn't wandered the mountain alone and afraid. She hoped that Aiden didn't feel the impact at the bottom, that he had died clean and peaceful, knowing that she knew what he had tried to tell her. That in many ways... she had always known. She had just ignored it because she was afraid – afraid of what she might feel if she let him in closer.

Her vision faded in and out as the rain finally let up, and the first full rays of morning light filtered through the sky. Her head rolled to the east to look at it, the mud sticking to her hair and face as her neck grew limp. It was strange how even now, as breathing became painful, she still found the sunrise beautiful. Not everything in this world was terrible, and she still, even now, believed that there was hope for those that would remain.

She let out a sigh, then a massive gust of wind blew up the side of the mountain, and she struggled to breathe as the air was all but pulled from her lungs. Her body slid across the path in the blast, her eyes closing tight as mud splattered through the air, and she was rolled onto her stomach once more. She dug her fingers into the mud to stop herself from blowing clear off the path as her barely mobile feet scratched against the cold stone. She knew it wouldn't matter if she fell, she was going to die anyway, but her body fought reflexively as if it was incapable of doing anything less.

Then as the wind stopped, the ground shook beneath her body, and a rattled exhale filled the air. She froze, the few muscles she could still control going stiff as she opened her eyes and forced herself to inhale. The ground rattled again, and her bleary eyes went wide as she fought to lift her chin and look up at the large, dark figure that was blocking out the rising sun. It stood before her like a demonic angel, its black wings folding behind its back. Its dim red gaze met hers, and when it lowered something to the ground, Mizuki felt her heart seize in her chest.

"Aiden," she croaked, a low groan leaving her lips as she forced her right arm to move.

She dug her fingers into the dirt, dragging her body forward as her legs struggled to push through the heavy mud. Her vision faded once more, and her heart rate continued to drop, but she didn't stop.

"Aiden – I'm here."

She clawed her way across the ground, choking on the mud with each pull she made as the creature did nothing but stand and watch. She ignored it. She didn't care that it was there. She didn't care why it was there or how it had managed to find Aiden – all she cared was that she reached him before she took her last breath, so he wouldn't be alone.

Sharp shooting pains crept through her heart and chest as she pulled herself the final few inches to his side. She grabbed his cold, bruised hand; it was covered in dark tendrils of purple and black. He was dead, probably, or seconds away from it – but that didn't matter, and she collapsed on her chest into the mud by his side as she gripped him tight.

She struggled to inhale. The muscles through her chest were starting to fail, and her breath came in staggered gasps like a fish out of water as she turned her head to look up at the creature that was still lingering on the path behind Aiden's body. It was just standing there, unmoving and indifferent, as its gaze remained locked to her face with an unreadable expression. She could just barely make out some of Lilah's features, her nose, her cheekbones, and the thin white scar that ran along her forehead.

Mizuki's vision blurred. She gripped Aiden even tighter, and her throat began to burn. Darkness was creeping in from the edges again, but this time, it didn't fade in and out. It stayed, and she knew it was permanent.

Her shoulders sagged, and her eyes began to flutter as her heart thudded painfully one last time.

"Thank you."

The words slipped from Mizuki's lips as the fuzzy outline of three green eyes faded from view. Then her grip on Aiden's hand loosened, the last of the air left her lungs, and her head dropped to the ground with a heavy thud as her eyes fluttered shut.

Death

Everything hurt.

It was worse than the pain of being bitten by that wolf. Worse than the pain of falling down the ridge as a child, and worse still than the pain that had ached through her body as she forced herself to climb the mountain through the storm. She could feel it in her bones, like a deep thudding ache that made her body heavier than stone.

Surely she was dying, and these were just her final moments, though a part of her couldn't help but feel like it was a shame her subconscious had woken to feel it. Images of her life were rolling by, and she watched them with a sense of morbid intrigue as she wondered how long it would go on until her brain finally gave out. Each passing memory grew older, and soon those from a long-forgotten past began to bubble to the surface.

She saw her brother Ren chasing after a frog near the lake during the early spring as she played along the shore, and a taller young boy collected different shaped stones nearby. It was the day that she had fallen into the water off the small, wet rocks and nearly drowned. Ren had called for her father, who was collecting kindling nearby, but it was the other boy who had truly saved her life. He had jumped into the freezing cold depths without hesitation and held her head above water until Kazuki dove in and hauled them both out.

It was the first time that she had ever seen her father visibly terrified. He had clutched her tightly to his chest as he carried her, her brother, and the other boy back to the Altherr home. She had spent the remainder of the day wrapped in a blanket before the hearth. Keelin had been a mess. She wouldn't stop fussing, and she kept brushing Mizuki's tangled locks from her face as she made them all bee balm and lavender tea to warm up. She must have thanked the other boy a thousand times, and Miku had insisted that Kazuki teach them all to swim. Keelin hadn't liked the idea. She thought that they were too young and the lake was too dangerous. What happened was clearly proof of that in her mother's eyes, but Miku had insisted, and so that summer, Kazuki taught them all how to swim.

The memory twisted in her mind as the ache in her body fell away. She was getting closer. Soon this would all stop, and she would finally die. She watched the memory reshape, and with a start of surprise, Mizuki realized that the boy who had saved her life that day was Aiden. He had been tall for his age and thin like all the other children in the village. His childlike face was so different from how she knew him now, but his curious and friendly amber eyes were unmistakable.

She must have only been five or six at the time, which would have made Aiden only eight or nine. It was a wonder that he had been able to hold her up for as long as he did, and as she watched the memory shift into a string of others, she realized that had been the moment that Aiden O'Kane entered her life.

Up until then, he had always just been a boy who occasionally played nearby while she and her brother ran around. Maybe he had always wanted to join them? Maybe he had been hoping that they would invite him to play along?

Maebh would have yet to be born, and so Aiden would have been an only child who was probably lonely. His da was gone for extended periods to hunt for food, and his ma was often busy working in the crops during the spring and summer.

It was no different than her own family or any of the others within the village. Life was hard, everyone worked – Kazuki was gone for long hours during the day, and Mizuki was often left unattended as her mother made and repaired clothing from within their home. The difference was, she'd had her brother and Miku, so she had never truly felt alone in those days. Aiden had his cousins, but they would have been too young or too old for him to befriend.

Something heavy and sombre shifted over her chest as the old memories continued to flow through her mind. She had never asked Aiden about that day, about why he had come to save her or why he had wanted to be their friend. She had thanked him as they sat around the fire of course, because it was the polite thing to do, but at the time, as a child, she hadn't understood the full gravity of what had happened. She hadn't fully understood the risk that he had taken by jumping into the lake.

Worse yet, she had forgotten about it.

Just as she had forgotten that her father had taught them to swim that summer and that her mother used to fuss about and dote over them with worry. Kazuki used to laugh, and Miku used to smile. Her brother put the frogs that he had collected in her hair and chased her with bugs. She had forgotten that Keelin and Miku brought Aiden home that day wrapped in a thick blanket and that they thanked Mrs. O'Kane so profusely the woman grew uncomfortable and flustered.

After that day, Aiden started to come by to play, and they would welcome him with open arms. He would sit around the fire outside and listen to Miku's stories while Keelin rolled her eyes and made them all food. She had forgotten just how happy they had been, how close they were, and how full of life her home was when she was a child.

She thought that these memories were lost, but in truth, she had pushed them all down along with the pain of losing her brother, Ren. For ten years, she never let herself think of him, and in many ways, she had all but erased him from her history. She never spoke of it. She never tried to remember him, save for a few occasional reflections, but those were never more than fleeting. Aiden never mentioned him either, and she wondered if that was because his own memories of her brother were painful or if it was because he knew how much it had hurt her and her family to lose him.

Did his ma tell him never to speak of it?

Or had he forgotten too?

A sharp flicker of pain jolted through her body as more memories flittered within her mind: Aiden helping them build a fort, Keelin braiding her hair, Kazuki teaching them how to carve, Miku making them tea and telling them the best places to find berries. She saw herself hugging Mrs. O'Kane tightly as she and her brother dropped off a new leather jacket that Keelin had made for Aiden's da.

She had forgotten how impressive her mother's work was, how intricately Keelin could wield a needle and how tight the stitching would be. Had she always hugged Mrs. O'Kane so freely in the past? She couldn't recall, and as more memories spun to the surface, Mizuki's heart constricted with grief. Her parents weren't the only ones that had changed the day that her brother died.

She had changed, too.

She could hear Aiden calling her name as she chased after him through the trees. Her brother was laughing – they were both so much faster. She was panting for breath, and her lungs were getting sore. She was frustrated that she couldn't keep up, so they both slowed down. Then Aiden helped her climb the tree; her brother helped her tie her shoe. Aiden was still calling for her. It was echoing in her mind like a physical pull on her body. She reached for the long black feather that she saw on the ground, planning to bring it home and show it to Miku and Keelin. Aiden's call grew louder as her brother's voice faded in her head.

She turned to look at him, at the smile that she had not seen in over a decade.

She felt her heart breaking, and the pain was worse than the first time when she had lost him because now, she understood.

He had been such a good kid. So kind, so caring, and so thoughtful. She reached out to touch his hand, but he was running again through the trees. He was getting further and further away, his messy black hair blowing in the wind as he blurred in the light that streaked through the forest, and Aiden's voice grew louder still. She called for her brother, but no sound left her lips. Her legs were starting to slow against her will because they were heavier than stone and stiffer than wood. The pain was coming back now. The world around her was fading into darkness and agony ached through her bones once more.

This was it.

Mizuki.
Mizuki.
Mizuki.

Something was touching her arm. Maybe she was going to be picked clean by a wolf in her final seconds. She tried to move to pull away, but her limbs refused to cooperate. The pain was getting worse. She could feel it inching down her spine as the smell of burnt flesh registered in her nose, and fresh memories began to flood her mind. Her pulse spiked, panic surging through her core as a massive mountain exploded and liquid fire poured from the sides. People were screaming. They were dying in the heat. Water was boiling. It was drowning her. Suffocating her. The earth beneath her feet buckled as she moved, and great stones shot into the air higher than the trees to block out the sun.

Mizuki.
Mizuki.
Mizuki.

Something was touching her arm again, but this time when she moved, a groan left her lips, and her eyes fluttered open.

"Mizuki!" Aiden's voice rang in her ears.

Dim light flooded her eyes. Her skull throbbed as if it had been hit with a stick, and she shot up from the ground gasping for air.

"Woah, slow down!"

She cringed, shutting her eyes tight once more as every muscle in her body pulsed with pain. She must have pulled them all and ripped them to shreds, because it felt as if she had fallen down the ridge and been pummeled by every rock on the way down. She clenched her teeth hard, forcing her breath to slow before she cracked her eyes open once more, and Aiden's face came into view.

"Mizuki, are you alright?" Aiden asked, his eye searching her face with concern as his hand continued to grip her arm and keep her steady.

"Aiden," she breathed, blinking her eyes as she reached out to him in disbelief.

Her shoulder throbbed at the movement, but she ignored it and raised her hand to his face. Her fingers shook as they touched his cheek. It was real, warm – he was there – and then before she could stop herself, she was grabbing him tight and hugging him hard.

"I thought you were dead," Mizuki whispered, her face pressed against his chest as a wave of emotion rolled through her body. She clung to him, not caring that she had just thrown herself into his arms as her eyes stung with tears, and he gripped her tightly in return. "I thought you had died."

"It's okay," he murmured. His voice sounded roughly above her and hearing it again after she thought that she had lost him only made her grip him tighter. "I didn't die."

She held him for a moment longer, almost afraid that if she let go, he would slip from her grip and fall into darkness once more. But the second the thought reached her mind, questions began to surge, and she pulled away to look him over.

"What happened?" she asked, blinking away her unshed tears and forcing her eyes to focus as they skimmed over his body.

He looked terrible. Dried blood and mud caked his clothes. The fabric was ripped and torn in multiple places, worse than his da's. There was fresh linen wrapped around his hand, arm, head, and leg – which was also braced with sticks to keep it straight. Her brow furrowed at the sight before she looked up to meet his one-eyed gaze.

"Your leg–" Mizuki faltered. "What happened to your leg?"

"It was wrapped when I woke up," Aiden said, his uncovered eye darting to their right. The gesture made her still, and her scattered thoughts rapidly assembled.

"No," Mizuki whispered, her eyes growing wide as suddenly the rocky walls and warm flicker of firelight registered in her mind.

It was familiar, eerily so, and as her eyes landed on the thick green vines behind Aiden's head, she stiffened completely. Before Aiden could even open his mouth to ask her what she was doing, she had twisted around, her vision swimming and her body swaying as she struggled to stay seated upright on the cold stone ground.

Aiden gripped her shoulder to keep her from falling over. She could hear him telling her to slow down, but she ignored it as her eyes rapidly and desperately searched the familiar cavern until they landed on the tall, semi-feather clad, but mostly humanoid being sitting in the chair by the hearth.

"You," Mizuki rasped, her hands shaking as they shifted against the stone, and she struggled to turn around to face the creature completely. She tried to stand up, but her legs folded beneath her weight, and she collapsed back onto her knees in front of Aiden as she looked at the creature with distrust. "What did you do?"

It stared at her in silence, and she felt Aiden grip her arm more tightly.

"Mizuki," he murmured as he shuffled nearer to her side. *"That's* what fixed my leg."

She froze at his words again, staring at the creature, which remained motionless by the fire as the final threads of daylight moved across the stone. It was watching them, its gaze slowly flicking between her and Aiden as the fire sparked by its side – but as Mizuki truly looked at it, she couldn't believe her eyes.

Lilah was sitting in that chair.

At least, the majority of her was.

Her ears were still too pointed to be human. Her hair was still too thick and too long. Her legs bent the wrong way, and her feet were still bare, scaled, and terminated into three dangerously sharp claws – but her wings and antlers were gone. Her entire upper half resembled the woman that Mizuki had seen from the clipped memories. The once vivid dark black quills and feathers that still extended from her neck and back were now fewer, and the ones that remained were dark grey and dulled in colour.

Her face was entirely human. It was thin and worn, somehow looking exhausted and ancient even though she hadn't appeared to have aged a day since her accident. Mizuki's eyes trailed over the familiar features as the woman's memories flickered through her mind: the eyebrows, the nose, the high cheekbones, and the thin white scar that trailed down the center of her forehead. Seeing it tugged at her heart and made her throat burn, but the most striking feature of all, and the one that she could not look away from, was the two dull and seemingly entirely green eyes that met her gaze.

"You did this?" Mizuki whispered as she stared at the woman in disbelief.

She didn't understand. Why had this thing saved their lives? Did it want something? Or had Lilah finally managed to gain some control after nearly a century of burning in the flames of her own rage? She watched as Lilah shifted, the woman sitting forward in her chair and resting her elbows on her knees as she continued to watch them closely.

"Yes," Lilah responded in a voice much more like the one from her old memories, though Mizuki still felt Aiden flinch at her side.

"You fixed his leg," Mizuki murmured, but then she struggled to find her next words.

Her gaze moved down to her left arm that was hanging by her side. Holding her breath, Mizuki tried to move her fingers, and her eyes widened as they twitched upon command. She reached for the ripped and muddy sleeve of her shirt and tore it up her arm.

"Impossible," she breathed, her head shaking as she took in the absence of purple and black tendrils. It was like they were never there, and a fresh linen was wrapped around her hand. Her gaze flicked back up to Lilah's. "And you cured the poison."

Lilah didn't speak, but she nodded, and Mizuki frowned.

"Why?" she pressed, her gaze boring into the dull green eyes as she tried to understand what was going on. "Why would you do it?"

"Why not?" Lilah countered, and Aiden cringed again. *"It was the right thing to do."*

"That doesn't sound like something you would say," Mizuki whispered, swallowing hard as she felt Aiden's gaze land on her temple.

If they lived through whatever was about to happen, she would explain this to him. She couldn't even begin to imagine what it must have been like for him to wake up in this cave, next to this creature, with her unconscious by his side.

"I suppose that it isn't," Lilah said, a low sigh leaving her lips as she sat back in her chair once more and fixed them with a look that Mizuki could not decipher. The woman stared at them for a long moment, only the crackle of the fire filling the silence as the evening light continued to fade. Then, she closed her dull eyes, and her next words were but a whisper. *"It is something that Ren would have said."*

"I don't understand," Mizuki murmured, shaking her head as Aiden looked between the two of them in confusion.

"You remind me of her," Lilah whispered, and she opened her eyes once more.

The green was brighter now, but they were laced with a deep sadness that pierced through Mizuki's heart. This was Lilah – the *real* Lilah – the tormented woman who had spent nearly a century alone.

"There is nothing up here for you," Lilah said quietly. *"And the lands to the north are largely barren. By tomorrow his leg will be nearly healed, and you should be able to return to your village."*

"You healed us, but you still want to get rid of us?" Mizuki asked, a small scoff leaving her lips. "Why? Because it's what Ren would have done? Why bother doing it if you're going to send us back? They'll kill us the second that we get within range of the gates."

"I did it because I wanted to," Lilah said, her cold voice taking on a stern tone as her green eyes flashed. *"They will not kill you when you go back."*

Mizuki opened her mouth to argue, but Lilah sat forward in her chair, and the words were lost on Mizuki's lips as a dull whisper filled the air. It was the same one she had heard before, and she could feel her muscles stiffen in response. She watched as Lilah stood, her brain struggling to process the unnatural movement; it was like the woman was unfolding from her seat and expanding into the air around her. She towered above them at her full height, and Mizuki had to fight the instinct to cower before her.

"I've spent nearly the last century of my life reliving that moment over and over," Lilah murmured, her green eyes shimmering in the dull light. *"Wondering if Ren was right."*

Her gaze locked to Mizuki's face as she took a step forward and flora erupted from the ground beneath her clawed foot.

"I'll never know," Lilah continued, her gaze unblinking as the vines around her claws crept across the stone floor. *"You were right that this power is great, but there are some things that even it cannot do. I cannot go back – I've tried and failed many times because curiosity got the best of me over the years, and I needed to know. Since then, the question has haunted my mind like an itch that I cannot scratch. It digs under my skin, no matter how hard I try to ignore it."*

Lilah took another step, and Mizuki flinched as the stones cracked beneath her clawed feet.

"I try to picture it – to imagine what might have happened if I had left with her. I wonder what the world would be like if I had done things differently," she said, her voice filling the cavern around them as the dull whisper spun through the air. She blinked, her eyes narrowing as a small sound left her lips like a scoff. *"It is impossible to know, and it will forever be unanswered. I'm not sure I believe that things would have been better. But maybe that's why it picked me – maybe what happened was needed in order to start over."*

Lilah paused, her eyes sliding over Mizuki's small frame. The whisper was growing louder, and the air was getting cold. Mizuki could feel Aiden's fingers digging into her skin, but neither of them seemed capable of moving, and her gaze remained fixated on the woman before them.

"Or maybe not," Lilah said, her eyes growing even brighter as she began to move across the stone once more.

Each step was slow and smooth like liquid as green life burst from the ground and crept across the cavern. Mizuki couldn't look away. She could feel her lungs starting to stutter as the distance between them grew smaller and smaller. The murmur in the air was just out of earshot, and she felt like she could nearly make out the words as Lilah took yet another step forward.

"It is wild and untamed, uncompromising and vicious – but I've come to learn that it is not biased," Lilah admitted, her voice getting lower as Mizuki's skin prickled in the cold. *"It is truly neutral. So maybe the pull was always within my soul, and I was simply given the means to let it out. I'll never know for certain, and I will carry the burden of what I did until the end regardless."*

Lilah paused two feet away, the gleam from the fire circling her body like a warm flickering halo as she stared down at Mizuki with burning determination in her eyes. She was so close now that Mizuki could see the tiny outer rim of red that still encased her irises and her thin, slitted pupils.

"But I will make sure that it is given a more mindful keeper," Lilah murmured, and something unearthly shifted behind her gaze as the whispers doubled in volume. *"We didn't always see eye to eye. I was not always there for her the way that I should have been, but I loved Ren more than anyone else. She was everything that I wasn't, everything that I wanted to be – and I destroyed her.*

"I've spent the last ninety-four years of my life wishing to see her again," Lilah whispered and her eyes creased. *"Agonizing over our last words and longing to apologize for all the pain that I caused her, but by the time I regained control, she was dead. I lost my chance. I left her alone in the world that I broke. She and your ancestors suffered so much more than you know, and I will have to live with that burden too."*

She paused once more, a rattled exhale escaping her lungs like a windstorm.

"Yet even after all this time, after all that pain – I cannot honestly tell you that I regret it," Lilah admitted as she took one final step closer. *"But I want to believe I was wrong."*

Mizuki stiffened as Lilah's human-shaped hands stretched into the air between them, and the whispers morphed into a chant. The pain of the cold stone against her knees faded away as the words filled her mind like a heartbeat. It blocked everything else out, and Mizuki's body grew numb as her breath began to crystalize in the air before her lips. The cold was inching down her spine, freezing her bones and chilling her blood. Her lungs failed to inhale, her body refused to move despite the alarms going off in her mind, and her eyes latched to Lilah's unblinking stare.

"My body is dying and won't last much longer. It needs a new vessel, someone stronger who can resist the pull and find balance within the chaos. That person was never going to be me," Lilah said, her voice distorting into the cacophony of noise that made Mizuki cringe once more. The woman's green eyes grew unbearably bright as her slitted pupils dilated wide. *"You were right, Mizuki Altherr. I am a monster, but you don't have to become one – and I want to believe that you won't. I want to believe that you will be better than I."*

Lilah moved.

It was so swift and so fluid that Mizuki would not have been able to do anything to evade it even if she could have moved her body. The woman's scaled hand grabbed Mizuki's shoulder, tugging her away from Aiden's grip as one long index finger brushed against the center of her forehead – and Mizuki's entire body seized.

Her blood ran cold.

She could feel her eyes growing wide in shock as ice penetrated her muscles and ran through her veins. It froze, almost like a burn, and her mouth fell open in a silent scream as the chanting consumed her mind. Green and red flooded her vision, wrapping around her body like a thick blanket as it snuffed out her surroundings. She could feel it. She could taste it. It sunk into her skin like sunlight as the smell of fresh rain and wind filled her nose. The bitter tang of blood touched her tongue. A hint of something bigger, something *enormous* and filled with a hellfire rage that threatened to burn her alive. But it was wrapped in the wind and soothed by the ice water that rushed through her veins and pumped through her heart.

She could see it.

She could hear it.

The words were anger and joy, bitter and calm, melted together into a blur of colours that danced through the night and into the light. Every nerve in her body tingled with the rush, and then... there was nothing.

Nothing at all.

Veles Reborn

Light and darkness. It moved within her like a constantly swirling pool. She could feel it in her chest. The rage, hotter than the lava that had burst from the earth and angrier than the storms that ravaged the lands for the last ninety-four years. The calm, cooler than the water of Glass Lake on the coldest winter day. It was steady and even, placid like a sheet of ice that reflected the world around it. Together they churned, bubbling like hot springs in a winter storm, stuck in a never-ending loop of life and death, wrath and peace – it was chaotic and volatile, yet it was patient and tolerant.

Neutral.

Unbiased.

And *ancient.*

Older than she could comprehend. It transcended humanity, and it carried the memories of thousands, a complete history of its time and the existence of all those that had been its keeper. The recollections floated through her mind as if they were her own. She could feel the emotions attached – the pain, the joy, the disgust, and the anguish. She saw things that she had never known – buildings taller than the sky, waters bigger than the Dead Zone, temples, pyramids, forests, fires, and light. She could see it all, and more than that, she knew it all as if those moments were her own, and she could experience them with a single touch.

It didn't ask for anything, and it did not want anything.

She didn't know what it was or where it had come from. It simply sat there within her chest like a weight on her heart, existing in silence, waiting until it was needed again. It had been called a thousand names. It had been worshipped, feared, revered, abused, and hunted. It had spent centuries in solitude, millennia simply lurking while taking no action at all. Then, there had been moments where it soothed, seeding the earth with new life only to burn it all to the ground in a different century when it had been pushed to the breaking point.

She wasn't sure that she would ever fully understand it. There was so much there to sort through that it was difficult to know where to start. Her fleeting glimpse through the memories that filled her head suggested that to understand would be impossible. As if this thing's very essence was beyond the realm of human comprehension, floating just out of reach of their reality. Yet, just below the surface – she felt like she could nearly see the answer, like a shimmer of light off the water or a shadow moving in the dark.

Others before her had tried to understand, and Lilah had been one of them. The woman had spent years trying to wrap her head around it as she tested the limits of her new abilities, but her experience seemed to be one of the worst. When it sought her out, the chaos was reigning, the rage was burning, and Lilah had not been able to see past it to find the peace that was drowning in the middle of the storm, desperate for air.

It wasn't until much later that the woman realized the calm even existed.

Every experience was different, and some only lasted for very short moments. They ranged from human to creature, and each of them gave a view of the world that enlightened and terrified Mizuki's mind. A mouse, small and unknowing, wandering the underbrush of a thick forest in search of food, where every sound was a threat of death. An elk, bypassing a dried stream in search of water until it stumbled upon an injured and dying man. A creature of the deep, giant and dangerous, lurking beneath hundreds of feet of water and using its many legs to explore and catch food. A man seeking vengeance, and a woman, who had used it to protect her child.

The number of keepers seemed endless, and each had their own story. All of them were unique, and yet all of them were the same, marked by the two symbols and bound to the entity until their bodies finally failed. Drawn to the call of the mountains, which had always been its home as images and symbols flooded their minds. That's why they were marked on the walls. This was not the only one, and the symbols were something more. It was wonderful and terrible – it was horrifying, and it was extraordinary. It was, in many ways, the embodiment of nature's energy and the purest representation of life itself.

A cool breeze drifted across her skin, and a deep inhale filled her lungs. The smell of night air and dew filled her nose as a thousand other scents followed.

She could feel it.

The moonlight on the ground and the wind shifting through the trees of the forest that surrounded the village at the base of the mountain. She could feel the water – the massive ocean to the west that lay beyond the Dead Zone, which she now understood was the ruins of the coastal city where Lilah and Ren had lived. Their village was built around the cottage that her great-great-grandmother had fled to while pregnant with Miku, and they had barely escaped the ruin that Lilah had wrought across the earth. Whether that was intentional or not, she would never know; even Lilah had been unsure if she had managed to spare them purposefully, so the woman had refused to give herself that credit.

Yet they were not the only ones who had survived.

There were others out there. More than the first betrayers to the east or the deserters to the south. Hundreds of them – thousands. She could feel them moving across the earth like ants on her skin, but it wasn't painful; they were simply there. She could feel the creatures too, and she could tell that those of the sea had fared far better than those that had roamed the lands.

It was yet another thing that Lilah had regretted for the last century as she was consumed by loneliness and pain. It wasn't just people she had annihilated… it had been the other animals of this earth too, countless numbers of whom were lost in the fires or drowned in the seas.

Mizuki let out the breath.

Water was falling from a rock to her right. She could hear the *drip, drip, drip* as it landed on the stone. There were so many heartbeats. So many movements. So many things happening all at once that if she focused on them, they flooded her mind and became overwhelming. It was no wonder that Lilah had struggled, that the woman had been inundated by it and lost within the current. Mizuki couldn't imagine what it must have been like. Lilah hadn't understood what was happening to her – she'd had no warning, no explanation or hint as to what she had become. The thought made Mizuki feel sick, so she tried not to focus on it and instead turned her attention to her own body.

It felt strange.

Heavier and lighter, all at the same time.

She wasn't sure how she felt about it – or how she felt about Lilah giving it to her. She didn't want this, but it seemed like many before her hadn't wanted it either. It was unclear how it picked – whether Lilah had made the decision herself or if she had simply done what the thing had suggested. She would never know the answer, and the only thing she knew for certain was that this thing had been searching for the last few months. It knew that Lilah was dying, and as the woman had used the last of her strength to help them, it had been planning to leave her. If Lilah had not given it to her, it would have transferred on its own, to Aiden or to some other living thing.

She let out a quiet mental sigh.

It was such a strange feeling to both understand it and yet know absolutely nothing at all about it. She would need time to figure this out, and the stress of that was daunting. A part of her wished that she could just stay like this forever and never open her eyes, avoid the responsibility and die like she had been meant to on the barren mountain path. But another part of her, the part that Miku had taught to be compassionate, resilient, and kind, knew she had no choice. She had to face this, and more so than that, she had to make this right because she knew where things would go if she didn't.

She may not understand, and she may not know the full truth yet, but she knew in her core that the keepers were supposed to be its protector. They were not just empty vessels to be used and tossed aside – their role was much greater than that.

She inhaled again and felt the air flow through her lungs, cool and soothing. She could feel the whole of her body now as the wind brushed lightly against her bare toes. The collective memories were subsiding, and her mind was beginning to return to the present. She tried to twitch her finger, and she felt it move against the rough stone.

"Mizuki?"

The voice was soft, and it made her heart flutter. She knew this voice. She would recognize it always, and it flooded her mind with memories as her eyes fluttered open. The familiar sight of jagged rocks filled her vision as she stared up at the cavern ceiling. The smell of fresh rain filled her nose as the cool breeze brushed her skin once more. She blinked, then her gaze slowly shifted to the warm heartbeat that was thudding gently by her side.

"*Aiden,*" she breathed, watching as his worried and dirt-covered face crumpled.

His single uncovered eye was brimming with tears. He was warm and glowing in the dim flicker of the firelight, the beacon of hope and kindness that he had always been in her life. He helped her sit up from the ground, and she let him tug her against his chest. She could feel his pulse racing as he gripped her tight, and she buried her face into the crook of his neck.

"It's okay," Mizuki breathed, closing her eyes once more and inhaling deeply. "I'm okay."

"It's not okay," Aiden choked, and he gripped her tighter for a moment, then pulled away to look at her. He continued to hold her arms as his eye traced over her face with concern, and he seemed to struggle to find his words. "Nothing about any of this is okay, Mizuki. What happened? What was that thing? Why did you seem to know it? What did it do to you?"

"Aiden," Mizuki said, her voice gentle as she brought her hand up to grip his shoulder and halted his stream of anxious questions. "I'm okay – I promise."

"Please, just tell me what's been going on," Aiden whispered as he searched her gaze. He stiffened as he looked at her, then he leaned forward, and his eye narrowed. "Mizuki – your eyes are different."

"Different how?" Mizuki asked, worry flooding her body as Aiden shifted even closer.

"They're still blue," he murmured, his gaze shifting between hers. "But there's yellow – like a golden ring around your pupil."

"Gold?" Mizuki asked. "Are you sure? It's around my pupil – not the iris?"

"It's definitely gold," Aiden confirmed as he leaned back once more. "And there is a scar on your forehead. Mizuki – what happened?"

"Why would it be gold?" Mizuki muttered, her mind racing as she thought back through the snippets of memories that she had seen. Her eyes dropped down to her chest, and she stiffened. Then without pausing to think, she let go of Aiden's shoulder and grabbed the collar of her muddy shirt to pull the material down.

"Wait, what are you–," Aiden's panicked words cut off as the faint black symbol came into view, and she heard the air leave his lungs.

She swallowed as she looked at it, her hand trembling as the fabric remained poised several inches below her collarbone.

"Mizuki," Aiden whispered, his mouth falling open as he struggled to find his words again. His gaze was locked to her sternum and the symbol that now resided under the mud that caked her skin. "What – is that – is that Veles's symbol?"

"Yes," Mizuki whispered, already knowing that the companion symbol would be on her back between her shoulder blades. She looked up to meet his gaze once more. He was staring at her in shock, but concern was building behind his gaze.

"Mizuki," Aiden breathed, a tone of desperation filling his voice as he leaned forward and placed a shaking hand on her knee. "*What* is going on?"

"She transferred it," Mizuki said as she let go of her muddy shirt and dropped her hand to her lap.

"Transferred *what*?"

"Veles – her power," Mizuki said, struggling to figure out how to say it as strange feelings continued to overwhelm her senses.

To Lilah, in the rage, it had all been blurred together, and it had felt like being burned alive. To Mizuki, in the calm, each feeling was like a flutter within her body, and if she focused on them, they were distinguishable.

"Aiden, I – I don't know how to explain it." Mizuki faltered, her head shaking as she met his familiar gaze. "It doesn't have a name. Not truly. People named it Veles ages ago and adopted the symbol, but it's had other names before. Different names for the different sides, but it's one and the same. It's been around forever. Lilah was its keeper for the last hundred years until she gave it to me."

Mizuki twisted on the ground, turning to look over her shoulder, already knowing what she would see before it came into view.

"Wait – who is Lilah?" Aiden's voice sounded to her left, but Mizuki's eyes were glued to the lifeless body that was sitting in the chair before the hearth.

"*She* is Lilah," Mizuki whispered, her heart thudding in her chest. She stared in silence for a moment, then shifted to pull herself up from the ground. "Aiden, how long have we been here?"

"I'm not sure," Aiden replied, his brow furrowing even deeper as he struggled to his feet by her side. He leaned against the cave wall for support, keeping his weight off the leg that was still wrapped with linen and braced with sticks. "The last thing I remember was the air growing cold and it touching your forehead. I woke up just a short while ago, and that woman was sitting in that chair. Mizuki, I don't understand – what is going on? What did she do?"

"She saved our lives," Mizuki murmured, her hand instinctively reaching out to steady Aiden as he swayed on his feet and tried to step toward her. "And she ended the world. She was Ren's best friend – my great-great-grandmother, Aiden. She knew her. Lilah was Veles, and *she* was the Great Destruction."

"Mizuki, I–" Aiden's voice faltered, and she could hear his frustration as she turned to look at him once more. He looked so desperate and worried. Stress lines crinkled by his eye as his gaze searched her face, and his shoulders dropped as he looked at her in defeat. "I don't understand."

"I know," Mizuki said, nodding in understanding as she took a step towards him. She paused right before him, craning her neck to look up into his eye. She knew that he was struggling right now. She could practically taste his anxiety in the air. She wanted to put him at ease, but he deserved to know every detail, and that would take time – and there was something that she needed to do first so she could give him the consideration that he deserved. "I know you don't – and I promise you that I will tell you everything, Aiden. I promise I will explain. I'll answer every question you have, and I'll tell you everything that I know – but I can't leave her in that chair. I just – I need a minute. I need you to trust me."

"I do trust you," Aiden whispered, his eyes searching her unfamiliar ones. "I just want to know that you're okay."

"I'm okay," Mizuki said, giving him a small smile. She gripped his arm reassuringly, then slowly stepped back. "I promise."

She moved away from him, watching the perplexed expression on his face grow as he begrudgingly nodded and gripped the stone wall for support. She hadn't been lying – she would tell him everything. She would tell him what happened when she got to the top of the mountain, and she would tell him what Lilah had shown her. She would tell him what she had become, and if she could figure out how to do it, she would even show him the memories because more people needed to know what had happened. They needed to understand what had led to the world's destruction so they could ensure that it never happened again. She would share every single piece of it and tell him the truth.

But as she approached that chair and her heart clenched in pain – she knew that she would never be able to explain this feeling to him. She would never be able to explain the rush of conflicting emotions or the heartbreak in her chest.

This was Lilah.

The *real* Lilah.

The woman underneath all the anger and pain. The person who had slaughtered billions of people in a matter of seconds.

She was death, she was rage – she was the fury that had nearly ended the world, and yet now, she looked so fragile.

Not a hint of anger or stress lingered on her motionless face as she sat in the chair staring at the fire. She looked exactly like how she'd looked just before the accident. Her hair was back to normal, and not a single feather or quill covered her body. Her bare feet rested against the cold stone ground, and her hands sat in her lap. She was wearing the same clothes that she had been wearing before the Great Destruction. Mizuki recognized the jacket and the shorts, but they were old now, worn and threadbare. She was thin, dangerously so, like she had been before the accident, and the only thing that remained from the change was the thin white scar that ran down the center of her forehead.

The same scar, Mizuki knew, that now ran down her own.

She held her breath as she approached, nervousness sliding down her spine as the distance closed because she felt like she knew the woman.

How could she not?

Lilah's memories were in her head, and a piece of her would forever be carried within Mizuki's heart. Still, there were so many unanswered questions. How long had Lilah lived after making the transfer? Was it just long enough to return to her seat, or had she had time to sit and think? Had she been scared to finally face death? Or had she been relieved?

Mizuki stopped just a foot away, staring down at the woman in silence as she struggled to understand the bizarre feelings that were surging in her heart. She could feel Aiden's gaze on the back of her head as he watched in confusion, and the truth was, she felt just as lost. She didn't have all the answers, and she already knew that she wouldn't be able to answer all his questions. She swallowed hard, her gaze flicking over the woman's tattered frame. Her green eyes were open, but now they were dull and staring lifelessly at the flames that flickered from the hearth. Her shoulders were slumped as if the weight of the world had finally been lifted, and she had let out a great sigh of relief.

Mizuki took another step forward and froze when she saw the worn paper card that was clutched within Lilah's cold hand.

"The photo," Mizuki murmured.

386

Without stopping to question whether she would be able to do it, she reached forward and lifted the woman from the chair. It didn't even cross her mind as curious that she could lift Lilah with such ease or that she could carry the woman's body down the hall to the smaller cavern that she had found two nights before. She didn't stop until she reached the large, matted nest in the corner of the small room, and then she placed Lilah in the middle, surrounded by the large black feathers.

Mizuki crossed the woman's arms over her chest, then she collected the two other pictures from the small stone shelf and laid them by her side.

"You're not alone anymore," she whispered, and her eyes started to sting.

She didn't know why it hurt so badly, but the unnameable feeling hit her hard like a physical blow as her fingers instinctively clutched her necklace. She wasn't sure that she could ever forgive her, and yet she wasn't sure that she could ever fully condemn her either. Lilah had been the cause of so much death, so much destruction and pain. Yet Mizuki refused to believe that Lilah was the abomination that she claimed to be, not when all of the woman's memories were circling within her mind.

There had been moments of kindness, moments of self-sacrifice – countless examples of Lilah's strength, love, and desire for good. Maybe that was why Ren had stayed by her side all those years, because beneath the ugly and twisted surface, in her own way, Lilah had cared, and she had wanted to change. She had just gotten lost along the way – but buried beneath the hatred and the pain was a mountain of regret.

Mizuki's stomach knotted as she pushed Lilah's memories to the side and as she leaned down to brush the stray locks of brown hair from her face. She would never forget this woman, and she knew that her own life would never be the same. Pausing only for a moment, she let out a slow breath then closed the woman's eyes before making her way back to the main cavern. Aiden was standing exactly where she had left him. His gaze was locked to the tunnel, and it fixated on her the second that she came into view. He opened his mouth to speak, no doubt planning to ask another stream of questions – but not a word left his lips as he watched her wipe the tears from her eyes. She quickly closed the distance between them, then wrapped her arms around his middle as her chest split in two.

He held her.

Not moving. Not speaking. Not understanding what was going on or why she had been crying as she clutched him harder than ever and closed her eyes tight. He just let her do it, his arms tentatively wrapping around her before he gripped her tightly and tried his best to comfort her. She didn't know how long they stood there or how long it took until her heart began to slow, but eventually, the words came, and she told him everything.

She told him how she had climbed the mountain. How, against all odds, she had reached the top and staggered inside. She told him what she found, and she told him about the vines. She told him about the creature, what it had said and what it had been. She told him everything that Lilah had shown her, then everything that she had seen. As she told the story, she knew it sounded unbelievable, yet somehow it felt like the truth could be nothing less after the last seven days.

Aiden let her speak, not interrupting the flow of words as they gushed from her lips. Instead, he sat there unmoving like an anchor, and eventually she found herself sitting right next to him, nearly leaning against his side as she continued to try to explain what had happened. She rambled until she ran out of breath, and she didn't even question it when Aiden took her hand and held it tight.

"So, you don't know what it is?" Aiden asked when she had finally run out of words. It was probably the most she had ever spoken in her life, and it was certainly the most that she had ever said to him. Yet he didn't seem to mind, and maybe that was why he had listened so intently.

"No," Mizuki said, her voice hoarse as she let out a sigh. Her throat ached after talking so much, but she found it difficult to stop now that she had let so much out. "I don't – I feel like the answer is there, just out of my reach, but I can't get it. I don't think anyone has ever managed to figure that out."

"But it – does it affect you?" Aiden asked as he looked at her cautiously. "It's not controlling you, is it?"

"Not as far as I can tell," Mizuki answered, shaking her head again as she leaned back against the cold stone of the cave by Aiden's side. She let out another breath, watching as the first morning light started to stream into the cave. "It's just there, waiting – from what I can see, it only takes control in extreme situations. Otherwise, it's completely neutral. I can't explain why. It's just a feeling, but I don't think it's supposed to be in control like that. What happened with Lilah was unlike anything else from what I could see, and it didn't feel right. I don't think something of that magnitude will happen again so long as it's kept in balance."

Mizuki frowned, her stomach knotting with unease as she unconsciously gripped Aiden's hand tighter.

"Or at least, I hope that it doesn't," she whispered, her gaze dropping to their intertwined hands as doubt filled her mind. "Aiden, I just don't know – I don't know if I can do this."

"You can do it," he said, and she felt his fingers tighten around her hand in return.

"Aiden," she breathed, looking up to meet his warm gaze. "There's no way that we can be so sure."

"It won't happen again, Mizuki," Aiden said, and from the look in his eye she nearly believed him. "We'll make sure it doesn't. I'll help you."

She nodded, but the uneasy feeling in her stomach remained as she let out a slow breath.

"I'm still me, Aiden," Mizuki whispered, her throat growing tight. She wasn't sure if she said it to reassure him or herself, but as she spoke the words, she doubted them.

"I know." Aiden nodded, a small smile tugging at his lips. Something shifted behind his eye, and she recognized it as the same look he'd had back in the swamp. "That's why I know it won't happen again, because I know you. I know you're still you, and I know that you would never let that happen."

"I hope you're right," she whispered, leaning her head back against the stone and letting her shoulders drop. She watched the light dance across the cave again as the sun rose, and they sat in silence until the final remaining words that she had been avoiding bubbled to the back of her throat. "Aiden?"

"Yes?"

She could feel his gaze on her temple once more, but she couldn't seem to make herself look at him. Even after everything that they had been through together, even after everything that she had seen, she still felt sick with anticipation. In some ways, she was more afraid of this moment than she was of anything else. It terrified her to her core because it changed everything – but she didn't want to avoid it, not anymore, and she knew that if she didn't say this now, she would lose her courage completely.

"I'm sorry I left you on that ledge," she whispered, and she gripped his hand tighter. "And I'm sorry that it took me so long to come back to you."

"Mizuki don't, I–"

"And I'm sorry that I didn't tell you about the poison." She cut him off, swallowing hard as the nervousness in her gut doubled.

"I knew about the poison," Aiden said, and she felt him shift at her side to face her. "The second that my hand went numb, I knew what they had done."

"I still should have said something," Mizuki murmured as she desperately tried to push down the nausea building at the back of her throat.

"It wasn't your job to take care of me," Aiden replied, and Mizuki finally turned to look at him.

"And it isn't your job to take care of me," she breathed, her chest tightening as she forced herself to say the words. "But you do it anyway – just like you did all those years ago when you jumped into the lake."

Aiden stilled at her words, and she felt her stomach knot.

"Why didn't you say something?" Mizuki whispered as her throat started to burn. "Why didn't you tell me?"

"I thought you had forgotten," Aiden said, and that only made it hurt worse.

"I *did* forget," Mizuki breathed as she tucked her loose hair behind her ear. "I blocked it all out with everything else – Aiden, I never even thanked you."

"Yes, you did," he whispered, a tiny smile tugging at his lips. "You thanked me nearly ten times before I went home that day."

"Maybe, but it doesn't count if I don't remember it," Mizuki retorted. "Why didn't you remind me?"

"Because it didn't matter," Aiden said, his voice gentle as he looked at her in a way that made her pulse flutter. "It has nothing to do with me wanting to spend time with you, and I didn't want you to feel like you owed me – besides, you were just a kid. I assumed that you forgot because it was such a long time ago."

"But it wasn't the only thing I forgot," Mizuki whispered, her eyes searching his face. She swallowed nervously as her heart began to race. "I forgot we used to be friends beforehand. I blocked out everything that happened after Ren died, and then I forgot how to feel."

"You didn't forget how to feel," Aiden said, shaking his head in disagreement. "You just stopped showing it – it's not the same thing. It's always been there, Mizuki – I could see it, but I knew that you were struggling. I'm sorry I didn't try to talk to you about what happened. I thought about bringing it up so many times, but I just never knew what to say."

"I probably wouldn't have wanted to," she whispered, her voice catching in her throat. "It hurt too much."

"I know," Aiden said, and she saw the pain behind his eye. Ren may have been her brother, but she wasn't the only one who had lost him. "I'm sorry, Mizuki – for everything."

"So am I," she whispered.

He was staring at her so intently that she could feel a blush creeping across her face. The final words were burning at the tip of her tongue, the ones that she had truly wanted to say. She opened her mouth, closed it, and struggled to find her nerve.

"I never told you–," Mizuki faltered, the words cutting off as her hoarse voice broke. His eye was searching her face now, confusion in his gaze as he watched her struggle.

"Never told me what?" he asked hesitantly, and her skin tingled as his thumb brushed along the back of her hand.

She knew if she didn't make herself say it now, she would never say it, and she would never forgive herself. She had nearly lost the chance. She had almost lost him once already, and even though it was hard, the truth was undeniable: Aiden was and had always been the only person that she could count on. He had been her friend before her family was torn apart; he had stuck by her through the pain and remained her ally even though a large piece of her had been crushed beneath the anguish. His faith in her and Miku's final wish for her to live with compassion were the only things that had kept her from falling into despair and losing herself entirely. Without him, she was lost, and he meant more to her than she could ever say. More to her than even she had realized until this moment, and she refused to do anything else without letting him know for fear of losing him again.

She swallowed hard, desperately trying to find her words as her entire body began to tremble. He watched her closely, his hand gripping hers tightly as her heart started to race so quickly, she could hear it in her ears.

"Aiden, I–," she stammered, her voice catching in her throat again.

Why was this so hard? She could feel his steady heartbeat in her mind if she concentrated on it, and somehow his calm demeanour was only making her more nervous. It didn't help that she could feel *everything* outside as countless creatures walked across the earth.

How had Lilah managed this? How did any of the past keepers deal with the overwhelming influx of signals while trying to focus on the person right in front of them?

She tried to calm her heart, forcing herself to exhale before she started again.

"You know that I–" she faltered, her eyes starting to burn with frustration as she clenched his hand tight. She could see understanding shifting behind his gaze, but she refused to use that as an excuse to give up. "Aiden, I – I've always – I – *ughh* – why can't I say it?"

His eye creased, and she saw his lips twitch.

"It's okay, Mizuki," Aiden said, his voice soft as his eye filled with warmth. "You don't have to."

"No, it's not okay," she said, her voice trembling almost as much as her hand in his grasp as she shook her head in irritation. She tried to fight the blockage that seemed to prevent the words from coming out, but she could tell that it was a losing battle. "Aiden I–"

Her voice cut out again, but this time as her brow furrowed in frustration, Aiden smiled at her, and his thumb pressed into the back of her hand.

"I know," he murmured, his free hand slowly reaching up to touch her face. She shivered as his thumb brushed her cheek, his gaze met her nervous eyes, and his voice dropped lower. "I love you too, Mizuki."

She swallowed, unable to speak as he bent forward and leaned his forehead against hers. She gripped his left hand tighter, closing her eyes and letting out a breath as her pulse continued to race. They sat that way for a moment, neither one of them moving as Mizuki's heart ached. She hadn't been able to tell him with her own words – but she knew that he knew, and right now, that would need to be enough.

Someday she would try again, and she knew that he would be patient with her. She shivered as his fingers brushed her loose hair behind her ear, and she leaned into his hand. His touch was gentle, soothing – nothing like the burn that Lilah had experienced. She let out a deep breath as her heart finally slowed and her mind moved back to the situation at hand.

"We need to go back, Aiden," Mizuki whispered, forcing herself to open her eyes and meet his gaze once more. He pulled back to look at her, but his hand lingered on her cheek. "There's nothing up here for us – no food or water. You'll need to eat before I do, and I'm not sure that I trust myself to figure out how to grow anything yet. Besides, we have to go back to the village and tell them the truth about what happened. We have to make this right."

"We will," Aiden said, his gaze growing serious. "It won't be easy, but if we do it right, not only can we tell them the truth, but we can fix the crops and change the entire village. We can stop the Elders, go find Dante and Anya – we could look for the first betrayers."

She nodded, but she felt her nerves flare with anxiety at the thought of facing the entire village with this thing in her chest. She didn't know what would happen if they returned to find the village in uproar – or what she would do if anything had happened to her parents or Aiden's family.

"Aiden," Mizuki said, fixing him with a serious stare. "You have to promise me that if you see me changing – if the gold in my eyes ever becomes red – that you'll tell me."

"It's not going to," Aiden said, his voice firm.

"You don't know that," Mizuki breathed, her eyes pleading with him. "I'm serious, Aiden – if it turns red, you have to tell me so we can find a way to stop it."

"And I'm being serious, too, Mizuki," Aiden said, gripping her hand tight. "If it happens, I'll tell you – but it's not going to happen. We'll take care of each other – it's what we do."

Her eyes creased at his words, and she couldn't stop the small smile that tugged at her lips. He was right. It was what they did – even if she hadn't realized it before, it was what they had been doing silently for over a decade.

"Okay," she sighed, closing her eyes and leaning her forehead against his once more. "Then let's do this."

They took the time to unwrap their wounds and check over the state of their bodies. Mizuki was entirely healed; not a cut or bruise lingered on her skin from the climb up the mountain. She didn't even have a scratch on her face from the Wild, and the wolf bite was gone. She looked completely untouched, save for the scar on her forehead.

Aiden was improved. His shoulder was healed, and his leg didn't appear to be broken anymore. Once they had removed the linen wraps and sticks, he was able to stand on it with no issue. His eye was still damaged, but when she washed away the herbs and dried blood with the clean water dripping within the cave, the swelling was gone, and he was able to open it.

It looked foggy, like the mist that covered the mountain range. Two scars ran across it, and one slit down the center of his eyeball like a jagged red line, but he assured her it didn't hurt, and he couldn't feel it.

She took the herbs that were hanging from the ceiling by the hearth just in case and packed them into her pockets before they moved toward the mouth of the cavern. With one final look over her shoulder, she steeled her heart and said a final goodbye to Lilah. Then, she and Aiden stepped out into the sun, and she blinked her eyes in the bright rays of light.

The sensation was unlike anything she had ever felt. A rush of warmth and life flowed through her veins as the wind tugged at her hair. She stared out into the open, speechless at the beautiful calm blue skies that filled the air around them. It was clear; it was bright – she could see forever into the distance as a thousand heartbeats fluttered all around her. The Dead Zone wasn't dead. It was teeming with life, and her heart surged with joy as her eyes began to sting from the overwhelming feeling in her chest.

"Aiden," she whispered, her throat clenching tight as she moved toward the edge of the plateau and looked out at the incredible world around them.

She didn't understand how anyone could have ever seen this any other way or how anyone could have ever believed that this wasn't worth fighting for. She felt alive – more alive than when she first climbed the ridge in the spring after a long, cold winter. She inhaled deeply, the fresh air filling her lungs and making her heart swell.

"It's beautiful," she murmured, finally turning to look up at him.

She thought that he would be looking out at the lands around them, but he wasn't – his mismatched eyes were fixed on her, and they were wide with awe. Her eyes narrowed in question, and she felt her heart start to flutter once more as he took a step closer.

"What?" Mizuki asked nervously, watching the way that his gaze moved over her small frame with unhidden emotion.

"You," Aiden whispered, shaking his head as a small smile tugged at his lips. "You're going to be incredible, Mizuki – you're already sprouting green."

She turned to look down at her bare feet, her mouth falling open in surprise as her gaze landed on the patch of wildflowers that were swaying in the wind beside her muddy toes. They were delicate and colourful, ranging from shades of purple so light that they were nearly white to ones so dark they were almost black. She had no idea how she did it, but for the first time since she had woken, she felt the underlying fear fade away.

"Let's go home," Aiden whispered, wrapping his arm around her shoulder and pulling her closer to his side.

She couldn't stop the smile that tugged at her lips as she looked up at him in the bright morning light. He smiled down at her, then his head ducked toward hers, and his lips grazed her temple in a soft kiss. The sensation rushed through her body like a wave, tingling down her spine in a rush of energy that made her heart soar. She wrapped her arm around his waist as she reached up to grip her necklace tight. For the first time in her life, she felt at peace.

There was beauty in the chaotic storm within her chest, and she knew that she would always choose to see it.

"Let's go home."

THANK YOU!

Thank you for supporting my work and taking the time to read VELES! I hope that you enjoyed the story.

Please consider leaving a review on Amazon or Goodreads to let me know your thoughts! Reviews are extremely helpful to authors and new readers, and they are greatly appreciated. You can share your reading experience on social media with the hashtag #Veles and encourage others to read the story, too!

About the Author

Engineer by trade, P. J. Marie has always been a storyteller at heart. Inspired by the captivating tales that her Ukrainian grandfather used to tell about settling the Canadian prairies, P. J. has always looked at life through a narrative lens.

An avid creator, P. J. loves the design process from start to finish and is always working on projects that meld the structured world of engineering with her creative passions. Whether through world-building, crafting cosplays, or building custom bookshelves for her ever-growing collection of novels, manga, and terrible monster movies, P. J. is always working on something.

In her spare time, she enjoys collecting new skills, drinking copious amounts of tea, and spending time with her family and adorable doggo.

Sign Up

To get in touch with P. J. Marie, please visit https://www.pjmarie.com and subscribe to the newsletter for updates on upcoming works, release dates, and events.

Future books in the Veles Saga:

Veles: The Great Destruction
Veles: Reborn

For a sneak peek at a NEW upcoming trilogy, visit
https://www.pjmarie.com/upcoming

Lightning Source UK Ltd.
Milton Keynes UK
UKHW010011040522
402455UK00012B/766/J